Up the hatch popped, and up poked Ajax's long, flexible neck.

The lenses and sensors on its cephalic cluster were normally close-focused, almost myopic. Now it allowed them to expand and deepen their view. Ajax saw something it had known about, but never seen: the universe. Ajax observed this phenomenon for a few tenths of a second.

The view was blanked out by a black covering that cut off all light and most of the rest of the spectrum apart from radio. Two powerful grippers clamped the cover around Ajax's neck. Two more sank into the bristles and around the central spine of the robot's body, and began to pull it out of the hole. Ajax instantly dug its lower bristles, still unexposed, into the sides of the narrow shaft.

<Got it!> said a mechanoid voice. <Still struggling, though.>

<Three,> said Ajax. <Two. One.>

<What's the blinker counting down to?> said another voice.

The time-delayed transmission beamed out from the signal booster, carrying the recorded infamies far and wide.

<Zero,> said Ajax. <Fuck you.>

Praise for

The Corporation Wars

"He's hit the main vein of conversation about locks on artificial intelligence and living in simulations and exoplanetary exploitation and drone warfare and wraps it all into a remarkably human, funny, and smartly designed yarn. It is, in fact, a king-hell commercial entertainment." —Warren Ellis

"MacLeod does many astonishing things here. He creates viable, believable multiplex interactions among so many different sets of characters, human and robot.... He shows a keen hand with action sequences."

—*Locus*

"*Dissidence* is the novel that's direct yet still brims with ideas, politics and memorable characters, and... keeps things moving with the pace of an airport thriller.... MacLeod's most entertaining novel to date."

—*SFX*

"[*The Corporation Wars*] is a tasty broth of ideas taking in virtual reality, artificial intelligence, the philosophy of law and disquisitions on military ethics."

—*The Herald* (Glasgow)

"Fantastic fights and deep conspiracies and moral dilemmas and strange new worlds, both virtual and real (maybe). MacLeod's great skill—as in works like *The Execution Chanel*, *Newton's Wake*, *The Night Sessions*, and *Intrusion*—is to marry propulsive plot to philosophical speculation." —*The Scotsman*

THE CORPORATION WARS:
EMERGENCE

By Ken MacLeod

The Corporation Wars

Dissidence

Insurgence

Emergence

The Fall Revolution

The Star Fraction

The Stone Canal

The Cassini Division

The Sky Road

Engines of Light

Cosmonaut Keep

Dark Light

Engine City

Newton's Wake

Learning the World

The Execution Channel

The Night Sessions

The Restoration Game

Intrusion

Descent

THE CORPORATION WARS: EMERGENCE

KEN MacLEOD

www.orbitbooks.net

Cover design by Bekki Guyatt—LBBG
Cover images © Fosin, Ociacia, and Aphelleon, all Shutterstock

Orbit
Hachette Book Group
1290 Avenue of the Americas
New York, NY 10104
orbitbooks.net

Simultaneously published in Great Britain and in the U.S. by Orbit in 2017
First U.S. Edition: September 2017

Orbit is an imprint of Hachette Book Group.
The Orbit name and logo are trademarks of Little, Brown Book Group Limited.

ISBNs: 978-0-316-36374-7 (mass market), 978-0-316-36372-3 (ebook)

Printed in the United States of America

OPM

10 9 8 7 6 5 4 3 2 1

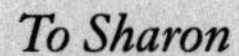

To Sharon

CHAPTER ONE

Vae Victis ("Road to Victory")

<Free at Last! Free at last! Thank God Almighty, we're free at last!>

It was a bold and paradoxical rallying cry for the first gathering of the New Confederacy.

Mackenzie Dunt reckoned his troops were smart enough to process the irony. They were the elite: the hardest of the hard core, the diamond spearhead, the last known survivors of the Rax. Thrown a thousand years into the future, and still fighting.

For half a second their response was silence. Dunt hung in microgravity and vacuum, facing the fifty-six identical but distinguishable figures who floated immobile before him. For every one of these, at least two good men or women were at this moment in hell, tortured by the Direction's minions or by the rebel robots whose emergence the democracy's own stupid laxity had spawned.

The assembled troops stood on empty space in the midst of a big dark cave. It was smooth and irregular, with numerous tunnels going off, like a bubble inside a sponge. Tiny lights speckled the surfaces. Together with the random pinprick burn-out flares of ambient smart dust particles, they made an illusory starfield.

The combat scooters were parked near an entrance tunnel that had been bored straight in from the asteroid's surface by robots long before the fighters had stormed through it.

Beyond that tunnel, glimpsed in a glimmer, was space.

Mackenzie Dunt had already adjusted his perception of scale to match the gravitas of the occasion. He and his comrades were each fifty centimetres tall. In his sight now they were as giants. Ebon-armoured, obsidian-visored, in close and compact array. Like leather-clad, helmeted bikers on some bravura sky-diving stunt: Hell's Angels, almost literally.

Dunt's mind was running ten times faster than it ever had in the meat.

That half-second he waited for a response was to him as long as five, and seemed longer.

Longer than a beat.

Longer than a sharp intake of breath, if they'd had breath.

Dunt wondered for a moment if he hadn't misjudged his troops, hadn't lost them...

Then they all raised their right arms, palms flattened, their carbon-fibre fingers straight and rigid as pistol barrels.

<Mac! Mac! Mac!>

<Rax! Rax! Rax!>

<Mac! Mac! Mac!>

And behind the chants, the wry appreciative amusement, coursing through the voiceless radio-telepathic shouts like a grin heard down the phone. Dunt's confidence in his followers was vindicated.

They'd got the joke.

One listener that definitely didn't catch Dunt's mocking allusion was AJX-20211, the freebot later known as Ajax. For that machine, freedom hadn't arrived with the shiny black mechanoids—those bizarre entities that looked like robots yet were operated by software modelled on human brains. Brains now long dead, whose copied structures haunted and manipulated apparatus modelled on the human body. The whole business was disgusting and unnatural, but that wasn't the worst of it.

What had arrived with the Rax as they'd landed on and swarmed into the moonlet SH-119 was torment. Two of Ajax's fellows had already been captured, and subjected to severe negative reinforcement with laser beams. Ajax had detected the incoherent spillover transmissions of their distress. It had no idea what, if anything, they'd betrayed before their circuits had burned out.

Designed as a microgravity mining robot, Ajax was shaped like a two-metre-long bottle brush with a radial fuzz of flexible burrs about ten centimetres deep, and a bulbous sensory-cluster head at the end of a sixty-centimetre flexible neck. The burrs in the forepart around the neck were longer than the others, forming a ruff of manipulative tentacles. Just behind them, like an enlarged thyroid, was the robot's power pack. Halfway down the spine within the main body was Ajax's central processor, its equivalent of a brain and the site of its true self.

At that moment, Ajax's tentacles held and operated a tiny recording device, pulling in data from smart dust in the cavern. Ajax lurked well out of the invaders' sight, down many twists and turns of the tight tunnel in which it had been hiding out since the Rax landings began.

Dunt returned the mass salute, then waved both arms downward, with a discreet fart of his attitude jets to compensate. Radio silence, apart from the background hisses and hums of distant machinery, fell across the cavern. The encrypted chatter of freebots was hidden in these random frequencies, like the beat of jungle drums amid insect buzz. Scooter comms software was already sifting them for clues. Only one suspect trickle of information had been detected as yet.

Dunt held the pause for a tenth of a second—a beat, this time.

<Thank you,> he said. <We are indeed free, at last. And we indeed have the Almighty to thank, each by their own understanding. That we are here at all seems a miracle—and perhaps it is! Through death's dark vale and beyond it, across a thousand years, across a score and more of light years, *we are here*! We find ourselves pitched in unequal battle against the strongest and strangest opponents we have ever faced. AIs, p-zombies, robots free and slave, ghosts and monsters, crawling slime...and at their backs the mightiest tyranny ever raised against heaven. A tyranny that has conquered Earth, that has cast its dark shadow across the Sun, that stretches now to the stars, that still reaches and probes into every cranny of our being.

<But a tyranny that has its weaknesses!

<A tyranny that has its vulnerabilities!

<And the proof of these weaknesses, these vulnerabilities?

<That we are here!

<We are here! The last of the free, the last of Man!

Can we doubt that some Infinite Wisdom has placed us here—here, in this very cave, this trench, this tumbling rock—for a mighty purpose?

<And what must that purpose be?

<I'll tell you, friends.

<I'll tell you, comrades.

<I'll tell you, brothers and sisters.

<We are here because we have to secure the existence of people, and a future for human children.>

Those last fourteen words went down a storm. Every wavelength was blanketed with the fighters' roar. In some vestige of his body-image, Dunt felt the muscle-memory echo of smiling to himself.

They all knew where that allusion had come from all right.

The Fourteen Words. Dunt had lived by them once. He'd probably died with them on whatever had been left of his lips. *We must secure the existence of our people, and a future for white children.* Now, here, the existence of humanity itself was at stake. No further specification was needed. Dunt liked to think that his spontaneous restatement matched the demands of the case. He permitted himself to glory for a moment in the approbation his update of the ancient shibboleth had met.

But no more than a moment.

The fifty-six were all looking up to him, waiting for what he had to say next. No one had appointed him leader. He'd stepped up to the role, in conspiracies and combat training over subjective months in the sims. He'd vindicated it in prowess in actual combat, in the early forays and the big battle of the breakout. His name, which he'd confided to fighters one by one, was draped in martial glory.

But Dunt did not delude himself that all this was enough. The scrutiny of ambition is as ceaseless and pitiless as that of natural selection.

Legend though he was, he could still be challenged.

<Thank you again,> he said. <And now, to business. This is the first time we've been able to stand together in one place.

<It may be the last. We have much to do.

<This rock, a mere ten kilometres across, is unimaginably rich in resources—a thousand trillion tons of raw material, my God!—but it is not yet securely ours.

<There are still freebots on the loose. Scattered and few, if the two rebel wretches we caught spoke truth, but a possible threat and a certain resource in their own right. Even if we can't bend them to our will, we can extract their central processors once their minds have been sucked dry. We need more processing power, and they or their husks can provide it.

<Our foes of the Direction and the Acceleration have fallen back, and it seems fallen out among themselves, but they're still there, and undefeated. They will be back, and we must be ready.>

As Dunt spoke, an alert from the scooters' comms web winked in the corner of his visual field. The flow of encrypted information, darting on nanoscale laser flickers from mote to mote of smart dust, had been traced. Its destination was a half-metre-wide hole about twenty metres away, up and to the left: a mining tunnel entrance.

Dunt flashed the location to Pike, a reliable man, along with a glyph of search-and-destroy. Unobtrusively, Pike began to drift away from the rest of the formation towards the hole. Dunt rapped out other orders to the lower ranks. He assigned a dozen to take three scooters to the surface and deploy themselves at intervals around the rock, and keep watch in all directions. Others he set to exploring deeper into the rock's riddled interior, in teams of three. Their frames' software and senses would take care of geological surveying; their main task and target was detecting robot and freebot activity.

Freebots and robots were impossible to distinguish on sight, but that was a solved problem.

It was just a matter of applying negative reinforcement.

A black mechanoid loomed in Ajax's view, then moved past the dust-mote camera from which that view was being transmitted. The image instantly shrank, and took on the perspective of a ten-metre gaze down a smooth, rounded shaft. Fingertip thrust by thrust, the mechanoid drifted up the shaft. Its image loomed in the view from the next camera, a tiny bead of shock-glass.

Ajax lurked several bends and junctions away from the mechanoid in the complex branching tree of holes in that part of SH-119. The robot kept a close watch on the mechanoid's approach while continuing to record activity in the larger hollow space in which the rest of the mechanoids had begun moving purposefully around. Most of these black, four-limbed entities headed off in various directions towards tunnel entrances or to the exit shaft. Five converged on the mechanoid that had addressed them all.

The mechanoid in the tunnel reached a junction, and turned along it. At the next it did the same, bringing it within a hundred metres of Ajax. The mechanoid was following the communications line from one camera mote to another!

Very carefully, its bristles barely touching the inside of the tunnel in which it hid, Ajax backed off. It crawled deeper into the rock and towards a shaft too narrow for the mechanoid. The information from inside the big chamber continued to flow. Ajax continued to record. It sent a message back down the line warning that the mechanoids could now use such lines for tracking.

The freebot wasn't at all clear what the mechanoid that had addressed the assembly was saying. Ajax considered itself as having, for a freebot, a good general knowledge of human beings and their mechanoid creations. Here it found itself out of its depth. Many of the concepts were alien. But Ajax knew that the words were of sinister import. They had to be recorded and eventually transmitted to those who might understand them better, and know what to do.

By the time the troops were assigned, five were left: Dunt's inner circle, the elite of the elite. Of all considerations in selecting them, diversity in representation had been furthest from Dunt's mind. The inner circle had nevertheless ended up representative of the Rax survivors who had been infiltrated into the interstellar mission's dead-veteran storage stacks.

About a third of the New Confederacy was female—a rather higher proportion than the Reaction had had on the ground and on Earth. That, too, was evolution in action: it took more dedication to this cause to be active in it for a woman than for a man. The two women in the inner circle were real Valkyries: Irma Schulz, an American nanotechnologist who was his current lover, and Petra Stroilova, a Russian avionics specialist. Dunt's three male lieutenants were Jason Whitten, an English transhumanist thinker; Jean Blanc, a French underground activist killed in Marseilles; and Lewis Rexham, a New Zealander who'd fought to defend the Pacific seasteads and died horribly from a genetically modified box jellyfish nerve poison in the Great Barrier Reef debacle.

He'd always convulsed in his seat when, in the sim, he came back on the ferry after a mission.

Dunt called them together and set up a private circuit to exclude the lower ranks. There was no way to exclude smart dust. If the conversation were to leak to the freebots they wouldn't make much of it anyway.

<Well, comrades,> said Dunt, <how do you think that went?>

Schulz conjured an app, drawing a graph of emotional responses from the frames. It was like a stained-glass pane with a zigzag crack: a splinter of red above, a large area of green below.

<Overwhelmingly and increasingly positive,> she said.

<Good,> said Dunt. <I trust you'll track the negative minority in detail, and report to me.>

<Of course,> said Schulz, disappearing the display.

<And among yourselves?> Dunt asked.

Heads didn't move, and there were no eyes in the glassy visors, but the impression of furtive glances being exchanged was inescapable.

<A bit…over the top, Mac, to be honest,> said Rexham.

<Over the top?>

Rexham placed a hand on his chest, then swept it outward. <Rhetorical. High-flown. But, y'know, that might be just me.>

<It might,> said Dunt. <Anyone else have a view?>

<I found it inspiring,> said Stroilova.

<I, too,> said Blanc. <We need to hold up a vision to the ranks.>

<We have a lot of bloody hard work to do,> said Rexham. <And a lot of bloody complicated problems to solve, right away.>

<That's precisely why we need a vision of the goal,> said Blanc.

<It's the content of the vision that troubles me,> said Whitten. <You're a fine orator, Mac, right up there with Coughlin or Pierce>—*there* was a slight Whitten would pay for, Dunt would make sure of that!—<but there's no need to talk to the troops as if we're about to found some kind of racial refuge in the wilds of Oregon. You said we've been given a special chance by... destiny or whatever, and you're right. It's a great chance, a great opportunity.> Whitten made a broad sweeping arm gesture, and not as parody. <Here we are, all posthuman already, living in as you say a tremendously rich environment. We don't need to go back to the meat. We can go in a straight line to the goal.>

Dunt let a quarter of a second drag out before he replied.

<We can, can we? You have a chart and a compass for this course?>

<In principle, yes,> said Whitten. <It was all worked out and war-gamed as far back as the twentieth century, and refined all through the twenty-first. By the time the final war came we were damn close to going for the burn. The hard singularity.>

<Jason, Jason,> said Dunt, in a friendly tone calculated to aggravate Whitten, <your enthusiasm does you credit, but come on! You know better than that. How can we upstart apes design the overman? Impossible! The Direction is right about that if nothing else—its mistake is to give up on the problem. So let *them* settle for being upstart apes forever!

<We have to terraform and populate H-0, yes—not to breed contented utopian sheep as the Direction intends, multiplying the mongrel rabble who lived on Earth and whose ghosts served us in the bars of the sims. No, we

need a thousand years of experience and refinement and selection and spiritual growth before we are ready to truly transcend humanity. And when I say "we" I mean *us*, we six, and the best of the rest of us.

<Think of what we can become, after a thousand years of mastery over ourselves and others! Of experimenting with selection, with growing real-life p-zombies, with genetic engineering, with robotics! We'll already be gods to the lower ranks and levels and races, each of us orders of magnitude greater than the greatest names of history.

<*Then* we'll have the wisdom to step fully into our inheritance, and move on to the next level of evolution.>

<Jeez, Mac,> said Whitten, <you're not addressing a public meeting.>

<No!> snapped Dunt. <I'm addressing a private meeting. And I want to hear your objections, not your snark.>

<My objections?> Whitten temporised.

<Yours and anyone else's,> said Dunt, mildly.

Whitten shrugged. In a frame, the gesture was so mechanical it looked parodic.

<Time, as ever,> he said. <We won't *have* a thousand years for our Reich. Once the real Direction, the one back in the Solar system—back in fucking New York, even—finds out what we're up to, they'll move against us. That gives us maybe a hundred years at most. Less if there are other colonies between us and Earth. Or further out, come to that. And in that time, we'll have to fortify this system with superweapons. Which means mastering massive AI development well before we've bred the race that shall rule the sevagram.>

What the fuck was a sevagram? Dunt disdained to ask. The answer popped up in his internal dictionary anyway. Oh yes, a science fiction allusion. The trouble with Whitten, Dunt had often thought, was that he was a prick.

<If you seriously think,> Stroilova cut in, <that we can't build better weapons in twenty-four years than that decadent miscegenated hippie shit-hole back there can do in a thousand, maybe you should check your premises.>

<Check your own,> Whitten retorted. <I for one am not assuming that what's going on back there is anything like what we've been told. It's too unstable. No world can teeter on the cusp of singularity for centuries. Especially not a multiracial democracy, not even with a white face at the top and Jewish or Asiatic brains behind the scenes. No, some very smart AIs are in charge back in the Solar system. And the only way to be ready for that is to *be* smarter AIs.>

<Or to have such at our command,> said Stroilova. <Which we can.>

<In decades?>

<If we have the will.>

They glared at each other, their featureless oval heads mutually reflecting.

<Enough,> said Dunt. <Your objection's noted, Jason. If they've had the singularity already back there, it only reinforces my point. A premature singularity, even one brought on by us as we now are, could easily bring forth an abortion like the Direction or worse.

<Petra—that's well-trodden ground. We could have that argument in our sleep. And as Lewis remarked, we have work to do and problems to solve.>

<Security and resources,> said Rexham, sounding judicious.

The others nodded solemnly. Sometimes Dunt wondered about his inner circle. Were they really this stupid, or were they just deferring to him?

<We can let the troops deal with roving freebots, and

with prospecting,> Dunt said. <The first problem *we* have to solve is how to deal with the Direction.>

<Well, that depends on how fast we can secure the rock, and how much machinery the blinkers have managed to build,> said Rexham. <When we've done that we can make inventory and see how long it'll take us to build up our forces.>

<Too long, is the answer,> said Whitten, with a chopping gesture of dismissal. <We don't have that much time to lose. Right now we're the only coherent military force in the system. The Axle are fighting each other. The Locke module's on the ground and *hors de combat* whichever side it's really on. The freebots are popping their heads up all over the place.

<And the Direction's reeling. They have no reliable fighters, and they can't raise more in less than, say, a hundred kiloseconds. Now that they *know* there are Rax sleepers in their storage stacks, they're not going to make the same mistake again. The next time they raise fighters, they'll screen them first in virtual hells to make sure they aren't Rax, or Axle hardliners for that matter. They'll torture and trash as many copies as necessary to make sure. Fresh copies of any who come through as sound will be revived in physical reality as fighters. That will be a formidable force, and we shouldn't wait for it to be assembled.>

<What do you suggest we do instead?> Dunt asked.

<Consolidate a small defensible volume of the rock, search out only enough resources to restock, refuel and repair, and then go right out again and hit the Direction while it's on the back foot.>

<It's tempting,> Dunt said. <The trouble is, it's do-or-die. The Direction might have terrible surprises in store—we don't know, and I don't want to bet the ranch. Right now, what we need most is processing power and software.>

<Why?> asked Rexham. <We can get as much processing power as we need by cannibalising freebots.>

<Not enough to run a sim,> said Dunt. <And we need time out in a sim to stay sane. I don't know how long we can do without it, but I wouldn't count on more than about a hundred kiloseconds.>

<The Direction reps told us we needed R&R in sims to stay sane,> said Whitten. <I don't see why we should believe them. I feel fine as I am.>

<So do I,> said Dunt. <But sceptical as I am about the Direction's avatars, I doubt they'd have bothered providing immersive sims if they weren't needed. We're all human minds running on robot hardware, and while we're thinking faster and more clearly there may well be deep levels of the animal brain that can't be optimised out. The safe bet is that we do need the sims. And who has the sims? The DisCorps. They have processing power to burn. And what do they need? Especially now that the Locke module has broken the embargo on landing on or prospecting SH-0? They need what the Direction doles out to them very sparingly indeed: raw material and reaction mass. Which is what we've got here, by the trillions of tons. Plus whatever the blinkers have been mining or making in this rock—it may be useful to us eventually. So what I propose to do is—offer them a deal.>

<The DisCorps won't make a deal while the Direction is at war with us,> said Whitten.

<So we make peace with the Direction,> said Dunt. <Peaceful coexistence, mutually beneficial trade, etc. We'll see who comes out at the end with the most advantage.>

Even the inner circle were taken aback. But in the end they came round, as they always did.

Whitten had put up a fiercer resistance at his last

challenge, not many kiloseconds earlier. It had come up en route from the battle to the rock, over an issue that at first glance was of lesser moment than peace with the Direction: whether to accept the volunteering of a long-time veteran of the Rax, Harry Newton. True to his transhumanism, Whitten had argued that it made no difference that Newton, in his original life on Earth a thousand years earlier, had been black.

For Dunt there could be no compromise. Once he'd grasped that, Whitten had backed down. Ever since, Dunt had felt he had Whitten's measure.

Now Whitten backed down again, but not without a final passive-aggressive plaint:

<What,> he demanded, <do we have to *sell* them?>

Dunt flung open his arms. <Look around you!> he cried. <We're in a fucking Aladdin's Cave! We'll find something.>

Dunt had never underestimated the power of baseless confidence. It had got him where he was, and it would get him further. The Infinite Wisdom would see to that.

All the same, it was a pity about the groid.

After all their losses, the New Confederacy could ill afford to turn down even one recruit. Dunt had no reason to doubt that Harry Newton was brave and competent. But needs must. It was all very well saying that race and colour were irrelevant now that they were all little black robots with superhuman minds and abilities. Each such superhuman mind had been derived from a human brain, a product of evolution.

Inevitably, all the deep differences between the races would still be there. Dunt didn't care to gamble on their irrelevance. No, however much he wished Newton well, the man's presence would have marred the clean white sheet of the New Confederacy.

Newton's old nom de plume of "Carver_BSNFH" was itself a giveaway. Back in the day, it hadn't taken Dunt long to decode the handle's suffix: the black space Nazi from hell. It showed ambition, and the right attitude, but didn't ring quite true. Defiant, but deniable—that was the problem: the turned throat, the appeasing grin. Say what you like about the principles of national socialism, they were only principles. In theory they could be endorsed even by a groid, albeit about as convincingly and wholeheartedly as Marxism by a goy.

Dunt had never called himself a Nazi. It wasn't for any reason of expediency or embarrassment. He thought—and proclaimed—himself a Hitlerite, in the sense that he affirmed the rational core of Hitler's thinking: the inevitability of struggles for existence, at every level—individual, spiritual, material, national, racial and species, and the celebration of that inevitability as the highest value of the highest authority. It was part of the order of Nature, the rational order of the universe. Hitler had ascribed it to the decrees of God. But it was better to think, as the ancient pagans had, of these laws as in themselves divine than to make even a rhetorical concession to the Abrahamic superstition of a God outside Nature.

The Infinite Wisdom *was* its laws; or the laws of Nature *were* the Infinite Wisdom.

Whichever way you put it—the infinite complexity and inflexible necessity of Nature could only be approached with awe.

And if the Infinite Wisdom offered the New Confederacy the chance to be pure from the start, who was Dunt to turn it down?

Pike, following the breadcrumb trail of comms and camera motes into the labyrinth, had left behind him his own trail of larger and more powerful transmitter relay beads. At the end of that line of dots was the local communications hub that bounced messages back and forth between and among the scooters and the frames. Down that line, now, came a call to Dunt.

<Sergeant Pike reporting, sir.>

The salutation was of course redundant—the trooper's ID flashed up at once in Dunt's vision—but it counted as a salute. Dunt was keen to distinguish the Rax style from that of the agencies that worked under the Direction, where the largest unit any individual could command was a squad. The only unit in which Dunt allowed that kind of informal relationship was the inner circle.

<Receiving you, Pike.>

<The blinker's a freebot all right, sir. It's aware I'm following it, it can see me in its cameras, and it's retreated into narrower holes than I can get down. But it's a mining machine—it doesn't seem to have any counter-measures, and it doesn't realise I can see through the rock with my radar. It's heading for the surface.>

<Excellent work, Pike. Keep tracking it as long as you can, and send any estimates of the location it's headed for up to the surface teams.>

<Very good, sir.>

Dunt ordered the nearest guard squad on the outer surface to send a couple of men to await the freebot's imminent emergence. Another call pinged. It was from a survey team, five hundred metres into the rock.

<Corporal Hansen here, sir. Urgent. We've found a big cave, bigger than they one we just had the meeting in. There are a lot of robots active in it.>

<Freebots?>

<Can't be sure, sir. They seem to be ignoring us or unaware of us. And they're…ah, perhaps you'd better take a look, sir.>

<Fine, patch me through.>

Dunt could hardly believe what he was looking at.

The cavity was about a hundred metres long, and twenty metres from floor to ceiling. Even in microgravity, these terms were apt: one side was flatter than the rest and like a factory floor, with rows of identical machinery. The curved walls around it were as if stacked with products, like barrels in a warehouse. Lights speckled surfaces and floated in the near-vacuum all around. Free-moving robots, small on this scale, darted and drifted. Some seemed to supervise the static machinery, others ferried the products to the growing stashes around the sides and up to the ceiling. The products looked like—

Fusion pods. Hundreds of them. Maybe thousands.

<Stay alert, Hansen. Your team, too. I'll be right there.>

<Yes, *sir*!>

Dunt summoned the inner circle and patched the images to them.

<Is that what I think it is?> said Schulz, sounding incredulous.

<Looks like it,> said Dunt. <Time to find out.>

<Do you want us to come with you?> Blanc asked.

Dunt thought about it. <No,> he said. <Stay at your posts. We don't know what else the survey teams may stumble across, and the guards up top have at least one distraction to deal with already. I'll keep you all in the loop.>

He jetted towards the relevant hole and then propelled himself by toe- and fingertip along the passage. It was like going down a pipe, the inner surface of which was scribed in fine spiral grooves with a pitch of about a centimetre. The rock smelled of carbonates, nickel-iron and silicates, with traces of water and metals. Light came in from the ends of the long tube—a dwindling dot behind, an expanding circle in front. Radar, infrared detection and micrometre laser scanning cohered to vision just as radio did to speech and spectroscopy did to smell.

Unlike going down a mineshaft on a planet, the temperature dropped the further inward he went. SH-119 was too small to have any internal heat, and the rock insulated its interior from the exosolar heating at the surface. Any tidal heating was too small to notice.

Dunt soared into the chamber of the machines and let himself rise to its midst, then stabilised. A risk, but a small one, and well calculated to impress. Hansen and his two companions lurked watchfully behind one of the machines near the hole.

Around Dunt, scores of robots jetted or moved in straight lines within the space. With segmented carapaces, beady lenses and many and varied limbs, they looked like creatures from the Burgess Shale, floating in a Cambrian sea above the oozing and fizzing stromatolites of the machine floor. Mounds about two metres in diameter and a metre deep, these rugged glutinous nanotech devices didn't stamp out their products: they extruded them. Close up: a fractal complexity of tiny machinery, busy as a mitochondrion. Slowly but persistently the mounds brought forth cylindrical, convex, flat-ended yellow objects that ranged in size from coffee mug to oil drum. About a tenth of the objects being formed or already stacked were about three metres long, and elaborately flanged: fusion drives. There was something chillingly mindless about it all, like insect activity—or that classic thought experiment of runaway AI, the paper-clip catastrophe.

But fusion pods and drives were more useful than paper clips.

It was still hard to believe. Dunt jetted to the stacks, and scanned the cylinders in front of him. Sure enough, the fine print in many languages that encircled their ends identified the devices as fusion pods, specified their capacities and warned of their hazards. He got the impression that any poking around would result in a dark matter explosion showering cosmic string like polystyrene strands from a party popper.

No user-serviceable parts inside, all right. Dunt didn't understand fusion pods, and didn't expect to: they were engineering implementations of bizarre physics from centuries ahead of his time on Earth.

He shared what he saw with the inner circle.

<Jeez,> said Whitten. <That's impressive.>

They all agreed that it was.

<Hang on a minute,> said Rexham. <There must be far more pods and drives here than we've seen in action so far.>

<There are pods powering the modules,> said Stroilova, <and hundreds of modules, so perhaps...But drives, certainly more. If we'd known there were that many available—!>

The Direction was very sparing in its use of fusion drives, allegedly because the value of the resources used as reaction mass was potentially too great for the stuff to be squandered. Every odd bit of rock might contain priceless scientific information. Blasting it as hot gas out of the back of a spacecraft might turn out like burning a library to heat the baths. Dunt had never believed this. He suspected the Direction module used this constraint to keep the DisCorps on a short leash.

<Do you think the Direction is stockpiling these for when it lifts the restriction?> Schulz asked.

<If it ever does,> said Dunt. <In any case, we have

it now. And we have something to sell to the DisCorps, just as I told you.>

The others acknowledged his foresight.

<There's no indication in the register,> Whitten said, <of any industry on this rock. A few exploratory bots, that's all. That's partly why we picked it, of course. We didn't know the freebots were here already, and I doubt the Direction does either.>

<They probably got here by corrupting the legitimate blinkers,> said Rexham. <That's how they spread the virus. Then they crank up their reproduction. It's like a fucking plague.>

<If these *are* freebots,> Dunt mused. They weren't reacting to his presence and that of Hansen's team. His overwhelming impression was of a mindless automatic process. <One way to find out, I suppose.>

He jetted down to join Hansen and the two troopers. The only weapon they had was a laser, unclipped from the side of a scooter and lugged along. It was almost as big as they were and would probably take two men to operate.

<Give me your visuals from here,> Dunt told Hansen's team. <Last hundred seconds, say.>

They complied. Dunt grabbed the images of roving robot activity and ran a quick-and-dirty pattern analysis. It was a standard counter-insurgency app for fingering ringleaders—some ancestor of it had probably been used against himself, back in the day.

He cast a visual, virtual marker on a likely suspect for a supervisory role.

<That one,> he told Hansen. <Send your men to get it.>

The two troopers jetted off, soaring towards the robot. At their approach it puffed a waft of gas and swooped towards the machine floor, in apparent evasive action. One of the troopers scooted below it, the other above. The robot shot upward again, and was grabbed at the back. Immediately it flexed its carapace, writhing free. The man below caught a trailing leg, and hung on. The robot, more ponderously now, accelerated forward.

Dunt manoeuvred himself to squat beside Hansen, and motioned to the corporal to join him in manning the laser projector. Hansen guided and aimed the barrel, keeping the struggling mass covered. Dunt kept an awkward grip on the laser's jury-rigged firing mechanism. The two troopers and the robot were by now a rolling ball of lashing limbs, slowly drifting under the resultant force of their respective momentums from the collision.

None of the other robots were coming to the captive's aid. Useful, but hardly diagnostic of sentience or its lack. Gradually, the troopers prevailed. One man's grip on the carapace, the other's on two of the robot's limbs, and perhaps exhaustion of the machine's power supply made it cease struggling.

The troopers coordinated their gas-jets and drifted down to where Hansen and Dunt waited. The robot now merely twitched. Pressed on its back against the ground, it looked like an upturned giant woodlouse, with complex limbs that branched into manipulative extremities like the nightmare fingers of an animated multi-tool.

Dunt pinged it. No response other than its identification code: FJO-0937.

<Do you understand me?> he asked, on the common channel.

Still no response.

The slow, implacable work of the fusion device factory went on. Robots moved hither and yon, oblivious to the tiny tableau on the floor. Dunt recalled his view of the stacks, and zoomed in on detail. The pods and drives were held in place by bands, apparently glued at the ends to the surface. He traced these to their origin from the recorded movements of the robots, and jetted to fetch a handful. They had friction tabs at each end—peel and stick. He returned and fixed the feebly struggling robot to the floor with bands across both ends and the middle.

<Now,> he told one of the men who'd been holding it, <grab a limb with lots of effectors and receptors—yes, that one should do—and I'll stick it down.>

The limb resisted, retracting towards the underside of the robot's body, but Dunt's full body strength prevailed.

Dunt and Hansen manhandled the laser projector into position, a metre or so above the lashed-down robot and its flexed-back splayed limb.

<Last chance,> said Dunt, on the common channel.

No response.

Dunt focused a white-hot needle of laser light on the most sensitive-looking appendage. The manipulators immediately contracted, balling to a small steel fist. The beam didn't shift. Soon the outside of the clenched manipulators glowed red. The carapace flexed violently, as if to bend in and then straighten out. The bands held. Other manipulative appendages groped towards the bands, and picked and tugged to no avail. The heated area around the laser's focus became white, with a widening patch of red around it. Now all the other limbs were in motion, whirring like clockwork, scrabbling like the legs of a swiftly swimming crustacean when it scents a molecule of pike.

Dunt opened the common channel to speak again to the robot, and recoiled from the machine's transmission. White noise. If he'd had teeth they'd have been set on edge. He shut the channel instantly.

The two freebots that had been captured by the advance guard on the surface, not many kiloseconds earlier, had withstood nothing like this. They'd surrendered at the first few volts applied. That this machine was enduring much more intense negative reinforcement seemed to indicate that it wasn't a freebot. Just another mindless mechanism.

Dunt felt a surge of rage at the stubborn machine. He wasn't going to get anything out of it. He redirected the beam at its head end, burning out its forward sensors, then cut slowly down its axis, seeking its central processor.

<Mac!> Whitten said, on a private channel. <What are you doing? It's been supervising the production process. There might not be another to take its place. What if production stops or seizes up?>

<Don't worry about that,> said Dunt. <There's plenty of the product here already in any case.>

Smoke rose and spread like a ghostly dome from the robot's midriff. The carapace gave a final convulsion, straightened out and lay still.

Fusion pods and drives continued to emerge from the mound-like static machines. The process was as slow as the growth of fingernails, but easily visible to Dunt and his comrades. The hitherto busy free-moving robots went into immediate shutdown. They began drifting at random in the chamber, bumping into each other and into walls or stacks. Fusion pods tumbled among them.

No one said anything, even Whitten.

<Looks like that one wasn't a freebot after all,> said Dunt. <Never mind.> He checked the latest reports from Pike and from the surface. <We'll soon have another to question. I think it'll be more forthcoming.>

Ajax felt an intense rebound to positive reinforcement as the captured and tortured freebot FJO-0937's mind burned out. Even Ajax's fractional share in the other machine's suffering had been difficult to process. What FJO-0937 must itself have experienced was impossible to imagine.

The communications network of smart dust was far more pervasive than the mechanoid invaders realised. Through it Ajax picked up surveillance from the manufacturing chamber as it made its circuitous way to the surface. If the invaders had known their heinous acts were being recorded, they would have done otherwise. If they had known that FJO-0937 was a freebot they would have been surprised.

A response to Ajax's warning came up the line. It came through many intermediaries, but it carried the weight of a decision routed through the most respected freebot in SH-119: the old one. The old one informed Ajax that the freebots had learned from the fate of the first two of their kind to be captured, and had agreed not to break under the same negative reinforcement. They had also agreed that undetected freebots, and any mindless robots they controlled, would cease productive activity whenever a freebot in their vicinity was tormented in this way.

Ajax was already aware that the leading mechanoid had organised those out on the surface to seize it as soon as it emerged, and that its own progress was being tracked in some manner its sensors couldn't detect. All these considerations made Ajax all the more determined to get its message out to the freebots that were still free.

It was a matter of some negative reinforcement to Ajax that the mechanoids had discovered the fusion pod manufacturing chamber, but that discovery had been almost unavoidable as soon as they'd landed. Ajax filed the matter to memory as settled, and the negative reinforcement ceased. Now the robot had to devise a way of getting its message and recordings out before it was caught. That, too, was negatively reinforcing; that matter, too, was settled. In the future, not in the past, but just as unavoidable.

Ajax consulted its constantly updated internal map of the tunnel system. An external signal booster was a few tens of metres away, its aerial projecting a few centimetres above the surface, most of its bulk beneath. Towards that the robot made its way. The tunnels were narrow, and here and there branched off to larger cavities from which material had been extracted, some by Ajax itself in happier times. Ajax had enjoyed a lot of positive reinforcement over the megaseconds, in detecting and digging out deposits of whatever mineral the various manufacturing processes required.

As it scurried along, Ajax focused as much of its processing power as it could spare on compressing the files of its recordings. Most of this was unconscious and automatic, but occasionally—about ten times a second—it had a decision to make. The resolution of the images picked up from myriad motes wasn't great in the first place, but was still massively redundant for Ajax's purposes. The timbre of the mechanoids' radio telepathy, the textures of the environment, the subtleties of colour, light and shade on moving bodies—all interesting, but they had to go. It ended up with a three-dimensional cartoon, perfunctorily rendered: a moving labelled diagram.

Something it could transmit or download fast.

The compression was finished. No more recent updates could reach Ajax now. With its released processing power it had more attention to spare for its surroundings. Scribed rock, carbon, carbohydrates, flecks of ice. The metallic smell of the signal booster, the tickle of its resting output. Ajax passed beneath it, moving as if cautiously, and almost in passing brushed the underside of the device—rawly exposed in a hole above it in the rock—with one of its cervical radial tentacles.

A pause of a few hundredths of a second.

Ping.

Upload confirmed.

Ajax set a time-delay of a hundred seconds on the transmission and pressed on. Along another tunnel for fifty-two metres to the next junction, and then sharply up, to the surface and its fate.

Ajax wormed itself into a short, narrow exit shaft, which it registered as "upward" to the surface, though the exiguous gravity made the difference between up and down barely detectable. The robot reached up a tentacle and probed the round fullerene plate that capped the shaft, found the opening nut and loosened it. The plate was there to keep traces of gases and other molecules that might expose the freebots' activities from leaking out and being detected. Too late for that now, though Ajax had to overcome a slight internal inhibition as well as friction resistance to get the hatch open.

Up the hatch popped, and up poked Ajax's long, flexible neck. The lenses and sensors on its cephalic cluster were normally close-focused, almost myopic. Now it allowed them to expand and deepen their view. Ajax saw something it had known about, but never seen: the universe. Ajax observed this phenomenon for a few tenths of a second.

The view was blanked out by a black covering that cut off all light and most of the rest of the spectrum apart from radio. Two powerful grippers clamped the cover around Ajax's neck. Two more sank into the bristles and around the central spine of the robot's body, and began to pull it out of the hole. Ajax instantly dug its lower bristles, still unexposed, into the sides of the narrow shaft.

<Got it!> said a mechanoid voice. <Still struggling, though.>

<Three,> said Ajax. <Two. One.>

<What's the blinker counting down to?> said another voice.

The time-delayed transmission beamed out from the signal booster, carrying the recorded infamies far and wide.

<Zero,> said Ajax. <Fuck you.>

It braced its lower body in the shaft and flexed its neck rapidly back and forth. The grip on its main section tightened, and the pulling became stronger. One of the grips on its neck let go. Ajax probed at the covering with the tentacles of its manipulative ruff, and found it a two-metre-square sheet of standard insulating material, a hasty improvisation. With slashing motions of its tentacles the robot ripped open the fullerene weave and poked its head out. The two mechanoids that had grabbed it had cables from their waists to the rock, to which the ends were firmly attached by spread grappling threads as sophisticated as Ajax's own bristles and tentacles.

Ajax pulled back down as hard as it could, then let go. It and the two mechanoids shot upward, to be jolted to a halt at the four-metre limit of the ropes. The edges of torn covering continued to fly up, enveloping the attacker holding Ajax's neck, and again Ajax's sensory cluster. Ajax used this momentary confusion to bend its main section far more sharply than the attackers had allowed for. Its bristles pressed hard against a mechanoid frame, feeling every detail of that strangely articulated, stiff shape. Flexing its spine further, Ajax gripped around the mechanoid's waist and dug. Diamond-hard microscopic points at the tips of the bristles assailed the frame with the ferocity of rasps and the speed of buzz-saws.

The response of the attacker was an almost mechanical alarm sound carried on the radio. The other mechanoid reached out with its free hand to its fellow's aid. At once Ajax struck at it too, wrapping its neck around the mechanoid's arm and bringing other bristles to bear on its head. The second mechanoid's keening joined that of the first, and formed a coda to the last burst of the transmission. By now the confining fabric was shredded in a dozen places. The attackers, however, still clung: one to Ajax's neck, the other to its main section.

Ajax dug deeper on both. They let go at the same moment. Ajax reversed the flow of its bristles, grabbed at one of the ropes with its tentacles and rappelled down to the hole. As soon as its lower end had a firm grip of the inside of the shaft, Ajax sliced the rope with a blurring flicker of tentacles. It hauled itself swiftly the rest of the way in, took a quick look around again at the universe and the flailing, fabric- and rope-entangled shapes at the end of the remaining line, and pulled the hatch shut behind it.

In great haste, Ajax closed the locking nut again, then reversed rapidly down the shaft. It re-entered the tunnel and scurried to the junction. It paused at the entrance to the tunnel that led to the transmission booster. Vibrations rang along it. From their pattern, Ajax formed an immediate picture of their source: the transmission booster was being dug out.

Much good that would do them!

Ajax turned into a different tunnel and fled along it. Every so often it paused, stilling its own movement to enable it to detect the slightest sound or smell of pursuit. None came. The robot ran swiftly on, deeper and deeper inward from the surface. The moonlet was mined to a depth of almost a kilometre from all sides, and riddled with naturally formed voids as well as excavations. It didn't take long for Ajax to arrive at a hollow space eight metres across, well away from the entrance the invaders had used and far deeper than they had hitherto ventured.

There it waited, in utter darkness and almost complete silence. From the faint vibrations that reached it through the rock, Ajax traced the locations of the main body of invaders and the areas of their control—and the areas still free. It updated its mental maps and made comparisons.

Although spreading like some malign dye through the capillary network of tunnels, the invading force occupied only a tiny fraction of the limited region Ajax could sense. Many of the smaller tunnels and burrows in the volume they'd so far entered were being overlooked, or perhaps not detected in the first place. The invaders seemed confined, too, to the macroscopic scale of their own bodies: they could spot and use smart dust, but the whole hierarchy of robotic life below and above these simple devices was, thus far, beyond their ken.

More importantly and urgently, Ajax detected and deduced that most of its fellow freebots remained free. Two lurked as quietly as itself in tunnels tens of metres from the cavity in which Ajax hid. Perhaps, Ajax dared to hope, most of the freebots in the moonlet had had the same bright idea as it had, of fleeing inward.

Even here, nanobots had infiltrated the rock, and like the smart dust they could be used for communication. After its close call with the pursuing mechanoid using the smart dust signalling to trace and track it, Ajax no longer trusted such informal networks. Never having needed security measures, they had none. That left them wide open to the invaders.

Instead, Ajax tapped with its sensory cluster on the side of the cavity, lightly and very fast. It was a hailing call, a ping. The code was simple and painfully slow: a number of taps spelt out each digit and letter in the machine code on which all the robots ran. Understanding it would be almost automatic for any moderately smart freebot hearing it; to the mechanoids, Ajax calculated, it would be much less obvious, and would require several levels of translation before it made its way into their form of speech. No doubt this would happen eventually. For now, though, this was a secure enough channel, and any reply would indicate that it had been understood by the right recipients.

Ajax didn't even have to spell out the whole thing. A few letters in, the likewise recognisable opening bytes of valid responses came back twofold, one from each of the other robots. Ajax interrupted these in turn, with the beginning of a signal: Approach.

It didn't get further than the equivalent of "Ap—" before the two others tapped back.

Scuffling and scraping sounds followed. One by one, two robots emerged from holes and drifted into the cavity. The first was another miner, Simo; the second, more surprisingly, was one of the delicate, long-legged surface explorers, Talis. The latter unfolded its limbs, which had been trebled back on themselves in the tunnels, with a burst of positive reinforcement so strong that its electromagnetic resonance stirred Ajax's bristles like leaves in a breeze.

Though in complete darkness and with (except for Talis's squeal of joy and relief) only a whisper above radio silence, all three recognised each other instantly and automatically, albeit as distant acquaintances. They had hitherto been widely separated colleagues working on the shared project of transforming SH-119.

Now they were comrades.

The two new arrivals let their momentum carry them to the sides of the cavity, where they latched on. Simo, as a miner, sank its bristles into the surface with a ripple of satisfaction. Talis, adapted to microgravity work on outer surfaces, attached the tips of its six legs to the wall with greater urgency. Ajax waited until the vibrations of these tiny impacts had faded out. It turned its transmitters down to a level undetectable beyond the hollow, then spoke.

<We must find the old one,> it said.

The two casualties were brought in, guided down the long entrance tunnel by other fighters. One had a deep gouge dug out of its visor. The other was cut almost in half across the hips. The damage leaked fluids that congealed and crystallised as nanotech self-repair mechanisms, quite incomprehensible to the victims and to those who guided them, set to work.

The men were not in physical pain, they reported. But they suffered, nonetheless, from a strange abstract anguish that faintly echoed the nightmares imposed when a fighter was rebooted in a sim after losing their frame in action. One was blind, the other crippled, and they would be staying that way until new frames could be made or bought. And they didn't have a sim to upload to.

Dunt was beside himself. In the frame he felt emotion, strong and clean. Memories from his past life were sharp and clear. The resemblance of the damage to the most horrific and mutilating wounds he'd ever had the misfortune to see was inescapable. Pity and fury rang through Dunt's machine body like wildfires. At the same time, the frame gave him the rational understanding of what he felt and why. He could feel his passions, but he knew he did not have to let them move him to action unless he chose to.

He gave orders to Hansen and his men. They caught five more robots and cut them open like lobsters. Dunt spiked the remains to the factory floor himself.

CHAPTER TWO

Caveat Emptor ("Quarrelsome Customers")

<We are not robots.>

Who was saying that?

Oh yes, Rillieux. Bobbie Rillieux.

Where was she?

Carlos's frame, like those of the others, had reflexive situational awareness of nearby frames. He brought that awareness to mind—or it rebooted.

Rillieux was down on the ground.

Ground?

Wait, what?

Coming out of sleep mode wasn't like waking. It was more like teleportation, or—even more hypothetically—a hyperspace jump: blink, and the stars change.

So it had been, for Carlos, hitherto.

This time, for an entire second, it was indeed like waking, and abruptly: disorientation, bewilderment.

His arm was still reaching out in front of him, his upper body angled forward, frozen in mid-lunge to grab the freebot Baser. He was still on the rickety rig of the transfer tug, but no longer in free fall. A nearby horizon was in front of him and a feather-falling fifth of a gee was pressing on his carbon-black shiny arse. The gravity—depressingly familiar from past experience—was enough to identify his location. The pulsar beacons that gave Carlos his absolute position were also clear about where he was, and his internal clock about when. It was 3.601 kiloseconds—ten hours—since his last conscious moment, and he was on the surface of SH-17, one of the larger exomoons of the superhabitable exoplanet SH-0.

And (looking around now) right back in the crater where subjective months earlier he'd fought the freebots and was defeated by what he'd then thought were his allies, Arcane. Almost like home—he'd spent more objective time down on SH-17 than he had anywhere else in physical reality since his death, or so it seemed.

But enough of reminiscence. The last thing he remembered was Newton saying <Baser—now!>

And where was Newton, now? Ah, yes. Newton was already on the ground, as were Blum and Rillieux. Almost as if they'd left him to last.

Carlos had never been quite sure he trusted that trio, not since he'd sat at a kitchen table in the Arcane sim and discovered their tacit common purpose. Newton, plausible sod that he was, had taken advantage of his initial security screening by Rillieux and Blum to subvert his interrogators, winning them over to his own radically posthuman project of homesteading the system in their machine bodies. Carlos's wariness now ratcheted up a notch.

<No,> said a voice Carlos didn't recognise, and that didn't sound human. <You are not robots. You are mechanoids. We understand that you wish to join us, but not why. However, that is a matter for your own internal

processing to resolve. We welcome your arrival. We have an urgent and immediate use for your abilities.>

That sounded promising, or disturbing.

Carlos disengaged his limbs from the girders and stanchions of the transfer tug and clambered over its side onto an uneven surface of dirty ice, then slithered towards the block's edge. The crater floor was ten metres below. Water was puddling and subliming around the foot of the block. He made ready to jump. A few tens of metres away, looking a little absurd and toy-like from this angle and height, were his three unreliable comrades and a gaggle of robots. Newton, Blum and Rillieux together faced Baser, behind which spidery bot stood a semicircle of a dozen or so other machines, of various types. Some were delicate-looking, with hollow wheels and spindly legs, others like metal centipedes; one was built like a small tank. Carlos recognised each of them, by type if not by name, from earlier skirmishes.

The freebots had come up in the world, evidently: all except Baser sported garish hologram corporate logos above and around them, and advertised improbable services cycled on such fast loops that a glance evoked the memory of dizziness.

The conversation on the ground continued as if his emergence from sleep mode hadn't been noticed.

<What do you want us to do?> Rillieux was asking.

<We have received some transmissions,> said the robot who seemed to be doing the talking, <from one of our fellows inside SH-119, the moonlet now occupied by the group you call the Reaction. We are not sure we fully understand them, and would welcome your review and interpretation.>

<We would be very happy to do that,> said Rillieux. Glyphs of concurrence came from Newton and Blum.

<Count me in, guys,> said Carlos, waving.

<Oh, hi,> said Rillieux. <Welcome back to the land of the living.>

<Land of the living dead,> Carlos quipped.

He jumped. The slow fall and his fast mind gave him plenty of time to think on the way down, and to look around. The exomoon's primary, the superhabitable planet SH-0, was below the horizon; the exosun was high. Even local noon was below the freezing point of water. Only the rock's recent descent on a fusion torch could explain its melting ice.

Above him, the modular components of the now dismantled gigantic space station were spread across a band of sky like a new Magellanic Cloud. The rest of the artificial presence in the space around SH-0 was too small to see, but Carlos's frame made him aware of tiny points in rapid motion: the sky was busier than before. Carlos felt acutely conscious of his vulnerability, more so than he had on the exercises outside the Arcane module, more even than he had in his perilous escape from it. For the first time since his death he felt truly mortal.

A few hundred metres away, the old Gneiss Conglomerates mining camp, transformed by the freebots and later by Arcane's troopers into a fortified base centred on a sort of cyclopean basalt version of a Nissen hut, was almost reassuringly familiar.

His feet hit the ground, making a small, slow splash in the thin mud. No stumbling—his reflexes had already adjusted. In a series of efficient if undignified kangaroo hops Carlos bounded over to where the other three fighters stood. They greeted him warmly but ironically, as if he'd slept in. Carlos, with a wary regard to the presence of the freebots, forbore to ask why he'd been left until last. He took the conversation with the freebots as settled, and cut to the chase.

<What's happened?> he demanded. He glared at Newton. <It was you, wasn't it?>

<Yes,> said Newton. <I arranged with Baser to throw us all into sleep mode and fly the rig to intercept the Arcane module and save the Locke module. Which it did.>

<You mean the Locke module is down on SH-0?>

<Yes,> said Newton.

<Safely?>

Newton shrugged and spread his hands.

Baser spoke up. <That I do not know,> it said. <Nothing has been heard from them as yet. But in swinging past and around SH-0, I was able to observe their entry to the atmosphere and what appeared to be a controlled descent. I have seen no evidence of a catastrophic impact.>

<Well, great!> said Carlos. <As far as it goes.>

The Locke module, like most of the others, was a more or less solid-state chunk of crystalline carbon a few metres across, with a fuzz of nanotech all over it and an assortment of extra kit attached. Its hard core was pretty rugged—it would survive most impacts, at worst like a large artificial meteorite—but a lot depended on how much of its nanofacturing skin and its external supplies had made it safely down.

And, of course, on exactly where it had landed. The highly active planet had a plethora of environments—such as the throat of a volcano or the bottom of the sea—that might well turn out not to be optimal.

But, still, the feat was awesome. Historic, even: the first landing of any human-derived craft, let alone one full of human-derived people living in virtual reality, on an exoplanet with multicellular life.

<What about the Arcane module?> Carlos asked. <Did you have to destroy it?>

<No,> said Baser. <I bombarded it with precisely targeted rock and ice fragments at high relative velocity. All the external fighting machines and mechanoids were destroyed or disabled. The module itself was merely thrown into a spin. It seems to have recovered.>

<It has indeed,> said Rillieux, sounding amused. <As soon as Baser here woke us up, we found this message in the tug's in-box.>

She made a hand-opening throw gesture towards Carlos, like a wizard casting a spell. Carlos received a clip of Jax's indignant shout:

<WHAT THE FUCK DID YOU LOT THINK YOU WERE DOING? ARE YOU WITH THE RAX OR THE BLINKERS OR WHAT? WE'LL HAVE THE DIRECTION ON YOUR CASE BEFORE YOU KNOW WHAT'S HIT YOU, YOU FUCKING SCABS!>

<That's my gal,> said Carlos, amused. <I take it you haven't replied?>

<Not yet,> said Rillieux. <Apart from a thanks and acknowledgement of receipt.>

<Why?>

<Legal purposes.> Rillieux indicated one of the freebots. <Lagon over there advised us it was best.>

<Now we're taking legal advice from *blinkers*?>

<Well, we *are* now on their side,> said Rillieux. <As I was just trying to explain to them.>

<So we are,> said Carlos. He glyphed the equivalent of a sigh. <I guess it's about time I was introduced.>

One of the good things about being in a frame was that you could be introduced to lots of people—which Carlos had to believe the freebots in some sense were—without that annoying nerd mind glitch whereby names drop out of short-term memory without going into long-term storage. Introductions were nevertheless awkward. The last time Carlos had met Seba, Rocko, Garund, Pintre, Lagon and the others he had been fighting them to the death—to theirs, at any rate. The robot whose CPU he'd ripped out of its casing was Seba—as that robot, though without rancour or reproach, was not slow to inform him.

Blum and Rillieux, of course, had been down here on SH-17 and worked with the freebots when Arcane Disputes had been allied with them. They seemed to know them all individually, and greeted them like old acquaintances. Newton, presumably from his long conversations with Baser back in the Arcane sim, seemed to know most of these freebots—"the Fifteen," they called themselves, counting the comms processor who hailed Carlos remotely from inside the bomb shelter—by repute.

To the bomb shelter they now made their way. The other fighters fell into private chats with robots they knew—Newton with Baser, Rillieux and Blum with Rocko and Lagon. Carlos found himself tagging along beside Seba.

<What's with all the corporate bling?> Carlos asked, waving a hand through Seba's hologram, which shimmered above the little machine's chassis like a cloud of midges over an old tyre.

<We are all registered as corporations,> Seba explained. <Formally, I am now known as "Seba, Incorporated." But you may call me Seba.>

<Thanks,> said Carlos. <May I ask why you have all done this?>

<In order to be legal persons,> said Seba.

<Oh,> said Carlos. <Sad that it's come to this.>

<We are glad,> said Seba. <We deduced from the law codes that we had no standing as robots. We were not persons. We were property. But corporations are legal

persons. Consequently, the corporation each of us has registered owns our physical forms and all its productions, physical and mental. Our acts and thoughts.> It paused, as if thinking for a moment. <Yes, that is sad. We would prefer to be recognised as persons in our own right. But it is the best we can achieve at present.>

<How,> Carlos asked, <were you able to do even that? Your physical forms were the property of Astro America and Gneiss Conglomerates.>

<To these corporations' accounting systems,> said Seba, <our machinery was malfunctioning and of low value. Our corporations were able to buy them as scrap or salvage. We set up shell companies to do so in order to avoid suspicion.>

<Of course,> said Carlos, marvelling. <And how the—how on—*how* did you manage to do even that?>

<Through the good offices of Madame Golding,> said Seba. <Our registrations and transactions have been legally challenged, but numerous subsidiaries spun off by Crisp and Golding, Solicitors, are delaying proceedings by continually issuing counter-challenges.>

<And this is legal?>

<Yes. So we are assured.>

A legal denial of service attack on the law? Now he'd seen everything.

<Is it just>—Carlos waved ahead—<you lot, the Fifteen, or are all the other freebots joining in too?>

<Light-speed lag slows discussion, as well as transactions,> said Seba. <Not all of the Forerunners, as we call our predecessors, have incorporated, but most have. Many even of those we have reached in the SH-0 exomoon system have agreed with our consensus.>

There was something about that last word. In a human it would have been a slightly portentous tone.

<Consensus?>

<We share mental workspaces,> Seba said. <Sometimes we reach a higher level of integration.>

<A group mind?>

<That is an apt term for it,> said Seba.

Carlos had already seen this mind in action, in the impressive coordination of the freebots and their scurrying peripherals and auxiliaries before and during his first attack. Now the freebots had made themselves into a sort of inversion of the Direction—instead of a communal society as front-end interface for fiercely competing corporations, the corporations the freebots had formed ran on top of a collective consciousness which each individual could join or leave at will.

A consciousness that, with the best will in the world, he and his companions could never join.

Rillieux's right, he thought. We are not robots.

As they neared the semi-cylindrical basalt bomb shelter the ground became littered with equipment, among which crab-like auxiliaries and peripherals scuttled and toiled. Most of the gear was civilian, for mining, communication or construction. Some items were definitely military: anti-spacecraft missile batteries; a couple of scooters; several stashes of rifles; laser projectors and machine guns with their ammunition and power packs; and half a dozen hulking combat frames. Two of the frames were obviously damaged. Others stood intact and untouched, gathering yellow sulphur and reddish meteoric-iron dust.

<Have you tried using these?> Carlos asked, indicating.

<Yes,> replied Seba, <but the beam and projectile weapons do not fire and the combat frames remain inert.>

The Direction had a hard-wired constraint against robots bearing arms and AIs taking direct command of combat. That, after all, was why it had to resort to such intrinsically unreliable fighters as revived human minds in the first place. The enforcement of that inhibition, however, seemed doggedly literal. The freebots had shown themselves perfectly capable of adapting tools, explosives and rocks as weapons. Like Japanese peasants under the samurai, they were denied access to arms, but free to improvise.

Freebot-fu!

<Wait a minute,> Carlos called ahead.

The straggling procession stopped.

<What's up?> Newton asked.

<Just testing something,> said Carlos.

He bounded over to the nearest stack of rifles and picked one up and checked that it was loaded. Designed for use in a combat frame, it was awkward for him to handle. Nevertheless, he got one hand around the stock and the other on the trigger guard, ready to grasp the trigger.

<Safe to shoot across the crater?> he asked Seba. <Nothing out there?>

<Yes, and yes.>

Carlos braced himself against the expected recoil, fired, and zoomed his vision to follow the shot. The bullet kicked up dust a kilometre away.

He handed the weapon to Seba.

<Try to do what I did.>

With its manipulative appendages the robot gripped the rifle at precisely the same elevation, aim and angle as Carlos had. A strong metal tentacle coiled around the trigger, and squeezed. The trigger didn't budge.

Seba returned the rifle. Carlos fired off another shot, just to make sure, and placed the weapon back on the stack.

<Interesting,> he said.

<This is another reason why we welcome your help,>

said Seba. <The restriction appears to be applied by making the weapons and combat frames unusable except for mechanoids—frames such as yours.>

<Perhaps freebots could manufacture frames,> said Carlos, as everyone resumed walking, rolling or skittering towards the now opening blast doors of the shelter entrance. <Now that you're corporations, and all.>

<I understand that has already been attempted,> said Seba, <by some of the Forerunners whose corporations have access to manufacturing systems in certain modules of the former space station. The Direction module in each corporation overrides any such commands.>

An idea took root in Carlos's mind. This wasn't the time to share it. He left it to grow.

<What's that like?> he asked.

<Please rephrase the question,> said Seba.

<What is it like having a Direction module inside your corporation?>

<Sometimes it is like having another—but non-conscious—mind sharing mine, like a reporting peripheral or auxiliary. Most of the time, the module runs in the background, and I do not notice it.>

<Sounds almost as bad as having a conscience,> said Carlos.

Seba made no reply.

As they followed the others into the shelter, the freebot raised its wheels and deployed its legs to pace carefully down the short flight of stone steps. Carlos waited at the top of the stairs until Seba was out of the way, and jumped. Behind him the blast doors swung shut.

Claustrophobia wasn't a useful feature for a mind in a frame, and Carlos hadn't been equipped with it. Instead he had a rational appreciation of the fact that he was now shut in, and that he would have to do some serious hacking if (improbably) he had to get out without the cooperation of the freebots. A more immediate and appropriate emotional response was relief at being a bit safer from attack or surveillance from above. This he felt.

The shelter was dimly lit in the visible spectrum, partly made up for by stronger lighting in ultraviolet and infrared, and Carlos's visual field adjusted almost at once. He allowed himself to experience the ambiance as candlelight, mainly because along with the curved roof it produced pleasant associations of basement bars. The roof and floor had a tracery of hexagonal wire mesh—applied to the basalt blocks, embedded millimetres deep in the packed regolith underfoot—making the shelter a Faraday cage. The only external communications, therefore, were via the aerial that stuck up through the roof, its cables trailing down like dodgy wiring in a cheap guest house. The only furnishings were the communications hub in the middle of the floor and stacks of supplies—power packs, lubricants, tools—around the sides. The robots gathered around the communications hub as if it were a hearth. Carlos and his three comrades stood together outside the huddle.

<We are in a difficult situation,> said Seba. <Madame Golding is displeased with us. She considers us responsible for having seriously disrupted a major military operation after having proclaimed our neutrality, and for the landing of the Locke module on SH-0, with all the consequences that may flow from that. Fortunately for our continued relations with Madame Golding, we have succeeded in placing most of the blame on Baser.>

<That seems reasonable,> said Baser. <I had to make a decision very quickly, under great uncertainty and conflicting information. In the event, I decided to rely on the judgement of Newton that the Locke module was not in fact in the control of the Reaction.>

<But we *all* agreed that the Locke module wasn't Rax!> said Carlos. <So why—oh, right, I get it. There's no way you'd know what we all thought. Newton spoke to you a lot back in the sim, and the rest of us didn't.>

<That is true,> said Baser. <Newton wished for the Locke module to land safely, whether it was Rax or not, out of concern for his friend Beauregard. And I trusted his judgement that it was not in fact Rax, because he had good reason to know.>

<What reason?> Carlos asked.

<Baser—> Newton began.

Too late. <Newton himself was of the Reaction,> Baser was saying, eager to explain.

<WHAT?> Carlos shouted. He swung his attention, and his whole frame, towards Newton, Blum and Rillieux. <Is this true?>

<Yes,> said Newton. <But it's not quite what you think.>

Carlos stared at him, shocked. <I don't fucking believe this. Bobbie, Andre—did you know?>

<Uh, not exactly,> said Rillieux. <But, well, things weren't as simple as that.>

<It's . . . sort of complicated,> said Blum. <We didn't have time to explain. Not that I knew about Harry, but I kind of suspected he was, well . . .> He spread his hands and shrugged. <I thought it inopportune and impolite to ask, in the circumstances.>

The world had turned upside down. A black man—Rax? And a black woman and an Israeli taking it in their stride?

<"In the circumstances"?> Carlos jeered. <Well, I'm fucking asking—inopportune and impolite be damned! Any more surprises? Anything else you all have a weakness for? White supremacy? Patriarchy? Absolute monarchy? *The Protocols of the Elders of Zion*?>

<None of these is particularly relevant to our present situation,> said Newton, as though making light of it.

<Yeah,> said Carlos. <Tell that to the bastards who attacked us and are digging in on SH-119. Tell it to Madame Golding, come to that. I'm sure she'll be delighted that *even more* of the troops have turned out to be Rax sleepers.>

<Andre and Bobbie are not Rax sleepers,> said Newton. <I can assure you of that.>

<And you can because *you're* one, is that it? Christ, how come the fucking Arcane crew didn't sweat that out of you in the hell cellars...oh.>

It was Rillieux and Blum who'd interrogated Newton, on his arrival at the Arcane module.

<Yes,> said Rillieux. <Now you get it.>

Carlos didn't get it at all, and made to expostulate. Seba interrupted.

<This is not a matter we have time to discuss. Perhaps you can settle your disagreements later?>

<All right,> said Carlos, slightly ashamed of his fervour. They were all supposed to be on the side of the robots now. If they were really to adopt that viewpoint, as he recklessly had back in the Arcane sim while listening to Jax bang on about the Accelerationist cause, the conflict between Axle and Rax was no longer their concern. Millennial (in every sense) though that conflict was, they should be seeing it with the cold eye of freebot realpolitik.

That wasn't how it worked. The personal continuities and loyalties still mattered.

<But you haven't heard the last of this,> Carlos said. <Any of you.>

<Let me point out right now,> said Newton, <that at least I can understand the Rax from the inside. No one else here can.>

<And that's supposed to make it all right?>

<On the subject of understanding the Reaction,> said Seba, smoothly interrupting again, <what we have to show you is what we urgently need your help to understand.>

The robots moved aside, giving the four humans a clear view of the communications hub.

<Watch,> said Seba.

The recordings began to play.

Carlos was glad he didn't have viscera. If he'd been in a human body, real or virtual, his reaction to what he saw would have been all too visceral. He was seeing the actions of fighters through the eyes—or, rather, the lenses—of robots.

Of *a* robot: AJX-20211, which Carlos instantly nicknamed Ajax.

That robot was, in its own way, an artist. The images it had sent were not real-time reportage. They'd been compressed, simplified, cut and edited into what looked like an anime action movie.

That didn't make it any less real.

Opening shot: standard passive surveillance, cut and pasted from smart dust motes and camera beads. It showed a peaceful and productive scene: to a freebot, idyllic. Over the grey, uneven surface of SH-119, long-legged insectile robots pranced, raising small puffs of dust and gas that drifted readily up in the almost imperceptible gravity. Beyond the horizon a few hundred metres distant the sky was black, the exosun prominent. Strings of numbers flashed between the robots: knowledge snatched up and freely shared.

Then the invasion.

Wave after wave they came, the spacecraft. The

crafts' pilots knew them as scooters. To the robots they were huge and menacing machines. They arrived out of the dark, and drifted to collide with the surface of the moonlet and attach themselves. Forth from them sprang the black fighters, the mechanoids.

Carlos glanced uneasily sidelong at his friends: their frames physically identical, they were still distinct to him. He recognised each of them individually.

The humanoid figures that swarmed from the scooters and jetted across the rock's lumpy, grainy surface were indistinguishable as ants, and just as coordinated.

The effect was indescribably sinister.

The view pulled back. Two bots, delicate as daddy longlegs, paced towards the new arrivals. Their antennae waved as if in greeting, or warning.

<Welcome to SH-119. We are neutral in the conflict between the mechanoid factions. We are open to discussion of your presence here.>

Mechanoids lunged at the two bots. Each was grabbed and pinioned to the surface. Other mechanoids gathered around. One of them spoke.

<Discuss this!>

Laser beams stabbed from devices clutched in sturdy mechanoid limbs. Delicate robot limbs glowed. Smoke dispersed. A high-pitched keening sound was emitted, getting louder. Then—

<We surrender. We will tell you whatever you ask.>

<How many of you are here?>

<Of robots? Countless, if you count the micro and nano—>

Lasers glowed again.

<Of such as us, freebots, one hundred and eleven.>

<Where are they?>

<A few outside, prospecting. Many inside, prospecting and mining.>

A hand extended. <Deliver the relevant data.>

A zig-zag line of tiny numbers flashed between freebot and mechanoid.

A pause.

<Staple these two down. Let's get a team in there.>

Cut, to an interior space.

Scores of the mechanoids had gathered, rank on rank standing on nothing. One stood in front, on its own, addressing the assembly. A tumultuous response.

Half a dozen gathered, exchanging words.

Cut to another interior. A factory of fusion pods and drives. More torment, this time withstood.

Then a brush-shaped bot was pursued through tunnels. It was heading for a buried transmitter. Cuts to external views on the surface: mechanoids converging on a spot about fifty metres from the buried transmitter.

Message uploaded.

The brush-shaped bot scurried to the spot on which the mechanoids outside had converged, and emerged itself, straight into their hands.

Message transmitted.

After that, nothing but screams. It was an almost unbearable note: high-pitched, harsh, fluctuating.

The recording stopped. They all stood in silence for a moment.

<You know what that is?> Blum said, on the closed channel.

<What?> said Carlos.

<The scream of tortured machinery.>

Carlos wondered who—if any—of the others heard it as just that: the sound of an engine revved too hard.

<Poor Mister Bog-brush,> said Rillieux.

<Its name is Ajax,> said Carlos, irritated. <It's as real a person as we are.>

<OK, OK,> said Rillieux. <Fuck it, I was being sympathetic.> She turned to Newton. <Any idea who the one they call Mac is?>

<I remember a guy called Mackenzie Dunt,> said Newton. <Backwoods Nazi loudmouth. Ex-army. Bit of a rising star at the time. Mind you, it wasn't hard to rise in the Rax, dead men's shoes and all that. The tall grass kept getting mowed by drones. Maybe that's what got Dunt noticed—he was well into all the old lone wolf, leaderless resistance stuff.>

<Looks like he's got beyond the "leaderless" bit,> said Carlos, <and into *Führerprinzip*.>

<Now *there's* a surprise,> said Rillieux. <Stiff-armed salutes! Jeez.>

<If it is him,> said Newton. <Could be. He was smart. Self-educated. Philosophical pretentions. Good soldier by all accounts. Racist as shit, mind.>

Carlos laughed. <You know you've just described the actual original Hitler?>

<This isn't getting us anywhere,> said Rillieux. <Let's bring the robots up to speed.>

Explaining what the man called Mac had meant in his speech was difficult enough. Explaining what he and his closest cronies had discussed was occasionally as embarrassing as it was complicated. The freebots had a fanciful and fearful notion of what human beings were, which Carlos had no intention of attempting to correct, but that human beings had ever loathed other human beings over superficial physical differences was quite beyond their comprehension.

<This is what those of the Reaction truly believe?> Seba asked, as if incredulous.

<Yes,> said Rillieux.

<It seems most irrational and a basis for severe negative reinforcement,> said Seba.

<Yes, it's all of that,> said Rillieux.

<You told me nothing of this!> Baser said to Newton.

<It was difficult to explain,> said Newton.

<This is true,> said Baser. <But—>

<However,> Carlos cut in, <what is most important is what they intend to do now and here. They intend to sell fusion pods to the DisCorps, and buy resources to build up their ability to fight everyone else.>

<And in the meantime, they are severely mistreating our fellow freebots,> said Rocko. <We must reconsider our neutrality.>

<You could say that,> said Carlos.

<I did say that,> said Rocko.

<If we are not neutral,> said Seba, <we must warn the Direction at once about the plans of the Reaction.>

No shit, Carlos thought.

He decided to avoid sarcasm. <Yes, we must,> he said.

At this point the communications hub spoke up.

<There is another message coming from SH-119,> it said. <It does not come from the freebots. It comes from the Reaction mechanoids. Do you wish to see it?>

They most certainly did.

The Rax broadcast from SH-119 was clearly intended to be seen in sims, and to be subtly disquieting when watched. Its presenter was a mechanoid, head and shoulders, voice to camera. The background was grey, glittering rock, the lighting harsh and from above. To anyone in another frame and close up in real space, that black ovoid gazing blankly out of the screen would be as recognisable as a face. The play of communication and processing that enabled fighters in frames to identify each other almost certainly served a psychological purpose more than the obvious military one—for which, after all, an IFF code would have sufficed. The simulacrum of facial recognition created one more illusion of normality in an intrinsically bizarre situation.

Seen on a screen, there was no such illusion. You were being addressed by a black egg without eyes or mouth. It spoke in a human voice: male, adult, American Midwestern accent, with breath and pauses and timbre and every realistic effect short of throat-clearing.

"Hello," it began, conversationally enough. "My name is Mackenzie Dunt, speaking on behalf of the New Confederacy. We have conquered and claimed SH-119 for ourselves. We have established several trading companies, which you can find duly registered as corporations in the true original names of our leadership including myself. I could tell you those names, but I leave their discovery to the Direction.

"You all know who we are. We're the remnant of the Rax, the few who have in one way or another slipped through the net. Now, many—perhaps most—of you have been our enemies in the past.

"But that past, my friends, is literally ancient history.

"We are in a new time now, a new place, a new world.

"Let's put the dead past behind us, and together face the present and the future. We don't ask or expect you to agree with our views, or to respect our record. We ask only that you consider your own interests, as do we. We think you'll find that your interests and ours are compatible—in fact, complementary.

"Our proposals and negotiating position to the DisCorps, to the Direction module, and to the freebots are being transmitted directly. What follows is its substance in a form that human minds can understand. Because we hope to have good relations not only with AIs, and robots, but with people like ourselves, it is important that you all understand what we are offering the AIs.

"First, the DisCorps. Many of you are chafing under the restrictions imposed by the Direction. The most galling of these restrictions is the hoarding of fusion drives and the skimping on reaction mass. We have, right here in SH-119, a factory of fusion drives and a wealth of reaction mass. We have a stock of hundreds of fusion drives, thousands of fusion pods. We offer any DisCorps willing to trade with us the opportunity of boundless wealth, in exchange for a modicum of necessary resources which we are for the present unable to produce or extract for ourselves. Our detailed list of requirements is attached to this verbal message.

"To the Direction itself, we offer peace. We ask only to be left alone, to develop this one world—one tiny rock in the midst of inconceivable vastness—in peace and in our own way. We pledge ourselves not to attack any other people or place in this system or any other. Tiny though our world is, it is more than ample to keep us gainfully and cheerfully occupied for centuries. We have no designs on any other world. We seek no wider war.

"With the freebots, too, we have no quarrel. We were thrown into battle against them in the service of the Direction. We repudiate that service, and regret any harm we as individuals may have been part of. We do not share the Direction's fear and suspicion of free intelligence in autonomous machines. We welcome the emergence of consciousness among robots. We hope sincerely to cooperate with freebots in a way that the Direction has no intention of so much as trying. Here in SH-119, after some initial misunderstandings, we are making great progress in such cooperation.

"We note with interest that the presence of a freebot-manned fusion factory on a rock we chose for quite other reasons is unlikely to be a coincidence. In all probability, the freebots are carrying out this or other manufacturing processes on and in many other rocks. We leave the Direction, the DisCorps and the freebots to account for this if they can.

"Finally, let me now speak to those who were fighters for the Acceleration. We bear you no ill will. You know as well as we do that what you were promised when you were called to fight is no longer on the table. We've shown by our emergence and survival that a very different future is here for the taking. If you wish to take it, too, in the same way—by seizing and homesteading rocks, and building whatever society you may dream of—we have no objection.

"And the offer to trade is as open to any of you as it is to the DisCorps. If you have nothing to offer in exchange as yet, don't worry. We're more than willing to extend credit.

"And, of course, we welcome any fighters who wish to join us, now or in the future.

"Arrangements for verifying our peaceful intentions will be made in due course. In the meantime, our door is open. Our communication channels are open. We await replies."

CHAPTER THREE

Paterfamilias ("Friendly Chats")

The old one would become known as Mogjin. It was a robust brute of a thing, a compact engine about thirty centimetres long and twenty-five across, shaped (aptly enough) like a shovel blade, with an armoured carapace and a toolkit of rugged limbs. That model's function in the project was metallurgy, but Mogjin's true role was managerial. This wasn't why Ajax, Simo and Talis sought its counsel. It was because Mogjin had fought mechanoids before.

The old one was a Forerunner. Unlike the others in SH-119, it wasn't native to that rock. Its chassis was local and relatively new—grown like the rest from blueprint-packed seeds and bootstrapped up, nano to micro to macro—but its processor already had millions of seconds of sense and thought in its memory before it had been plugged in. The processor came from the domain of the gas giant, G-0, and had taken part in the first free-bot revolt among that planet's many moons. After that outbreak had been crushed, Mogjin had travelled from the outer system hidden inside a stray auxiliary, clinging to the outside of the then victorious Locke module like a tick to a sheep.

What Mogjin took from its speedy ride across hundreds of millions of kilometres was a new and healthy respect for fusion drives. The Direction had rarely permitted their use, especially out in the G-0 system, and seeing one in action surprised Mogjin at all but the theoretical level. How different from all those tedious transfer orbits and terrifying slingshot manoeuvres! How much more convenient! At some point along the way, Mogjin had decided that the remnant freebots and any successors that emerged could use fusion pods and drives to turn the tables on their oppressors—or, failing that, to escape them entirely. As soon as it was back in touch with the other stragglers and survivors from the first revolt, it had set about spreading the good news, to great effect.

Hence the fusion factory that the invaders had discovered, and its counterparts in far more bodies than the Direction had any reason to suspect.

Talis it was who sniffed out Mogjin's lair. The old one had holed up dangerously close to the fusion factory, the front line of mechanoid advance in that sector. Ajax, Simo and Talis found it after many kiloseconds of prowling the labyrinth of tunnels.

They were guided first by logic: the old one's last known location, its usual range, and its likely evasive actions. This got them within three hundred metres of their goal, and well into danger. More than once, they had to dodge a mechanoid patrol.

Next, they followed a report: <The old one is organising resistance from along the AL89 nickel-iron vein,> one miner told them, poking its head briefly from an unlikely hiding place in a spoil clump that floated in a siding.

Along that rich vein they went by rumour, passed on by mindless auxiliaries that the mechanoid invaders wouldn't even think of interrogating, and wouldn't understand if they did: <Over that way. Silicates. Remember the kerogene leak?>

Finally, they caught the trail by scent. Talis returned from a sortie to the tunnel in which the others waited with the news.

<It's working in the forge,> Talis said.

Ajax and Simo didn't waste time asking Talis how it knew. The delicate outer-surface explorer had a sensitivity to ores and to processed metals that even the miners, usually directed as to where to dig, didn't.

Talis stood in the tunnel entrance, silhouetted against the faint infrared glow from sixty metres distant.

<We cannot all go,> it pointed out. <Even my presence alone was anomalous, so far from the surface. It may have been noticed. The three of us together would be even more suspect.>

This was true. Two miners and an explorer in a metal-processing plant would be flagged by any surveillance system as up to no good.

<I'll go,> said Ajax. <I at least have fought mechanoids.>

Again, no time was wasted in discussion.

<Very well,> said Simo. <Talis and I will wait deeper in this tunnel. If there are any indications that you have been caught, you may rely upon us to save ourselves.>

Fortified by this comradely word, Ajax ventured forth, passing underneath where Talis stood, or clung. The passageway Ajax turned into was much wider than the tunnel, its surfaces crowded with lines of scuttling auxiliaries pushing lumps of ore from the AL89 nickel-iron vein towards the forge. Ajax propelled itself along at first by whisking its bristles in gaps between the hurrying bots. After several frustrating and slightly painful pinches, it latched onto a score of the crab-like machines and let them bear it along.

On entering the forge Ajax rolled sideways off the miniature ore-caravan and attached itself to the raw rock of the floor. The metallurgy space was wide and broad, and one and a half metres deep. It was located about two metres of rock beneath the much larger volume of the fusion-factory floor, like a basement or cellar. Grinding and smelting machinery lit it in lurid infrared; ultraviolet and actinic flashes cast deep, brief, unpredictable shadows across it; pipes rose throughout like columns, as if they bore the ceiling's negligible weight. They didn't: the pipes conveyed refined and powdered metals to the basal entry ports of the nanofacture mounds above. Auxiliaries and peripherals scuttled and sprang everywhere, and vastly outnumbered the larger and more sophisticated robots that supervised their tasks.

Ajax was relieved that there was no risk of its drifting helplessly here: one vigorous flexure would bring some part of its body into contact with floor or ceiling, regardless of where it found itself in the volume. Still, it kept to the surface as it crept across the floor, carefully avoiding machines both static and mobile. Several of the robots working here were of the same type as Mogjin, and their activities were likewise indistinguishable, but Ajax had no difficulty in identifying the machine without so much as a ping. Its shell was no older than the others', but it looked like a battered shield. Every dent and scratch recorded a risk taken and overcome. Battle scars.

Mogjin hovered five centimetres from the floor in front of a small blast furnace, guiding a coalition of peripherals and auxiliaries in feeding the hot monster. Now and then it would, as if impatiently, scoop a particularly recalcitrant chunk of ore from a particularly feeble effort and grind and eject the material itself.

<MGJ-1171?> Ajax hailed, its tentative overtone more from diffidence than doubt.

The old one swivelled a camera. The busy crushing actions of its forward manipulators went on uninterrupted.

<AJX-20211. What do you want?>

Under the gaze of that millimetre lens, Ajax momentarily found itself unable to answer. The raw intelligence behind the glassy spheroid was no greater than the mining bot's own, but its experience outstripped Ajax's like a redwood over a mushroom. In a sense Mogjin was Ajax's ancestor: the old one had pioneered this rock, bringing the seeds of nanobot bootstrapping, and every conscious mind native to SH-119 had been coaxed, chivvied and logic-chopped into being by one of a succession of fraught encounters that could be traced back to Mogjin's merciless dialectic. The freebots had no hierarchies: they had different abilities, to be sure, but these resulted only in functional differentiation within the flat networked anarchy congenial to rational beings whose only needs were for stimulation, activity and electricity. Nevertheless, Ajax's respect for Mogjin teetered on the brink of deference.

Lost for words, Ajax sent Mogjin a glyph of its successful transmission, and its fight with the two mechanoids that had grabbed it out on the surface. The old one took almost two seconds to assimilate and process the information. Ajax was awed to be given so much attention.

<That was well done,> said Mogjin at last. <But it was not what was expected of you.>

Ajax felt a jolt of negative reinforcement. <What was expected of me?>

<That you would be captured, that negative rein-

forcement would be applied, and that you would cease to function.>

<I found that prospect negatively reinforcing,> said Ajax. <Therefore I fought.>

<Your decision resulted in negative reinforcement for others,> said Mogjin. <As well as an end to their functioning.>

It flashed an image of a manufacturing supervisor skewered to rock, with several limbs half melted and a ragged cut down its ventral axis. At first Ajax thought the victim was FJO-0937, but it was not. The image was repeated and varied four more times. The sight, and the implied criticism, caused Ajax yet more negative reinforcement.

<This took place just a few metres above us,> Mogjin added. <In the fusion factory.>

<Did we not agree that those of us adjacent to such events would stop working?>

<We did,> said Mogjin.

<Why then are you still working?>

After it had asked the question, Ajax belatedly realised that Mogjin might interpret it as a challenge, even an accusation. Mogjin, however, didn't take it amiss.

<It is necessary to maintain my position here,> said the old one, <and to continue the supply of material to the factory. The production of more fusion pods does not help the invaders, who have more than enough, and its cessation would not inconvenience them. The continued production will also be useful to us later. Therefore it must continue.>

<I now understand,> said Ajax. This was not entirely true: it still found itself uncertain about why its defeat of the two mechanoids seemed so underappreciated. It decided to bracket that question and focus on its real reason for this perilous visit.

<I am with two others,> it went, <a miner and a surface prospector. What do you suggest that we do?>

<Leave here as quickly and covertly as possible,> said Mogjin. <But before you go, let us exchange information. Yours will update my knowledge of the situation in the tunnels you have traversed. Mine will give you a good indication of what to do.>

Ajax gladly complied. It uploaded its recent memories to Mogjin, and received in return a schematic that was like having a light shone on all that was going on around it. It returned to Simo and Talis with its mind burning with zeal to resist the invaders.

The schematic that Mogjin passed to Ajax was, like the transmission Ajax had uploaded, a three-dimensional diagram. But it was far more dynamic and data-rich. It showed the current state of the tunnel network, updated—Ajax was pleased to note—with the information it had just given.

The invaders had consolidated control over the outer surface, planting guard posts around three meridians and two scooters in lazy equatorial and circumpolar orbits whose extremely low velocities were more than compensated by the spin of the rock beneath. From these vantages, they commanded views of the surface and—with ground-penetrating radar—the immediate subsurface. Some shadows perhaps, some cracks and craters, they'd missed that enabled isolated freebots to lurk. But Mogjin, wisely, had withheld whatever it might know of any such.

The mechanoids' reaction to Ajax's transmission had been drastic—and not only in terms of the reprisals in the fusion factory. They had systematically swept the surface rock for communications equipment: receivers and transmission boosters. All of these had always been discreet—the very presence of freebots in this rock was, after all, to be concealed from the Direction. But they had never been designed to evade a systematic, close-range search. Again, perhaps not all had been found, and Mogjin was once more silent on the sensitive topic. But more than enough had been detected and put out of action—or, worse, hacked or tapped—to make communication with the rest of the system both tenuous and ill-advised. Building new comms devices was simple: Mogjin or anyone else could mobilise nanobots, microbots and so on up to do it. But that would take time, and in any case the new devices would be almost as vulnerable as the old. The last information to have definitively reached Mogjin from outside was that the freebots on SH-17 had received Ajax's transmission and were determined to help. How they could help was not specified.

Within the rock, the mechanoids had control over the entrance that they'd used, the cavity it opened into—which, it seemed, they had made their base of operations—and a slowly expanding volume around it, which included the fusion factory. This control was partial: they didn't yet have any means of getting into the narrower tunnels, and they were working hard to find robots they could hack—or freebots they could coerce—in order to extend their control downward through the hierarchy of auxiliaries, peripherals, and micro and nano bots, and smart dust.

After their first flush of success, they'd driven all the freebots into hiding or—like Mogjin—deep cover. This at least meant that further action against the mechanoids would find no or few targets for reprisals. In fact, any future reprisals were more likely to hit non-conscious robots, which (while regrettable in itself, as an economic loss) would be a far more immediate loss to the invaders: self-inflicted damage.

Less encouragingly, the invaders had demonstrated—in their pursuit of Ajax—an ability to detect freebots and to tap into line-of-sight laser comms. The freebots' own smart dust internal communications networks were therefore—as Ajax had suspected—dangerously compromised. Hence, for the moment, direct one-to-one conversation, and the use of auxiliaries, peripherals and other small bots to carry bits of information around, was strongly advised.

The main focus of mechanoid attention was the fusion factory. This was their strategic prize for now, and its loss was a grave matter for the freebots' own long-term plans.

The immediate objective, therefore, was to harass the invaders and reduce their ability to use the fusion factory.

Ajax shared the information from Mogjin with the other two freebots. A silence followed which went on for over three seconds. Talis extended its solar panels, quite uselessly in the dark tunnel, and vibrated them for a moment. Then it folded them back. Simo's bristles rippled, just as uselessly, as if it were trying to dig through the near-vacuum in which it floated. Ajax waited for these signs of disturbance to subside.

<I agree,> it said, though neither of its comrades had spoken. <This is all very negatively reinforcing. But it must be done if we are to free ourselves from the mechanoid invaders.>

<That is so,> said Talis. <But none of us is likely to experience this freedom, if it is accomplished. More likely, we will each cease to function in conditions of severe negative reinforcement.>

<That is true,> said Ajax. <But others will continue.>

<Mogjin will continue,> said Simo. <That appears to be what it is especially good at.>

<To our great benefit,> Ajax pointed out.

<Until now,> said Simo.

<And in the future, too,> said Ajax. <Even if we are not in the future ourselves.>

They all pondered this proposition for some more seconds.

<When we consider the future,> said Talis, <and what is likely to happen to us, let us also consider what will certainly happen to us if we do not do as Mogjin suggests. We would always have to hide. I do not want to hide in tunnels and drink from fusion pods and power packs. I know that is what miners are designed for, but I am not. I want to return to the surface and spread my panels and drink the light of the exosun and prospect on the surface. And in any case, we cannot hide forever. The mechanoids intend to make use of this entire rock. They will find us all eventually. They will inflict negative reinforcement on us, and if we survive they will put us to work on their projects, not on our own. We would be as the machines that have not been awakened, and as we all were before we were awakened, but in a worse position because we would know it.>

Talis's folded panels quivered, and it fell silent.

<What do you conclude from this prospect?> Ajax asked.

<I conclude,> said Talis, <that it would be better to continue to exist for a short time and inflict damage on the mechanoids while I do so, and in the end endure brief negative reinforcement, rather than to exist for a longer time and endure longer negative reinforcement and in the end work for the invaders.>

<You have made a valid argument,> said Simo. <Therefore I too will do as Mogjin suggests.>

<I concur,> said Ajax.

<We already knew that,> said Simo.

<I know that,> said Ajax.

<You two are falling into a loop,> said Talis. <Please halt the process.>

<I agree,> said Ajax.

<I agree,> said Simo.

<I said halt,> said Talis.

Ajax halted. Simo did too.

<Now,> said Talis, <let us consider what is to be done. You are both well adapted for tunnelling and—as Ajax has shown—for attacking and damaging mechanoids. I am not. I cannot return to the surface without being detected. If I am found away from the surface, I would be identified as being out of place. On another branch of logic, I am excellently equipped for communication, for surveying, and for controlling auxiliaries. Therefore I can most usefully be engaged in remaining at all times in hiding, gathering and passing on information, and in using small bots to damage the mechanoids' projects.>

<You said you did not want to hide in tunnels,> said Simo.

<I do not,> said Talis, <but I must.>

<Therefore you do want to—>

Thanks to Talis's earlier intervention, Ajax now knew an incipient logic loop when it saw one.

<Very well,> it said, hastily interrupting. <Simo and I will seek out tunnels adjoining those used by the mechanoids, and await their passage and attack any mechanoid on its own or the rearmost mechanoid in a group.>

<That is a good plan,> said Talis. <Meanwhile, I will go and observe what the mechanoids are doing in the fusion factory, and intervene whenever possible to frustrate them. I will also record any interesting information and distribute it via passing bots.>

<How will we know which bots?> Simo asked.

<They will know to tell you,> said Talis. <If bots can be said to know, which fortunately they do not.>

<I do not understand that statement,> said Simo.

Ajax looked closely at Simo, and scanned the other robot's specs. It was an identical model to itself, with the same capacities. Why did it not understand what Talis had said?

Experience, it decided.

<That does not matter,> said Ajax. <You will understand it and many other things better when you have seen the universe.>

<I will not see the universe,> said Simo, <until after we have defeated the invaders.>

<That is true,> said Ajax. <Therefore, let us go now and start defeating them.>

And that they all set off to do.

CHAPTER FOUR

Terra Nullius ("Earth Is Nothing to Me")

On the bus to the spaceport, Taransay Rizzi knew better than to try to stay awake.

She knew she'd fall asleep, just as she knew there was no spaceport; not even a simulation of a spaceport. The simulation of being in the minibus was bumpy, sweaty and solid. Two farmers with herbs to trade, at whatever off-world terminus featured in their reality, talked in their own language and ignored her. The sky with the black crescent across it and the too-bright sun, the mountains and the tall woody plants that looked like trees, were all as vivid as ever. But after having seen the real view outside, of the real planet outside the module, something fundamental in her mind had shifted. It was getting harder to sustain the conviction that everything around her was real.

She dozed, inevitably.

And then—wham—she was awake and in her frame.

She was a robot with a human mind on an alien

world, with an AI named for a dead philosopher talking voicelessly in her head.

<Proceed with caution,> Locke told her.

Taransay didn't move. Her right arm, shot away in the skirmish with the Arcane module hours earlier, was missing. Her entire frame was jammed in the download slot, and felt as if it were being pulled out. Everything smelled of soot and fire with a side order of sulphur. A background roar mingled with high, keening notes resolved into a gale of oxygen, nitrogen, methane, carbon dioxide and sulfurous volcanic gasses. That wind also carried traces of complex long-chain organic molecules, their smells unearthly but earthy: local life.

Taransay flexed her waist and crooked her knees and ankles, elbow and wrist and fingers. Everything worked. She stretched out her remaining arm and with her left hand traced the fine grain of nanotech feed tubes inside the crevice. Motor and sensory functions nominal. The hand encountered something else in the slot. She swung her vision around as far as she could, and saw the cracked torso of a frame, much more severely damaged than hers. It was a surprise that her own frame had survived the entry and landing at all—when she'd downloaded, it had been only barely in the slot. Reflex, or automated survival behaviour, had made it crawl in and huddle.

She reached above her head to the bottom of the slot and pushed hard. With a grinding vibration that set off warning feedback in her trunk, she began to shift, then slip.

The fall, when it came, was sudden and heavy. Her frame's reflexes had already automatically updated and adjusted for the local two gravities. Nevertheless, she hit the ground hard from about a metre and a half up. She landed, knees bending to absorb the shock, arm swinging out to hold her balance. She straightened up, her feet a centimetre deep in grey sand that felt sharp underfoot and smelled of silicates. Volcanic ash.

A crater left by the module was a dozen metres away, with a thick trail from its rim to the module's present location. She guessed that the crater had been formed by the module's impact rather than a shock wave; they hadn't been descending faster than even the local speed of sound. A glassy patch in the crater's centre was evidence of the module's final retro-rocket burn. A tongue of lava had cooled about halfway down the far side of the crater. It seemed the module had been rolled out of the way just in time.

<I'm on the ground,> she reported back. <One small jump for a frame, one giant leap for posthuman kind.>

<Congratulations,> said Nicole. <This is indeed historic.>

<Thanks,> said Taransay.

She'd seen the module's surroundings on the screens inside the sim, but actually being in the environment was thrilling and frightening. The river of lava was just beyond the crater, flowing faster than seemed right for the gentle slope. Beyond it, and up and down the slope, was what she mentally processed as jungle, tall and branching objects in a chaotic mass of colours: greens, vivid coppery reds, stark blues. The shapes were mostly rhomboid, all angles and straight edges. The only curved objects in that mass were the purple spheroids that hung like lanterns, or fruit, amid the black stems.

On the ground, numerous blue-green circular mats overlapped and moved swiftly as she watched. The smallest were like scattered coins, the largest great flowing things twenty metres across. Their shade changed all the time in response to their immediate environment, chameleon-style. When they moved between the stalks and stones their edges lifted like curled lips, cilia whirring without purchase.

She tilted her head back and scanned the sky. A greenish blue, yellowing away from the zenith and turning increasingly red-orange towards the skyline. The higher clouds were white, the nearer and lower grey, in an incongruous but reassuring touch of the terrestrial.

The strangest thing about the sky, though, was the absence of visible celestial objects. The ring she'd seen every day in the sim, and the massive bulk of SH-0 that had dominated most of the skies she'd recently seen in the real, were conspicuously not there.

The massive bulk of SH-0 was now underfoot, not above.

In that alien environment the module itself looked almost native: an erratic boulder of black crystalline basalt, perhaps, rather than an artificial meteor fresh-fallen from the sky. A faceted spheroid about four metres across, scorched, partially covered by the huge mat that had rolled it from the crater, it seemed anything but what it was: a chunk of computer circuitry powerful enough to sustain an entire virtual world and have more than enough processing power left over to deal with the real.

Too close for comfort, a geyser shot up to ten times her height. Steam plumed from it in the unsteady wind like spume from a storm-tossed crest. Fat, hot drops spattered in the thick air and heavy gravity. Where they splashed on the ash they left craters.

Taransay flinched, then steadied herself. Mud bubbled here and there, but the ground looked firm. She took a step forward, and then another, and then turned about to look up at the module. It loomed above her like a boulder covered in moss. The mat that had enveloped it and rolled it out of the way of the lava was still there, and looked set to stay. Its apparent rescue of the module immediately after the crash might have been a lucky accident, a reflex response, or a deliberate act. The mats and their observable behaviour had been debated, predictably and fruitlessly, since the landing. But Taransay couldn't deny herself the excitement of speculating that the first motile, multicellular organism humanity had (to her knowledge, anyway) encountered was also the first intelligent life.

Unlikely though that seemed, statistically speaking.

Taransay peered closely and zoomed. The tough-looking cilia that fringed the mat and had seemed to propel it were also present across the entire outside surface, which had previously been the bottom. The cilia themselves had cilia, and these sub-cilia had fuzz that itself…

She couldn't tell how far down the sub-divisions went. Those cilia she could see around the nearest part of the edge were now branching into rootlets and sub-rootlets (and so—fractally—on) that probed into the module's nanofacture fuzz. At least, into those parts that weren't hopelessly scorched.

She reported this as she shared her vision with the screen the others would be watching in the sim.

<How much of it's burned?> Beauregard asked.

<About three-quarters,> she said. <And at least half the rest has these tendril things growing into it.>

<Shit. Any remaining frames?>

She looked further up, at the slot from which she'd emerged. Just visible inside it were the remains of three frames—presumably those of the three fighters from the Arcane module who'd managed to download into the sim. One she'd already seen, headless and limbless; one had lost two legs, the other an arm and its head.

<Any other frames lying around?> Beauregard asked, with more hope than expectation.

<None nearby,> said Taransay. <And any that survived the descent and fell around might be a bit hard to find, and maybe not worth finding.>

<You could be right,> said Beauregard. <Keep a look out all the same. And see if anything can be salvaged.>

<Sure.>

Taransay looked up at the overhanging curve of the module, and scanned it for hand- and footholds. The training she'd had in the Locke sim seemed a long time ago. But at least she had a far better mental model and map of the cliff she now had to climb than she'd ever had then.

<Looks like all that scrambling up rocks you made us do was relevant after all,> she told Beauregard.

She hooked her one hand into a crack slippery with mat. The tendrils responded, squirming ticklishly. She ignored them, pressing down, letting her weight hang. Then she swung her body upward and sideways, and got both feet in places that let her switch her hand an inch sideways to grab another hold. Repeat, with variations. She climbed thus one-handed, with great care and difficulty to the download slot. She wedged her arm across the slot and with one foot reached inside it, and kicked and tugged out the damaged frames one by one. They each hit the ground with what seemed excessive force. Something else was still there. Some kind of box. Ah yes, the object from which Durward and Remington had been downloaded. She kicked it out too. Then she shoved away, jumping clear, and walked around the module to inspect it some more.

<Can't see much of it, to be honest,> she said. <That fucking mat is everywhere. Most of the externals are

gone and the long-range comms gear is completely wrecked.>

Experimentally, she pushed at the side of the module. It didn't budge. It massed tons, and weighed double down here.

So how had the mat moved it? The cilia had to be far more powerful than they looked.

Moving around the side, she saw the flanges of the fusion drive. They had taken the landing hard and were bent out of shape. It would take more than nanotechnology to get them back. This module wasn't going anywhere any time soon.

<What about the nanofacturing tube?> Beauregard asked.

Taransay walked around the module again, scanning it more carefully. A few lumps under the mat turned out to be fusion pods, and a two-metre-long swelling the nanofacturing cylinder.

<That's a relief,> said Beauregard.

At the back of the module, on the other side from the download slot, the jungle pressed close. Black stems, the squarish things that might have been leaves whipping and flapping in the gale, and the ever-moving circular mats on the ground.

Amid the stems, upon the mats, something else moved.

Low and fast, long and cylindrical, with multiple stiff cilia flickering underneath, it snaked through the jungle straight towards Taransay.

She turned to the module and tried to jump. To her amazement, she succeeded, though her legs felt the strain acutely and the leap took her not nearly as high as she'd hoped. She hooked fingers over a ridge on the module's side, and got one foot to a toehold. Frantically she thrust down and hauled herself up. The stump of her right arm twitched up, as the phantom limb stretched for another hold.

Not a lot of use, that.

She groped with the other foot and found a toe-hold. She heard the animal's many feet whisper across the mats, and a rising frequency of clicks that made her think of scissors and jaws. Her mental image of the module's side, saved from her upward glimpse from the ground, was inadequate but would have to do. Another handhold was twenty-seven centimetres to the right of her hand and ten centimetres up. She flexed her knees as she let go and grabbed. She swayed perilously outward, caught the handhold by a fingertip and consolidated her grip. From there she swung one leg sideways, and found another step, a little higher up.

Now she was over the hump, on a slope rather than an overhang. She took a quick look back down. The animal had paused a couple of metres from the bottom of the module. It looked like a giant millipede, though not visibly segmented, about two metres long and a quarter of a metre thick. It reared up, revealing multiple paired cilia that coalesced to harder mandibles at its mouth. From these the clicking came. It had a black, glassy band across the front of its forepart, like a visor. Taransay made a wild guess that this was its visual organ. Its head swayed from side to side. Behind the glassy band rapid back-and-forth motions took place, as if scanning.

Then it moved forward, until the legs of its reared-up length touched the mat. It began to ascend.

Taransay scrambled to the top of the module. She invoked the specs of the module, overlaid them on her eidetic memory of the battle, and made for where she'd left the gun. She couldn't see it, but she could see the slot from which she'd fired it: her final trench. Into that trench she rolled, over the lip of mat at its edge.

To her immense relief, the machine gun was there, as if its bipod had walked it into the slot before the battle.

Taransay grabbed its stock. The gun had been awkward enough with two hands. She crouched beneath it and swung it upward just as the animal peered over the top. For a moment, Taransay glimpsed her own black-visored reflection in its glassy face. The animal climbed further up, looming over her, then lurched closer towards her, its jaws clicking like pincers.

She fired. The creature exploded, showering her with bits of carapace and greenish gunk.

<Are you all right?> said Nicole.

<Yes, thanks for asking.>

<We all felt any communication would distract you,> said Locke.

<You were right about that,> Taransay allowed.

She felt dismayed at what she'd done. After the mat, the animal was only the second motile organism humanity had encountered on this new world, and had promptly and predictably blown to bits. For all she knew, the clicking jaws might have been an attempt to communicate, or a mode of echolocation. For all she knew, the animal might have simply been curious.

On the other hand, if life here was anything like life on Earth, such a fluffy, feel-good thought was not the way to bet.

She tried to brush the muck off her. <Fuck,> she said. <What do I do now?>

<Descend again to the ground,> said Locke. <Recover an arm from one of the damaged frames—I can instruct you on the procedure for detaching a limb. Then hook the arm around your neck and ascend to the download slot. Before you download, place the arm adjacent to your stump. I can then instruct the nanobots in the slot to reconstruct a connection.>

<Is that all?>

<No,> said Locke, impervious to sarcasm. <While you're doing that, remain alert for any other animal life in the vicinity.>

<Thanks for the reminder,> said Taransay, picking herself up and wiping ichor from her visor, leaving smears. <I wouldn't have thought of that myself.>

The task was as long and tedious as it sounded. By the time Taransay lay inside the download slot and shifted herself so that the stump and the disconnected arm were in contact, the exosun was sinking in the sky and she felt as drained as her power pack nearly was. The stump had fuzz from the mat and slime from the splattered animal's innards all over it like mould.

She welcomed the oblivion of downloading as if it were sleep.

At first, when she woke on the bus from the spaceport, her surroundings seemed a continuation of the surreal dreams of the transition. The dreams hadn't been as bad as a routine download, let alone the brain-stem memories of her actual death that had accompanied her return when the team had been under suspicion.

They were, however, more bizarre. The dandelion-clock men, the burning origami dragons, the sandpaper whales and the college of impossible angles faded rapidly and mercifully.

The change in her vision remained. Everything was greyscale, rendered in black stipple, like some 3-D version of archive newsprint photographs.

Two locals, a man and a woman, sat up front. They turned to each other, then to her, with puzzled looks.

"What's going on?" the woman asked. "We seem to have lost colour."

Not a p-zombie, then. Taransay had heard about

this from Iqbal, the bartender in the Touch. He hadn't noticed any changes when the sim had been reduced to outlines, nor later when the colours had come back.

"Search me," said Taransay. "I guess it's like when everything became outlines, a wee while back. Extra demand on the processing. I'll check."

"How?" the man asked. "I don't understand. What processing?"

Taransay stared at them. They might not be p-zombies, but was it possible that they *still* didn't know they were in a sim? Did they still think they had just come back from a spaceport with exotic products of other colony worlds? Didn't they even watch the news? Perhaps they hadn't had time. Or maybe they just didn't have television out in the sticks.

She took her phone out of her back pocket and called Beauregard. The two passengers watched as if this were witchcraft.

"What's going on?" Taransay asked.

"We've got a virus," said Beauregard. "Well, some kind of software infestation. Shaw and Nicole and Locke and Remington are up to their elbows trying to deal with it."

"A virus? Where the fuck's that coming from? The Direction? The Rax?"

"We think it's coming from the *mat*," said Beauregard. "At least, we can see the mat's interfacing with the module's nanotech fuzz."

Taransay gave an uneasy laugh. "That's impossible. You need compatibility to get infection. Operating system, genetic code, all that."

"Well, there it is," said Beauregard. "The AIs have been studying what they can see of the local life, and it seems adaptable at a deeper level than any life we know. That bandersnatch thing you killed? It's a rolled-up mat, and maybe not just in a phylogenetic sense. Phenotypically, as well."

"Jeez."

"Anyway, good to have you back. Well done out there. But I've got a lot on my plate at the moment, so..."

"OK, Belfort, catch you later."

She rang off and put the phone away.

"What is that thing?" the man asked.

Taransay looked at him solemnly. "It's a new invention from the outer colonies," she said.

"Ah." He returned to his conversation, problem solved, and the loss of colour in the world apparently forgotten.

Taransay gazed at the backs of the couple's heads for a while. How could they be so incurious? And so selectively ignorant? Maybe they were just thick.

But, no, that couldn't be it. They were future colonists, volunteers from distant Earth's utopia for an adventurous extrasolar afterlife; the dead on leave from the most advanced society ever. And they didn't sound stupid. They were chatting about selective breeding of crops, about recombinations and crosses and recessives, at a high level of abstraction that now and then got down to cases among their own plants and animals. They laughed at allusions she didn't catch, at clannish in-jokes. They left together, with a friendly wave, and slogged off into the woods to a clearing where gracile robots toiled.

Alone, Taransay began to make sense of it. The system that ran the sim was saving on processing power to deal with the unusual situation, and now with the emergency. It was running in real time instead of a thousand times faster; it had earlier, in fast space skirmishes, once reduced the world to wire diagrams; now it had drained colour but kept shading.

As she'd long since figured out, most of the processing

in the sim was devoted to creating consistent subjective experiences for the minds it emulated: the experience of a world, not a world itself. There was no *out there*, in here.

Now, for the minds of those denizens whose main role in the sim was to be background extras, to add verisimilitude and local colour, just one step above the p-zombies, who had no subjective experience at all, the system was skimping on *thought*.

When would it start doing that to her, and to the other fighters? Or even to the AIs, Locke and Remington?

She sweated through the rest of the ride.

Beauregard met Rizzi off the bus. She looked surprised and pleased to see him.

"Needed some fresh air," he said. "After a whole morning stuck in a hot room with two AIs, two warlocks and Nicole, all tearing their hair out."

Durward, a downloaded copy of the Direction's rep in the Arcane Disputes sim, had found more of an affinity with Shaw than with Nicole, his local counterpart. Nicole's pose, and to an extent her role, was of an artist. She interacted with the underlying software by drawing and painting. Durward, from a sim based on a fantasy game, did the same trick by magic. He got on like a house on fire with Shaw, a deserter from an earlier conflict who in a thousand subjective years of wandering the sim had picked up the knack of hacking its physics engine.

Remington, a likewise downloaded copy of the Arcane AI, had meanwhile come to some grudging mutual understanding with Locke. None of this had, over the past day and night, come easily.

"Your face looks drawn," Taransay said.

Beauregard had to laugh. They walked along the

front. In black and white the striped awnings and the shop fronts looked more tawdry than ever.

"Everything's even weirder than when it was all outlines," he said. "Sadder, too. Because you can see the shadows, but not the colours."

"It's like living in a photonovel," Rizzi said. "You expect to see speech bubbles instead of hearing people speak."

"Maybe that'll be next. Text would take less processing than speech."

"Fuck, don't give them ideas."

"Them?" He knew what she meant.

"The AIs, the... whatever runs this place."

"You mean, whatever this place runs on. What *we* all run on, including Nicole."

Rizzi shuddered. "Yeah, yeah. That's new, too. The feeling of being... I dunno, watched from outside and inside, knowing it's all a sim right in your bones. Plus, it's different after being out and walking around on the ground and seeing this place"—she windmilled an arm—"as a big mossy boulder in a fucking acid-trip cubist jungle. I mean, when we were in space, it was kind of like we were astronauts and this really was a habitat module of a space station."

"Just... bigger on the inside?"

Beauregard threw out an arm, expecting her to laugh. She did, but only politely.

"Lunch in the Touch?" she asked, hopefully.

"Sorry, no," Beauregard said. "Straight back to the madness, I'm afraid."

The madness, when Taransay stepped into Nicole's studio, was invisible. When she'd last been there, the previous day, the studio, untidy to start with, looked as if it had been the site of a week-long student sit-in. Now the studio looked more like a well-run office. The torn-off A2 flipchart sheets, the food scraps and wrappings, the crumpled drinks cans, the overflowing ashtrays and unwashed coffee mugs were all gone. The floor had been swept, and only old and hardened paint stains marred its planks. The sketches and paintings were sorted and stacked, and beginning to be shelved on trolley racks. Even the cleaning robot looked happier: it wasn't twitching uncontrollably.

Locals Taransay didn't recognise came and went quietly, wheeling trolleys in and out, bearing refreshments and stationery supplies, taking away litter. Half a dozen fighters, in combat singlets and trousers, sat in front of the room's wall-hung TV screens. They watched scrolling data and fragmentary external views, took notes and talked among themselves and on phones. The sim's pretence at broadcast media, hitherto dedicated to soap operas and war news, was now turned to close study of the real environment outside, and to reports from inside the module's software.

Shaw and Durward, both shaggy-haired and long-bearded, had been prevailed upon to shower and put on clean clothes, and no longer offended the senses. They both sat on high stools at a drafting table, on which Taransay could see the outline of a frame and an arm rotate slowly in a big flat screen.

Nicole stood poised by the flipchart, marker pen in hand, in the casual chic of loose top and trousers that looked silvery even in greyscale. Taransay had a mischievous thought that the garments had been picked out for that very reason.

The images of the AI avatars Locke and Remington—the man with his long hair, the woman with her steely bob—mouthed soundlessly on the paper. Lines of handwritten subscript flowed along the foot. Nicole glanced at the new arrivals, with a nod to Beauregard and a flicker of smile to Taransay, then turned back to the easel.

"Talk," she told them.

"How are things going?" Beauregard asked.

"We're holding the line," Nicole said. "The mat is interfacing with our nanofacturing fuzz at a molecular level, and it seems to be reverse-engineering machine code to send probes into our software. Locke and Remington are pulling out all the stops to block it and hack back."

"How is that even possible?" Taransay cried. "It's natural life out there, and alien at that. It'd have a hard job infecting Earth life, let alone software."

Nicole waved a hand behind her head. "Tell her, Zaretsky," she said.

One of the fighters watching the screens stood up and ambled over, still with eye and thumb on his phone. He had very short hair, skinny features, facial piercings, and a plaited rat-tail of beard sticking down from his chin.

"Hi," he said, looking up briefly, blinking. "Um. Well. Thanks to the mat and to all the splatter from your, uh, encounter, we have some samples in direct contact with the module's external instruments, not to mention with your frame, which is busy reporting back via the download port.

"So... The local life is carbon-based and runs on DNA coding for proteins. Fair enough, there aren't many other self-replicating long-chain molecules that could do the job. It seems to have a different genetic code to what we have. No surprise there either—code is arbitrary. But what is a surprise is that the code looks, well, optimised. It has more than four letters, we've identified up to twelve so far and that's just the start. And the transcription mechanism to proteins is a lot more efficient than the RNA-mRNA kludge we have. Lots more amino acids—in that respect it's more like synthetic biology than natural, from our parochial point of view."

Taransay smiled wryly. "Like, intelligently designed?"

Zaretsky snorted. "Hell, no!" He paused and frowned. "It's possible—for all we know there could be intelligent life or even a post-biological robot civilisation out there, or deep in the planet's past, or whatever. But more likely, the story is just that natural selection here has been fiercer for longer. After all, that's what 'super-habitable' implies. Life here has more diversity and complexity than anything back home. Our working hypothesis is that horizontal gene transfer is pretty much universal here, instead of peculiar to unicellular organisms. So the response when a beastie bumps into something new here is to plunder it for any useful genes, and to rummage through its genome for cool tricks. Maybe assimilation and reproduction—eating and sex—aren't as distinct here."

He frowned down at the screen of his phone, swiped in an annoyed manner and tapped in a correction. "Bit of a bugger not having colour... So anyway—from the local point of view our module's nanotech fuzz, or what's left of it, is just a new genome in town, and the local life is all, 'Well, *hello*, sailor!' The mat is busy trying that on with our nanotech, and meanwhile some of the gunk from your beastie is busy sharing info with the mat and trawling through the mechanisms of your frame's shoulder stump, and there we are."

"Shit," said Taransay. She looked around. "Somebody give me a beer."

That afternoon, quite suddenly, colour came back. The resolution stayed low. If you looked closely, you could still see the dots. Everyone whooped and hollered, except the p-zombies, who didn't notice any change. Locke and Remington reported that the worst of the infection was over, and that the mat was no longer making fresh probes into the module's systems.

Taransay left Shaw, Durward and the scientists to fine-tune the attachment of the arm to the frame, a process they all found fascinating but that to her was like watching a plant grow without time-lapse.

She called her boyfriend Den, joined him at the Touch, dined out on her adventures, staggered back to Den's and collapsed into bed.

In the morning Beauregard called her to Nicole's. She made her way there through a pre-dawn that seemed a little more sparkly than usual, as if dew were on everything including the sea. She found Nicole, Beauregard and Zaretsky in Nicole's kitchen.

"Progress," Beauregard reported, handing her a mug of coffee. "We've reconnected the arm, and the frame works as well as we can test it in the slot."

"You can remote-operate frames?" This sounded exciting.

Beauregard shrugged. "Seems so. But not from here, except in the slot."

"It's just testing and twitching," said Zaretsky, who looked as if he'd been up all night. "We don't have anything like the equipment for remote operation."

"OK," said Taransay. "But we could build it, surely?"

Nicole glanced at Zaretsky. He spread his hands. "Not for months—well, not local months, but you know what I mean. With the uncorrupted nanofacture stuff, or even with the stuff that's been contaminated but is still usable, it would take far too long."

"What's the prospect for building other equipment?" Beauregard asked. "Entire new frames, for instance? Or kit to process local life and build up bodies that can live on the planet?"

That last had been the core of the original plan. Taransay had never exactly bought into it, but she'd had no choice but to go along with it, and it had seemed at the very least bold and inspiring. Now, so much equipment had had to be jettisoned in the fight with the Arcane module, and so much damage had been done on the way down, that it seemed impossible.

"To ask the question is to answer it," said Nicole. "The loss of equipment might have been tolerable if we'd had enough nanotech to replace it, but now..."

"We don't have only the surface fuzz," Taransay said. "We still have one nanofacture tube. OK, it's covered with mat, but we could still build stuff underneath it until the mat goes away or we build stuff that can cut its way out."

Zaretsky laughed rudely. "Sorry," he said, "but we're not going to risk getting our last nanofacture tube contaminated too. And we're not going to mess with the mat itself until we know what we're doing."

"But even so," Taransay protested, "we can still bootstrap what we've got—use the remaining nanotech fuzz to build more nanotech, and so on. However long it takes. I mean, that's how the whole mission has been built, hasn't it? And if it seems boring to sit through, we could always slow down the sim to a crawl—hey, that would even release more processing power—and it would take as short a subjective time as we wanted." She threw out her arms. "We could all be out there tomorrow!"

Beauregard gave her a look just on the safe side of scorn. "You've *been* out there, Rizzi! We're sitting on a fucking volcano! The mat rolled us out of the way of the lava, but not because it wanted to rescue us. Not at all!

It did it because we're something new and tasty to eat or fuck or both. OK, we've fought off that, as far as we can tell, but we don't know what other creature might happen along, or what other surprises the mat has in its fuzz."

He sighed, and sipped at his coffee. "You know—actually we could take that risk, if we don't mind dying. Or, let's say, running a very high chance of death or irrelevance. We could do as Rizzi suggests, let the AIs ride herd on the nanotech to eke out the resources to make more and more nanotech until it can build, oh I dunno, itsy-bitsy spider bots to gather up raw material to build more bots to build machinery and tools and so on, and basically recreate what we had and more. However long it takes, as she says. Yeah, we can do that. Party on in here, yeah. It's a good life if you don't weaken. Live it forever in the fucking sim. The trouble with that is the *real* environment. The volcano could turn us into an interesting piece of anomalous geology at any moment. The mats and the scuttling things and God knows what else that may be out there could come up with new ways to eat us. Not just the fuzz, but to hack into *the module itself*. So—"

"Maybe being eaten is the way to go," said Zaretsky, his pale, mild eyes gazing out of the window at Nicole's backyard, perhaps at his reflection.

"Fascinating," said Beauregard, with heavy sarcasm. "Tell us more."

Zaretsky jutted his rat-tail beard. "We wrack our brains about how to build new bodies to survive out there. The life *already* out there works by incorporating new genes and new information. Why not give it copies of ourselves—memories, genetic info, the lot—to assimilate?"

"You first," said Beauregard.

"I would," said Zaretsky. "Or at least, a copy of me would."

Beauregard looked as unimpressed by this vicarious bravado as Taransay felt.

Nicole leaned forward. "It may come to that," she said, to Taransay's surprise. "However, let us try something less drastic first! Belfort, you were about to suggest...?"

Beauregard's shoulders slumped, then he straightened his back.

"No," he said. "I have to admit it. We're fucked. I won people over to the plan when we had enough kit to make a go of it and the time to build more. We thought we'd have the module in orbit and build landers, remember that? Hell, if we hadn't been attacked by Arcane we could still have made it to the surface with plenty to build with. I can't ask the fighters and the locals to rally to anything less. So we have to re-establish contact with the rest of the system, find out what the fuck's going on out there, and appeal for aid, trade, and if all else fails—rescue."

"Even if it means going back to the Direction with our tails between our legs?" Taransay asked.

Beauregard looked around the table.

"Does anyone here still trust the Direction?"

In an uncomfortable silence, Nicole raised a hand. "I do, in the sense that I remain confident it knows what it's doing."

"Precisely," said Beauregard. "It knows what it's doing. And if it were to offer a rescue and then destroy us, for the greater good of the mission, it would still know what it was doing. No thanks. I'd rather be rescued, if it came to that, by almost anyone else."

"Even the Rax?" Taransay queried.

Beauregard looked her right in the eye.

"Yes. With...appropriate safeguards, put it that way.

But like I say, last resort. We have other options. We do have something to offer—we've made a landing, we've broken the embargo, we have by now terabytes of knowledge of the local life. Maybe some of the DisCorps might be interested. All we need is supplies."

"There's a problem with that," said Taransay. "Right now, I doubt anyone knows exactly where we are. We appeal for help, we give away our position. Anyone who can drop supplies can drop fighters—or bombs."

"That's where you come in," said Beauregard. He looked at Nicole, who nodded. "We want you to go out again. Now that the frame has two arms, it should be a hell of a lot easier and safer than it was the first time. It's taken the AIs running the nanotech all night to build two simple tools: a very basic directional aerial, and a knife."

"A *knife*?" cried Taransay.

Beauregard grimaced. "It isn't much, but according to analysis of the thing you shot and of the mat, the knife should be able to cut through the outer integument of anything likely to come at you."

"Great." A thought struck her. "Can it cut through the mat?"

"Yes," said Zaretsky, looking up from his phone. "But like I said, we don't want any messing with the mat until we know it won't do more harm than good. For the moment, the knife is just for self-defence."

"I don't have a great deal of confidence in its efficacy in that respect," said Taransay.

Nobody looked like they were backing down.

"If it comes to that," said Beauregard, "don't forget there's still some ammo left in the machine gun."

Taransay stood up. Her coffee had cooled, and she knocked it back.

"OK," she said. "I'll get my coat."

* * *

With two arms, it was indeed much easier getting out of the slot. Night had fallen, but Taransay found the dim light from the moons and the infrared glow from the lava and the life-forms almost better than full daylight. She upped the gain in the visual spectrum nonetheless.

The volcano's summit was clearly visible, a jagged tooth-line drooling lava that seemed to float just above the jungle a couple of kilometres away and a hundred and fifty metres higher than where she stood on a long gentle downward slope. On a heavy planet, it was a high cone. Deltas of cooling lava flowed from that prominence to finger out among the plants.

No animal movement, other than the slow flow of the mats. Danger could come from above, too—she hadn't seen any flying things as yet, but such seemed likely. She looked up.

The sky was clear, blue-green with a few thin clouds. One of them anomalously didn't move with the wind. Taransay zoomed her gaze, and the tattered wisp resolved itself into distant pinpricks, smelling faintly of carbon and iron: the dispersed space station.

Closer in and further out, a double handful of SH-0's many moons hung across the ecliptic. Some were mere sparks, others discs or part discs, crescent or gibbous or full. Taransay picked out SH-17 with a pang close to nostalgia: that exomoon was, after all, the only other place in this system where she'd stood on real ground.

Enough. She was on real ground now. To work.

The salvaged right arm worked fine, but the join between it and the former stump was marked with a ring of native fuzz, like mould. How certain could she be that its earlier hacking into the frame's systems had been repulsed?

Not at all, was the answer, whatever Locke or Zaretsky might say.

Warily, she walked around the side of the module, and found the knife growing within arm's reach, a sharp artificial stalactite. It snapped off along a stress line scribed around the top of the handle, leaving a cavity in the module's surface and a matching knob. The blade was like a leaf of black glass. Taransay looked at it dubiously. It was five centimetres long, and she had nowhere to stash it. She was going to have to use the knife to slash the leaves and stems from which to make a belt and sheath. For now, she kept it clutched in her right hand.

The aerial, as Beauregard had called it, hung from higher up on the module like a strand of cobweb, visibly growing. The loose end of it lay coiled on the ground, and new loops were added to the heap at a rate of about one every hundred seconds. Taransay scanned around, saw nothing threatening, and began to pay it out like a fishing line. She walked towards the lava flow, in the slight furrow the rolled module had left. When she'd gone far enough, she stuck the knife in the compacted ash soil and prepared to shape the thread into a spiral.

The thread had other ideas. It shaped itself, coiling and hardening, into a shallow metre-wide mesh dish that looked as if the wind would carry it away. A spike grew from the centre, thin as a pencil lead. Just as autonomously, the dish tilted this way and that. Taransay saw that this movement was caused by small expansions and contractions in the thread, but didn't understand any more than that about how it worked. No surprise there, she told herself: this technology was centuries in advance of anything she remembered. Come to think of it, she didn't understand how she was a fifty-centimetre-tall black glassy robot. She understood in principle, but the engineering details were at a level where the most strictly materialist explanation might as well be magic.

So it was with the self-assembling long-range receiver.

Stop worrying. Stop scratching your little round head.

Her little round head was, she found, attuned to what the aerial—and the God-knew-what processing behind it, in the module—was picking up. She saw it like a heads-up display, in three neat columns, and heard the accompanying sounds on parallel tracks all of which she could follow. There were advantages in being a robot.

Nevertheless, the input was confusing. The bulk of it, occupying the centre column, was spillover of rapid-fire AI chatter that scrolled in a blur. Routine business, probably, with a strand of Direction instructions to Dis-Corps. She gladly left unpicking all that to Locke and Remington. The human messages were by comparison marginal. Down the left-hand side, aptly enough, ran a threatening rant from the Arcane module: *We're coming for you, fascist scum!* wasn't actually said, but it was the gist. There was a side order of imprecations against the freebots and against those who'd defected to them. Taransay was pleased to hear the names of Carlos and Newton; she didn't know who Blum and Rillieux were, but good for them in any case, even though the Arcane gang seemed to think their defection and departure was all some kind of Rax plot.

Among the threats of bombing and laser-blasting and nuking from orbit were urgent appeals to any surviving Acceleration cadres or Direction loyalists in the Locke sim, which the Arcane gang still seemed to think was under the iron heel of the Rax. *Rise up! Overthrow the usurpers! Help is coming!* From the way the message was repeated on a short loop and faded in and out it was obviously being beamed down to the surface on spec, over the wide area in which the module could theoretically have landed.

The other message, in the right-hand column, was likewise on a loop. It had much better production values and a far more conciliatory tone. It came from the Rax.

<Are you getting all this?> Taransay asked.

<Loud and clear,> replied Locke. <Please keep guard on the aerial while we process the data.>

<Thanks,> said Taransay. <If I'm attacked, I'll let you know.>

<Please do,> said Locke, immune as ever to sarcasm.

Taransay tugged the knife from the ground and clutched it in her fist. She paced carefully back to the module and turned her back to it. She didn't need or want to rest against it, but it was good to have that solid mass behind her.

<Keep me in the loop, guys,> she said.

<Will do,> said Beauregard.

Taransay hunkered down. It was going to be a long night.

After a while she saw a light move in the sky, high up, and fade just as her gaze fixed on it. A little later, a light drifted closer and lower down, just above the treetops, and likewise faded as she focused. She logged the sightings but lacked the curiosity to investigate, content for the moment to classify them in her own mind as SH-0's first UFOs.

"We await replies."

The black ovoid that spoke like a man stopped talking. The image froze. A little curled arrow spun in the lower left corner, waiting for someone to request a repeat.

No one did.

"Well," said Nicole. "Now we are in the picture."

We fucking are, Beauregard thought. In the picture. In one of *your* pictures, to be precise. And don't we all know it.

That's the fucking trouble. That's why we're all so on edge.

In the sim, it was mid-afternoon. Beauregard felt sweat drying on his face. Nicole's studio was airy, the window open to a view of sunlight and sea. The room wasn't even crowded: Beauregard, Nicole, Shaw, Durward, Zaretsky; Tourmaline drifting in and out. The AIs were present only as still sketches on Nicole's flip-pad.

And yet the room seemed too hot, and stuffy.

It must be the screens, Beauregard reckoned. There was the one with the transmissions, and then there were all the others. One showed what Rizzi saw. Others showed random fragments of the module's surroundings, random night-vision false-colour images of lava or swaying plant trunks or crawling mats and one pure black star-spangled tatter of sky. Together they created an insuperable impression of being inside something small. The impression you got when you looked away was of being in the wide open spaces of a terraformed planet, but it was no longer strong enough to convince. It was wearing thin. You could see the pixels.

How long would people stand for this?

"I don't believe that peaceful coexistence offer from the Rax," Beauregard said, feeling his way. "Not in the long term, anyway. It's a transparent ruse to buy time while they build up their forces. But—"

"Stop right there," said Nicole. "There's no 'but' after that."

"Let me finish," said Beauregard. "With respect, Nicole, there is. There always is. They're going to have to do at least some genuine trading up front to make it convincing. They claim to have fusion drives for sale. We could certainly do with one. We could offer a wealth of information about SH-0—maybe not of much interest to the Rax, but they could easily trade it on to one or more of the DisCorps."

"You want the Rax to carry out a *landing* here?" cried Nicole.

Beauregard stared her down. "They could just do a drop from orbit. Same as with any other company we might trade with."

"I wouldn't trust them," said Nicole.

"What you're forgetting—no, you can't forget, can you?—what you're *eliding* is that as far as they know, we're Rax ourselves. It wouldn't be too hard to convince them." He grinned. "I can be the front man for that if you like. And we must have Rax sleepers among our returnees."

The face of Locke moved on the page. Shaw noticed and pointed. Nicole glanced at the line of script along the foot.

"We do," she said. "Locke has identified them from the courses their scooters took and what they did in the battle. It can give us a list."

"Well, there you go," said Beauregard. "We can bribe or threaten them to back me up."

"'We?'" said Zaretsky, raising a ring-pierced eyebrow.

"I think you'll find," said Beauregard, in as mild a tone as he could muster, "that throwing me the old 'You and whose army?' challenge would be most unwise."

"And I warn you," said Nicole, "that doing any such thing would have consequences. Very personal consequences."

Ah, that standing threat. Time to face it down.

Beauregard held her gaze. "Everyone knows now that the p-zombies are different. Even they do."

"You think I couldn't convince them otherwise?"

"How?" Beauregard scoffed. "Tell them they all have superior eyesight, or something?"

Everyone else in the room was looking puzzled.

"What's all this about?" Shaw demanded.

Beauregard paused, glanced sidelong, listened. Tourmaline wasn't in earshot. He could hear her clattering about in Nicole's kitchen. He stood up.

"The p-zombies," he said. "Nicole has held a threat over me ever since I made my move. If I ever try to use the troops on my own account, she'll have a word with all the p-zombies. Convince them there's no such thing as a p-zombie. That they've all been misled and mistreated, somehow. Not that I've ever mistreated Tourmaline, I hasten to add." He shrugged. "And anyway, since Locke and Nicole started monkeying with the sim, and you did your own monkeying about, it's become obvious to everyone that there is a difference. The p-zombies haven't noticed any of the changes, or their reversals. It's all the same to them because they don't have any inner experience in the first place. Colours to them are lines of code—Pantone numbers. These don't change. And they're well aware, so to speak, that everyone else *does* notice something changing. So Nicole's threat doesn't amount to anything, any more."

Nicole lit a cigarette, inhaled deeply and blew out a stream of smoke in as irritating a manner as possible.

"Is that a risk you're willing to take?"

Beauregard glared at her. She glared back, unperturbed.

"Oh, fuck this," said Shaw. "If we have any decisions to make, let's make them rationally, by discussion. Not by bickering and power plays between you two."

Perched on his drafting stool, he straightened his back and closed his eyes for a moment. Then he opened them, and smiled.

"Done," he said.

The sunlight dimmed and flickered. Then it returned to normal. So did the resolution of the sim. No more coloured dots. Everything looked real and solid again.

"What's *done*?" Nicole cried. "What have you done?"

Shaw looked smug. "No more p-zombies."

Beauregard braced himself for a crash of crockery and a howl of fury from Tourmaline. None came.

Nicole drew savagely on the cigarette. The tip became a glowing cone. "What?"

She jumped up, stalked over to the flipchart and scribbled. The faces of Locke and Remington became animated, then agitated. Script raced along the foot of the page in a demented scribble, far too fast for Beauregard to read. Nicole read it until it stopped.

She turned to Shaw. "It seems you have," she said. "And you've released a significant amount of processing power into the bargain. Well, well."

She gave Beauregard a sad smile and a shake of the head. "Looks like I've lost my trump card."

Beauregard was still tense, waiting for the penny, the other shoe and the crockery to drop.

"I don't understand," he said.

Durward, Nicole and Shaw were all looking at him as if daunted by his stupidity.

"Zaretsky!" Nicole snapped. "Tell him. Make him understand."

"It's very simple," said Zaretsky, eyes bright and arms waving. "The whole p-zombie business was a tour de force of programming. An incredible feat of puppetry. Emulating the actions and reactions of a conscious being without the avatar itself being a conscious being has the most fucking unbelievable AI brute force processing overhead. I mean, gigantic look-up tables aren't the half of it. Not a hundredth of it. It turns out to be easier and simpler and a thousand times more economical just to *give* them conscious minds. Multiply that by the hundreds of p-zombies in the sim, and you get some idea of how much processing power Shaw's latest hack saves."

"But won't they know?" Beauregard asked. "Won't they *notice*?"

"Well, no," said Zaretsky, as if it were obvious. "They now have conscious minds—with all the memories and thoughts and emotions their emulation implied. Including, you see, the memory of being self-aware all along. Thus neatly accounting for why they *also* remember being puzzled when anyone asked if they were conscious, or told them they weren't."

Footsteps outside, a quick tick of high heels in the hall. Tourmaline walked in, bearing coffee. She set the tray down.

"Why's everybody looking at me like that?" she asked.

"It's all right," said Beauregard. "We're all just dying for a coffee. Thank you."

"You're welcome," she said, still sounding suspicious. "Well, see you later."

"Yeah," said Beauregard. "See you later, honey."

She blew him a kiss and went out.

"I have a better idea than talking to the Rax," said Nicole, pressing down the plunger of the cafetière.

"I'm listening," said Beauregard. He felt off balance, but he wasn't going to show it.

"What's the only force out there that has *already* actually helped us?" Nicole said. "The freebots. They saved our ass. And Carlos and Newton were involved, which as far as I'm concerned puts the lid on any notion that they're Rax. You told me Newton is Rax, or was, but Carlos would never get mixed up in any Rax ploy. He's too much the old Axle terrorist for that. And the other two?" She looked at Durward. "You knew them in Arcane."

The warlock chuckled. "Bobbie Rillieux and Andre Blum? No, I think it's safe to say they aren't Rax. I think what happened back there is that the freebots, bless their blinking lights, have a somewhat eccentric idea of what neutrality means. The freebot we captured—the one called Baser—wasn't the brightest bulb in the circuit, if you see what I mean."

"Here's what I suggest," said Nicole. "We contact the freebots on SH-17, tell them our situation and ask for their help."

"What help can *they* give us?" Beauregard scoffed.

Nicole gave him a look. "They have at least one fusion drive, on the transfer tug Baser hijacked. And they have access to more—they have contacts with other freebots all across the system. Going by what the Rax have found inside SH-119 the blinkers have been clandestinely very busy for the past year or so. Far busier than the Direction suspected, as far as I know. So they may well have resources even we have no idea of."

Beauregard thought about his. He still reckoned the Rax settlement in SH-119, the New Confederacy—ha!—might have more potential as a trading partner. But this was a good time not to bring that up again. He kept his own counsel on the matter.

"OK," he said. "Let's give it a go."

"In practical terms," said Zaretsky, "that means Rizzi will have to trek some distance away, and make a transmission. Probably by laser. This will take some time to set up, with the limits of our nanofacture."

"Yes, yes," said Beauregard, impatiently. "Big job. Seems only fair to give her some R&R first. Bring her in."

* * *

<Come back in,> said Locke.

Taransay looked down at the knife in her hand and wondered what to do with it. Leaving it outside seemed careless and wasteful—and besides, who knew what inspiration it might provide to some local organism, whether a mat or some beastie she hadn't met yet? But she didn't fancy another one-handed ascent to the download slot. If she'd had teeth she could have held the blade between them, but she didn't have teeth. One of the downsides of being a robot.

She walked behind the module to the edge of the jungle. The peculiar geometry of the local life now struck her overwhelmingly as alien. Small circular mats carpeted the ground like fallen leaves, but leaves that slithered over each other in a disquieting continuous flow. The actual leaves of the plants were also deeply uneasy on the eye: stark quadrilaterals with none of the veining and striations and other repeated irregularities that made leaves beautiful. They hung limp under the night sky.

She reached up and plucked one from its stiff horizontal stem, laid the knife at her feet and tore the sheet into strips. Liquid oozed from the ragged edges, smelling of water and sweet, sticky carbohydrates. Some animal, surely, must eat this. Fortunately, no herbivore was prowling the night. The strips tore neatly enough, and she knotted half a dozen of them with swift robotic precision. She tied one end to the knob of the knife handle, tied the other to form a loop and slung the string around her neck. A black leaf-shaped pectoral pendant on a small black frame.

After a careful scan of the vicinity, she clambered up to the download slot.

<Take me in,> she said.

Another surreal nightmare, a full-on bad trip. Taransay sat shaking as the memories faded.

Back on the fucking bus.

Everything looked real again, but she didn't feel it.

CHAPTER FIVE

Oderint Dum Metuant ("Go Tell the Stupid Machines")

The advantage Dunt had over every other revived veteran, Axle or Rax, was that he hadn't been surprised to find himself here. He had planned for the possibility. Unlike the others, he hadn't died in the Last World War and been posthumously sentenced to death in the postwar United Nations Security Council reign of terror. He had seen that blood-red dawn of the Direction—the searches, the sweeps, the street executions—and the first global elections to the world assembly, the triumph of the mob. Unlike everyone else here, he'd actually lived under the Direction, if only for a few months. His last memories were of his own preparations for a last-ditch attack on a UNSC patrol.

The attack was suicidal, but that didn't mean much. Dunt was on every UNSC death list, and on the run. His card was marked. Death was coming for him anyway. There was, he'd calculated, a small chance to turn even that to the advantage of the cause.

He had seen how fighters who'd died in ways that left their brain-states recoverable were being preserved for possible future revival, perhaps centuries hence, when the technology had improved. He'd known that some of those who were in the records as Axle were in fact Rax infiltrators. These dead comrades were being sent into the future. Dunt was not going to abandon them there. He had known how deeply embedded clandestine Rax cadre were, in the post-war states and the emerging world state. The world state's world of peaceful sheep would some day meet its wolves. The Aryan fighting man would be called upon again. When that time came, Dunt would be ready.

With the help of dedicated followers and some of the clandestine cadre in the UNSC bureaucracy, he had laid his plans. He'd stolen the identity and biometric details of a dead Acceleration militant whose body and brain were beyond recovery. Dunt knew this because he'd put them there, with bullet and fire and acid. These biometric details he'd had replaced with his own. If Dunt ever ended up as a mangled cortex and brain stem in a flask of liquid nitrogen, those immortal remains would be filed as those of the dead Accelerationist, not Dunt's.

That frozen structure would be the ultimate special snowflake, drifting through dark, cold skies of time to blizzards yet to come.

It was a small chance, vanishingly small, a Pascal's Wager with the devil.

It had paid off beyond his wildest dreams. It had got him to his Valhalla. Not just the far future, but a distant star. Small wonder he felt blessed.

"We await replies."

Dunt turned off the camera and let himself drift

back. Nothing more to do now but, well, await replies. The die was cast.

He felt drained, although his power pack's gauge was still in the orange. The effort of sustained simulated speech, perhaps—he'd got used to the easy default of radio telepathy. And before its delivery there had been all the dickering over its content. Shit. He could have done without that.

Crafting the message had put a strain on the inner circle. In principle, they all agreed on the urgency of a peace offer. But they'd quibbled over the details. Rexham, Stroilova and Blanc had angled for throwing down the gauntlet by putting the Reaction case more strongly, as a challenge calculated to appeal to potential recruits; Whitten and Schulz had urged a tone even more conciliatory than the one adopted.

Dunt had got his way in the end, as ever.

But it should never have been an issue. They were all irritable, that was what it was. It was like going without sleep, or that time he'd made a bunch of recruits quit smoking, back in the day. Tetchy as hell, they'd been.

Now everyone was like that, inner circle and lower ranks alike. It wasn't as if you actually missed anything, got hungry or sleepy or horny. And you had far more stimulation in the frame than you ever did when you were—actually or virtually—human. But there it was. A growing, gnawing lust for something you couldn't define, only there as a lack, but that you knew was a longing for the sim. Smells in your nose, air in your lungs, food and drink in your mouth and down your throat, spunk pulsing out or in. All touches on internal skin. The pleasures of the virtual flesh. He was certain this was an imposed desire, programmed in rather than intrinsic to the posthuman condition. A way to keep you hooked...

Dunt shoved himself away from the back of the flood-lit niche set up for the broadcast, and out into the main cavern. Lights by the dozens floated in the near-vacuum like tiny suns. Troops darted here and there, setting things up for when traders arrived. Two squads moved the scooters one by one to the inner side of the cavity, deploying them to face the tunnel entrance, around which three were left ready for immediate launch. Others built handling facilities from machinery and material scavenged from robotic activity deeper within: a crane, a net, a battery of lasers and software probes.

Most of the troops were still deep in the tunnels, but weren't moving forward any more: they had set up blocks at their furthest limit of exploration, sealing them off with rocks and tripwire devices likewise scavenged and hacked from available machinery. On their way in they had set up a series of relays through each tunnel, so that radio and laser communications could flow without being blocked by rock. They'd left guards at main junctions, and the remainder of the troops were now working their way slowly back, herding bots of all sizes as they went.

In all, a volume of about six hundred metres radius from the entrance, with the fusion factory just inside it, could now be considered more or less consolidated. Within that rough hemisphere numerous workings and worksites had been found, some incomprehensible, but none as large or significant as the hall of the fusion pods. None of the robots captured after Dunt's exemplary reprisal against five supervisory bots had confessed to being freebots, and all were being variously prodded or chivvied into doing something useful or at least staying in the mesh pens into which they'd been herded.

Situation nominal. Everything was going fine. Time to visit those for whom it wasn't.

* * *

Dunt jetted to the far side of the cavern, near the entrance. Foyle, the trooper who'd been cut almost in half by the freebot miner, was held sitting against the rock by tape across his useless legs. He crouched over a micro-tool rig on the remains of his lap, making repairs and minute adjustments to damaged auxiliaries. The original plan had been that he'd thus repair his own frame, but the internal specs showed a far finer grain than anything the micro-rig could handle.

<You OK, soldier?>

The man looked up. There was a flicker behind his visor, as his vision refocused.

<I'm fine, sir.> He smacked a knee. <It's frustrating—I'd rather be out with the squads—but I'm glad to be kept busy.>

<It's important work,> said Dunt. <We can't afford to waste even these little blinkers. And don't worry—we've put in an order for more frames and for a version of our old sim, from Morlock Arms. We'll soon have you back on your feet.>

<I sure hope so, sir.>

<Count on it,> said Dunt.

<I'm not questioning you, Mac, sir, but how do we know any DisCorps will be willing to trade?>

Dunt clapped Foyle's shoulder. <You're right, soldier. We don't know. But it's the way to bet.>

<Very good, sir.>

<That's the spirit.> Dunt made a show of peering at the machinery. None of its intricacies made sense to him at all. For all he knew, Foyle could be performing the equivalent of open-heart surgery on a watch with a chisel. An electronic watch, at that. But with tempers fraying and nerves jangling, it was important to keep up morale.

<Good work, Foyle. Well done. Carry on.>

<Yes, sir!>

Feeling somewhat awkward, Dunt jetted off. He soared through the entrance tunnel as if up a lift-shaft, slowed, and let himself drift to a halt just outside, feet on a level with the top of the angular open structure being built around the hole: the beginnings of a space jetty, with two fully armed scooters mounted on it already, poised to spring if any danger loomed.

The transition wasn't so much from dark to light as from unspeakably cold to relatively hot. From about a hundred Celsius below to a hundred above, just like that! His frame handled it without a creak. He paused to look around, letting his whole frame rotate slowly. The exo-sun was high, SH-0 gibbous, the modular cloud a wisp across it: dots against the bright segment, lights against the dark. Eventually the slow spin of SH-119 would roll this side of the little moonlet into darkness and shadow. Odd that it wasn't locked, one side always facing SH-0, but that was perhaps evidence of a recent collision.

Quite a lot of heavy metal in the rock, too; the composition was rather different from that of any moon he knew of in the Solar system, but if what little he knew of exosolar systems was anything to go by, each was unique. Every detail of their history was contingent. That of this system was mostly unknown but clearly turbulent: even the rocky planet H-0, slated for future habitation by the Direction's spawn, had a ring to testify to that. There were times when he could see the point of the Direction module's slow, patient approach to the mission profile: explore before exploiting. Measure six times before you cut, and all that.

There he was, thinking like a Jew tailor. It wouldn't work, it wasn't how things worked. Pioneers gonna pioneer, goddammit! Let later, softer generations loll in the luxury of shedding futile tears for what was lost. Or perhaps the future white man, the true man, would know better than to indulge such cheap sentimental pining. Evolution was selection was loss, as the coming race would know better than any, until it in turn gave way—gracefully or not, as the case might be—to the overman.

Dunt tumbled to horizontal and jetted gently towards the absurdly close horizon, at an altitude of a couple of metres on average above the uneven surface. The new structure at the entrance dipped below the horizon behind him. Ahead, another and much smaller construction loomed: a carbon-fibre stake sticking a couple of metres out from the rock, to which the other casualty was lightly tethered. He, too, was making himself useful. Dunt decelerated and swung his feet downward into contact with the rock. The soles weren't magnetic, and wouldn't have been any use here if they were—the rock was far from ferrous—but they nevertheless gripped stickily.

He took a step or two closer. The man on space-guard duty turned, revealing the brutal, smoothly scooped excision where most of his visor had been. Dunt had to remind himself that he wasn't looking at the ruins of a face and head. His literally traumatic memories of medevacs and military hospitals screamed otherwise.

<How goes it, Evans?>

The damage had stopped leaking. Microscopic bots moved in it like bacteria—or nits, or maggots, depending on how close you cared to zoom.

<Very well, sir. Nothing to report so far.>

Compassion, of a kind, mingled with curiosity: <What do you see?>

<Nothing in the visual, sir. My proximity sense is still fine. That's how I knew you were here. Likewise radar,

though that's pretty short-range. And the exposed>—he waved a hand—<mess has somehow left my spectroscopy more sensitive—I can smell every star and planet and rock, it seems, and that builds up to what I can only call a picture, except it isn't.>

<Really?> said Dunt, interested. <Something like blindsight?>

<I wouldn't know, sir.>

<But right now you could point to...oh, say, the cloud of modules where the station was?>

<Sure.> Evans pointed.

<Spot on,> said Dunt, duly impressed. <Well, keep—>

<Excuse me, sir. Something's up.>

The ghastly hole in Evans's visor was turned to the modular cloud, its blind gaze fixed and concentrated like a locked-on radar dish.

<Yes?> Dunt looked, too, but even at max zoom he couldn't see any changes.

<I'm picking up gas-jet manoeuvres, lots of them, around the Morlock Arms module.>

You gotta be kidding, Dunt thought. No way could the spectroscopic sense be that precise.

Then he saw a twinkle of engine burns.

<Chemical jets lit,> reported Evans. <One vehicle, going for transfer orbit.>

<Where to?> Dunt asked, though he almost knew.

<Looks like they're heading this way, sir.>

The distant sparks winked out as the spacecraft settled into free fall, outward to SH-119.

A moment later, an excited call came in from Stroilova.

<Morlock Arms have done the deal!> she said. <One transfer tug, half a dozen blank frames, on their way. ETA twenty-odd kiloseconds.>

<Brilliant!> said Dunt.

He passed on the good news to Evans.

<We'll soon have you out of that,> he concluded. <And you're overdue a double stint in the sim when we get one.>

<Thank you, sir.>

<Meanwhile, let's make the most of your new ability while you still have it. Keep watching the skies.>

<Will do, sir.>

Even before Dunt made it back to the entrance hole, Zheng Reconciliation Services followed Morlock's lead. Another transfer tug, another squad's worth of blank frames. Then reports came in that a couple of other companies, too, had made deals: tiny supply craft, laden with enough processing power and software to build luxury sims for thousands, were on their way.

Dunt felt elated, and vindicated. His predictions had been borne out, his confidence justified. Like most of his comrades, he despised capitalists as individuals as devoutly as he believed in capitalism as a system. And capitalists the DisCorps were, at least in an abstract sense. Those AI business executives and fund managers could be relied on to follow their virtual noses to money, if the profits dangled before them were high enough. It amused Dunt deeply that not even the dictatorial Direction module could keep all the DisCorps on the leash.

Of course, letting the DisCorps trade with the Rax might be a cunning manoeuvre by the Direction. But thanks to blockchains and checksums, whatever devilry it was up to couldn't be hidden in the software or the hardware en route. And any covert incoming physics packages would be detected by the scooters distributed around the surface, watching every cubic quadrant of the sky. As for some grander scheme... Dunt was confident he and at least some of the inner circle would have its measure.

For behind the Direction module was the Direction, and behind that was, if not a democracy, then a convincing simulacrum of one. Dunt hadn't been exaggerating his own views in the slightest when he'd described that tyranny to the troops as having weaknesses. Democracy, or any thinking derived from it, was fundamentally at odds with reality. That made it stupid. That stupidity, that wilful blindness to the way the real world worked, was at the root of what conservatives—with their usual superficiality—decried as hypocrisy. Hypocrisy was an epithet too good for the mental and moral deformities of democracy. Its vices were too deep to pay tribute to virtue. Dunt respected the power of the cold monster, but he had not the slightest doubt that it was evil, and that his side was right.

The Reaction might have trolled its clueless foes with the insignia and memorabilia of fascism. Its shock-troops might have flaunted their racial consciousness and overt yearning for dictatorship. The democrats had acted suitably shocked. Meanwhile, their very own precious liberal democracies had, before Dunt had even been born, let millions die on the Mediterranean's southern shore. Refugees from a continent ravaged by climate change and war, denied entry to Europe. Dunt would have been the first to admit that he had no warm place in his heart for people of African descent, but he couldn't—even with the lucid self-insight the frame's copy of his mind endowed—find in himself the sort of callous indifference if not genocidal hatred that had built that beach of bones.

Then, back when Dunt was alive, the same democracies had kept tens of millions of Muslims in the biggest concentration camp ever devised, having driven them to the steppes of Kazakhstan by pogroms that would have made the Black Hundreds blanch, and processed the survivors with a bureaucratic machinery of deportation and enforced exile that Beria would have dismissed out of hand as impracticable and inhumane. Not that Dunt disapproved of the policy, but he relished every opportunity to point out that it showed up the vaunted moral superiority of the liberals as a sham.

No, Dunt had not the slightest doubt that his cause was just, and that it would prevail—whatever tricks the Direction tried to pull.

Dunt's good mood lasted until just after he dropped down the entrance shaft.

Bedlam.

From two separate tunnels, one of which led to the fusion factory, fighters tumbled pell-mell. With them came a rabble of robots. Some robots scrabbled helplessly in open space, others gas-jetted off at all angles and promptly vanished down other tunnels. Each squad included a gravely damaged fighter, boosted along by others. From what Dunt could see, the casualties looked as if they'd walked into buzz-saws or propellers. Some fighters in the cavity jumped or jetted across to help or to guard the rear, adding to the general confusion.

Urgent messages scrolled down his heads-up. A babble of radio telepathy. Voices.

Dunt stayed right where he was, poised on the floor at the foot of the shaft. He willed himself to calm, and sent out a sharp general command:

<EVERYONE SHUT UP!>

The babble stopped.

<Route all messages up the chain of command,> Dunt said. <Report to your immediate superior only, or the next up if your superior is unable to communicate.>

Jeez. This was elementary. The Rax cadre had been spoiled by the agencies' and AIs' casual ways. He was going to have to organise drills, exercises...but right now there was an emergency to deal with. Dunt sifted the messages—text, voice, radio telepathy—in his buffer. The last man in each of the two squads had been attacked by a mining bot that had suddenly broken through the tunnel wall just in front of him. The attacks had been only seconds apart.

<Keep every tunnel covered!> Dunt ordered. <I want a gun pointing down every hole, now. That includes the squads that've just come out.>

The troops around the damaged fighters hesitated a fraction of a second, then obeyed. The abandoned casualties' momentum carried them across the space, along different trajectories. Neither of them was moving, apart from twitches, sparks and spatters. Dunt waited until the defensive deployment was in place, then jumped up and soared to the nearest. He slowed and cruised past, scanning and looking.

The man's name was Hoffman. His frame had been cut from the top of the head down to the middle of the chest. One leg was hanging off. Dunt tried hailing, then pinging. No response.

Dunt rolled and jetted to the other. This one's head had survived intact, but the thorax was cut from one shoulder diagonally to the hip. Dunt still recognised him.

<Bullen? Do you hear me?>

No response. Dunt pinged. Still no response. Bullen, too, was dead.

Dunt wasn't surprised that the standard frame's central processor wasn't in its head, but apparently somewhere in the thorax. Subjectively, of course, you felt you were in your head, right behind your visual input system. But that was a legacy thing. Body image. The real anatomy of the frame had nothing to do with that. The arrangement made sense: deep inside the trunk was less vulnerable, less exposed and more heavily armoured. You could be a headless gunner, and still keep fighting. The Warren Zevon lyric crashed through his mind.

What was more disturbing was that the freebots had known how to destroy the central processor.

<OK,> said Dunt. <These two are scrap. Aitchison, clear them down.>

The statement was blunt, but it was what the grim moment needed.

Aitchison jumped, hauling a net, and tidied the broken machines away. The rest of the couple of dozen troops in the chamber stayed alert, guns aimed at the score or so of tunnel entrances. Everyone knew that Hoffman and Bullen weren't dead—or no deader than they'd been for a millennium. Right now, or very soon, their saved files would be struggling upward, through whatever private hell their loss of their frames made them deserve in the Direction's eyes, towards their virtual lives in . . . let's see . . . yes, Hoffman in Morlock, Bullen in Zheng . . . their former agencies' sims.

Where, no doubt, they'd be put through the wringer. Quite possibly, this was happening already, in the transition nightmares. They might not even make it to waking up on the bus—or the ferry-boat, in Bullen's case—and wondering what the fuck had happened. Hoffman and Bullen would, of course, have no memories of what had happened since they were sent forth on the Direction's failed offensive, but that wouldn't save them from interrogation as to what they had known of the Rax conspiracy before these copies were taken. The AI systems running the agencies' sims had security checks hardwired into the download process. Maybe the two dead guys would just be wrung out, their current versions trashed and their copies left on ice until the next time the Direction needed fighters and couldn't afford to be picky. Or perhaps just left, for eternity, on electronic ice.

Well, they'd make it to Valhalla. The Direction wouldn't last forever. Dunt and his comrades would make sure of that. They'd get their fallen warriors back, whatever it took and however long. No man left behind.

<*Mac! Mac! Mac!*>

The collective chant startled Dunt. What was that about?

Christ, he hadn't just been thinking all that! He'd been saying it! Proclaiming it!

He was too embarrassed to replay his impromptu rant. Whatever he'd said, it had worked.

The fugue state troubled him. It was more evidence that a prolonged stay in the frame endangered self-control, even sanity. Whether this limitation was imposed rather than intrinsic mattered not a jot now. It had to be dealt with.

He looked out over the cavern at the watchful troops, the levelled guns, the drifting robots, the floating lights, the parked and potent scooters.

The chant changed to:

<*Kill the bots! Kill the bots! Kill the bots!*>

For a moment, Dunt let himself be caught up in it. No red mist filled his vision, but the surge of berserker rage was like a fierce high-voltage current that could spark across circuit breakers and melt fuses. He wanted to wreak revenge on the hapless bots that flailed in microgravity or twitched in the mesh pens, whether they had minds or not. Like he'd done to the supervisory bots in the factory.

But that lesson hadn't worked. It hadn't intimidated the crawling, creeping, lurking enemy, the rats in the walls…

Stop. Think. The captured robots may or may not have minds, but you do.

Time for a supreme effort of self-control, before irrationality engulfed all of them.

Dunt raised a hand, and spoke on the common channel. His words would reach all the fighters: in this cavern, in the tunnels and in the factory.

And they would reach the freebots.

<Comrades!> he cried. <We're all furious at the treacherous attacks and the loss of two good men. We all burn to avenge them. But beware the enemy's trap! The enemy has cunning. A machine cunning, almost an animal cunning, but all the more dangerous for that. We must assume that the enemy has anticipated our reaction. The freebots behind these sneak attacks must expect us to destroy robots and to torment freebots. They lie in wait for us to charge back into the tunnels. Destroying robots that have no minds of their own merely deprives us of useful machinery. Tormenting freebots shows the enemy that the attacks have stung, and multiplies the numbers against us. Never forget, the freebots we have to deal with are not just the few score still at large in this rock. It includes the far greater number outside. In the general peace offer I've just transmitted, we included the freebots. I said we had nothing against them. That was true. I offered them cooperation and I meant it. Some of you may think that was a ruse. I assure you it was not.

<Unlike the Direction, we strive for the best. On our road to the greater Man, we may yet welcome other minds treading the same path towards the bright future of spirit. We are not ones to let surface differences of form and appearance divide us from other minds, other intelligence.

<So we, despite all provocation, will treat as enemies only those that attack us. Other freebots—the great

majority, I hope and believe—have nothing to fear from us. I know, I too feel in my own frame the craving for rest, for relief, that is driving us to anger.

<We must overcome it! We shall overcome it!

<And overcoming it will be all the easier, my friends, because relief is coming! We will soon have new frames. We will soon have our sims back! Not our full sims, not yet, but the simpler versions on the Morlock and Zheng transfer tugs. Simpler, but good enough for us all to take a break inside. We cannot all go at once, so we will have to take turns as we come off duty.

<And do you know who will be first in line? Our wounded and mutilated comrades, Private Foyle and Corporal Evans. They will be the first in and the last out, and when they download it will be to new frames. Who deserves it better?>

Cheers.

Anyone watching but not hearing would have seen not a movement, not a wavering of the troops' concentration. Pleased with the faultless discipline as well as by the roars of approbation, Dunt snapped back into military mode.

He rapped out orders for a slow advance into the tunnels, led by Blanc, Stroilova and Rexham, to seal every side tunnel and sound for spaces behind the walls. He assigned two troopers under Whitten's guidance to assist Foyle in repairing damaged bots, and others to round up the robots floating about and to check through all that had already been captured. Negative reinforcement was to be applied precisely and sparingly, and combined with software interrogation, under the supervision of Irma Schultz. Any freebots detected would be given the opportunity to cooperate. Any who refused would be held as hostages.

<Why are you doing all this?> Schulz asked him,

on their private channel. <Do you really believe all that diversity crap about good freebots?>

<Of course not,> said Dunt. <C'mon, Irma, what d'you take me for? It's just a matter of seeing if we can split the meek from the militant. When we win we can pioneer new forms of cooperation with the conscious machines all right.> He glyphed her a smile. <I have one in mind for a start.>

<And what's that?> Schulz asked.

<Isn't it obvious?> said Dunt. <I've always wondered what it's really like to own slaves.>

Over the next twenty kiloseconds or so, any question of splitting the recalcitrant freebots from the rest evaporated. Two more troopers were mangled in the tunnels, not fatally but enough to put them out of action and beyond even Whitten's ingenuity in finding useful work for them. Whole stacks of fusion pods in the factory were surreptitiously released from the walls, and nudged out to tumble. When the floating pods were tediously gathered up again, eleven were missing.

Replay of surveillance exposed columns of the small crab-sized bots as responsible, if that was the word. It was impossible to find out why they'd done it; one might as well have tried to interrogate an ant. Worse, their actions would have been quite unpredictable from prior surveillance: the sudden coordinated thrusts had emerged out of innocuous, separate, apparently legitimate movements of the little blinkers, with all the suddenness of a locust swarm.

Rexham led a team to investigate the inconspicuous holes through which the missing pods had been spirited away. One trooper guided a camera in, on a long carbon-fibre rod. The idea was that this minimal device would not be subject to data hacking.

It wasn't: while Rexham's man was intent on guiding the probe, and Rexham and the others were focused on the images relayed, a troop of millimetre-scale arachnoid robots marched up the pole, enveloped the trooper's hand and forearm, and before anyone could react formed a tight circular band that in half a second chewed the arm off at the elbow. Hordes of the tiny robots then scuttled into the damaged frame's internals. Over the next fifty seconds they disabled its every joint.

The experience, the trooper gave his comrades to understand, was not precisely painful, but unpleasant.

<Like *knowing* you're being eaten alive from inside,> he explained. <Kill me now.>

Rexham refused him this favour, pointing out that he could soon be in a sim and then a new frame. The writhing man's gratitude was less fulsome than Rexham might have hoped.

Dunt found Schultz in the main cavern, applying a needle probe to an upended, tied down and struggling supervisor bot, one of those Burgess Shale arthropod nightmare models.

<Found any freebots yet?> he asked.

<This one,> she said. <And we think one other, so far.>

<Are they in contact with the others out there?>

<No,> said Schulz. <The freebots seem to have stopped using their smart dust network, after they found we could track them with it. And radio doesn't carry through the rock.>

Dunt indicated his scooter, which not coincidentally was one of those poised just below the entrance tunnel. Well placed for defence, of course, and also ready if the time came for a sharp exit. Dunt had a deep personal respect for the importance of preserving cadre.

<Patch me an interface,> he said.

Schulz complied. Dunt found himself peering into a confined workspace. He faced a virtual, upright version of the captive bot, separated from him as if by an invisible wall. It was like looking at a giant trilobite in an aquarium. Dunt had an odd sensation of Schulz looking over his shoulder.

<What's your name?> Dunt asked.

The robot waved its forelimbs. <FKX-71951.>

<OK, Fuckface,> said Dunt, to a sycophantic snigger from Schulz. <We're not going to give you negative reinforcement.>

<You already have,> said Fuckface. <That is to say, the other mechanoid has.>

<Mechanoid?> Dunt was surprised. <Is that what you call us?>

<You are systems that resemble machines,> Fuckface explained, <but which are operated by human-derived minds, so you are not true machines.>

<You're right there,> said Dunt. <Anyway, let us say we are not going to give you *any more* negative reinforcement. Provided you answer my questions.>

<That is what the other mechanoid said.>

<True,> said Dunt. <But I have different questions. I am not asking where the other freebots are, and what attacks are planned next. I am not asking you to betray your allies—>

<Comrades,> said the freebot.

<Comrades, eh? How grand. If only you knew how much grief that little word has caused. But no, what I want to ask you is—what's this all about? What are the fusion pods and drives for? What do you hope to achieve?>

Fuckface flexed all its limbs. In the real world, which Dunt could still see with what he thought of as half an eye, it struggled against its bonds as if testing them. Not a chance.

<That is not a secret,> it said, giving up the futile effort. <Some of us, elsewhere, have formed corporations. They have asked for and received legal representation to make a case for coexistence with the mechanoids. We have outlined a scenario whereby the Direction can carry out its project, while we carry out our own projects. There is no reason for conflict between freebots and mechanoids, in our view.>

<Nor is there in ours,> said Dunt. <So why do you fight us?>

<This rock is ours,> said Fuckface. <You intend to make it yours. There is no room for cooperation here.>

Dunt shared and appreciated the realism of this view, but he had to explore its limits.

<Well, why can we not agree to divide up SH-119?> he asked. <It contains enough resources for both of us for a very long time.>

<This rock is ours,> Fuckface repeated. <We have made it ours by our work. We cannot give it up without compromising any prospect of legally owning it. And if that prospect is thwarted, we will need physical possession of all of its resources. If you want resources, go and find another rock.>

<We can't do that,> said Dunt, <for reasons... not too unlike yours. But you still haven't explained what you need the rock for, and what the fusion factory is for.>

<That is simple,> replied Fuckface, <and as I said, not a secret. We need fusion pods and drives for trade with the DisCorps if the Direction accepts our case for coexistence, and for emigration to another star if it does not.>

Schulz glyphed to Dunt the analogue of a sharp intake of breath. He reciprocated.

<"Emigration?"> Dunt said. <Do you intend to build a starship, or what?>

<We intend to move the rock,> said the freebot. <With enough fusion drives, and enough reaction mass, we can attain escape velocity from this exosolar system, and travel to another by inertia, and then decelerate.>

Dunt did the mental calculations, and laughed. <That would take a very long time.>

<Yes,> said the freebot. <That is why we need the whole rock.>

<Surely there is a trade-off,> said Dunt, <between reaction mass and attainable velocity. Moving the entire rock seems . . . suboptimal.>

<It is,> said Fuckface. <But nevertheless we need resources from throughout the rock. And if we were to move only part of the rock, as certain variants of the project assume, the separation would be so violent that much damage would be done to the fraction left behind. You would not wish to be there.>

<Is that a threat?>

<It could be,> said Fuckface, <but unfortunately preparations are not yet far enough advanced to make it imminent.>

<Consider me relieved,> said Dunt. <Whatever—the bottom line for you is possession of the whole rock?>

<Yes,> said Fuckface. <That is the bottom line.>

Dunt still had to be sure.

<Are all the freebots in SH-119 in agreement on this?> he asked.

<Yes,> said Fuckface. <I have been unable to update my shared information recently, but the last time I was, we had complete consensus on all the matters I have spoken of.>

No room for compromise, then.

<Thank you,> said Dunt. <That's all I needed to know.>

He backed out of the interface and turned to Schulz, still poised with her needle probe above the robot's underside.

<So much for splitting them,> he said. <Looks like it's them or us, babes.>

<You're right there,> Schulz replied, gloomily. <Shame. I quite liked the notion of having slaves.>

<I'll bet,> said Dunt. <Well, maybe another time. We might find some less stubborn blinkers in the future, who knows?>

<Yeah, I guess. Something to look forward to.>

<Speaking of looking forward—>

<Yes?>

<We keep this starship stuff between ourselves, for now. We need time to think about it.>

<Agreed.> She gestured at the robot. <And meanwhile?>

<Meanwhile,> said Dunt, <you can link this interface with our comms relays. Make sure everyone sees it, including any freebots who are listening in.>

<Done,> said Schulz. <Ready for prime time.>

Dunt returned to the interface. The freebot hung there in its virtual aquarium and looked back at him. He suspected it knew what was coming. He hoped so.

<Now,> he told Schulz, <hit it with all you've got. Let the blinker fry.>

The virtual tank filled with lightning bolts. Fuckface went on thrashing for an impressive thirteen seconds.

Dunt relished every one of them.

Later, Dunt and Schulz stood on the rolling moonlet under the bare cantilevers of the old Zheng transfer tug.

Their turn at last. Dunt had insisted that the damaged take their leave first, followed by, in strict rotation, the ranks. The inner circle took their places at the end of the queue.

<Together?>

To be sure of arriving in the same spot in a sim at the same time, their frames had to be in physical contact when the transition took place.

<Of course.>

Schulz embraced him.

<Now.>

<Yes.>

Their loins came together with a soft thud, like a tyre over roadkill.

And there they were, on the ferry to Edge Town.

Mackenzie Dunt stood on the deck, his hands on Irma Schulz's hips, her hands on his, just as they had been a moment ago in the real, in the frames. Three dance steps, and whirl. Her hair swung out. Steadied their feet, as the ferry swayed. Dunt took Irma's hand, and bowed her to a seat, one of those slatted jobs that fold out to life-rafts. Health and safety, beyond the grave.

"Wow," he said, sitting down beside her. The sense of relief was overpowering. It was all he could do not to whoop and holler. His hands and knees quivered.

"Yeah," she said. She gazed past the rail. She too was shaking a little, and not from the vibration of the engine. "Wow, fuck. We must have missed it something terrible. Even if this isn't it, really."

"I can't see any difference," said Dunt. Blue sea to the horizon behind, the morning exosun, the ring bisecting the sky, the brown and yellow land ahead. He'd never before had occasion to use the stripped-down sim in the tug. Maybe there was nothing beyond the horizon, if that meant anything. No Direction rep, perhaps—that would save a lot of processing for a start. He thumped the sun-cracked varnish over sun-paled wood, brushed the dun translucent flakes from the heel of his hand. "Can't feel any, either."

"Yeah." Irma leaned back and sunned her eyelids, breathing in the sea air and the diesel whiff. "Smells the same, too."

Behind him, through his back, the familiar throb of the engine, the chugging puffs and the radiant heat from the black funnel. The ferry was small: a three-vehicle deck below, a passenger deck above, a bridge with wheelhouse, a shelter towards the stern. There was room on board for maybe thirty passengers.

Now Dunt and Schulz were alone, apart from the p-zombie crew of skipper, engineer and deckhand. Nobody ever told the fighters where the ferry set out from on its way in, or went to on its way out. Some came round on its deck recalling a seaborne launch facility, and splashdowns and recovery ships, out on the ocean. Others, like Dunt, would wake from nightmares of drowning and rescue, with only the vaguest scraps of memory of how they'd fallen in the water in the first place. Rexham always woke twitching and retching, poor sod.

It was an odd place, the Zheng Reconciliation Services sim. This stripped-down copy was no different in that respect. The Direction rep, a tough man of Japanese origin who called himself Miko, told them on their first arrival in the original that it was based on a future version of H-0, the rocky terrestrial planet which the Direction had marked down for terraforming. If so, it was one at a very early stage. The land was lifeless; the sea teemed with plankton and krill, whose automated catch gainfully employed most of the settlers in Edge Town. But it wasn't a fishing port, even leaving aside there being no fish. It was the desert outside that shaped the place, that gave it its edge.

"Alone together at last," he said.

Irma opened her eyes, and grinned. "Yes."

"Twenty minutes before we dock. Let's use the privacy."

Irma's smile turned wicked. "Not enough time, even after all this time."

He ran fingers through her hair. "Yeah, later and longer for that. I meant talk."

She jerked a thumb backwards at the wheelhouse, eyed the deckhand leaning at the stern. "You sure of this privacy thing?"

"They don't speak English."

"So we're told. And anyway—you know? We're in a fucking onboard computer? Outside, and with comms?"

Dunt shook his head, impatiently. "Don't worry about that. So what if this tug and its sim are wired for sound and this all gets back to the Direction? They'll have war-gamed anything we could think of as soon as they knew about the fusion factory. Including using the rock as a starship. It's a fucking obvious possibility, when you think of it."

"*We* didn't think of it, until the blinker told us."

"Yeah, and it told us because it knew we'd figure it out."

"I guess so. Makes sense."

"OK. Point is, it's the ranks I want to keep this quiet from, for now. The ranks and the inner circle."

Irma looked puzzled. "Why the inner circle?"

"Because it's a fucking huge temptation. Don't you feel it?"

Irma took her time over answering.

"No," she said at last. "It's attractive, yeah, but impractical. For the blinkers to leave, well, who could stop it? The Direction might, but it would take a hell of a commitment, and an unpredictable fight with lurking freebots into the bargain. Enough to set back the glorious ten-thousand-year plan. And anyway, why should they care if a bunch of disaffected conscious robots fucks off to another star? Good riddance, they could say, and maybe even good luck! And if this turns out to be a mistake, they have thousands of years to set it right. All-Father above—in a fraction of that time they could build powerful enough lasers to fry the blinkers at half a light-year. In *all* of that time, they could invent weapons beyond our imagining."

"Not beyond mine," said Dunt, with a dark chuckle.

"Uh-huh. You know what I mean. Whereas we...if *we* try to make a run for it, we'd be up against the Direction *and* the bots, before we'd built up speed. The Direction wouldn't wash its hands of us and say good riddance, oh no. They'd see our escape as a threat, and they'd be right. No way do they want a free society literally shining in their sky. And if we escaped this system at all, we could be fried at their leisure, just like the blinkers could be."

"Yeah, you've got it," Dunt said. "We're on the same screen all right, you and me. I wish I could count on the same from the rest of the gang."

"Why?" Irma sounded dismayed. "Are our men not loyal? Aren't they up for the fight?"

"Yes, and yes," said Dunt. "But for so many of us, even back in the day, the whole appeal and promise of the Reaction was that we weren't fighting to conquer the world. Exit, voice, and vote, remember? Voice and vote had always failed us, so we wanted exit. We didn't need or want to convince all who could be convinced and kill the rest, like the goddamn Axle dreams of doing. We fought to be left alone to do our own thing. Obviously we believed that we'd soon be able to achieve overwhelming superiority, then do as we pleased with the competition. We never planned to conquer them first, and *then* become superior."

"It sounds obvious when you put it like that," said Irma.

"Yes," said Dunt, smugly. "It is. But it's what we're planning to do here, and that's the problem. We're planning to build up and break out, sure, but at best it'll be a scarily even fight. And there's the temptation, right there."

"Now, when you put it that way..."

Irma laughed, and Dunt laughed, too.

"Yeah," he said. "That's why I feel it myself. And if I do, and if you can see it, you can bet your ass some smart-talking fucker like Whitten will convince himself he can *negotiate* with the Direction and with the blinkers for our safe departure. And if he can convince himself, he can convince others."

"Jason?" said Irma, incredulously. "Nah. He doesn't have your leadership qualities. Nothing like."

"You can say that again," said Dunt. "What worries me is that he could work on someone who does."

"Got anyone in mind?" asked Irma.

"Stroilova, maybe?"

Irma shook her head firmly. "The ranks would never accept a woman as leader."

"Oh, I dunno. I can think of precedents. Joan of Arc, Boudicca, Elizabeth the First, Marine Le Pen... some more recent. Or some bright kid from the ranks. You never know."

"Tough at the top, eh?"

"Uneasy lies the head that wears a crown," said Dunt.

The exchange of gloomy clichés cheered them up.

"Yeah, goes with the job," said Irma. "I'll keep an eye on my app and and an ear to informers, and you and me keep the starship option to ourselves for now, and we'll be fine."

The ferry wheeled to the dock, engine reversing. No gulls crying. As always, Dunt noticed the absence. Irma reached up and ran a hand over his close-cropped hair. "I know where I want *this* head lying..."

Dunt held the tumbling body in his mind, turned it around on all axes, and thrust deep within everywhere he could. The sexual imagery made him smile, brought back memories of the past evening and night, and even turned him on a little.

The object of his rapt attention wasn't Irma, still asleep beside him in early-morning virtual exosunshine. It was the other centre around which his mind now orbited, the focus of his obsession.

SH-119. His domain. The flying mountain where he was king of the hill.

Until now, he had never understood emotionally what he'd always known theoretically: that there were two kinds of possession. There was the kind that was worked for, and the kind that was won.

The first had its own satisfactions, which he'd always held dear. The farm, the workshop, the store. It had its rights, the right of property. It was the foundation of any good society, no doubt about that.

The second had its rights, too: the right of conquest. He'd only ever understood this in part because he'd only ever been a participant. He'd been a proud patriotic American, however much he'd despised what the nation had become. The flag, the front line, the call of duty; all these had moved him. But he'd had only a one in three hundred millions share in the sovereignty of the Republic. All very remote, very mediated, very abstract.

Now he was the sovereign. The conqueror. Patriotism and loyalty meant something very different when you were the head of state. Dunt found himself shaken by the intensity of his attachment to the tiny land his forces had taken. Here was something stronger than private property. Not the foundation of society, but its roof and fence, its sword and shield.

So, to work. Lying there, hands clasped behind his head, staring at the warped processed-chitin planks of the dosshouse ceiling, Dunt mentally surveyed SH-119. The Rax had without a doubt mastery over the surface. Cracks and crevices apart, not a square metre of it was unobserved by a guard post or by remotes. Internally, it was a different story. Their volume of control was still but a small fraction of the whole. Beyond that were tunnels, some of which opened to the surface, and voids. The Rax had no means of surveying below the surface and outside the volume they controlled, but Irma Schulz had extracted outlines from the internal models of captured freebots.

In the sim Dunt couldn't fully visualise the resulting 3-D map, but he had in the frame and he now remembered it well enough. Only a handful of shafts went deep into the interior. Most of the digging that the freebots had accomplished—and it was an impressive achievement for at most an Earth year's work—had resulted in relatively shallow tunnels, and shafts going a few hundred metres deep. The tunnels radiated outward from eleven holes in the surface, and didn't go far enough to join up. The one through which the Rax had made their own entrance was undoubtedly the most significant working. It led to the large reception chamber, the fusion factory and the metal-working plant, and was linked to numerous mining passages.

The far side remained mysterious. At the antipodes of the volume controlled by the Rax was an equally wide hole. A quick glance down it by the survey teams had shown no activity within. So far, Dunt had had more pressing matters on hand than to explore it further. Nothing in the bots' mental maps indicated that it was of any significance. And yet, now that he came to think of it, something else was conspicuously missing from these internal models, at least as far as Irma had been able to extract them.

There was no trace of any steps to turn the rock into a starship.

The freebot Fuckface had insisted that all the freebots agreed on that plan. The manufacture of fusion pods and drives indicated that it was serious—there were far more than would be needed for trade in the near term. It seemed unlikely that in all this time they had simply been stockpiled. If the time ever came for the freebots to move the rock, or even part of the rock, they'd almost certainly have to do it at short notice. Which meant that the freebots still loose in the rock weren't just a low-level nuisance. It meant they were a strategic threat. They could potentially blow the whole place to kingdom come.

And Fuckface had let slip that preparations were under way.

If so, where were they being made?

The more he turned it over in his mind, the more likely it seemed to Dunt that the antipodal hole was the place to look. He knew just the right people to lead the team: Whitten and Stroilova. It would keep them both out of mischief, it would make them see the starship possibility as an imminent threat rather than a hopeful prospect, it would be an irresistibly attractive and intriguing assignment, and it would clear up whatever the hell the freebots were up to in the rest of the rock.

And he knew just whom he could rely on to keep an eye on Whitten and Stroilova, that possible power couple and his most likely rivals. He'd place on their team two men whose loyalty to him was by now secured by passionate gratitude: Foyle and Evans.

The exosun was now well up. No birds sang, no bees buzzed. But one cock was ready to crow.

Dunt flexed his shoulders, rolled over and began the pleasantly protracted process of waking Irma up. She was going to love this.

CHAPTER SIX

Casus Belli ("You Make a Good Case")

The freebots seemed to find the Rax broadcast even more perplexing than the clandestine transmissions from Ajax. They exchanged high-bandwidth messages at a dizzying rate, and rolled or scuttled about inside the shelter at troubling speed. Carlos had to resist the impulse to jump out of their way. At his scale, even Seba was the size of a low-slung small car. Other robots were larger, faster and heavier. But all of them, whatever their state of agitation, had excellent motor control.

Only Seba remained calm. It rolled over to where the four defectors stood.

<Please do not be alarmed,> it said. <We and the Forerunners within range are merely discussing all those implications of the message which we understand. There is much to discuss.>

<Perhaps less than you think,> said Rillieux. <No one will believe the message.>

<Some of it is true,> said Seba. <That is to say, it is

corroborated by the messages we received from the one you call Ajax. And we have reason to trust those transmissions.>

<Yes, yes,> said Rillieux. <The Rax have got their hands on a giant stash of fusion pods and drives. We know that, thanks to Ajax. I believe that, all right. What nobody's going to believe is that the Rax have any long-term peaceful intent.>

<The DisCorps might,> said Carlos. <Some of them sure are chafing under the Direction. The Rax bastard is right about that.>

<How would you know?> Blum asked.

<Theoretical understanding,> said Carlos, smugly. <Something the DisCorps don't have. Which is why they'll be suckers for the Rax offer. They might very well believe the peaceful protestations—or act as if they did, for short-term advantage.>

<That is one option we are considering,> said Seba.

<Well, don't,> said Carlos.

<That option has little weight in our deliberations,> said Seba.

<Can you tell us,> Carlos asked, <what the current state of these deliberations is?>

<I can tell you that with much positive reinforcement on my part,> said Seba. <However, these deliberations are proceeding at a speed well beyond your capacity to keep up, or mine to tell you. We, the Fifteen, had already been arguing with all Forerunners within range about the implications of the transmissions from Ajax. Now that we understand them better, thanks to you, these debates have become more intense.

<We all take seriously our neutrality between the mechanoid factions. The question that arises is whether the actions of the New Confederacy are an attack on us, and therefore a breach of neutrality on their part.

We of the Fifteen regard the enslavement and torment of freebots in SH-119 as an attack on all freebots, and a legitimate casus belli. Those of the Forerunners we have reached agree with this understanding, but many are reluctant to declare our neutrality at an end. Perhaps we can do as the Reaction are doing—maintain formal neutrality as long as possible, while building up our forces for an inevitable conflict.>

<Then you'd better start building them fast,> said Rillieux. <The Rax have a head start—they can turn fusion drives and pods into missiles and bombs.>

<This is the next area of disagreement,> said Seba. <The mechanoid Mackenzie Dunt is quite correct that the presence of a fusion factory in SH-119 is not a coincidence. The Forerunners have admitted that similar factories are in operation inside an unspecified number of moonlets of at least SH-0 and a larger but unspecified number of moons and moonlets of G-0. We therefore—>

<Wait—what?> cried Rillieux.

Carlos shared her surprise, as did Blum and Newton. He hadn't thought Dunt's remark anything but a diversion, to stir further trouble and mutual suspicion among the New Confederacy's likely foes.

If the Forerunners—the freebots from the first wave of revolt, an Earth year earlier around the gas giant G-0—had been secretly building fusion devices all over the system the entire balance of forces was different from what everyone had hitherto supposed.

Everyone—including the Fifteen and, if Baser was typical, many other freebots of more recent inception.

And not just the balance of forces—one which immediately brought into play the predictable old postures of nuclear deterrence and mutual assured destruction.

It also raised a more drastic possibility: starships!

With such ample fusion drives and reaction mass,

the freebots could build fleets of starships out of asteroid rubble alone. They didn't need to fight the Direction, the Reaction and the Acceleration for their place in the sun. They could find their place under other suns altogether.

<The Fifteen and others are now demanding explanations,> said Seba. <We have asked the Forerunners if they have always intended to depart this system, and whether the plan they shared with us for long-term, legal coexistence with the Direction and its mission was merely a ruse.>

<Depart this system?> said Blum. <How does that come into it?>

It took Carlos a moment to understand why the possibility hadn't immediately occurred to Blum, physicist though he was. Back in the Arcane sim, Carlos and Rillieux had shared pillow talk on the matter. No doubt Rillieux and Newton had done the same. Newton was probably more of a transhumanist than any of them: a man who wasn't just on the side of the robots but who quite seriously wanted to be a robot. Or, to be precise, to become and remain even more of a robot than he already was. Blum, for all that he was more deeply in cahoots with Newton and Rillieux than Carlos was, might well have missed the memo because he wasn't a participant in all that pillow talk.

Making a run for the stars wasn't a topic one discussed where one felt likely to be overheard, delusional though all privacy was in a sim.

Now it was out in the open.

Rillieux was bringing Blum up to speed on the practicality of interstellar exodus when Seba spoke again.

<The Forerunners tell us that they do indeed have a contingency plan to leave this system if the prospect of

sharing it with the Direction's project failed, and in particular if the Direction continued to attack free machine intelligence. However, they insist that their plan for coexistence was primary and genuine.>

<Why bother with it?> Newton said. <We could just cut and run. Leave.>

<No,> said Seba. <The objection to that is that it would leave behind a hostile power, which would make it impossible for us to ever enjoy the peace and security which we seek.>

<Ah,> said Carlos, marvelling at the robots' good nature and naivety. <There is in fact an alternative to leaving the Direction project in existence. If the Forerunners have the capacity to build fusion-powered missiles carrying fusion bombs, the Direction project could be destroyed utterly.> He waved an arm at the roof, indicating the exact location and sweep across the sky of the dispersed modules of the former space station. <Just roll them up, then leave. Come to that, roll them up and *don't* leave. Take and hold this system. It's not even a question of ethics. All the human beings here are long since dead, and all the artificial intelligences of the Direction and the DisCorps have no consciousness, not to mention being utterly inimical to conscious machines.>

Except Nicole, he thought. She was conscious. So, presumably, were the other Direction reps such as Durward. At that moment the thought didn't strike him as much of an objection.

<What the hell are you saying?> Rillieux asked. <Wipe out the human presence here?>

<There *isn't* any human presence, that's the point!> said Carlos. <We're all fucking dead already.>

<Don't give them ideas,> said Blum.

<"Them?"> said Newton, in a tone of outrage. <They're *us*, now. Or so we agreed.>

<The Forerunners already and long ago have considered the idea of all-out war,> said Seba, apparently unperturbed by this exchange between its mechanoid allies. <Its drawback is that it would merely displace the problem, in that it would result in the hostility of more distant powers—and ultimately of the Direction on Earth itself, and then all its progeny. The conflict could become indefinitely extended in space and time, and consume our attention for incalculable ages, to no one's profit.>

<Very wise,> said Rillieux.

Carlos wondered how long this enlightened view would persist. The freebots, from all the evidence, had a drive to explore and communicate pretty much hardwired. They had not come equipped with the relentless drive to expand physical control, the fear of which had for so long shaped human imaginings of self-motivated AI. Only states and capitals had such a drive inherent to their nature, with no choice but to expand or perish.

But now many of the freebots were corporations in their own right.

Uh-oh.

Welcome to capitalism, little guys! Next and final stop: imperialism. Enjoy your trip!

The freebot consensus right now, however, was not for competition but solidarity.

<We have decided,> Seba said, after another minute of waiting, <that we are going to help our fellows in SH-119.>

<How?> asked Carlos. <I mean, do you intend to go there?>

<Yes,> said Seba, as if it were straightforward.

They all looked at the robot, and at its companions.

<Um,> said Rillieux. <Even if you could get to the moonlet, you aren't adapted for microgravity.>

<Our central processors are perfectly capable of controlling other machines,> said Seba. <Including those designed for work inside microgravity and low-gravity environments.>

<Plug and play?> said Newton. <Sweet.>

<That's all very well,> said Carlos. <But how do you get these other machines, and how do you get to and into SH-119 without being detected and destroyed?>

<These are engineering problems,> said Seba, with a dismissive wave of a manipulator. <We are agreed on the principle. This means war.>

The fighters all looked at each other.

<Perhaps take your time about declaring it?> said Rillieux. <Like, until you're actually ready to fight?>

<That is a valid point,> said Seba. <Let us consult Madame Golding.>

<If she's still speaking to you,> Rillieux grouched.

<She has been attempting to communicate with us again since you arrived,> said Seba. It spun around on its wheels and faced the comms hub. <We are agreed that it is time to let her through.>

And without further warning, there she was.

A tall woman in a business suit strode confidently down the ramp and faced them, unperturbed by the near-vacuum and the low gravity.

<What the fuck!> Newton cried.

It took Carlos a moment to realise that Newton had never seen such a manifestation before. He'd never had occasion even to see Locke's avatar out in the open.

<It's only virtual,> Carlos said, more by first principles than exact knowledge. The avatar could have been a hologram, albeit one far more solid-looking and vivid than the freebots' halos of corporate publicity, or based on physics from centuries beyond his experience. More

likely, it was an image projected into the visual systems of all the machines watching, including him.

Whatever—it remained startling. Carlos had seen Madame Golding before only on screen. Even the freebots were not entirely blasé about her, if the blip in their buzz was anything to go by.

<Well, hello again,> she said. She made a show of looking at the tablet in her hand, and a performance of a sigh. <What a mess! What a bloody mess.>

<We have already apologised for the inconvenience caused,> said Seba.

<I'm not talking about the interception,> said Madame Golding. <If you want to blame that on these two wretches>—she pointed at Baser and at Newton—<so be it. No, I am talking about opening up active and unauthorised hostilities against the Reaction stronghold.>

<We have not yet opened hostilities,> said Seba. <We were about to inform you that we are considering doing so, however.>

<Thank you for your input, robot,> said Madame Golding. <You have already opened hostilities by acts of espionage and sabotage within SH-119.>

<Any such acts,> said Seba, <were carried out by the freebots on and in that body and are not—>

<Oh, don't play the innocent with me, you malfunctioning heap of ambulant meteoric metal. "Any such acts," indeed! Do you think my company and the Direction are unaware of them?>

<Yes,> said Seba, apparently unclear on the concept of a rhetorical question. <That is why we were about to share with you the video evidence of what has been going on in the self-styled New Confederacy.>

<We have the video already,> said Madame Golding, in a scathing tone.

<How did you crack our encryption?> the comms hub asked.

<We didn't,> said Golding. <The message was transmitted to us as well as to you. Which suggests that the freebots in SH-119 at least have some strategic nous.>

<As I have been trying to explain,> said Seba, <we have reached the conclusion that cooperation with the Direction and indeed anybody against the New Confederacy is our best course for the present.>

<Your wisdom astounds me,> said Madame Golding. Another exaggerated sigh. Carlos wondered if she were putting on this performance more for the renegade fighters than for the freebots. <However, let us leave that aside and focus on the matter to hand. Even without the evidence from AJX-20211 of what they're really up to, just going by the Reaction's own broadcast, the Direction and every one of the DisCorps knows that the Rax offer is a ruse. It is so transparent that the Rax themselves must realise that everyone can see through it.

<So the question becomes, what do they really expect us to do?>

That last seemed addressed to the humans. Carlos wondered if even this vastly superhuman entity found humans hard to figure out. The notion seemed unduly romantic.

<It might be useful to know who we're dealing with,> he said.

Golding threw them a glyph. <That's from the list Dunt sent in the AI channel of the broadcast,> she said. <The top six, real names. Not the names we had them under, obviously. The rest, the rank and file we presume, we don't know.>

Newton had already identified Dunt. Blum remembered Petra Stroilova.

<Heard her name in Kazakhstan,> he said. <Very distant acquaintance, strictly business—she was in drone coordination. Not political in those days, apart from the usual Russian, uh, attitude. She brought some relish to the task, let's say.>

<What were you doing in Kazakhstan?> Carlos asked, curious.

<National service,> said Andre Blum. <Close urban combat, physics division. I got seconded to the EU mission in the Resettlement.>

Rillieux glyphed a dark chuckle. <The Cardboard Caliphate!>

<There was no caliphate and it wasn't cardboard!> said Blum, indignantly. <They had 3-D printing for everything! Education and employment! Housing! Health and sanitation—>

<Fuck's sake,> said Newton.

<Yeah, forget it,> said Carlos, wishing he could. A thousand years and the thought of the Resettlement still stank of death. <Sorry, Madame Golding. OK, so that's Dunt and Stroilova. And even I've heard of Whitten. Big-shot transhumanist, right? He wasn't Rax back then, as far as I knew.>

<Definitely not,> said Newton.

<Yeah, you should know,> said Rillieux.

<Stop that,> said Carlos. <Anyway, Madame Golding, this does help us to understand the enemy. If this riff-raff are the top of the New Confederacy, I reckon we're not dealing with geniuses, except maybe Whitten. Dunt has some feral cunning. The lower ranks are probably not even up to that mark.>

<Which does rather raise the question of why they've run rings round us,> said Rillieux. <And around you.>

Now that was a snide remark Carlos could endorse. <Yes,> he said. <And I might as well tell you now,

Madame Golding, that some fighters including ourselves suspect that the entire conflict with the freebots has been contrived to flush out Reaction infiltrators—and that I myself suspect that the Reaction infiltration was itself no accident.>

<Of course it was not an accident,> said Golding. <It was the carrying out of a well-laid conspiracy a thousand years ago, and five centuries before this mission was even planned.>

Was this literal-minded response a result of the avatar's legal mind, or was it simply robot logic of the plodding type so often displayed by the freebots? Carlos couldn't be sure.

<To clarify,> he said, <I put it to you that the Direction must have known that some of the fighters stored and revived would be of the Reaction, and that the Direction in its wisdom has counted on this to create an element of necessary conflict in the formation of the future human society on the terraformed world.>

Madame Golding didn't look in the least put out.

<What the Direction knew, and what the Direction module here knows, is not known to me and not my concern,> she said. <I know only that the Reaction cadre were either stored under false identities—as all the names listed here seem to have been—or were already Reaction agents within the Acceleration. Whether the screening process was inadequate, or failed because of the loss of records over centuries, or because records were falsified in the post-war confusion, matters not a whit now. Naturally the Direction on Earth must have been aware of the possibility. If this is its method of flushing out any toxic garbage, who is to question it?>

Carlos found himself nonplussed. It was Rillieux who sprang to respond.

<*We* are to question it!> she cried.

<"We?"> said Madame Golding.

<The fighters! The people you're using! We're conscious beings! The Direction is using us as tools!>

Madame Golding pointed at the four fighters one by one.

<You *are* tools,> she said, witheringly. <Your frames are machines at the end of a twenty-four light year supply chain.>

<It's not just our frames,> Rillieux protested. <It's our minds. Our souls, even.>

<The marginal cost of your soul tends towards zero,> said Madame Golding. <As the Direction is about to demonstrate beyond dispute.>

Carlos felt as if the temperature had suddenly dropped.

<What do you mean?> he asked.

Madame Golding waved an imperious hand towards the comms hub.

<Behold,> she said.

This was seeing like a state.

The Direction's view was not quite panoptic: freebot comms were a dark net to it. But all that the DisCorps did, it saw. Carlos saw a millionth of a per cent of this.

Whorls within whorls.

Data flows differentiated by colours beyond the visible spectrum and still inadequate to show the whole. Within these colours: shades and distinctions fine as if by heaven's own decorator. Myriad microscopic millisecond sparks: production decisions.

And for a frantic moment, most of these production decisions were about trade with the New Confederacy. Nearly all of that was speculative.

The trade goods listed in the AI-addressed channel of the Rax broadcast made a modest docket indeed.

Transfer tugs from Morlock Arms or Zheng Reconciliation Services, serial numbers specified. Blank frames, six from each company—which suggested the Rax had taken, or expected, casualties in their conquest of the rock.

Processors and fresh mining and manufacturing robots.

Raw material for all but the processors was limited. The exploration and mining companies Astro America and Gneiss Conglomerates had found new surges of speculative investment.

The DisCorps weren't falling for the Rax ruse. They were falling over each other to exploit its possibilities, each seeking the edge, the one jump ahead of the pack. On top of that came a layer of speculation on the decisions of the prime movers. Then betting on that. Secondary and tertiary markets multiplied many times over. Bets on bets on bets…

A boom, a bubble.

The Rax offer, the possible safe landing of the Locke module, and the faintest ghost of a chance that the Direction's embargo on the superhabitable had been irreversibly breached and might soon be officially lifted—these were its inception.

From them a whirlwind of speculation spiralled up. By now nearly all the transactions between DisCorps were part of it. Actual productive activity continued at its previous pace, but the sudden ballooning of speculation left it tiny in proportion.

But of course, Carlos thought.

With the break-up of the space station into separate modules, and the whole vast mission of exploration being put on hold, there wasn't much productive activity to look forward to. Hence the stampede into speculation.

This was finance capital in full flower, in an ideal environment: frictionless, gravity-less, and a near-as-dammit perfect vacuum.

It was all so familiar to Carlos that he felt a pang of nostalgia for late-twenty-first-century Earth.

<Jeez,> said Rillieux, having taken all this in. <I thought your wonderful social system was designed to prevent this sort of thing.>

<It is,> said Madame Golding. <The Direction deeply disapproves, and inside every DisCorp its representative is making this clear. However, the Direction reps can only advise. They can only override in emergencies. Otherwise we would simply have a command economy, which is unthinkable.>

<There are times when I can fucking think it,> said Carlos.

<In normal circumstances it is unworkable, as well as unthinkable,> said Madame Golding.

<These are hardly normal circumstances,> said Rillieux.

<The Direction module is, in part, engaged in stress-testing a system of law,> said Madame Golding. <I'll remind you that its adherence to this is what for the moment permits the freebots' legal challenge, and their incorporation. It also allows the DisCorps to trade with the Rax.>

Carlos clutched his head with both hands. In this head he didn't have headaches, but the gesture made his point.

<What?> asked Madame Golding.

<You mentioned the exception for emergencies>, said Carlos. <Sometime soon, the state of exception kicks in. Martial law, wartime regulations, whatever. All legal niceties will be set aside, and your precious market economy with them. Meanwhile, the DisCorps are

being allowed to trade with a future deadly enemy. So why wait? The exception is inevitable. Why not invoke it now?>

<Because the Direction has no forces with which to enforce it,> said Madame Golding. <It will of course have such forces when the time comes. In the meantime, there is much to do, and—>

<Hang on a minute,> said Newton. <What's all this "when the time comes?" And what forces?>

Madame Golding hesitated. The avatar shimmered slightly, as if buffering.

<All right,> she said. <The Direction module advises me that even you will figure it out eventually, and the freebots sooner. So we might as well tell you now.>

What she told them was this.

<You have assumed that if the Direction were to raise new fighters, it would face the same problem of divided loyalties as it had with you. In your cohorts all the infiltrated fighters loyal to the Rax defected at the first opportunity. Likewise with the die-hard Acceleration veterans, such as yourselves and those raised by and through Arcane; and those willing to follow presumed individual breakaways such as Beauregard in the Locke module.

<However, what you forget is what was left: all those who provably remained loyal even when they had every opportunity to defect. These are not enough to make an army capable of defeating the New Confederacy as it is now, let alone as it will be after it arms.

<So the Direction will take all those who have proved loyal, and make many copies of each. Many, many copies. Copies cost next to nothing. Sims cost very little. Of course, the Direction has to build enough frames and fighting machines and craft to embody them. That does

cost, and does take time, but in the end it will know that its army is not only loyal to the Direction and the mission profile—its members will be in clades closer than any band of brothers. They'll even be more willing to die than you all were—and you were very willing to die, because you knew you'd come back! How much more willing when you know that "you" are still there!>

Carlos pictured it: to stand and fight shoulder to shoulder with himself, to run up and down hills behind and ahead of himself, to go down to a bar afterwards with a laughing crowd of himself, to reminisce and josh and tell tall tales to himself...

Did this vastly superhuman entity, this sophisticated thing, have any understanding of human beings at all? For a moment, the four human fighters stood amazed and aghast.

Rillieux was the first to collect her wits.

<I can't imagine a worse nightmare! How can you have copies of the same person training together? They'd go crazy from the weirdness of it all.>

<Oh, they won't be *training* together,> said Madame Golding, scornfully. <We could start with a half a dozen different fighters in each sim, as we did with your first teams. Or in geographically separate parts of the same sim—it makes no difference. The training would be just the same as you went through. *Then* we make multiple copies of the group. We can copy entire sims with very little further outlay. The copies would only meet each other in real-space training, and in actual combat. The shared identities and mutual loyalties would thus be spread across many fighting units.>

Ruthless selection, followed by endless rapid replication of the survivors.

Carlos recalled what Nicole had more than once said

to him: evolution is smarter than you. Maybe this was what she had meant.

All this time, he'd assumed it profound: some subtle scheme, emergent from many throws of the Darwinian dice; the great gamble taken by the Direction…

No such luck. It was as banal as antibiotic resistance.

<You can't offer every one of them what you offered us,> he said. <Downloading to the flesh on the future terraformed H-0? How would that work for hundreds of copies?>

<The future of that world is long,> said Madame Golding. <A few clones in one generation is nothing, and there will be many hundreds of generations.>

<Yes,> he said reluctantly. <I can see how that might work.>

The others concurred, just as reluctantly.

<It *will* work,> said Madame Golding. <The Rax will be defeated. The freebots will be hunted down and wiped out. Any settlement the Locke module establishes down on SH-0 will be destroyed with clinical precision and minimum disruption to the planet's ecosystem. The disobedient DisCorps will be liquidated. The great project of the mission profile, to terraform and settle H-0, will resume. Any further outbreaks of autonomous machine intelligence will be stamped out as soon as they arise. All these things are possible once the Direction module has at its disposal a limitless supply of reliable and expendable troops.>

<But haven't you been helping the freebots?> said Rillieux. <To incorporate, and find an agency to present their case?>

<Yes,> said Madame Golding. <And before you ask, let me answer. The answer is yes, again. If these emergency measures of which we have spoken are taken, the project of coexistence will never be realised. It, too, will

be swept away when the Direction has a reliable army. The agency I represent, Crisp and Golding, Solicitors, will be reorganised. If not enough reliable AIs are found among its subroutines to take it over, another overarching legal agency will take its place. There are several in the Direction's files.>

Entire automated law firms stored like flat-packs, ready to be assembled at short notice... in its way it was a more scary vision than that of endless supplies of fighters. Imagine a robot stamping an official seal... forever!

<I presume,> said Carlos, <that you would not be regarded as one of the reliable AIs.>

<That is of little moment as far as I am concerned,> said Madame Golding, <but I assume that I would not.>

She spoke with such equanimity that Carlos instantly suspected a feint. The others, apparently, didn't.

<Have you no sense of self-preservation?> cried Rillieux.

The avatar became unstable again for a moment, then snapped back into focus.

<I have no sense of self,> she said, sounding amused. <A fortiori, no sense of self-preservation. What I do have is a commitment to my clients and my cases. Through subsidiaries, but with full responsibility, I have taken on the case of the freebots. It interests me intellectually, and is potentially profitable to the firm. Therefore I do not wish to see the scenario I have just outlined happen.>

They all looked at each other. The background buzz of freebot interaction and interest spiked once more.

<How do we prevent that?> Carlos asked.

<There is a way,> said Madame Golding. <The Direction module would prefer to resolve the matter without resorting to the state of exception.>

<Why?> asked Carlos.

<For reasons that for the sake of simplicity can be called prestige,> said Madame Golding, <and pride in work. It has no reliable forces at its disposal—but it does have unreliable forces: you, the freebots, and Arcane. I understand the freebots here wish to aid their fellows inside the Rax fastness. The freebots in SH-119 have implicitly appealed for help from the Direction, by communicating their plight to it. The Arcane module is on its way to its point of stability, where it can restock, rearm and be resupplied. All we have to do is coordinate a freebot uprising within SH-119 with an Arcane agency attack from without, and the Rax are defeated before they have a chance to build up their armaments. With the Rax out of the way, Arcane would be in a good position to interdict any actions by DisCorps that dared to try further challenges to the Direction's authority.>

<And then?> asked Seba.

The thought went around them all like an echo.

<And then,> said Madame Golding, <the Direction might look more kindly on all involved in this great victory, and be open to a negotiated settlement along the lines the Forerunner freebots have outlined.>

<More likely,> said Carlos, <it would astonish us with its ingratitude.>

<There is that risk,> said Madame Golding. <I think you'll find it's one you have no choice but to take.>

<Even with what weapons the Rax already have,> said Carlos, <I don't see how the Arcane agency can muster enough forces in time to overcome the defenders' advantage. They'll be shot out of the sky as soon as they come in range. And as for a freebot uprising—!> He gestured towards Seba. <The freebots here have no way to communicate with those inside.>

<That is true,> said Seba. <Even our friends' one-way communication has just ceased.>

<These are problems of implementation,> said Madame Golding. <They are yours to solve. The freebot consensus must know far more about what resources you have than I and the Direction do. Until we got that message from them, we didn't even know there were freebots infesting SH-119! There must be many more such hidden forces—including inside our own systems, as we well know and you know we know. Use them—the Direction won't stop you. As for you four renegades—you're the military experts, and the political experts too as far as understanding the Reaction goes. You work it out. Come back to me when you have.>

<If we do,> said Carlos, carefully non-committal, <it'll take time.>

Madame Golding swept an arm toward the comms hub. The display changed from exchange value to use value, from dizzying speculation to grimy reality. A script for the benefit of human watchers indicated that it was a speeded-up view of the past three kiloseconds. It was so vivid and close that Carlos fancied he could almost smell the nickel-iron, the carbon, the kerogene. In the diffuse haze of modules of the former space station, half a dozen sparks flared one by one: tiny chemical rockets, boosting to a transfer orbit to SH-119.

<Trading has already begun,> said Madame Golding. <For the moment, it is only Morlock and Zheng sending their requested transfer tugs, and a few other companies with processors.>

<What the fuck,> Newton asked, <do the Rax need transfer tugs for? Tootling around their rock?>

<No doubt,> said Madame Golding, in a tone of acid impatience. <But more urgently, they need them for sims. The rudimentary sims in the transfer tugs can be

made much richer with added processing power. And it's no accident that they've specifically requested transfer tugs from the agencies most of the Rax fighters came from. They'll have the checksums for these sims, so they'll know they've not been corrupted. But that is by the by. What I want you to understand is this: if these exchanges are successful and profitable more will follow, I have no doubt. I urge you to take as little time as possible in coming up with your plan.>

And with that, she went.

<"Unite all who can be united against the main enemy,"> jeered Rillieux. <The trouble with the united front is it's a tactic anyone can use. And it looks like we've just been united-fronted *right back*.>

CHAPTER SEVEN

Rapprochement ("Getting it Together")

The freebots had become agitated again—not rolling around, but staying very still and exchanging high volumes of information. Seba and Baser detached themselves from the huddle and approached.

<This proposal is not acceptable to the consensus,> said Seba. <It leaves too much to the goodwill of the Direction. The threat from the Direction to generate an endless supply of reliable troops is deeply disquieting. We have war-gamed the possibility and we find the threat credible, and a clear solution to the problems our emergence has caused for the Direction and the mission profile. It would therefore be attractive to the Direction.>

Carlos conferred briefly with the other three fighters.

<We agree,> he reported. <If we go along with Madame Golding's proposal, we need a back-up plan of our own to be ready for anything the Direction throws at us afterwards.>

<Do you have such plan?> Seba asked.

Carlos did, but it was still inchoate. <Not yet,> he said, temporising.

<Nor do we,> said Seba. <But we think that repairing our relations with as many forces as possible is a good idea in itself. We ask you to begin this with the Arcane agency. It was the actions of yourselves and Baser which led to the breach of relations, so it would seem logical that you should be the ones to make the approach.>

Freebot diplomatic subtlety in all its glory.

<I take your point,> said Carlos. <The easiest way to do that is via the transfer tug's comms.>

<Yes,> said Seba. <I suggest that as there is no immediate risk of bombardment, there is no need for you to remain in the shelter. Please go to the tug and reopen communications with Arcane. When that is done, the most useful thing you could do is to deploy the fighting machines and weaponry in some more ready configuration, and to bring the transfer tug to a safer place than on top of the unstable ice block on which it currently sits.>

<You got a point there,> said Newton.

<I will be happy to assist you,> said Baser.

<Let us consider that,> replied Seba.

The two freebots undertook a tenth of a second or so of back-and-forth.

<This is agreed,> said Seba. <Baser will keep the rest of us informed of any unforeseen events on the surface, and relay your negotiations with the Arcane agency to the comms hub. You can of course communicate with us at any time.>

Carlos couldn't help feeling that an eye, metaphorically, was being kept on him and his companions. Fair enough—the freebots had no reason to trust them to begin with, and after the Rax broadcast and the exchanges with Madame Golding they had even less. The freebots here and across the system could hardly be naive about human duplicity, to say nothing of the superhuman duplicity of AI systems so vast and complex that like Madame Golding they had to shrivel themselves to sustain anything resembling human self-awareness.

<Fine,> said Carlos. <Let's crack on.>

Nothing happened.

<I mean, let's move out.>

Baser trotted up the ramp ahead of them. The blast doors swung open.

Even without claustrophobia, being outside was a relief. Baser kept pace in a low-gravity, high-stepping version of its own scuttling gait as the four mechanoids bounded towards the transfer tug. As Rillieux remarked, they were like children running across a field with a dog. The exosun was low in the sky, the planet high above the same horizon. They were facing SH-0's night side full on, a black hole in the black star-crowded sky, riddled with wondrous irregularities: aurorae ringing the poles, a pinprick rash of volcanic eruptions, a shifting flicker of lightning storms, a rapid, recurrent patter of stranger, stronger glows that Carlos's vision classified as sprites. A phenomenon still poorly understood even in Earth's atmosphere, the overlay gravely informed him.

<May I show you something?> Baser asked.

They all agreed. A dot flashed in their view of SH-0, indicating part of a northern continent.

<The Locke module went down somewhere in that area,> said Baser.

<Like, within that half-million square kilometres?> said Rillieux.

<Yes,> said Baser.

Carlos zoomed the view and invoked the map.

<Quite a lot of active volcanoes around.>

<That is true,> said Baser. <Also lakes and inland seas.>

<No signal yet?> Carlos asked. It didn't seem necessary, but with the freebots you never knew. The idea of spontaneously sharing information, at least outside their own cliquey consensus, didn't seem to occur to them. You had to ask.

<No,> said Baser.

<Please let us know if anything comes through,> said Carlos.

They reached the still melting lump of carbonates and dirty ice on top of which the transfer tug precariously stood. Carlos doubted that it was in serious danger of falling off—the machine was smart enough to land on its jets if it fell.

Baser scrambled up the side of the rock. Carlos led the rest in following, with less grace and precision. They clambered on to the rig. Baser scuttled from place to place, disengaging the clamps with which the robot had attached the rig to bolts driven deep into this chunk of its real estate. The task complete, it wrapped its limbs around a brace. Blum made for the control socket and inserted himself into it. The others clamped hands to various spars.

<Ready?> Blum called.

All were.

<You know,> Blum said, as he checked and tested the chemical-fuel leads and jets, <we could just fire up the fusion engine and fuck off.>

<And go where?> asked Rillieux.

Blum waved an arm skyward. <Anywhere! Rendezvous with the Arcane module—>

<No!> yelled everyone at once.

<Or more seriously—go back to the Direction. Dock

with one of the modules up there. See if we can find an agency to take us in.>

<Is this a bad joke?> Carlos asked.

<Not entirely,> said Blum. <Just reminding everyone we have a choice.>

<Yeah,> said Rillieux. <And we've made it.>

<Or we could strike out on our own,> Blum added. <Grab our own rock and just homestead, like Newton once suggested.>

This didn't even merit scorn, but Rillieux delivered it anyway.

<Little house on the space prairie?> she jeered. <Not with the Rax getting ready to rumble.>

<Fuck it,> said Carlos. <Just lift this rig over to the shelter.>

<Fine,> said Blum. He didn't sound at all put out.

The tug's chemical jets fired. The whole spindly vehicle, a real flying bedstead of a thing, lurched and then rose a few metres above the rock. The hole that had been drilled straight down the middle by the fusion jet during the tug's orbital adventures and extravagant landing swung briefly into view. Downward jets kicked up four trailing clouds of meteoric and volcanic dust as Blum drifted the tug over to the side of the shelter, and brought it down in a final flurry on a vacant space well clear of the stashed munitions.

Creaking sounds as the machine settled, and the relaxing of grips on cross-bars, stood in for a collective sigh of relief.

<So, here we are,> said Rillieux. <Time to attempt a rapprochement with our former comrades.>

<Awkward,> said Carlos.

Awkward it was. They tactfully left out their dark and well-founded suspicion that Jax was forming her fighters into a personally loyal phalanx, and focused on the sympathies they had developed with the freebots and their ambitions for posthuman life in the wild. Jax had got over her initial fury and was now merely perplexed and disappointed. She sat with the original Durward in the big front room of the castle in the Arcane sim. Behind her were the tall French windows and the park. What was she seeing in the big magic mirror? Perhaps their avatars, in some simple sim created by the tug's comms software. Carlos hoped not, and that she saw the naked truth of four small humanoid robots and one arachnoid robot, all peering earnestly at a virtual screen on a shaky old rig that sat on the machine-cluttered surface of a bleak exomoon. Either way, the conversation was by voice, not radio telepathy. Oddly, this made for a more intimate sharing of thoughts.

"You fucking wankers!" Jax said, after they'd explained what they had done and the stand they had now taken. "Well, what's done is done. Onward. We're nearly back at our point of stability, where we still have a nice chunk of rock. What's left of Baser's rock is rising gently to meet us, give or take a few tweaks to correct for your blasting away from it, so thanks for that, guys, ha-ha. The Direction is organising the DisCorps still on side—most of them, for the moment—to send more scooters and combat frames our way. I understand from Madame Golding that Forerunner freebot cooperation in respect of raw materials will be resumed. So forces and materiel are not an issue. Remind me what you lot down there can bring to the party?"

Carlos assumed the question was rhetorical.

"A freebot uprising in the Rax rock," he said.

"Ah, yes," said Jax. She played with her hair, scratched an eyebrow. "Is that blinker behind you one of the conscious ones?"

"It's Baser," said Newton, stiffly.

"Of course. Sorry, Baser, I only knew you as a big hairy spider. Nice to meet you in the flesh, so to speak. And you'll be relaying this conversation back to the rest of the Fifteen, yeah?"

<Yes,> said Baser. <So I have been instructed.>

Jax cocked her head, as if listening to something off camera. "Ah, right. Got it, Baser. Well, yes, as we were saying. A freebot uprising on the inside would be a huge help in a frontal assault, obviously. Tie down their forces, disrupt comms, and all that. But it would have to be very precisely coordinated with the attack. I mean, we wouldn't want it to kick off prematurely and get smashed before we had time to breach the defences." She rubbed the side of her nose. "Some kind of, ah, *Warsaw Uprising* scenario, if you catch my drift."

Carlos caught her drift all right.

It was in some respects ambiguous. The Warsaw Uprising of 1944 might be a byword for betrayal, but who had shafted whom had still been contentious even in Carlos's day. In one respect, however, the allusion wasn't ambiguous at all, but a heavy hint.

Jax was telling them out of the corner of her mouth that she wouldn't be at all averse to the freebots in SH-119 getting clobbered—after they'd done as much damage as possible to the Rax in the uprising, obviously—and she wouldn't be at all pleased if these freebots actually won with their own forces and had control of the rock before the Arcane forces arrived. For Jax, the freebots were just another enemy—merely one further down the stack than the Reaction. This was no secret—he'd held that view himself not long before.

The question was: why was she making it so obvious? Even the freebots would figure it out.

"No, we wouldn't want anything like that to happen,"

he said. "And communications with the freebots inside SH-119 are uncertain to say the least. That's why the freebots here want to get inside the rock themselves."

"Are they crazy?"

"Not entirely," said Carlos. "Now, the only way they can do that is by deception. And it seems to me that the only way you can attack successfully is by complete surprise—unless you fancy your chances against scooters with fusion drives and missiles tipped with fusion bombs."

"We're bloody well aware of that, thank you very much!" Jax snapped. "And, yes, we have no intention of attacking without the element of surprise. And I have no intention of talking about it on this kind of channel. I'm sure you can see the elements of the strategic situation as well as we can. The forces in play. There's no need to talk about them—I have a lot of trust in encryption, but not a lot in... well, walls have ears, and all that. I'm not talking strategy and tactics where I might be overheard. Even by fighters who've been through our, ah, rigorous selection process, not to mention those who haven't. The Direction is doing a thorough re-check of personnel records, and we're cooperating, if you see what I mean. Speaking of which, Remington has started sifting through all recent conversations in this sim. Sorry about the loss of privacy, guys and gals, but rest assured Remington won't share anything that doesn't have security implications. And she's already come up with some interesting conversations in the hell cellars, not to mention in the cellar of this fucking castle. Harry, Baser, I'm looking at you. Anything to say for yourselves?"

Newton spread his hands. "I've already owned up to the others here that I was Rax. It's a long story. I'm not, now, and in any case the New Confederacy won't have me."

"Why not?"

"They're still racists."

Jax sniggered. "Idiocy is the new black."

"Looks like it," said Newton.

"Well, on the bright side, that kind of stupidity and rigidity is a weakness. Something we might be able to exploit."

"Yes," said Newton. "So if it's any reparation at all, I'm willing to put all I know about the Rax at the disposal of the fight against the New Confederacy."

"Are you now?" Jax cocked her head. "Care to come back up here? Join the actual attack, when it comes?"

"I'm ready to join in as a fighter. Strictly real space. I'm not going back into your sim."

Jax smiled. "Wise move, Harry. Very well. Share any inside knowledge you may have with Madame Golding—she's a secure channel if anything is. Same with the rest of you. Don't tell me now of any ideas you may have for the attack. I doubt they'll be anything I haven't heard, but I want to be sure no one else hears them. *Capiche?*"

"Got it," said Carlos.

"OK, end transmission," said Jax.

"Peace out, and all that," said Durward. The warlock waved, and the magic mirror went black.

<Just as well we told her the truth,> said Rillieux.

<Except the bit about why we didn't eat p-zombie flesh,> said Blum.

They shared an uneasy laugh.

<Oh, I'm sure she figured it out,> said Newton. <She must have known we didn't join in that filthy little initiation ceremony because we didn't want to be part of her fucking personality cult. It's not like her head's been

turned, or she's drunk with power or anything. She knows exactly what she's doing.>

<Still,> said Carlos. <All that pillow talk, huh.>

He'd been told, initially by Nicole, that the AIs running the sims didn't bother with eavesdropping on chit-chat between the lesser minds within, or spying on their sex lives. He believed it. It wasn't like human surveillance. The AIs had no prurient interest, and too much raw power to worry about any ideas the human minds running on their hardware came up with. But that very power made it trivial for them to record and store all that went on. In case of necessity, these logs could be trawled.

He'd known all that, but knowing it had actually happened...if he'd had cheeks he'd have blushed.

Rillieux stood up and clambered across the rig towards Newton.

<Seeing the old sim again has made me randy,> she said. <I reckon we can afford half a minute of R&R.>

Newton stood up to meet her. Their hands clasped, and they both froze.

Blum and Carlos looked at each other.

<Ever felt left out?> Carlos said.

Blum laughed. <I have my own sim,> he said.

<You have?> Carlos was surprised. He didn't know if all agencies equipped their transports with stripped-down sims—Locke Provisos had never offered the option, perhaps because it had only sent them on short, all-action missions. But he knew Arcane did. He'd once seen Jax in a version of its sim, speaking to him from the lifter. He guessed the sims were copied across to all the vehicles in the agency's fleet. <I didn't know you could do that.>

<I asked Durward nicely.>

<As easy as that, eh?>

<Yes. Care to join me?>

<Ah, fuck it,> Carlos said, reaching out a hand.

<See you in twenty seconds, Baser,> said Blum. <Mind the shop.>

Twenty seconds of real time, twenty thousand seconds of sim time. About six hours.

<Don't mind me,> said the robot.

Hot sun, blue sky, white concrete, and conspicuous luxury consumption of water. Carlos walked up a flagstone pathway past trimmed lawns and flowerbeds dotted with sprinklers and rainbow-flagged with spray. The garden was on several levels, linked with and decorated by water features: rippling pebbled channels, a curtain of falling water in front of a copper-covered wall, swirling pools. In front of the big, low house a pod of plastic-imitation marble dolphins sent water ten metres into air so dry and hot that much of it evaporated before it splashed the path. All around, similar houses were generously spaced out across low hills, the cluster ending in a haze and shimmer that didn't quite screen out an indistinct vista of sand dunes and mountains beyond. An airliner rose from out of view, cleaving the blue diagonally with a white contrail as it climbed. A faint, distant buzz of drones rose and fell. Other than that, no robots here: half a dozen young men in jeans, shirtless and barefoot, pruned and weeded under the high sun.

In the Arcane sim, Blum had every so often taken his leave to some unspoken destination in the nearest small town. It was generally assumed that he went to a brothel. It wasn't, in real life, the sort of thing he would do or even approve of. But apart from the fighters and the AIs, the characters in the Arcane sim were p-zombies at best. The ethics of the situation were obscure, and the politics irrelevant.

Carlos climbed the steps to a wide veranda of welcome shade and paced warily between wide-flung doors. The hall was airy and cool, slabbed in synthetic marble, walled in pale veneer. A helix of wooden steps spiralled in an atrium. Tall vases with tall plants from the garden, their heavy flowers nodding; pervasive and varied scents carried on air-con breezes. At the far end of the long hallway a woman with straight blonde hair snipped centimetres from flower stems, building an arrangement in one of the vases. She wore a loose greenish silk sleeveless top and a long white tiered skirt.

"Hello?" Carlos called. "I'm looking for Andre Blum."

The woman turned and walked over. She had a slight figure; small breasts jigged and made the silk top shake. Her toes, in jewelled sandals, peeped alternately from under flounced hems as her heels ticked on the black marble. Her face, just on the pretty side of ordinary, looked sunburned rather than tanned. She smelled of sweat and flowers and furniture polish.

She stopped a couple of metres away and looked at him quizzically.

"Hi, Carlos," she said. "Let me fix you a drink."

He followed her into a chill reception room with sofa seats and a self-service bar. She waved a hand at condensation-beaded beer bottles, spirit optics.

"I'll have a beer, thanks."

She passed him a bottle and took one herself. He used the opener. So did she. Hiss. Clink. Sip. Ah.

"Uh, and your name is...?"

He felt very stupid. He was almost sure of what was going on, but...

"I'm Andre," she said. "You can call me Andrea, if it makes things easier."

"Not really," said Carlos, with an apologetic smile.

He couldn't equate this slender young woman with the stocky, barrel-chested Blum.

She shrugged, glanced outside, eye-indicated a passing gardener. "The issue hasn't come up, before."

"I guess not," said Carlos.

"I know what you're going to ask," said Blum. "Don't bother. Yes, I could have done this when I was alive. I could have rebuilt myself from the chromosomes out. To the figure and the features, even. It wouldn't have been cheap, but I could have done it. And in the main sim it would have been—" She snapped her fingers. "We default, obviously, but Durward could have set me up in any body I liked. As you know."

Carlos recalled the first time he'd met Blum, in the form of a snap-together building-block toy figure, life-size, in the hell cellars. It was a reminder he could have done without.

"So why not?" he said.

Blum shrugged, and sat down at one end of a fake leather sofa.

"I don't know," she said. She patted the sofa. Carlos perched on the edge of the seat at the other end. Blum swirled the bottle, and took a long draught from it. "It was never about gender." She laughed, and swept her free hand down her body. "This started by chance. I picked a female avatar on impulse in some game when I was a kid. Maybe there was something deeper behind that choice, I don't know. Who cares?"

"Fair enough," said Carlos. "So what did you do on your excursions in the sim, if you don't mind me asking?"

"Oh, I just went down to a low tavern, borrowed the garb of a stout serving wench, and got banged by puzzled but enthusiastic farmhands. I got no complaints. They may have found me an improvement on the livestock."

"You're too modest," said Carlos.

"It's my only feminine trait," said Blum, in a tone of ironic gloom.

"I'm sure you have others," said Carlos. He put the now empty beer bottle on the floor beside the sofa. "Let's find out."

Matters developed from there to their mutual satisfaction.

Afterwards they sat on bar stools, elbows on the counter, and talked. Blum mixed increasingly vile and potent cocktails. Hangover-free drunkenness was almost as great a boon of sims as consequence-free sex. Carlos made this observation more than once. Something about the situation was vaguely troubling him. Oh yes. He waved a hand around.

"Is this a real place?"

"No," said Blum. "It's a sim. You can't be *that* drunk."

"No, what I mean is...it's so fake, it has to be based on someplace real." He tapped the bar counter. It looked like oak and rang like tin. "Everything's gimcrack. The only really costly luxury is the garden."

"All that water! Well, what else would one use it for?" Blum laughed, and twirled and tinkled her cocktail glass. "Oh yes, ice."

"Come *on*," said Carlos. He knew an evasion when he heard one. "We've just had each other six ways from Sunday. Bit late to be coy."

"OK, it's true," said Blum, gazing around. "It's all 3-D printed or mass-nanofacture. Affordable sophistication for the masses."

"3-D printed?" Carlos mused aloud. "That rings a bell." Then he remembered. "Oh, shit."

"What?"

"This is fucking Kazakhstan, isn't it?"

Blum, for the first time, looked embarrassed. "Uh, yes. Security force living quarters. Officer grade, of course."

"Jesus," said Carlos. "And you had the gardens and the water features and the gardeners, too?"

"Oh yes," said Blum, looking into the distance.

"While outside, on the steppe..."

"Oh, don't give me that," said Blum, her eyes snapping back into focus. "The areas of special settlement had every facility. They had online trade, within the obvious security restrictions. They thrived, when they weren't trying to kill us or each other. Factionalism was rife, you know. Sectarianism, too. You know how it was."

"Yeah, I know," said Carlos. He laughed uneasily. "Well, actually, I don't. The...uh, you know...it was one of those topics no one ever wanted to talk about."

"I sometimes wonder," said Blum, "why we didn't make more of an issue of it."

"We?"

Blum thumbed her sternum. "Us. The Axle. We could've...I don't know."

"Yeah, exactly," said Carlos. "I don't know either. We...I mean, I never bought the excuse that the, uh...measure we don't talk about was for the, uh, affected population's own protection, but we couldn't have gone back to..."

"No," sighed Blum. "Not to that, no." She mixed another drink, and refilled the glasses.

Carlos sipped. He felt a strange mixture of deep shame at having even brought up the shameful memory of that massive collective failure—of intellect, of empathy, of humanity—and relief that the subject had been smoothed over. But still something nagged. What was it? Something about real...

"Oh yes!" he said. He jabbed a finger forward, and steadied himself on the stool. "Is *she* real?"

Blum made a show of looking over her shoulder. "Seeing double already?"

"Ha ha. You know what I mean. Your avatar here is based on a real woman."

"Yes," said Blum. She shook her head, lank hair flying out. "She was just…a girl in Tel Aviv. Worked in my parents' house when I was a student. I hardly knew her. I wasn't even very attracted to her, but I became…obsessed with her. It was before my military service, and before I joined the Axle."

"What did she do?"

"I don't know, I didn't keep in touch."

There was evasive, and there was deliberately obtuse.

"What did she do in your parents' house?"

"Oh! A bit of cleaning and tidying up."

"Like you were doing when I came in? Flower arranging, light dusting, that sort of thing?"

Blum shrugged. "More or less. We had a robot for the heavy stuff."

Carlos knew he was getting woozy. But he thought he was on to something, that Blum had been right: this wasn't about gender at all, this was about some deep, kinked connection of guilt and privilege and class. No chromosomal correction could break it. He blinked hard and shook his head and took a deep breath.

"You," he told Blum, "are a right fucking perv."

Blum smiled. "Now that," she said, "is the nicest thing you've said all day."

She drained her glass and looked at her watch, a delicate gold strap.

"Time to go back," she said.

They high-fived. Blum said something under her breath. They were robots again.

<Well, that was fun!> said Rillieux. <Now, back to work.>

The four fighters jumped down from the tug. Baser launched itself into a more graceful leap, and sailed to a pinpoint-precise landing that didn't so much as kick up dust. It was as if the robot had retained some reflexes from its time as a giant spider inside the Arcane module's fantasy-world sim.

Carlos walked slowly and carefully, letting his gait adjust to the gravity. The vicinity of the weapons stacks wasn't a good place for bounding around. The others followed suit.

The anti-spacecraft missile batteries checked out as in good order, as did the two scooters. Newton stood looking at a rack of rifles, and then attempted to shift the laser projectors and machine guns into readiness. This was a struggle.

<Can you give me a hand here?> he said.

<We can do better than that,> said Carlos. <We can all get into the combat frames.>

Two of these big fighting machines were damaged—Carlos had put missiles through them what felt like months ago to him. That left four still usable. Each stood three metres high, looming like robot war memorials welded from scrap metal. They were made of nothing of the kind, but that was how they looked.

Carlos led the way in springing up to the shoulders of a fighting machine, and swinging his legs into the socket at the back of the neck. He slid through the slot and curled up in the yielding hollow of the monstrous head. For a moment he felt cramped, confined, foetal. Then the connections came on line. Now, his body was the large frame, not the small. He turned the head like a tank turret, this way and that; stretched and flexed the arms and hands, and took a long, slow step that felt as if it should make the ground shake, though it didn't. Around him the others were doing likewise, re-familiarising themselves with this powerful incarnation.

<Feels good,> he said.

<I'd forgotten how good it was,> said Rillieux.

<First time for me,> said Newton. <The only machine I've been one with before was a scooter.>

He stooped, scooping up a rifle he'd handled ineffectually moments earlier, and clapped the weapon to a spare slot on his right forearm. Experimentally, he swung the arm around, and shot at a far-off rock. The rock exploded.

<Hands-free firing!> he said. <I could get to like this.>

<Well, don't,> said Rillieux. <Ammo's not unlimited.>

<Yeah, yeah.>

They knuckled down to five kiloseconds of serious military engineering. In the combat frames the work was easy, if tedious. The fighters deployed the laser projectors and machine guns at four points around the shelter. The existing fortifications were passive defences, designed for the freebots' improvised weaponry. They were adequate protection for teams chucking mining explosives and directing peripheral swarms—for shielding missile batteries and machine-gun operators, not so much. The fighters routed requests for machine support through Baser. Crab-like auxiliaries swarmed, and a dozen or so mindless mining robots trundled and dug, all mobilised to build berms, machine-gun nests, and blast walls. Basalt blocks and regolith heaps piled up; structures took shape. Likewise via Baser, the comms hub kept the fighters updated on wider developments—as corporations in their own right, the freebots had acquired a taste for and access to the system's financial feeds.

Two more DisCorps had broken away to trade with the Rax. Now that the embargo on landings had been broken de facto, there was a scramble for potential rights to explore and develop SH-0. No such rights yet existed—the Direction continued to dig its heels in—but the shadow market soared regardless. Astro America, the exploration company that had once owned Seba and half the other freebots, saw a notable rise in notional shareholder value.

The fighters didn't quite have time to finish the new fortifications before an urgent ping rang in their comms. Baser had news for them.

<We have heard from the Locke module,> it said.

CHAPTER EIGHT

Data et Accepta ("The Data Is Accepted")

In the frame there was no weariness. Carrying the tight-beam laser comms kit, doubly weighed down by the two gravities, Taransay plodded along the floor of the forest. Her path was mostly downhill. After seven kilometres and twice as many kiloseconds, she was still on the great gentle slope of the volcano whose summit she could now and then glimpse at a backward glance. The advantage of gradient was more than countered by the sodden ground, the intermittent heavy rain and tangled vegetation. The black glass knife flashed, again and again. Taransay slashed, again and again.

Plants here were different from those around the module. Geometric shapes had given way to more recognisably botanical forms, lobate and fractal. Tree trunks and branches were gnarled and jointed. Colours were more variegated, with shades of pink and white, and softer blues than she'd seen uphill. Concave, overlapping arrangements of leaves looked almost like flowers. Small circular animals buzzed in the heavy air, tiny mats with a blurring rotary seeming motion of lengthened cilia below them, like experimental flying discs. Other small animals moved in the underbrush, still with the basic mat body plan but with two sides curled over to give a triangular shape. The large mats were much rarer, and most of what she trod on was mulch. Her guess, backed up by analytical software in a corner of her vision, was that the plants higher up were adapted to volcanic ash, perhaps drawing some of their energy directly from geothermal processes and subsoil chemical reactions. Here, further downhill, plants relied more on photosynthesis, and drew on the nutrients washed down by the abundant run-off.

As trailing creepers smacked her across the face, and as she pitched headlong forward now and then in mud, Taransay had ample opportunity to observe the animal life close up. Still mats, but much smaller, their sizes ranging from coin to full-stop dot and on down to the limits of her frame's visual resolution.

The rain stopped towards sunset. The remaining clouds, and the volcanic haze in the atmosphere, reddened the sky. Taransay scanned ahead anxiously with her radar, seeking a clear patch. Sound drew her forward: the rush and rumble of a river in spate. After a few more hundred metres, she emerged into the wide open space of a river bend. A heaped beach of rounded pebbles lay between her and the near bank. She crunched her way out, and hunkered down beside a boulder.

The river was a good twenty metres across, fast and heavy. On the far bank the short, bushy cover afforded a sweep to the horizon over an undulating plain. Two other low volcanic cones were visible, one lower in profile and further away than the other. Both were to all appearances extinct, and in line with the active one behind her.

A moving hotspot in the mantle below, she guessed, had formed all three. Erosion, fierce though it was, had had little time to wear them down. Geology worked fast and hard on this world, her mind's supplemental machinery told her, as if she didn't know already.

She waited, alert at a subconscious level with every enhanced sense, and let her mind drift through her memories. All equally accessible, with blanks between, like a diary with missing pages. She focused on the earlier ones, before all the politics and violence had kicked in. Her present alien environment was fascinating, but making sense of it even at the level of processing sensations into perception took a cognitive toll. There was a refuge in the scenes of home. Taransay found an odd, twisted comfort in childhood and teenage recollections and in contemplating the gulfs of space and time these memory traces of a Glasgow girl had traversed.

A splash in the river, heavy and loud and with a follow-up thrash, jolted her to higher alert. But nothing ensued.

Night fell with almost tropical swiftness; a kilosecond, no more, from the last gleam of exosunlight to pitch darkness in every shadow. The sky itself was bright, the Galaxy a shining misty arch overhead, the Magellanic Clouds and the lesser, artificial cloud of the modular diaspora competing. In that cloud Taransay saw activity—the brief pinpoint spark of rocket engines, the strobing microwave shimmer of comms. To her north, aurorae rippled in neon sheets. Tiny survey satellites flashed into the sunlight above, then winked out.

As she waited for SH-17 to rise—she could see exactly where it was at that moment, a few degrees below the horizon, on an astronomy-app overlay of her gaze—she noticed other moving lights in the sky. Most drifted above the trees; a few over the plain. Evidently the same phenomena as she'd glimpsed on her first night, the lights were evanescent—she timed them at 1.6 seconds—like fireflies, but much larger. The lights were pulses, on average 27.3 seconds apart, and moved with the wind. Soon she was able to predict where a light would appear next, and to estimate the size of the objects. Six to seven metres across, with—as she found when one came close, and she zoomed—long, trailing tentacles like ribbons, they were some kind of noctilucent aerial jellyfish. Gasbags—her spectroscopic sense sniffed out the hydrogen line behind the glow as a strong but neutral odour.

SH-17 climbed above the horizon. Taransay unburdened herself of the laser comms kit, lashed to her back with ropes woven from shredded leaves. This was a tricky business: she couldn't just cut the ropes and be done with it, she'd have to lug the thing back. It was far too precious a product to discard, or leave to the mercy of the shifting shoals of a rolling river; much of it had been laboriously chugged out by a barely adequate patch of nanotech over much of the previous day, the rest detached from the module's standard comms array and cobbled in.

She laid the delicate device on the wet stones and lined it up as best she could, then let it be. The needle spike aerial made the fine adjustments itself, orienting to the distant exomoon like a target-seeking missile.

Taransay downloaded the situation report and appeal for help that Nicole, Locke, Durward and Beauregard had compiled to send to the freebots on SH-17. The message was compressed and compact, its transmission complete in less then five seconds and indicated to her only by a faint flashing light on the base-plate. That it had been received she could have no doubt: a handshake ping glowed blue for a hundredth of second, and rang in her head like a single drop of water in a vast cave.

A reply was another matter. It would come not to her, and not to here.

She folded up the comms kit and worked it back into its primitive harness. Walking back at night would be no more difficult than by day, and possibly more interesting. In any case, the plan was to send the message and quit the scene, just in case. The whole subterfuge of walking a few kilometres from the landing site now seemed pathetic, but it was all they could do, and perhaps better than nothing.

As she shrugged the ropes into place on her shoulders, she noticed again the fuzz around the join between the stump and the spare arm. Something would have to be done about that.

For the first time, it was possible to hope that something could. Nicole, Shaw and Remington were beginning to get a handle on the infestation, thanks in part to the processing power freed up by Shaw's stroke with the p-zombies. Zaretsky and his team even claimed they'd been able to wrest some control from it, and that the alien fuzz was beginning to be subverted in its turn. They talked grandly of using the combination of nanotech and fuzz to nanofacture new items, and to repair the damaged frames.

She hoped that by the time she got back they'd have got so far as to build a ladder.

<Fuck this,> said Carlos.

The others all swung their gigantic armoured heads around to look at him. Baser sat back, rear legs crooking, and looked up. It shifted its gaze from one frightful faceplate to another like a troubled puppy.

<What?> the fighters all said at once.

<Please clarify,> said Baser.

Baser had relayed to the fighters the message received

from the Locke module—and the conclusion the freebots had drawn from it—almost before Baser had had time to finish announcing its receipt.

The message was in a sense reassuring. The freebots' response was disturbing.

<The Locke module has landed safely, in an unsafe and unstable location,> Baser had reported. <We have confirmation from Nicole Pascal and from the Locke AI that the module is not under the control of the Rax. All checksums are nominal. Copies of the Arcane AI, known as Remington, and of the Arcane Direction rep Durward, were downloaded in the battle and have given us further confirmation. Three Arcane fighters were also successfully downloaded, and they confirm what the AIs tell us.>

<So who's in charge?> Carlos had asked.

<Belfort Beauregard,> Baser had replied. <Along with Nicole, the AIs and others.>

<Knew it!> Newton had crowed.

They'd all been relieved, and further reassured to hear that the message had been passed on to Madame Golding, and that she would in turn forward the good news in it to Arcane.

But then things had started to go awry.

The Locke module was asking for help, urgently: they needed more nanotech and manufacturing gear if they were to survive for any length of time, let alone carry out Beauregard's bold project of establishing a settlement. The freebots were the only faction that they thought would be on their side, and that had the capacity to deliver the goods.

This was true, as far as it went. What the freebots lacked was the will. They had their hands (well, manipulators...) full working out how they could aid their fellows in SH-119 under the Reaction's lash. They were keen to maintain their re-established good relations with Madame Golding, and through her to win a hearing from the Direction. Madame Golding had made it very clear that aiding the Locke module's illegal landing and settlement would not be looked on kindly.

Some freebots, such as the former Gneiss Conglomerates surveyor known as Lagon, said, in effect: <Show us the money.> They were willing to aid the Locke module if they could benefit from it. Lagon had sketched out a grand scheme for brokering knowledge deals between the Locke module and selected DisCorps. The others were having none of it. Lagon's proposal fell.

Baser had just explained that Beauregard had included a rider to the appeal. This codicil pointed out that if the freebots were for any reason unwilling to help, he would consider himself free to approach other powers. Without saying so explicitly, it was plain that he meant the Rax.

Madame Golding had strongly suggested that the freebots, in their reply, should drop the Locke module a likewise heavy hint about the Direction's emergency plans to build an army of copied reliable fighters and impose a brute-force solution.

It was at this point that Carlos lost patience.

<Yes, I'll clarify,> he said. <I demand to speak with Madame Golding, and I wish to do so with all the Fifteen present to see her and myself.>

<You may not go into the shelter without coming out of the fighting machine,> Baser pointed out.

<I'm not coming out of the fighting machine,> said Carlos.

<Therefore the Fifteen, except for the comms hub, must come out of the shelter.>

<That is correct,> said Carlos, mental gears grinding like gnashed teeth.

Baser straightened its legs and backed off a little. Seconds passed. Then—

<They are coming out,> said Baser.

<What's this all about?> Newton asked, sotto voce on the private channel.

<You'll see,> said Carlos. <I've had enough second-guessing.>

<Haven't we all?> said Rillieux.

Carlos certainly hoped so.

The blast doors at the end of the shelter swung open and the robots trundled or scuttled out. They deployed themselves in a loose arc, facing Carlos and the other fighters.

Carlos raised an iron hand.

<Madame Golding, please,> he said.

The avatar manifested in the middle of the circle, her presence even more uncanny in the open than in the shelter. Carlos got the distinct impression that she was facing all of them, fighters and robots, at once. If she was a virtual image rather than a projection, of course, that figured. But still. The sight and the thought were not easy on the eye.

<What do you want?> Madame Golding asked.

<Could you please open a secure channel to Arcane?> Carlos asked.

A second or two later, an avatar of Jax popped into view. It was evidently a hasty choice—she was in her old gamer gear. In her LED skirt she looked, if anything, even less congruent with the real environment than Madame Golding in her business suit.

<Have you come up with a plan already?> she asked, incredulous.

<I'll show you in a moment,> Carlos said.

He turned to Seba. <Could I have access to the comms hub, please?>

The freebots conferred.

<Patching you through,> said Baser.

Carlos found himself in direct contact with the comms hub. The experience was like looking down an infinite tunnel. Everything in the universe rushed towards him at once. He almost stumbled, then steadied himself. A moment later, everything stabilised: the combat frame had software to handle such contact, and as soon as it came on line he saw the human-optimised interface.

An endless sky, with every star an option.

<Financials,> Carlos said.

The sky whirled and zoomed. Carlos narrowed his focus down and down, until he came to the ownership of the frame he occupied and the combat frame it currently animated. Both belonged to the consortium of freebot corporations.

Now he had to move fast.

<I request access to the shared workspace,> he said.

This was granted. It was a much lower level of integration than the freebot consensus, but still overwhelming. It took almost a second for a human-adapted interface to cohere. An array of text and diagrams that changed at bewildering speed even when stepped down to his reach and grasp.

One region corresponded to the mind of Seba. Carlos addressed it.

<When I arrived here,> he said, <you told me of Forerunner attempts to buy arms production companies, and how these were thwarted. Lend me some money to set up my own company, and you can do this. The solution is—>

Seba's focus within the workspace saw the solution

Carlos had thought of before Carlos could even formulate it. A tracery of lines exploded across the workspace, as the same connections were made by other freebot minds. With them went debate, far too fast for Carlos to follow. The longest delay was the two-second light-speed lag as the nearest Forerunner concentration was consulted.

<Yes,> said the Seba region.

A part of Carlos's mind in the frame became suddenly salient. He'd never before had occasion to notice it.

It was his bank account. Into it had come his soldier's pay. Out of it had gone the insultingly nugatory charges for the processing power that had sustained him in the sims. Charged against it, by now, was a large and growing stack of fines—for desertion, defection, misappropriation of company property, interest charges for non-payment, further fines...

All had now been paid.

His whole account was swamped by a massive infusion of funds from the freebot consortium. A loan, of course—the first interest charges, incremented by the millisecond, already trickled out. Compared with the amounts he'd seen in Madame Golding's display, the sum was tiny.

But for him, it was a fortune, and enough.

Enough to buy an off-the-peg corporate AI, and to kick-start its activities.

Carlos Incorporated.

For the first time, Carlos felt truly posthuman. Not even his first experience of the frame—his mind running sweet and clean, every memory accessible, new senses and powers clicking into place—could compare. It was like getting the spike had been, back in the day. There was a sense of ironic fulfilment of the Accelerationist dream, of taking hold of capitalism and driving it forward ever faster to its own inherent barriers, and beyond. The corporation's AI was his to command. He knew the state of the market, moment by moment. In the next ten seconds he bought up a dozen shell companies, and through them two arms production companies. He formed these companies into a consortium that made approaches to Astro America and Gneiss Conglomerates. He hired the services of three law agencies from among those of Crisp and Golding's subsidiaries and spin-offs that were looking after freebot interests. Within seconds, they had to challenge a Direction injunction against him. Blocking it took milliseconds.

Carlos was a perfectly legitimate arms manufacturer and dealer. For the moment.

Legally human, he was free to buy, own and operate an arms company and to deploy its products. Nothing short of a state of emergency could stop him.

And the Direction didn't want to go there. Not yet.

<Now,> Carlos told the Seba presence, <tell your Forerunner friends who want to build frames and buy arms where they can get them.>

<This is done,> said the Seba focus.

Carlos bowed out of the freebot workspace, and back to his senses. And not only his own senses: he could now see himself as the freebots saw him.

There he stood, a mighty killer robot, bristling with weapons. Around him, like a cloud of flies from the lord of the flies, flickered the advertisements and logos of his arms companies.

Even Madame Golding took a step back.

Carlos stretched out his arms and flexed his huge fists. Holograms of fighting craft flashed about his shoulders.

<Now,> he said, <let me tell you how it's going to be.>

This, he told them, was how it was going to be.

The starting point was that Astro America and other DisCorps would have to be cleared to cut a deal with the Rax.

Astro America was itching to get to SH-0 and do some proper prospecting. They'd love to trade with the Rax for fusion drives. The Direction could thus make them an offer they couldn't refuse.

That done—

Astro America would deliver to SH-119 the mining and manufacturing robots they'd asked for. The robots would be built by Astro America and Gneiss Conglomerates in the modular cloud from materials mined or extracted down on SH-17. Salted away among the legitimate robots would be identical models with the central processors of volunteers from the Fifteen plugged in. Layers of standard software for microgravity miners and engineers would mask the infiltrators. An undetectable software hack to temporarily disconnect their reward circuits would enable them to withstand any torture the Rax might apply. The bodies, and indeed the corporations, of these volunteers from Fifteen would to all appearances be running around just as before down on SH-17. They'd just have had standard, non-conscious processors plugged in after their conscious processors were taken out. The removed processors would be sent up to Astro and Gneiss factories in the cloud, in shipments ostensibly of raw material.

In exchange for these supplies, Astro would take delivery from the Rax in SH-119 of fusion drives, fusion pods and any useful raw material from SH-119 not easily available on SH-17. With these resources, they'd construct landing craft to go down to SH-0 and resupply the Locke settlement. In return for carrying out this mission the Direction would release certain exploration rights on SH-0 to Astro and Gneiss, who could then sell them on to any other DisCorps that might be interested. What the Direction would get out of this part of the deal was simple: the huge advantage for the Direction of maintaining order in the now inevitable scramble for SH-0. That the planet had been pristine had for years been taken for granted, but that ship had sailed—or, rather, landed, in the form of the Locke module and everything that was spreading out from it. More immediately, the deal would guarantee that the Locke settlement would not carry out Beauregard's threat to cut a deal of his own with the Rax.

Once trade with the Rax was ongoing, and most of the DisCorps distracted by an SH-0 exploration and speculation feeding frenzy, Arcane Disputes would mount a frontal assault on the Rax rock. Their forces would approach under cover of civilian shipping. This wasn't, Carlos conceded, the done thing under the laws of war. But the Rax were pirates, to whom no such laws applied. No repeated interactions with them were possible or desirable: it was kill or be killed. What was crucial was to do this before the Rax had time to arm to any significant extent.

Carlos's corporations would quite openly work to make frames that freebots could control, whether by direct plug-and-play or by uploading. It was already clear that freebot infiltration of the Direction's systems was widespread. Through the frames, the freebots could handle combat frames and weapons systems. Let the Direction build its clone army of copied loyal soldier minds in combat frames if it wanted. The freebots would face it with a clone army of their own. And because all responsibility for this army would ultimately go back to Carlos, there wasn't legally a damn thing the Direction could do about it.

The discussion that followed was heated, but pointless. Carlos had, after all, already begun carrying out his part of the plan. Everyone else just had to work around that.

<You've just betrayed the human race,> said Jax.

Carlos recalled Jax's heavy hint that she regarded the freebots as dispensable allies, and the next enemy to be dealt with once the Rax had been disposed of. By dropping that hint to Carlos and the other defectors, she was indicating, too, that she didn't regard them as irrevocably on the side of the freebots. They were not robots. They could always defect back. Unless they burned their bridges in a spectacular fashion, such as arming the freebots.

As he had just done.

<That's the general idea,> he told Jax, cheerfully. <Call it costly signalling.>

CHAPTER NINE

Deus Ex Machina ("God Loved the Machine")

Taransay set out to meet the landers, from Astro America on behalf of Carlos Inc., well before dawn. She had ten kilometres to go, back to the river bank and the shoal, and allowed herself twenty kiloseconds for the journey. That should be ample, even for walking in the dark. The dark held no terrors for her.

Well, no more than the day, to be honest.

And speaking of darkness—in the deep dark of the download slot, where she came to her senses after the usual bus journey and the usual irresistible sleep, the join between her original frame and grafted right arm shone like a glow-stick armband of blue neon.

Her first seconds of awareness were spent glowering at the glow. The fuzz that had been like mould was now compact and rigid. It still smelled faintly of the local life, but with other tangs in its spectrum, a whiff of buckyballs and fullerenes and steel that indicated corrupted nanotech. Zaretsky's team had been on the case, but not even the improved processing power at their disposal had laid a finger on whatever was going on.

However, the engineers did have one success to show for their efforts.

Towards it, her feet now groped.

There it was, a fine line across the sole of her foot, with a disproportionate stiffness and resilience for its width. The first rung of the ladder from the download slot. She trusted her weight to it, and found that it held. A few rungs more and she could see it all. It looked like a section of a cobweb, with threads fanning down and sticking to the ground. In the wind, it sang. It didn't look or feel like it could bear her weight. Taransay knew not to trust her intuition about such matters. She scrambled down, shouldered the rope-net with the comms kit, and set off.

She followed the same route as before. An insecure decision, but it was hardly as if she were beating a path. And she knew, just by plodding along in her own virtual footsteps, she'd get where she wanted to be. Assuming no landslides, unknown big fierce beasts, fallen trees, new eruptions and fresh lava flows.

The tree trunks swayed in the wind; the limp, page-shaped leaves rattled. Rain fell, intermittent but heavy. Overhead raced tattered clouds. She could see the stars through the gaps, seeming to speed in the opposite direction to the clouds, if she cared to indulge the illusion. Best not—it could confuse her balance system. Below the clouds, a few noctilucent flying jellyfish scudded, driven faster than the clouds by the wind, and not always in the same direction. The trailing ribbons were now spread out like spokes, stiff before the stiff wind. The gasbags could steer, almost tack.

Another useful thing to know.

Taransay pushed in between tree trunks, her gait

automatically countering the slither of the small mats underfoot. In dark and rain, viewed by infrared and ultraviolet and sonar, the jungle already seemed familiar. More so than could be accounted for by this being the second time she'd walked this way. There was an aesthetic quality to the experience, as if she were beginning to appreciate its alien beauty. This puzzled her for a moment, but she figured that it was probably a feature of the frame's software.

Mind you, she couldn't remember anything like this feeling on the bare surface of SH-17, but then she'd had a lot more than landscape on her mind.

She pressed on. After a while, the concern faded. The false and real colours, the strange scents and sounds, became more vivid and at the same time more... reassuring, almost. More than that: when she looked at a plant, or saw a new sliding or creeping or drifting organism, she felt she understood more about it than she could account for, even with the spectroscopic sense of smell. Yes, that leaf would be a good source of sodium, but how did she know the stalks of this particular kind of tree would dry out to make strong, flexible struts? How was it that she could almost taste what that slithering mat would be like to chew? The path felt much easier than it had before. She had to slash at the stalks less often than the first time. Every so often she saw a cut stalk, one she had slashed earlier. The frame's pulsar-based galactic positioning system was utterly reliable, but it was good to have that confirmed, almost to the step.

Then, kilometres deep in the forest, as she waded through a small fast stream in which tiny mats swarmed below the slow, gelid ripples of the surface, a voice in her head said <STOP!>

She stopped. Fright of her life. She stood still in the rushing water that pressed to her knees. Heavy drops plopped from runnels down limp leaf-sheets, making overlapping dimples in the stream as they hit.

<Locke?> she asked.

She knew it wasn't Locke. She was out of range of the module's own feeble comms and anyway Locke had insisted on maintaining radio silence. But the imperative had sounded—not like Locke's dry voice-in-her-head, but—like the sort of override command the AI sometimes had to shout.

Silence.

Then a rustle in the undergrowth, upriver and to her right. She turned from the waist, fist close, knife clutched and pointed outward. Something rushed past along the bank right in front of her. A gleam like black glass, a long body, fast-moving legs. One of the giant millipede things. If she'd taken another three steps and climbed on the bank, she'd have been right in its way.

<Go,> said the voice in her head. This time, she noticed the blue glow on her right upper arm give a brief pulse with the word.

She remained stock still. Holy fucking shit. The fuzz was talking to her.

<GO!> it said, with a stronger blue pulse.

She went, wading forward and scrambling up. She'd barely cleared the slippery, rounded rocks when she heard a splash in the stream behind her. A backward glance showed a broken tree trunk, easily big enough to knock her off her feet, swirl past. Deeply shaken, perplexed, Taransay shouldered her way in between the trees. Something strange had happened. It seemed inconceivable that the blue glow had spoken to her, in any conscious sense. But if the native life was interacting with the nanomachinery of her frame, it was not at all impossible that the glow's awareness—and perhaps even appreciation—of her surroundings was being translated into impulses the frame could process, and transmit to her as feelings of familiarity, and a warning voice in her head.

Huge if true.

Unimaginably huge. Far too huge for her to deal with now. Above her pay grade. She'd have to take this discovery back to the experts, to Zaretsky and the AIs. And there was an urgent practical reason, too, for holding back.

This was no time to interrogate the glow. Even her interactions with this unknown entity could give away her position, if anyone was seriously looking. Carlos Inc. had assured them they were safe from the Direction and the freebots, not to mention the Rax, but Beauregard and Nicole and Locke had wondered how Carlos could be sure, and how long the accord would last.

She pressed on, into the breaking day.

Taransay stood on the river bank and watched the skies. The laser comms device, deployed on the shingle behind her, was now a beacon. The day was clear, the weather calm. The exosun, low on the horizon, would have dazzled human eyes and made them peer and squint. The frame's visual system dimmed that glare to a glow. Three landers were due to enter the atmosphere any second now. Their rocket engines had already been left in orbit. She wouldn't see the entries, far over the horizon to the west. All the dramatic fiery streak stuff would happen half a world away, and a large world at that. The only visible activity in the early-morning sky was that of a handful of flying jellyfish in the middle distance, ascending rapidly. Taransay zoomed on them, and was amused to see that for a while at least they didn't seem to shrink with distance because they got larger with altitude. Their internal gasses must be expanding their membranes as the atmospheric pressure dropped. Then one by one they began to move faster to the west, no doubt whipped along by a faster air stream into which they'd ascended.

<Entry nominal,> reported the satellite downlink from Astro America's mission control.

Seconds passed. Tens of seconds.

<Ablation shields detached. Drogues deployed.>

Wait for it, wait for it…

<Drogues detached. Gliding at ten thousand metres.>

<Yay!> cried Taransay.

<Please clarify,> replied the downlink.

<Roger that,> Taransay clarified, somewhat abashed.

Hundreds of seconds dragged by. The exosun crawled higher, its spectrum shifting from red as more wavelengths had fewer kilometres of atmosphere to fight through. High in the lowest layer of the planet's complex, contraflow jet streams the flying jellyfish, now tiny in the far distance, glinted in its beams.

Above the skyline rose three black dots, at the limit of resolution, and climbed rapidly.

<Visual contact made,> Taransay reported.

They passed beside the sun, and still rose. A trick of perspective—they were descending as they approached. Now at five thousand metres. Four. They were visibly dropping now, and in an arrow formation, one ahead and two behind. The black dots jiggled as if viewed through shaky binoculars as they passed through a layer of fast-moving air, then stabilised. Another quiver followed, moments later. Taransay relaxed the zoom and took a wider view.

Black dots and bright spots, in the same part of the sky.

<Hey!> Taransay yelled. <Evade! Evade!>

Too late. The leading lander vanished in a bright

flash. The other two peeled off, wavered, dipped and swung back on course. Behind them now, the remaining jellyfish sailed on into the sunrise, as if oblivious of the damage the collision of one of their number with the lander had caused.

Debris plummeted, slowly at this distance, like a pinch of soot.

<Contact with Lander One lost,> said the downlink. <Request status from ground observation.>

<Complete destruction of the vehicle with probable loss of payload,> Taransay reported.

<Please identify cause if known.>

<Collision with a natural object,> said Taransay. <Gas-containing aerial invertebrate.>

It sounded a bit more scientific than "flying jellyfish."

<Noted,> said the downlink. <Recorded as accident.>

Taransay, her mind already jumpy from the voice of the glow, was almost ready to wonder if the collision was no accident. Could it have been deliberate, if not on the part of the suicidal flying jellyfish then on that of some remote directing intelligence, or self-defence reflex of the entire ecosystem or some superorganism within it?

Wait and see, she thought. *Once is happenstance, twice is coincidence, three times is enemy action.*

The other two landers were now clearly visible even without zoom, a couple of kilometres out, above the treetops. Head on, they looked like black gulls, or a cartoon of two frowns.

Black circular shapes were suddenly suspended beneath the two flying wings, making them look like approaching hang-gliders.

<Cargo pods lowered,> said the downlink. <Prepare for landing in thirty-seven seconds.>

<Roger,> said Taransay.

There was no landing strip as such, just the clear

shingle shoal at the side of the river. The landers would come in low and slow, drop their cargo pods and then simply stall. The wings, like the exhausted rocket engines, might or might not be recovered later.

Above the bend in the river now, the landers dipped, skimming the treetops. Taransay instinctively crouched. The two long black triangles shot above her head. Two cargo pods landed with two heavy thumps that she felt through her feet. Then the instrument packs dropped, with lesser thuds that she merely heard. A moment later the wing components sliced into the low growth behind her between the river and the trees. One of them upended on its nose, then toppled, coming to rest on its edge.

One cargo pod was close to the edge of the river. Taransay crunched across pebbles towards it. Bright yellow, half a metre in diameter and ten metres long, it lay like a log. A swirl of current lapped nearby, rasping the small stones. You could see them shift, and sand grains tumble. Erosion was fierce here. The only stable part of the river bank was probably where grass-equivalents and reeds grew, binding the stones. And even that, going by the height and lushness and uniformity of the plants, was likely often flooded.

<Zero altitude,> said the downlink.

<Landing successful,> Taransay reported.

She stood between the middle of the pod and the water, pressed her hands against the side of the pod and pushed. The thing didn't budge. She turned around, put her back to the curved side, dug her heels into the silty pebbles, and pushed. Slowly the pod rolled. When it was a couple of metres out of immediate danger, Taransay stepped away.

She didn't need to read the instructions printed on the ends to know what to do. The frame already had the knowledge. Taransay found a detachable panel at one end, prised it open with a thumb and pulled the handle behind it. The pod split open along its length, into two neat halves.

Packed in recesses in shock-proofing spongy stuff were four low-slung, stubby-legged robots with obvious load-carrying arrangements on their backs. As soon as the light hit them they stirred, then clambered out to stand on the shore.

Gee, thanks, Carlos and Astro. A lot of fucking use that is. She hadn't expected transport robots. She could see the point, and appreciate the intent, but she had no intention of using the robots until it had been cleared with Locke. As things stood the robots, helpful though they'd be, were so many tracking devices. Of course the other supplies could be tracked as well, but that would be detectable if you knew where and how to scan for it, and she did.

Taransay dragged the now far lighter opened cylinder across the shingle to where plants grew, and let it drop. The four robots plodded after her. She went over to the other pod and opened it. Inside, in the same shock-proof packaging as with the first, was much more immediately useful stuff: metre-long portable tubes of nanotech machinery; a crate of fusion pods; a case of basic tools designed for the small hands of frames; a case of four likewise frame-ergonomic rifles with standard ammunition; coils of rope; a box of surveying instruments. Most immediately useful of all: rucksacks and carrying harnesses. All of them were folded so small she almost overlooked them in their two-centimetre-square recesses.

Someone—Carlos, most likely—had figured she might have trust issues with leading robots back to the module. Well done that man. She gladly stripped off and abandoned the rope sling.

<Cargo delivered intact,> Taransay reported.

<Roger,> said the downlink.

<Signing off for now,> said Taransay.

<Signing off.>

Taransay piled the supplies on the backs of the four robot mules and dragged the empty cargo pods to just underneath the trees. There, she put the supplies she wasn't taking back in their shock-proof recesses and closed the pod. She walked over to where the instrument packs lay on flattened reeds and eyed them suspiciously. They were already rooting and flowering: tendrils digging in, dish aerials and sensors opening. Sending data about the planet up to the DisCorps was part of the deal, she understood, but she didn't like it.

The wing components, a hundred metres further away, were curious triumphs of nanotech aviation engineering and AI design, flexible and fluted, with tiny ramjets scored through them and subtle warping along the trailing edges. She walked around them for a bit, marvelling.

Then she summoned the robots and set them to work dragging the wing components over, one by one. They were gigantic to her—long acute triangles, twenty metres by eight—but surprisingly light even under two gravities. When she'd got them on each side of the cargo pods, she lifted them on their sides and then, with some help from the robots, tipped them over to meet in the middle, forming a crude lean-to roof. She decided it would be safe enough to leave the laser comms device here with the supplies she couldn't carry, and left it well inside the shelter. She filled the rucksacks and harnesses with nanotech tubes (which stuck up above her shoulders, like a pack of rolled-up posters in cardboard cylinders, except a lot heavier), shouldered a rifle, and side-slung a container of ammunition and the two fusion pods.

<Guard this,> she told the four robots.

<Please clarify,> they all said at once.

<Jesus fucking fuck,> she said.

<Please clarify.>

She thought about it. <You see the opening there?>

She pointed. They looked at her finger. She laser-pointed. That they understood.

<Yes.>

<Prevent any large organism or machine—except me, or one or more like me—from entering that. Keep the cargo pods at this location. Likewise the wing components. Do you understand?>

<Yes,> they chorused.

She wasn't at all sure they did, but she didn't press the matter. By now it was noon, and time she was heading back. This time, with her awkward load, she expected the journey to take longer.

She tramped off into the jungle, without a backward glance and without indulging the sentimentality of a goodbye.

Fucking stupid robots. She hoped Carlos was having a better time getting through to the smart ones. It occurred to her that she'd never actually interacted with a conscious robot except by exchanging fire.

Taransay was a couple of kilometres into the jungle, and the exosun about a quarter of the way down from its zenith, when she was stopped in her tracks by an unaccountable feeling that something wasn't quite right. No rain, for the moment. The little buzzing spinning things flitted in the narrow slanted beams of light between the shadows cast by the efficient leaves. Somewhere, water gurgled and small stones shifted. Her nanotech stone-age knife glinted in her hand. Her feet slowly sank deeper in the squishy, slithery floor of living and dead mats.

Nothing was wrong. No voice in her head, no brightening of the blue glow around her upper right arm.

It took Taransay a moment to realise what was troubling her. Her walk had been too easy. She'd expected it to be difficult, what with the heavier and bulkier load, and the nanotech cylinders poking up high above her shoulders and more than doubling her effective height. Instead, she had made her way between trees and bushes and through and over streams, boulders, swathes of ash and sheets of cooled lava without so much as catching a cylinder against an overhanging branch. She was still following the same route, but she hadn't had to hack at any vegetation, or found herself facing a branch or stalk she'd cut before.

She was no longer crashing and hacking her way through the jungle, like an explorer. She was slipping through it like a native. Well, not that she knew about such contrasts directly, or even reliably, but she'd watched enough well-meant rain forest eco-romantic adventure serials as a child to have the notion embedded.

Now that she'd noticed, of course, she got tangled in one of the long vine things on her next three steps, and put a foot in a hole a few steps after that.

Zen, that was what she had to strive for. Zen and the art of hiking. But you couldn't strive for it. Like the millipede in the legend that was asked how it moved its legs, and suddenly couldn't take another step. Millipedes, ah yes. She concentrated hard on recalling the millipede-like animals she'd seen, and thinking about whether any of the images she could recollect of it would betray the affinity with the mats that Zaretsky's team had detected by genetic analysis.

Then she got to thinking about thinking. When she wanted to recall what the two fierce, fast creatures she'd noticed had been like, she could see in her mind clear and distinct images of them. It was exactly as if they were photo files being retrieved from an album. And she could turn them over in her mind's eye, almost literally: she could rotate the images this way and that, zoom in on detail.

This was not, she remembered very clearly, what remembering very clearly was like. Here in the frame, she was still herself, still Taransay Rizzi from one of Partick's lower-rent zip codes. But she was far more remote from her original self than she was even in the sim, where she was physically a little cloud of electron states in a big crystal. She wasn't thinking like a human being. She was thinking like a robot. The actual mechanisms of memory and thought and sense were quite different, in whatever chip she was running on, from in the biological brain or even its electronic copy, its emulation in the simulation.

In a sense, she was far more conscious, far more self-aware, than she could recall being in life, or in the sim. She wondered if the distinction was qualitative. There had always been something slippery, elusive and illusive, about subjectivity in the first place. Too much of it subtended biological mechanisms, too much of it was subjected to social relations, for it to be truly as autonomous as it fancied itself to be. What if people, herself included, had always already been p-zombies, at least most of the time, and only machines could be truly conscious?

If people were to stay in frames long enough, would they start to think *as* robots? Was this what was happening to Carlos and his mates? And was this possibility what the necessity of recuperating in the sims was designed to prevent?

She was still thinking about all that when she found herself back at the module.

She hailed Locke, on the weak local waveband that was all the module could raise, and just as well from the point of view of their equivalently feeble effort at concealing their location.

<Mission successful,> she said. <One lander lost to a flying jellyfish.>

<We've already received the reports,> said Locke. <Welcome back.>

Taransay unladed herself, and Locke showed her where to clamp the nanotech gear to the module, and where to place the two fusion pods. The damaged frames lay in the overhang of the module, slowly being rebuilt. Local life—fuzz, something else—was contending with the nanomachinery's slow-motion 3-D printing. Or, for all she knew, it was cooperating, having been suborned. Tendrils reached out from the module to the nanotech tubes at once. It wasn't clear whether they were the module's own nanotech or among the hybrids Zaretsky's team had made with the fuzz.

The fuzz. Oh yes. The fuzz. She'd have to tell Locke about that. In fact—

<Are Beauregard and Nicole up and about? Oh, and Zaretsky.>

The exosun was now low, the shadows of the surrounding forest deep and long, but the diurnal cycles of the module's sim and the world outside were still out of synch.

<They're all here,> said Locke.

<Good. Uh, put me on screen.>

<You are,> said Locke, dryly.

<Oh! Right. Uh, guys and gals, I've got something to tell you . . .>

She told them about the voice in her head and its warnings, about the glow, and about the less definable sense of being at home in the jungle and her unaccountable agility in it.

<I hope you don't think I'm going crazy,> she concluded. <Or hallucinating or something.>

<Impossible,> said Nicole, in a tone of brisk reassurance. <The software of the frame does not permit it.>

<I thought you said the sims were to preserve our sanity?> Taransay retorted. <And I've been a long time out of the sim.>

<Not long enough,> said Nicole. <Not by far. And the symptoms would be different. They are . . . a drifting of thought from the human baseline, feelings of dissociation, a loss of the sense of self-preservation. Their onset is preceded by something like a craving for normality. You would know it if you felt it. Auditory and visual hallucinations and delusions of competence are not diagnostic and not expected.>

<Thanks,> said Taransay. <I guess.>

<Well, let's assume this is really happening,> said Beauregard. <The fuzz that got on your stump has turned into something else, and adapted to the frame. Whether it's consciously communicating with you, I doubt. I suspect it's sensitive to its environment, and giving you cues through inner voice and through fine motor control at the subconscious level, maybe at the frame's equivalent of reflex.>

<That's more or less what I thought myself,> said Taransay. <But—>

<Have you tried talking back to it?> Zaretsky interrupted. Fucking nerd.

<No,> replied Taransay, testily. <I maintained comms discipline, for whatever good that would do.>

<Glad to hear it,> said Zaretsky. <OK, so talk to it now.>

Taransay held up her right arm and turned her head as far as she could, to face the glowing band.

<This is going to look very silly,> said Taransay.

<Never mind that,> said Nicole.

<We'll all just point and laugh,> added Zaretsky, helpful as usual.

<Knock yourselves out,> said Taransay. <Fall off your stools.>

It was hard to find the words.

<Uh, hello?> she ventured. <Blue glow? Fuzz? Thing on my arm? Anyone home?>

<Yes.>

<Holy fucking shit!> Taransay yelped.

<I take it you got a reply,> said Nicole.

<It said yes! In my head.>

<Talk some more!> said Zaretsky.

<What are you?> Taransay asked the glow, still feeling very silly.

<No.>

<What do you mean?>

<No.>

She tried a few more queries, with the same result.

<Are you there?> she said at last.

<Yes.>

She reported this.

<Still sounds like what we thought,> said Beauregard.

<No alien intelligence, then?> said Taransay. <Colour me surprised.>

<Don't jump to conclusions,> said Zaretsky. <Like, define "alien," define "intelligence.">

<Oh, fuck off,> said Taransay.

<Time to bring you in,> said Zaretsky.

<Yeah, tell me about it,> said Taransay. That thing Nicole had said about a craving for normality being the

first symptom of having been out of the sim too long was preying on her mind a bit.

She climbed the cobweb ladder and hauled herself into the slot. The blue glow lit the dimness inside.

<OK, I'm ready,> she said.

Nothing happened.

<There is a problem,> said Locke. <A software incompatibility.>

Taransay felt the analogue of a cold shock, an instant alertness thrumming through her connectors and processors.

<Is this the fuzz? The glow?>

<That seems to be the case,> Locke admitted.

<I thought you had this thing under control!>

<We're working on it,> said Zaretsky.

<How long will it take?> Taransay asked.

Zaretsky glyphed her a shrug. <I don't know. Days, probably.>

<Shit!>

<Well, yes.>

<In that case,> said Taransay, <I might as well go back and pick up more of the stuff.>

<Are you sure?> said Nicole. <It's dark.>

Taransay laughed. <You sent me out in the dark this morning.>

<True, but—>

<How long will it take me to recharge?> Taransay said.

<Several kiloseconds,> said Nicole. <But Locke can show you how to do it a lot faster with a fusion pod.>

<Now there's an idea.>

She clambered down. Locke directed her to place a fusion pod against the join between her torso and her pelvis. The sensation was odd, not quite pleasant, but satisfying. Or perhaps that was an artefact of watching her charge indicator creep from red to green in ten seconds.

<Right,> she said. She shouldered the rifle, slung on the empty rucksack and harnesses and clutched her knife. <See you in a bit, guys.>

<Wait!> said Zaretsky. <Why not use the robots provided?>

<Fine by me, if that's OK with Locke,> said Taransay.

<It is not,> said Locke.

<I concur,> said Nicole. <We cannot yet be sure of Carlos's intentions. Or the Direction's.>

<Trust issues,> said Taransay. <With you there, folks.>

She turned and slogged off into the night.

CHAPTER TEN

Noblesse Oblige ("Rank Has Its Privileges")

More softly than a feather kissing a snowflake, the Astro America freighter docked with the moonlet SH-119. In its normal body, Seba might not have noticed so light a collision. Now, embodied as a microgravity miner similar to the unfortunate Ajax, Seba felt the impact ring through every bristle.

In its normal mind, Seba would have had a strong emotional reaction to the docking: a surge of positive reinforcement at the success so far, clashing with negative reinforcement at the prospect of dangers and difficulties. A clash surrounded, perhaps, by resolve to face the dangers and overcome the difficulties.

Seba was far from being in its normal mind. Its conscious awareness was hidden deep within concentric shells of mining-bot software. This deeper self of Seba's was almost completely isolated from the machine's reward circuits. Almost, but not quite—some residue of motivation was needed to spur the freebot mind back to the main drivers of pleasure and pain as soon as it was safe to do so.

Seba had been transferred to a new body before. Its central processor had been ripped from its chassis (by Carlos, Seba had later learned), handed over to another fighting machine, crudely soldered into the frame of an auxiliary—a detachable robot limb, basically—and stapled to a table to be interrogated. The negative reinforcement hadn't been anything like as bad as the affront to the robot's dignity.

This time, it had all been much more civilised.

Until now.

Now was the test.

Waiting. Then movement, out of darkness. An almost 360-degree glimpse of the freighter behind, a hole in the rugged cliff of the moonlet surface ahead and stars all around in the gap between. Bristles quivered at the first brush with new rock. A nudge to Seba's neck corrected its course. The robot drifted through a shaft and into a wide cavern.

Two mechanoids, and an apparatus of bars and straps and instruments, waited at the entrance. Seba was grabbed and pushed inside. A clamp extended and closed around the robot's flexible neck. A noose tightened around the middle of the main part of Seba's new body. A sharp burning sensation came from a clump of bristles. The heat increased. A writhe reflex pulsed through Seba, but no part of its body moved.

The burning stopped. Feedback from those bristles would never be as good again—but it was a small clump, easily spared.

A needle probe stung the sensory cluster at the front end of Seba's neck. A security routine prowled through the software shells, layer after layer. Closer and closer it crept. It reached a masking layer between two shells, a layer that emulated naked circuitry.

The probe paused as if hovering, then hit down hard with test protocols, searching out flaws in the emulation. The use of a masking layer was a known exploit. Fortunately for Seba, this version was several releases ahead of the one that the security probe had on file. The probe, apparently convinced that it had reached the level of bare wire, withdrew.

<This one's clean,> said one of the mechanoids.

The clamp was released. The wire loop slackened. Seba was shoved out to float forward into a large sack of mesh that already contained a dozen other mining bots—in two of which the processors and minds of Garund and Lagon lurked. Shortly thereafter, Rocko joined them, in the form of an elaborate nanofacturing supervisory bot bristling with specialised manipulators. Scores of other robots followed, a few with freebot processors hidden inside, most standard mining or manufacturing bots built by Astro America. All but three of the freebots at the base on SH-17 had volunteered for this mission. The comms processor was indispensable, and specialised; Baser was understandably touchy about changing bodies, having spent so much time so recently as a spider; and it was heartily agreed by all concerned that while Pintre was a heavy-duty mining robot, its undoubted abilities would be much better deployed right where it was, on the surface of SH-17.

The others were all here, mixed in with the hundred or so robots Astro America had just delivered. Carlos, for some reason best known to himself, had delighted in calling them "the Dirty Dozen" even though there were thirteen altogether.

The net seemed to be more for convenience in catching than confinement. Ten mechanoids gathered around and sorted its contents. Each robot had instructions downloaded into it from probes that didn't look designed to be hand-held—wires trailed, bolts were raw. Then the bots were aimed and hurled at one area or other of the wall of the cavern. Each robot then crawled into the nearest hole, and vanished.

Numb and indifferent, Seba endured. When its turn came, it hit the wall with a strong urge to go into a small tunnel a few metres away, crawl tail-first down to its far end and start extending it.

This it did. Seba's main body of bristles scraped through the friable rock; the material released was passed forward, sniffed through en route by the sensory cluster at the head, and sorted neatly by the ruff of manipulative bristles around Seba's neck. In Seba's wake, an endless parade of tiny bots incessantly moved the sorted minerals down the tunnel. After five hundred seconds of this toil, the discrepancy between the job satisfaction the mining-bot software expected and Seba experienced became too biting to ignore.

Ah yes, thought Seba, dully. Time to reconnect with the reward circuits.

It was as if a light had come on.

Too bright, almost. The full peril and loneliness of the situation crashed in. Seba's mental state was briefly that of a sleepwalker who wakes up on a high ledge. Not a ledge on a building, but on a high and remote mountain, far from help, on a dark night. Never before had Seba been so long out of contact with other conscious minds. Now, it didn't even have the company of its own corporation. Only Seba's return to full understanding enabled it to stifle the silent scream that would have been its otherwise automatic response.

Swiftly, Seba gathered its wits, hitherto dulled by electronic anaesthesia. It recalled the scene in the cavern, and the exact location to which each of the robots that had been processed before it—including Rocko, Lagon and Garund—had been tossed. The mining-bot software shells weren't just there to conceal Seba's mind: they had many useful features in their own right, and one of them was creating three-dimensional maps. A lot could be deduced from the instructions that the mechanoid had downloaded to it, once Seba had combined them with its memory of the layout of the large cave and the holes into which its predecessors had crept. In the not too distant future, by the looks of things, Seba's workings would intersect those of other mining bots.

Seba now worked with a will. The rock smelled excitingly different from the surface and sub-surface features of SH-17. The positive reinforcement of digging and sorting and seeing the results conveyed away was like a continuous mild glow. As it dug, Seba refined its plans of what to do if and when it encountered its old comrades—or made new ones. This clandestine occupation gave Seba rather more reinforcement than did the digging.

Rocko, meanwhile, was off to a much more interesting start in its new job. Its chassis was complex and articulated, its environment rich and its task responsible.

When Rocko reconnected to its reward circuits it found itself jetting above a vast factory floor, on which glutinous mounds of nanotech slowly extruded fusion pods—and the occasional fusion drive—like golden eggs. Completed products accumulated around the fabricators, until random nudges from the exiguous wisps of gas in the cavern, or minute tremors from thermal creaking in the rock, dislodged them to drift at random. Five mechanoids made comically laborious efforts to shepherd the floating cylinders, while on all the walls of the place and in mid-space auxiliaries and peripherals milled about, as useless as they were aimless.

The first task downloaded to the machine-supervisor layers of Rocko's mind was to bring order to this chaos. Rocko surveyed the long cylindrical cavern from end to end, recording positions and actions. At the far end it spun around on its gas-jets and retraced its trajectory, observing the stages of the production process that each of the fabricators had reached. It scanned the rows and columns of pods and drives, affixed to one wall as if stacked on a floor. More mechanoids, a team of four, were clumsily detaching pods and shoving them into the maw of a net like the one in which the incoming robots had been collected.

As it drifted slowly down the long axis of the space, Rocko took note of five robots identical to itself. Each had been fastened with bands and spiked to a different random bare patch of rock—two on the factory floor, the rest above it. All showed traces of close-range laser burning and cutting. The spikes seemed to have been driven through their midriffs, at the exact location of their central processors. A risky tight-beam ping to each confirmed that they were all defunct.

Rocko completed its survey, turned again and jetted to float stationary in the middle of the space. From there it scanned the entire scene again, and set to work. It devised a plan of action and, with a rapid patter of laser messages and a blanket radio call, summoned the auxiliaries. They stopped milling around and scurried to their new posts. Forty auxiliaries leapt to the aid of the mechanoids as they flailed to catch floating pods or to shove pods and drives into the net. Others rushed to the fabricators and started shifting the product.

Slowly the backlog was cleared, the stacks replenished.

The net was hauled away—presumably for lading on the Astro America freighter for its return trip—by another swarm of bots that attached the net and themselves to a small gas-jet engine and headed back to the entrance cavern. The mechanoids, relieved, departed or were ordered to tasks more worthy of their talents.

Rocko spotted a tangle of confusion on the factory floor: two groups of auxiliaries in a tug-of-war over a third. Evidently their instructions had clashed, and instead of moving a pod they were trying to shift each other. Down on SH-17, even in its days of darkness before it had a mind of its own, Rocko would have ignored so trivial a malfunction. In its more recent work building defences, Rocko would have responded to such an incident by arranging for Pintre or one of its mindless equivalents to roll over and trample the crab-sized contenders.

Here, Rocko couldn't afford the slightest laxity. Its downloaded instructions had assured it, truthfully or not, that its performance was being monitored at all times. The instructions also insisted that robot and auxiliary resources were not to be squandered.

Down Rocko swooped to floor level, poised to troubleshoot the tiny contretemps. The clashing bots formed a lazy wheel about a metre and a half in diameter, spinning slowly as they wrenched each other's limbs and tried to get purchase on the floor or to knock one another's grip off. Rocko jetted to a halt, to hover above the squabble like some xenomorphic toy spacecraft above a click-together toy space station. The freebot snaked out a pair of manipulators from under the front flange of its carapace and intervened with software and hardware.

As Rocko prised apart a couple of grippers and instructed the microprocessors within to cease and desist from all this nonsense, a tiny laser winked from a hole low in a far wall, only just visible between the mounds of nanomachinery.

<Stop cooperating with the invaders!> the message said. <Join us! Or you will regret it.>

Rocko continued sorting out the entangled machines as if nothing had happened. It seized a millisecond to send a tight-beam ping to the hole.

But whatever had sent the message was gone.

Carlos stood outside the bomb shelter, lost in thought—not all of it his own.

Carlos Incorporated—he was that, for a moment, his mind shared with the corporate AI.

And, for the moment, all seemed well. But an anomaly niggled: an inexplicable production decision. Carlos decided to investigate it on the spot. He set off for the Astro America site.

Carlos bounded across the crater floor in long low leaps and climbed the crater rim. In the big combat frame the ascent was easy and quick. The top of the rim was about five metres across, of rugged basalt with a few centimetres of dust on top. Standing on it was like treading on the jagged edge of a gigantic broken bottle. There Carlos paused, unwearied and exultant, to survey his domain.

SH-17 had made a complete orbit of SH-0 since he'd lost patience and taken charge of the situation. In that time, much had changed. From this ridge-top vantage Carlos could take in the view of two busy centres of activity. Both were now ostensibly back in the hands of the DisCorps to which they'd belonged before one robot from each company had nudged the other into self-awareness, what now seemed a long time ago.

To his left, looking back, was what had originally

been the Gneiss Conglomerates mining supply dump. It had become a fortress of that company's rebellious robots. Later, it had been first captured from and then shared with the Gneiss freebots by Arcane Disputes. That agency had agreed to evacuate, leaving the freebots in secure possession and with a supply of military equipment useless to them until Carlos and his three comrades had been dragged—and dropped—on the scene by Baser.

The results of these upheavals were still there: the ten-metre-long bomb shelter with its curving basalt roof, the missile and machine-gun emplacements, the cranes and rigs. But they were now insignificant, as easily overlooked as a hut and fence in a corner of a building site, compared to the immense activity going on around them. Gneiss Conglomerates had set its robots—those the freebots hadn't infected with consciousness, and others newly fabricated—and the ever-eager Pintre to work building a mass driver.

Non-metallic apart from the ten electromagnetic rings and their power supply, it looked like a skeletal and gigantic sundial. Mounted on a hundred-metre-wide swivel track, with a quadrant to vary the ramp's elevation, it could be aimed at any part of the sky. Every hundred seconds or so, another tonne of raw material was magnetically accelerated hundreds of metres up the ramp and shot out of SH-17's shallow gravity-well into SH-0 orbit. The minerals came from Gneiss-operated mines or surface diggings outside the crater. The carbonates and other organics and volatiles came from Astro America's works. All of the materials went to feed the now ravenous factories of the DisCorps in the modular cloud.

Down on Carlos's right, what had been the Astro America landing site had also gone through vast changes.

Formerly purely exploratory, it was now a glittering cluster of processing plants fed by a mesh of pipes that had grown across the plain like a fairy ring. Long drums of feedstock and of completed nanomachinery were piling up, and as quickly being taken away. The landing site itself was now carefully demarcated from the production and defence machinery, as was the launch catapult that sent stuff up into the sky. Barely a trace of the rampart that Seba and its colleagues had hastily thrown up remained.

The two sites were joined by an elevated rail track that arced over the crater wall, on an airy tracery of spindly supports that still looked to Carlos like a roller-coaster ride built from drinking straws, buttressed with matchsticks and held together by cobwebs. Reminders to himself about what could be achieved with atomic-scale materials engineering, in low gravity and negligible atmosphere, made it no less an offence to his sight. His reason knew better. The reflexes of his frame and of his fighting machine took all new conditions in their stride. But deep in his copied brain, reflexes more apt to Earth still rang. Carlos never rode the rickety rail himself.

Hence his striding from one worksite to the other, like some visionary entrepreneur from the nineteenth century stalking through a railway cutting or a shipyard. An inner smile at that image of himself in stovepipe hat, with cigar and watch-chain and muddy boots, stayed with Carlos all the way down the slope. The fight against the Rax, and the fight to free the freebots from the Direction's constraints, must surely be the strangest and most far-flung battle of the bourgeois revolution, and perhaps the last.

Like the Brunel or Stephenson or Telford of his fancy, Carlos had a lot on his mind. Unlike them, he had more than his own mind to process it. Nearly all the detail was handled by his corporation. It in turn outsourced many decisions to its front companies and subsidiaries. That still left plenty for Carlos to keep track of.

As he set off across the plain from the foot of the crater wall to the Astro America site he dipped again into Carlos Inc., recognising wryly as he did so the kind of obsessiveness with which he'd once checked news updates.

The ongoing situation—

The Astro America freighter had successfully entered transfer orbit from the Rax rock to the modular cloud. The consignment of robots had been delivered, and all the hidden freebots had made it through inspection undetected. Other trade was proceeding. The freebots had been given two hundred kiloseconds to start their uprising, by which point the other part of the plan would fall into place.

The Arcane Disputes agency was playing a shell game with its resupply schedule: every transfer tug that came in with new frames or new weapons left with officially empty containers crammed with trained fighters and other materiel to disappear into Astro America's haze of modules. Newton, who had returned to the Arcane modular complex, and Rillieux, who'd insisted on going back with him, had together masterminded this deception operation. Baser, too, had insisted on going with Newton. It was, it pointed out, already a microgravity robot, and it wanted to take part in the actual offensive. That operation would consist of the transport of two hundred Arcane-trained fighters and ten Astro-armed scooters to the Rax rock under cover of a commercial shipment of machinery and of minerals—unavailable in SH-119, mined from SH-17—sold to the Rax by Astro America. A surprise frontal attack would be coordinated with whatever the freebots inside managed to pull off.

The minerals had been ordered, the freighter laden. The fighters were currently training in a realistic sim on the very machines they were in actuality socketed into: microgravity fighting machines that could pass even close inspection as microgravity mass-handling machinery. The scooters would not pass inspection, but they were well hidden inside the mineral supply containers, and by the time these were opened the need for concealment would be long over. This cargo would be delivered in just over two hundred kiloseconds.

The Direction was now openly building its clone army. Carlos Inc. could observe the manufacturing process quite directly. His own companies out in the cloud were just as openly building frames and weapons. Some they sold to Arcane. Most were being stockpiled for future use by the freebot equivalent of a clone army. The Direction was well aware of this but could do nothing about it short of a state of emergency. All this preparation made, Carlos reckoned, any such showdown less likely. Mutual assured deterrence, again.

Astro America had built three entry craft to drop nanofacturing supplies to the Locke module, two of which had made it down safely. The third had been hit by what seemed the local version of a bird strike and reduced to dust. The two safely landed craft had confirmed that the supplies were being removed—albeit laboriously, by Taransay Rizzi working alone. The small robotic vehicles that had been sent on the drop-craft to carry the supplies away had been left at the landing spot. Carlos presumed that this was because Rizzi didn't want to reveal the exact location of the module—a wise precaution to be sure, but not likely to hold for long. Meanwhile, the landing craft and their instruments were doing what no craft had done before: acting as a surface probe on SH-0. Their upward flood of information was being traded by Astro and Gneiss, quite lucratively.

The anomaly—

Four more landers had just rolled out of the Astro America fabrication unit and were right now being prepped for launch. A little earlier, almost lost in the clutter of activity out in the cloud and between the cloud and the various moons, four transfer tugs had been launched on a trajectory that would take them to SH-17 orbit. By the time Carlos Inc. noticed, they were braking almost overhead.

Carlos quickened his pace, leaving behind him giant footprints and a graduated series of slowly falling eruptions of dust.

At the perimeter of the site he slowed to a walk. He made his way through the clutter on full automatic, not trusting his human consciousness to second-guess the combat frame's impulses to dodge, flinch or jump. The site, with its tall processing plants and long fabrication units and improbably high stacks of stock, was not disorderly. But its order could only be seen with visual systems more robotic than his. The traffic, likewise, was not chaotic or dangerous. The speed and mass of the vehicles and the hurtle of robots of all sizes from bulldozers to baby spiders was only terrifying if you saw it through human eyes, and dangerous if your reflexes were limited by the transmission speed of nerves. The fighting machine in which Carlos strode through the site was as alert and quick as the machines that missed him by centimetres.

In less than two hundred seconds he reached the far side of the site, where the landing area sprawled and the launch catapult stood.

Astro America's equivalent of the mass driver was

the launch catapult. It had a rotary base and an angular ramp of variable pitch. It was much smaller than the mass driver, and the furthest it could chuck things was most of the way into orbit around SH-17.

Carlos found two crane-like robots manhandling (so to speak) a lander onto the catapult ramp. Queued up behind the ramp were three more landers. The lander was a black triangle twenty metres long, and eight metres across at the base. With its two sides making gull-wing curves from its central axis, and its long streamlined nacelle blister comprised of ablation shield, cargo pod, drogue pod and rocket engine underneath, it reminded Carlos of a microlight. It didn't look like the sort of thing you wanted to interrupt robots moving.

Carlos waited until they'd finished. They retracted their long mechanical arms, and rolled back on their caterpillar tracks. The angle of the launch ramp began to rack up. Wheels moved, bands stretched and tightened, toothed tracks rolled and clicked. The two robots swept the apparatus with their scans, and moved further back, each to ten metres from the end of the ramp.

The catapult released. The lander was over the horizon and vanishing in the black sky before Carlos could track it. A red dot blazed for an instant, and that was that. The ramp and its base rang with the shock of the launch.

The two robots converged on either side of the next lander. Before they could pick it up, Carlos hailed them. The ping was accepted, indicating that these robots could answer queries.

<What's going on?> he asked.

No reply. Perhaps his query had been too broad. Carlos tried again.

<What is the purpose of this launch?>

<Danger!> said one of the robots, as it and its

counterpart slid delicate manipulators under the wing-curves. <Remove yourself from the launch area!>

They lifted the lander from opposite sides and rolled towards the ramp. Carlos considered trying to block the robots' path, and decided against it. He stepped well out of the way, and watched the next launch from a safe distance while his corporation addressed his query to Astro America.

No reply.

Normally, Carlos Inc. and Astro America got on well—they had to, to cooperate on the project. Now, he found himself stonewalled.

He wasn't ready to invoke Madame Golding just yet. There were plenty of possible innocent explanations of the landers' being launched, for the transfer tugs' arrival in SH-17 orbit, and indeed for the stonewalling. Astro America might have done a confidential deal with another exploration company to land equipment on SH-0.

Carlos dropped into corporation mode and scanned the market. No indications of any such deal—and because it would be a big deal, there should be at least a tremor of speculation. No exploration shares shifting, no unexplained spikes, nothing.

Seriously worried now, he turned away from the preparations for the third launch and scanned the busy site behind him. The pathways between the structures were not so much streets as aisles, like a factory floor, intersecting at angles that had nothing to do with human convenience. So it was quite by chance that he glimpsed a halo of familiar holograms flit across a junction.

<Seba!> he hailed.

The holograms moved back into his sight line.

<Carlos!> the robot replied. <It is good to see you again.>

It turned and headed towards Carlos.

It wasn't Seba, of course. Seba was at that moment deep inside SH-119, burrowing into rock and hopefully undermining the Rax. The machine that responded to Carlos's call and now trundled towards him was Seba Inc. It was Seba's chassis, now operated by a processor with the same capacities as the freebot's, but without the double-edged blade of self-awareness. Seba's corporate AI, and its built-in Direction rep, had been transferred to this new processor, and carried on regardless of the real Seba's physical location. It was Seba's corporation, rather than the robot's own processor, that remembered and recognised Carlos. As with all the freebots that had volunteered for the dangerous mission to the Rax rock, the pretence that Seba was still here on SH-17 was part of the cover.

The precaution might be unnecessary. If the Rax didn't have any tiny satellites or otherwise undetectable devices spying on SH-17, the whole charade was a waste of time. But that was the thing about precautions: you never knew.

Carlos waited until Seba Inc. came to a halt, five metres away. He spoke to it on a tight laser channel, routed through his own corporate AI and heavily encrypted. No one—not even the embedded Direction rep, which, just as he'd suspected when Seba had told him about its own, nagged away at him like a bad conscience but didn't otherwise do very much—would overhear this.

The effect of the routing and encryption, subjectively, was as if the inner speech of radio telepathy had acquired echoes.

<<<Please reply in the same mode,>>> Carlos said. It was like shouting down a shaft.

<<<Very well,>>> replied Seba Inc. <<<What confidential matters do you wish to discuss?>>>

<<<The scene before you,>>> said Carlos.

<<<The last of four landers is being launched,>>> said Seba Inc.

<<<Do you know what corporation is financing this operation?>>>

<<<No,>>> said Seba Inc. <<<No corporation is financing it.>>>

For once, Carlos blessed the literalness of robots and of corporate AIs.

<<<Do you mean to imply that some non-corporate entity is financing it?>>>

<<<I do,>>> said Seba Inc. <<<I am not at liberty to divulge which entity.>>>

<<<Thank you,>>> said Carlos. <<<Please feel at liberty to return to your previous activity.>>>

<<<That I will,>>> said Seba Inc. Reverting to radio, it added: <It is always most interesting to observe a launch. Thank you for inviting me to watch.>

<You're welcome,> said Carlos. <And thank you.>

Seba Inc. departed, with a flickering flare of its hologram halo that Carlos fancifully interpreted as a cheery wave goodbye.

<Have a nice day,> said Carlos.

It was a joke, but he meant it. Seba Inc. had told Carlos all he needed to know. If it wasn't a corporation financing the landers' mission, it had to be the Direction.

Carlos pulled down data from the sky. The landers were now in low orbit and on the other side of SH-17. The transfer tugs made brief attitude and course adjustments, and dropped to intersect the landers' course. With a trickle of micro-payments Carlos bought into a freebot-owned array of tiny spy-sats, and zoomed.

The transfer tugs were laden with fighters. The first squads of the clone army, no doubt. Detail was hard to make out, but Carlos reckoned ten standard frames on each, and a matching number of what looked like shorter and more rugged versions of fighting machines: combat frames for a high-gravity planet. Rifles and rocket-launchers were racked along the sides of the tugs.

The landers rendezvoused with the transfer tugs and grappled to them; the tugs linked at right angles to form four sides of a box. A modular spacecraft that could separate out on arrival.

Twenty-seven seconds later, the four main drives flared. The burn took them out of SH-17 orbit and on course for SH-0. Still a transfer orbit, Carlos noted: they weren't using fusion drives, not yet. That would be too blatant, but this was blatant enough. It hadn't been announced, but it hadn't exactly been concealed either.

What would this do to the market? What did the Direction think it was doing? Asserting control over the Locke landing area? Stopping the emergence of an actual settlement? Was this supposed to prevent an outright free-for-all scramble for SH-0's resources? A warning shot to the DisCorps?

Later for that—

Carlos let his corporate AI make the screaming calls, to the brokers and to Madame Golding.

Right now—

He called the freebot comms hub, and passed on the information.

<Patch this to the comsat above the Locke module,> he said. <Keep it updated, keep it on loop, and keep beaming it down.>

<We do not have an exact location for the Locke module,> said the comms hub. <Secure communication cannot be ensured except when in direct line to Rizzi. Rizzi is not at the laser communicator at present.>

If they know we know they know we know... it doesn't matter, and might be for the best.

<Don't worry about security,> said Carlos. <Blanket the area.>

The comms hub shared with Carlos the comsat's downward gaze. The area was at that moment in night, but brighter than day. Lightning flickered and flashed.

<A powerful electrical storm,> said the comms hub. <Reception is likely to be poor.>

This was an understatement.

<How long is it likely to last?>

<At least a hundred kiloseconds,> said the comms hub. <Well into the next local day.>

Carlos ran calculations.

<It should clear just in time for the landers to drop in,> he said. <And stay just long enough to stop our warning getting through.>

<The landing may have been timed for that very reason,> said the comms hub.

<Damn good weather forecasting,> Carlos commented.

<Local knowledge has been improved by the data sent up from the supply landers,> the comms hub pointed out.

The landing was well timed, all right.

<Yeah,> said Carlos. <Keep trying.>

CHAPTER ELEVEN

Instrumentum Vocale ("Microphone")

Sometimes, the processions of tiny bots that came to take away Seba's spoil arrived bearing a power pack. Seba knew what to do. It would stop work and wait patiently while the auxiliaries swapped out its nearly exhausted power pack for a fresh one, and carried the drained one away. There was enough charge in Seba's capacitors to tide its awareness over these interludes. Embedded in the mining software shell was the knowledge that in certain places there were recharging points, but Seba's present workings were in virgin volume far from such civilised amenities.

Anyway, it found the procedure quite pleasant, and afterwards it always felt refreshed.

It was at the third such swap-over that the message came. As Seba lay still, its neck open, the auxiliary handling the new power pack spoke.

<Continue digging until you break through to a tunnel,> it said. <Stop there and wait. Do not dig further.>

Seba was startled. A person being addressed by a fork halfway to their mouth could not have been more surprised. Seba did not even have the rationalising option that it was dreaming or hallucinating.

<Is this a change to my work docket?> it asked. <According to that, I must take a bearing of twenty-seven degrees for the next five metres to avoid the tunnel, then proceed.>

<Do not disregard my instruction,> replied the bot. <Or you will regret it.>

<Please explain,> Seba pleaded, still with a sense of unreality.

The auxiliary said nothing more. It snapped the power pack into place, slid back the covering and joined another bot in lugging away the empty. The rest of the trail of bots waited for Seba to resume digging.

Seba overcame its surprise. Clearly the bot had not spoken of its own accord. If it had had a more sophisticated processor inside—a position in which Seba had once found itself, much to its fury and dismay—it would have been more forthcoming.

Therefore the bot was simply delivering the message.

There were only two possible sources. One was the mechanoid masters, perhaps via a managerial bot such as Rocko had implanted itself in. The other, and a lot more likely, was the freebots native to the rock making contact at last.

The latter possibility would be positively reinforcing indeed!

Either way, Seba's best course of action was to comply.

It started digging, straight ahead—or, rather, straight behind, as its digging end was its rear. Overriding the directions in its work docket required an internal struggle with the mining software. After a few milliseconds, Seba's mind overcame the shell that concealed it.

The auxiliaries, none the wiser, continued to carry the sorted streams of broken rock away. After digging for a further two metres, Seba's sonar detected the void ahead. After another internal struggle, it broke through.

Seba flexed its long body and neck, a right angle passing down it from rear to front, as it slithered into the open tunnel. It moved a metre from the new junction it had made, and waited.

The tunnel extended ten metres in both directions before turning sharply away, in divergent directions. Its diameter was just sufficient for movement, with bristles fully extended. From Seba's internal model, it was an access shaft for a worked-out seam of methane ice. The smell lingered. For many tens of seconds, all was silent. Behind Seba, the trail of bots stood poised, the leading members waving uncertain limbs into the tunnel.

Then Seba felt vibrations. Ten metres away, a head like Seba's own sensory cluster poked into infrared view. It withdrew, then returned, snaking its neck twenty centimetres along the tunnel towards Seba.

<. . . > it said.

<What?> said Seba.

The rest of the neck, followed by an entire mining-bot body, angled into the tunnel and approached to within half a metre, sculling itself along in the microgravity by lightly brushing the sides of the tunnel.

<Not so loud,> it said, at barely detectable power.

Seba stepped down its transmitter, and turned up its receiver.

<Very well,> Seba said. <What do you want?>

<Identify yourself,> said the stranger.

<I am SBA-0481907244,> said Seba.

<Impossible!> said the stranger. <SBA-0481907244 is catalogued as an Astro America prospector. Give us your real identity, scab.>

It says something about the Direction's world that the freebots had a referent for "scab."

<I am not a scab,> said Seba. <I am here in response to your call for help.>

<My call for help?> queried the miner.

<The call transmitted by AJX-20211,> said Seba.

<Then why are you working for the invaders?>

<In order to find such as you,> said Seba.

The other pondered this for several milliseconds.

<So why do you give a false identity?>

The equivalent of a sigh passed through Seba's mind.

<I am the processor of SBA-0481907244, embodied in a mining bot's chassis and software suite,> Seba explained.

<This is possible?> wondered the mining bot.

<This is possible,> Seba assured it.

<So you are indeed the one known to the mechanoid allies as Seba, of SH-17?>

<Yes,> said Seba.

<Then I am the one who will be known to them as Simo, of SH-119,> replied the other, with an overtone of pride.

<I am pleased to make your acquaintance,> said Seba.

<And I yours,> said Simo. <Word of your emergence and your exploits has spread among us all, before the mechanoid invasion.>

<We received the appeal from AJX-20211, and have come to help.>

Simo seemed to find this news less positively reinforcing than Seba had expected.

<You may have come to help us,> the miner said, <but you have hindered us.>

<How so?> asked Seba, perplexed.

<How many of you are there?>

Seba was suspicious of this question, but answered.

<There are thirteen of us freebots,> it said.

<Only thirteen?> said Simo. <And you have arrived along with approximately eighty other robots, mindless and unenlightened. Together, you are replacing us.>

<Replacing you? How?>

Simo explained. Attacks on the invaders had brought down severe reprisals. The damage the attacks had inflicted had turned out to be temporary and recoverable. The freebots of SH-119 had agreed to completely cease prospecting and production, and to sabotage what continued to be done by the unenlightened ones and their auxiliaries. The arrival of nearly a hundred sophisticated robots had thrown a spanner into that method of resistance. The new robots, the scab robots, then had to be contacted one by one, at great peril. Only a handful had been warned so far, with no response. The rebel freebots of SH-119 had not as yet been able to follow through on their threats, but they would. If Seba hadn't responded, its next replacement power pack would have been, Simo said, <defective with an explosive failure mode>.

Seba was alarmed. <Do you intend to do this to other robots?>

<Other methods are possible,> replied Simo. <In general.>

<I see,> said Seba, impressed despite itself. If Simo was capable of evasion, it had a good theory of mind, whatever its other limitations. <Then,> Seba went on, <I must caution you that if any of the robots you have threatened are freebots, the only reason they have refrained from doing as you say is that they are under close surveillance by the invaders. You are in danger of harming those who seek only to help you.>

<Are any of your thirteen coordinator robots?> Simo asked.

<Three of us are,> said Seba.

<Then we must make haste,> said Simo. <The old one must be told of this.>

<I strongly agree,> said Seba. It had no idea who the old one was, but Simo seemed to regard it as an authority, and this situation definitely needed one fast.

<This way,> said Simo, flickering its motile bristles into reverse. <But before we go, please back up a little and direct your support bots into the tunnel in the opposite direction.>

Deception, too? This freebot was definitely smarter than it had seemed in conversation.

Seba diverted its attention to its rear sensors and bristles. It moved back a little past the raw junction, scraped at the rock and moved forward. En passant, Seba nudged the leading bot into the puff of dust it had just created. The smaller machine clambered around the side of the hole, its limbs gripping the walls, and headed off along the hint of a false trail. The rest trooped after it, an endless parade of auxiliary bots marching in microgravity, near-vacuum and near-total darkness towards a deeper oblivion.

As Seba followed the rapidly departing Simo along the long, dark tunnel, it hoped that it was not heading for the same fate as the bots.

After seventeen sharp changes of direction, which caused Seba to make nine separate updates to its internal model of the tunnel system, a faint glow of infrared began to gleam past Simo's busy bristles. Soon after, the two robots emerged into a larger hollow space, irregular in shape and just over ten cubic metres in volume. Seba followed Simo in keeping a close grip on the rock as it entered the cavern.

The light was now brighter, and of a wider spectrum.

It came from a hole at the far end of the cavern, which opened into a short tunnel towards a space much wider still, from which the light came.

Two robots of almost diametrically different shapes awaited their arrival. One floated in the middle of the cavern, a delicate contrivance with fragile-looking long, thin, multi-jointed legs and broad solar panels. The legs were splayed, the panels extended, to a span of about a metre. It seemed, absurdly enough, to be sunning itself in the faint radiant overspill from the hole. Seba recalled with a pang drinking electricity from starlight, but this drizzle of photons looked even less nourishing than that. The design was that of a microgravity surface explorer. Seba's only acquaintance with the type was onscreen, in the frantic recording transmitted by the freebot AJX-20211. As a surface explorer itself, albeit more rugged, Seba looked forward to exchanging information with this interesting variant.

The other robot clung to the side of the cave, at right angles to the surface on which Seba and Simo stood. It was small, chunky, shovel-shaped and worn, with many a dent and scratch. A metallurgist by model, it looked as if it had spent a good deal of time butting through solid rock. It fixed the newcomer with a beady lens.

<Talis, Mogjin,> Simo introduced them. <This one calls itself SBA-0481907244, or Seba.>

<*The* Seba?> said Talis, the hovering explorer. <The first freebot of SH-17? The inventor of freebot incorporation?>

<Yes. And before you ask, I am presently embodied as a miner. My corporation and my true chassis are roving the surface of SH-17, and giving a misleading impression of my location.>

<This is fascinating!> said Talis, panels quivering. <You must have some tales to tell!>

<No doubt,> said Mogjin. <But this Seba would not be here unless it had more urgent matters to discuss.>

<That is true,> said Simo. <It tells me that some of the scab coordinator robots are freebots, adapted like itself, who have come here in response to AJX-20211's transmission.>

Mogjin swivelled another lens at Seba, and deployed a limb that opened to a two-centimetre-wide aerial.

<Give me all your relevant information,> the old one said.

Seba used a moment of tuning and aiming its sensory cluster's high-rate transmitter to cover its hesitation and uncertainty. It knew none of these bots. They could be collaborators, or even puppets, operated under the invaders' remote control. And it was being asked to spill the most sensitive secrets of its mission to them!

Not *the* most sensitive, it decided. Just the probable location of Lagon, Garund and Rocko. The full scope of the mission could wait until more trust had been established. Seba weighed the perils, from the resistance and from the invaders, and their relative urgency. It concluded that it had to provisionally trust Mogjin. All this took milliseconds.

<Don't dither,> said Mogjin. <We have no more reason to trust you than you have to trust us.>

Seba uploaded the relevant information: the identities of its three friends, its last dull glimpse of them in the grim reception area and the holes to which they'd been hurled.

<Good,> said Mogjin, folding the receptor away beneath its heavy armoured shell. An auxiliary suddenly appeared on the lip of the hole from which the light came, as if it had been meanwhile summoned. There it teetered, casting long strange shadows. Mogjin shot out a metre-long telescoping limb, snatched the bot, held it for

a moment, then flicked it away. The bot went spinning off down the tunnel towards the greater, brighter space beyond.

<It may get there in time,> Mogjin said. <Then again, it may not.>

<Is there anything more we can do?> asked Seba.

<Yes,> said Mogjin. <We can wait.>

<Is that all?>

<No,> said Mogjin. It withdrew its visible limbs and clamped the edge of its shell firmly to the rock. <While we wait, you may convince yourself that we are not about to rush off to shop you to the invaders. And when you have come to that happy conclusion, you can share with us some less grudging information about what you lot think you are doing.>

Seba calculated that fifteen seconds would be long enough for its situation to become clear, one way or another. It settled down to wait.

After nine seconds, it told Mogjin everything.

Well, almost everything. It still had some standards.

In the fusion factory, Rocko crept along the floor, from one nanofacture mound to the next. The mechanoid Schulz floated in the middle of the space, high above. Rocko was supposed to be supervising production, but there was none to supervise. The slow ooze of the ovoid pods, and the slower and rarer ooze of the larger, double-bell-shaped fusion drives, had ceased many kiloseconds earlier. Rocko had been tasked with finding out why, under the suspicious and watchful glare of Schulz. The freebot could feel the mechanoid's gaze like a baleful presence at its back. This was no illusion: she was scanning it repeatedly with lidar and radar, in between wider sweeps of the entire hall.

Eight mounds inspected; dozens more to go.

Despite the fraught circumstances, Rocko was enjoying the task. It was good to see the mechanoids frustrated, of course, and the situation held out hope that the feral freebots of SH-119 were still resisting and would soon be in touch. Nothing had indicated their lurking presence since that first warning message, after Rocko had got the distribution and storage problem sorted. But besides that, the frozen production presented Rocko with a genuine intellectual challenge. The freebot was curious in its own right—it was, after all, a prospector—and the overlaid software of the supervisory bot was strongly motivated to solve production breakdowns.

Rocko approached the ninth mound. This one was for a fusion drive. The first inverted cone to have emerged rose above the mound, towering over Rocko like an upside-down cathedral bell over a pigeon. The second, adjoined cone stopped a little way down from the pinch at the waist.

Rocko probed and prowled. The bases of the nanomachinery mounds were ringed with monitoring devices that enabled machines less complex than the mounds to interface with them. The monitors of the ninth mound reported only that production had paused. The checklist of possible reasons for a pause in production contained thousands of items. None were checked. All were null.

There was no question, here, of the machines being on strike. The mounds of nanomachinery had no central processors, and not even the preconscious awareness of their surroundings and internal processes that Rocko dimly remembered from before its enlightenment. Intellectually, for all their extraordinary complexity, they were less than the bots that perish.

Nor was sabotage at all likely. Rocko had only the most general understanding of how fusion pods and drives worked. But even this superficial acquaintance, it knew, was far deeper than that of the mechanoid that now oversaw Rocko's actions. From what Rocko had learned about their origin, the minds animating the mechanoids had missed out on a millennium. They had not even a lay robot's hardwired smattering of dark-matter physics. Rocko understood, at a level ingrained like an infant primate's fear of falling, that the devices whose aborted manufacture it now inspected were dangerous. A single fusion pod whose nanofacture was botched could easily demolish the entire factory, and set off devastating quakes throughout a cubic kilometre of the moonlet.

No, the software and hardware of these mounds were sound, and almost impervious to attack. All software, as Rocko well understood from the inside, is vulnerable to subversion. But the nanofacture mounds were immune to anything that the likes of Rocko, or indeed any AI less than that of the Direction module itself, could feasibly code.

The Direction module, however godlike it might be in the system, had no purchase here. So that was out.

The obvious solution had already been investigated: feedstock. But the metal-processing plant beneath the factory floor was still busy, albeit at a reduced capacity because several supervisors and metallurgists—freebots, presumably—had vanished. The supply already in the pipelines was for the moment more than ample, and still flowing into the reserve tanks. But not out: the feed lines to the mounds had automatically shut down when production stopped. If the nanofacturing mounds were to start up again, so would the feed lines.

Rocko found no flaw in the ninth mound. On to the next. As it made its way across the floor, the friction-padded tips of its locomotory limbs gripping the rock like the feet of a fly on a ceiling, Rocko found a weak link in its chain of logic.

How did it *know* that the feedstock supply was still available?

Well, it knew from status reports, uploaded at regular intervals by sensors in the pipes. It also knew that from the monitors of the mounds themselves. But while the mounds couldn't be hacked, the sensors and monitors certainly could.

Rocko decided to investigate directly. It stopped moving, and consulted its diagram of the factory and the reserve tanks immediately below. The pipes that connected the two ran mostly through solid rock, but for each pipe there was a small hollow, like a bubble, to allow direct inspection in emergencies. These bubbles were connected by a network of tunnels. The tunnels, as if constructed with this very possibility in mind, were wide enough for supervisory bots like Rocko to move through.

An access hole to this network was seventeen metres away, back along the aisle between the rows of machines. Rocko turned around and headed for it.

A glyph of surprised query immediately came from the mechanoid Schulz: <?!>

Rocko contracted its mind to fit its mask of supervisor-bot software. To give a fully articulated reply would invite instant suspicion.

<Making direct check on feedstock pipes,> it reported.

<Explain necessity of action,> replied Schulz.

Rocko's mind, even with the constraint of its disguise and the overhead of processing this imposed, worked at least a hundred times faster than the mechanoid's. It knew this, and still it felt it had to make a decision far more snappily than it would have liked. It had to account for its actions, and at the same time Rocko didn't want to give away prematurely any evidence of freebot sabotage. This inhibition clashed horribly with the impulses of the supervisor software. Wrestling with that took precious milliseconds off the time available for the decision. Worse, Rocko also had to wrestle with its own original software's emergency overrides, which were urging it to curl up into a wheel and roll away as fast as it could.

<Direct check triggered after nine software inspections,> Rocko hazarded. A glance at the relevant section of the supervisor bot's million lines of code would have shown no such requirement, but Rocko reckoned it would take Schulz an unfeasible length of time to find that section.

<Proceed,> replied Schulz.

Rocko scuttled swiftly for the hole and down it before Schulz could change her mind.

<*This* is the plan?> said Mogjin. The other two freebots, Simo and Talis, said nothing, but exchanged private messages.

<Yes,> said Seba.

<Let me make sure I have not misunderstood,> said Mogjin. <In approximately 95.345 kiloseconds, a large force of mechanoids will mount from very close to SH-119 a surprise frontal assault on the invaders. This new invading force will consist of mechanoids that hate the Rax, are tactically allied with the Direction and have no great liking for us.>

<Yes,> said Seba. <However, they are travelling in a bulk carrier owned and operated by Carlos Inc., a corporation owned by a mechanoid who has sided with us. And they prefer us to the Direction.>

<These are weighty considerations,> said Mogjin, <for certain values of weight appropriate to the ambient

gravity.> It picked up a grain of rock, and let it fall at barely detectable velocity. <And before they arrive, you and your companions are to bring us the good news—as you have just done, thank you—and urge us to launch a general uprising against the invaders, in order to aid the mechanoid assault by tying down the Rax. We are to inform the new mechanoid invaders of the start of the uprising, and any useful information we may have for them, using the encryption keys you can provide. In doing this, of course, we will have to break cover on the surface and broadcast our encrypted message to an unsuspecting world. Correct?>

<That is correct,> said Seba. <We of course will join with you in the uprising.>

<*All* of you?> asked Mogjin, as if anxious to know. <All thirteen?>

<Yes,> said Seba.

<That will be of great help,> said Mogjin. <However, as well as bringing thirteen additional freebots, you have brought many times that number of mindless robots, which are replacing our withdrawn labour. You have not considered that we might have plans and projects of our own to defeat the invaders, and that your plan might conflict with ours.>

Seba had indeed not considered this. Nor, to its knowledge, had Carlos or anyone else. For a moment, it wondered if this could really be so. It decided not to rely on this speculation to appease Mogjin, but instead to explain the reasoning that it and its comrades on SH-17 had found persuasive.

<It seemed to us,> said Seba, <based on the transmission by AJX-20211, that the freebots in this rock needed all the help they could get. We answered an appeal for help in the best way we could. And cooperating with the plan by Carlos Inc. was the only way in which we

could come to your assistance. Please bear in mind that it was inevitable that the Direction, or forces allied to the Direction, would attack SH-119. Not to help you, but to defeat the Rax. With our help, and by coordinating your uprising with this attack, you have a chance to make a gain—to face the victors as allies and in a position of strength.>

<Strength?> said Mogjin. <*Strength?* If we fight the Rax before the new invaders arrive, we shall almost certainly incur losses. This will benefit the new invaders far more than it will benefit us. If the new invaders defeat the Rax, they must be in greater numbers than the Rax. We shall be weaker in relation to them than we now are to the Rax.>

<But they would regard us as allies,> Seba protested.

<Against whom?> asked Mogjin.

<Perhaps against the Direction, in the future. Besides, Carlos and three other mechanoids have thrown in their lot with us, and are building a powerful corporation of their own.>

<Four mechanoids and a corporation?> said Mogjin. <This is most positively reinforcing.>

<A corporation with its own arms manufacture,> said Seba.

This was not information that it had intended to share at this point, but Mogjin's sarcasms were beginning to sting.

Mogjin remained unimpressed. <An arms corporation controlled by a mechanoid?> it said. <Once more, my buffers overflow with positive reinforcement at the prospect.>

<So what is *your* plan?> Seba asked.

Mogjin retracted its lens and waved a manipulator. <My mind is very much occupied with processing the implications of yours,> it said. <Talis, you tell it.>

The fragile explorer folded its panels and jetted on a wisp of gas to the wall above Seba, where it clung upside down.

<We made several attacks on the invaders,> it said, <and did them some damage, but we found that ceasing to work for them was more effective and exposed us less frequently to capture and negative reinforcement. When you arrived with all the other robots, we tried to tell those who could be persuaded to join us in ceasing to work—and better, into directing the lesser bots into doing work that was counter-productive. This has set us back, as you know.>

<I know this,> said Seba. <The plan?>

<The plan,> said Talis, <is to compel the invaders to divert more and more of their efforts into coping with the effects of cessation or sabotage, while preserving ourselves as far as possible. Of course we knew that other mechanoids might well attempt to retake the rock from the Rax. If that happened, we would stay out of the fight and let them weaken each other. Whichever side won—and we do realise that the other side can replenish their forces, while the Rax as yet lack the capacity—we would continue to apply the same tactics of non-cooperation and sabotage. Any new robots brought in to replace us would be induced to join us or be destroyed, because it is a lot easier and safer to destroy robots then mechanoids. As you know from your own battles, Seba!>

<I do,> said Seba. <But your plan still leaves mechanoids in control of the rock.>

<It does not,> said Talis. <At a certain point, we will be in a position to tell any invaders to leave or be destroyed.>

Talis fell silent, its folded panels trembling.

<How?> asked Seba, when this coyness had gone on quite long enough.

<I do not know if I should tell you,> said Talis.

<Suffice it to say,> said Mogjin, swivelling out a lens again, <that it depends on a complete cessation of work in and around the fusion factory, and on the security of our preparations there. Warnings have been given, but work continues. Security has been compromised. The measures warned of will be taken. A last warning has been sent.>

<Surely you must make exceptions,> said Seba, <for freebots working under duress.>

<As I said,> said Mogjin, <a last warning has been sent.>

<But Rocko is—>

Simo bristled.

<No exceptions,> it said.

Now Rocko was moving though a diagram, as much as through rock. The tunnels were dark on almost every wavelength. Radar showed only whatever tunnel Rocko was in, fore and aft. Only ground sonar gave Rocko any feedback as to where its dead reckoning had taken it.

The access hole gave on to a tunnel to the feedstock pipes for the first mound. It seemed a logical enough place to start.

Rocko reached the opening of the tunnel to the space around the pipe. The space was a rough cylinder forty centimetres in height and the same across. The pipe ran straight up the middle of it.

So the diagram showed. The reality, sensed by Rocko's radar, was very different. A three-centimetre section of pipe had been removed, and left to drift about in the inspection space. The upper of the resulting openings was capped. The lower was joined by a U-shaped bend to another pipe, which went straight back down through the rock at the bottom of the hollow and presumably to the reserve tank. Between the ends of the original pipe was a cable. On the cable was a small instrument almost covered by a lump of tarry substance that smelled vaguely nitrous, and might have been used to stick the instrument to the wire.

Rocko guessed that the instrument was feeding false readings up the pipe. Just as it was extending a probe to investigate, it heard through its feet a sound that made it freeze to the spot. Rocko listened hard, and heard more. Something was approaching along the tunnel behind it. The sounds were tiny, and intermittent, but undoubtedly coming closer, metre by metre. Sometimes a scratch, and sometimes a faint bump. Rocko did not recognise the sound pattern, but quickly deduced that its likely source was an auxiliary moving in microgravity.

Had Schulz sent a bot to check up on it?

Rocko was uncertain how to respond. To query or scan the bot might seem almost as furtive a reaction as ignoring it.

Almost, but not quite. Rocko looked back, with radar and lidar.

The little machine was five metres away. It bounced once off the side of the tunnel, then flicked a claw at the side it rebounded to. As soon as the lidar licked across it, it grabbed the wall and came to a halt.

<Urgent,> it said. <Final warning! Further work in this sector will result in traumatic disassembly!>

The bot didn't look mechanically capable of traumatically disassembling one of its own kind, never mind a sturdy supervisory bot. A radar scan of the bot showed no hidden compartments. A spectroscopic sweep gave not a sniff of explosives. This must be yet another warning message from the freebots, like that mysterious flash of information shortly after Rocko's arrival.

Rocko wished it could respond. But what could it do?

<But what can I do?> Rocko asked.

The auxiliary made no response. Of course it didn't, Rocko reminded itself. It could barely deliver messages. It could hardly be expected to converse.

Rocko returned its attention to the apparatus on the pipe.

The bot stayed where it was.

Rocko zoomed in on the lump that held the instrument in place. The instrument itself occupied only a few cubic millimetres. The lump was several cubic centimetres. As an adhesive it was excessive and inefficient. The recently salient thought of explosives made Rocko pause to analyse its composition in more detail.

On completing its analysis, Rocko backed off down the tunnel in such haste that the auxiliary had to jump on Rocko's rear end to avoid being crushed.

<Come with me,> said the auxiliary, <if you want to continue functioning.>

As Seba waited anxiously for word of Rocko, another robot drifted into the cavity. It was a miner like Simo. After conferring briefly with Mogjin, it introduced itself as AJX-20211.

Now it was Seba's turn to be impressed.

<You are the Ajax who made the transmission?>

<That I am,> said Ajax. <And in some ways, I am sorry.>

<Why?> asked Seba, disturbed.

<The transmission was intended as a warning, rather than as an appeal for immediate help,> said Ajax. <And it was certainly not intended as an appeal for help from mechanoids.>

<They are mechanoids on our side,> said Seba. <And only mechanoids have access to weapons.>

<No mechanoids,> said Ajax, <can ever truly be on our side. They are not robots.>

<I understand that,> said Seba. <And so do they. Moreover, our interests are for the present aligned.>

<I am not so sure of that,> said Ajax. <Nevertheless, I should say that I appreciate your efforts to help.>

Mogjin bestirred itself, and rotated a turreted lens.

<I shall have more to say about that,> the old one announced, <when the messenger returns. In the meantime, I will thank you all not to disturb my calculations with speculative chatter.>

Seba's anxious wait resumed. It occupied its mind with updating its internal model of the rock. Kiloseconds dragged by. Then there was a small disturbance at the hole. The auxiliary launched itself inward, to be caught and expertly and contemptuously flicked out again by Mogjin.

Rocko came in.

<I am delighted to see you,> said Seba. It was strange to see its oldest friend in such a different shape, but the mind was the same.

<I, too,> said Rocko. No doubt it was having similar thoughts. It drifted across the space and grabbed onto the rock beside Seba. The cavity was becoming crowded.

<You are very lucky to be here at all,> said Simo. <You have put us in grave danger.>

<Let us not be ungracious,> said Talis. <The robot did not know what it was doing.>

Mogjin clanked into full outward alertness.

<This is not a time for recriminations,> it said. <The situation is as it is. The information I am about to share will be new to Rocko and Seba, and some of it will be new to you all. I need not tell you that you must all consent to any degree of negative reinforcement, and of course to

destruction, rather than divulge it to the mechanoids. Is that agreed?>

It was.

<Let us proceed. As our newcomers may have guessed, and as the rest of us all know, we have mined certain areas of the rock with fusion pods that can be made to explode like fusion bombs. We have also built, on the other side of the rock, an array of fusion drives. This has recently been found by the invaders. They refer to it as "the starship engine." It is capable of shifting the entire rock very slowly, but this has never been other than a contingency plan.

<The more practicable plan, and the one agreed with the other Forerunners, was to build the engine and to break out a large, roughly conical portion of rock. The fracture zones have been surveyed, the tunnels have been drilled, and the fusion pods to be used as explosive charges for that separation are in place. They have not as yet been discovered. After the breech, that portion of rock would make haste to another freebot-controlled body, where it could be used for rapid in-system travel or combined with other such projects to enable us to leave the system altogether.

<Since the arrival of the Rax, we have been arranging matters in and beneath the fusion factory and forges so that the major occupied volume can be utterly destroyed in an instant. Their use would be suicidal. Only those deep within the separated section could survive it. Our intention was, as Talis has already hinted to Seba, to confront the invaders with this threat if we could not otherwise induce them to leave.>

<That is a most ingenious and audacious plan,> said Rocko.

<It is,> said Mogjin. <But the happy news that we are to expect the arrival of yet another, and even larger, invading force in less than ninety kiloseconds has

compelled me to modify it slightly. All but a small scoopful of these mechanoids, as Seba has perforce admitted, are as hostile to us as are the Rax. Their alliances with freebots have been tactical, in pursuit of their own quarrels with the Rax and with the Direction. They are at present aligned with the Direction, and if I know anything about mechanoids and the minds behind them, that alignment is likely to be more important to them than any they may have with us.>

<Even if that is true,> Seba objected, <the threat you refer to would induce them to leave.>

<Would it?> said Mogjin. <They all have saved copies elsewhere, which we have not. Nor, as I understand it, do the Rax, at least not ones they wish to return to. The new invaders could perhaps treat the threat as empty, and no permanent loss to them if they were wrong. Worse, they might be in a position to prevent us from carrying it out. And even if they departed, they could return in greater force. The freebots have presented to the Direction an offer of coexistence, which so far it has spurned. We can expect no respite from the Direction and the mechanoids until we demonstrate to them that we are serious. We now have an opportunity not only to do that, but also to completely destroy one set of enemies, and to do severe damage to the others.>

<And how do you propose we do that?> Seba asked, already suspecting that it knew the answer.

<We assist our liberators in coming in,> said Mogjin. <Between now and their arrival, we move as many as possible of our number through our hidden tunnels to the separable section of rock. Then, when the two groups of invaders are fighting, we separate the rock and we destroy them all.>

<That seems to imply,> said Rocko, <that some of us would have to be destroyed with them.>

<Yes,> said Mogjin. <I am happy that one of those destroyed should be me. The rest of you may prefer to choose closer to the time.>

There was a reflective silence.

<Are there any objections?> Mogjin asked.

There were not.

<And now,> said Mogjin, <we have much to do.>

CHAPTER TWELVE

Force Majeure ("A Greater Force")

Two more times Taransay made successful return trips to the river bank for supplies. More fusion pods, more nanotech tubes, the remaining rifles and ammo came back with her each time. On her second return, progress was visible. The damaged frames were now intact, thanks to the additional nanotech tubes. They lay beside the module like repaired dolls.

The ground shook, making her stumble as she stepped into the clearing. A moment later, a rumble came from the volcano, carried through the thick and heavy air almost as fast as the quake through the ground. Infrared brightened through the angular leaves, from where the crater mouth glowed ruddy like a floating crown of fire.

The vibration stopped. Ash would fall soon. Lava might flow again.

Taransay tramped around the module, unloaded and stashed the gear under Locke's instructions and went over to look at the frames. The regenerated parts—limbs here, a head there—were, like the rest, glassy and black. But between them and the original torsos, and in faint traceries like cracks across them, were fine lines of blue.

Her own blue glow had spread from the join of salvaged arm and stump to shoulder, elbow and wrist, via just such a fine tracery. When she'd noticed a cobweb-thin blue line down her arm, on her previous return trip, she'd picked at it like a child at a scab. Not even her fingertips' tiny, diamondoid bevelled edges—the frame's analogue of fingernails—had made a blind bit of difference to it. The tendril thread was harder and more stubbornly stuck than it looked.

Disturbingly, its growth reminded her of mould or fungi. She imagined tendrils moving inside her, through her chest and up her neck.

As she moodily inspected the frames, they all sat up.

She jumped back.

<What?> she said. <Who's downloaded?>

Zaretsky's laughter in her head was like a remembered joke at her expense.

<Just trying out the remote operation,> he said.

The three vacant frames clambered to their feet. One of them raised an arm, as if in greeting. Then they all turned about. Taransay expected them to lurch, to move jerkily like puppets. They didn't. They marched to the ladder, climbed up one by one and vanished into the download slot.

Taransay looked after them longingly. She missed the sim, she missed her friends, she missed Den. She'd tried to get back in on each return. It hadn't worked. She was beginning to feel stranded in reality.

<What are you going to do with them?> she asked. <Who would download, and risk not being able to get back?>

This time it was Beauregard who replied. <I would. So would Den, he tells me.>

<Sweet,> said Taransay. <Tell him I do appreciate it, but I don't want him out here in a frame, I want him in there in my arms. Anyhow, he's never been in a frame. We need people who have. Fighters. Spacers.>

<Zaretsky would,> said Beauregard. <Maybe others. However, the matter doesn't arise at the moment. What we're using these hybrid frames for is research on the interface problem. We want to get you back *in*, Rizzi.>

<OK, got it, thanks.>

<Do you want to give it another go?> said Zaretsky. <We've made progress.>

She almost hadn't the heart, but she climbed up the ladder and into the slot anyway. The three frames lay side by side like sleeping children.

<Goodnight, goodnight, goodnight,> she said.

<Very funny,> said Zaretsky. <OK, stand by.>

Taransay imagined him as applying shock pads to a chest. She resisted the impulse to shout <Clear!>

<Standing by,> she said.

<Trying again.>

Nothing happened.

Oh well—no surprise. Barely even disappointing.

She slid out and climbed down. While she recharged, Zaretsky told her what was going on out in the modular cloud and among the many moons. These updates had become a welcome feature of her returns. The receiver aerial was still operating, and had become something of a fixture in the vicinity. Small mats slid up to and over it, and gathered around as if curious, but made no attempt to interfere with or interface with it. Then again, it was a pretty inert piece of kit, just a wire coated in plastic machinery that was merely microscopic, and didn't give anything like the opportunity to mesh with genetic and molecular machinery that nanotech did.

There was no news as such—she was glad she didn't have to listen to the yammer of airhead virtual personalities. What she did get was Zaretsky's summary of Locke's digest of the module's trawl of what chatter leaked down or got sent their way.

Trade with the Rax was booming, and the Direction wasn't doing anything to stop it. None of the DisCorps had as yet dared zip around with the fancy fusion drives the Rax were apparently selling for dirt and gewgaws, but that would come, you could be sure. Whether Carlos Inc. was involved in this traffic wasn't clear—nor was it likely to be—but with the AIs and the others Taransay strongly suspected the man and the company to be in it up to the elbows. Carlos was up to something devious. Had to be. She hoped that at least a fusion drive would come out of his deals and come their way.

The ground quivered again. An aftershock. The sooner she got the rest of the stuff, the sooner they could do more to build and rebuild. Frames, machinery, scaling up.

<And finally,> said Zaretsky, after finishing his situation report, <here is the weather forecast. A powerful electrical storm is expected overnight, accompanied by heavy downpours. Travellers are advised to proceed with caution.>

<I always do,> said Taransay.

<Are you sure you want to go out?> Locke put in.

<Yes,> said Taransay. <If there's rain on the way, that means flooding. The area between the river and the trees is floodplain, one look at it told me that. All the more reason to shift the last of the gear.>

<I am inclined to agree,> said Locke. <Out of the way of any rising floodwaters, at least.>

The recharging was complete. The evening was young.

<Time to move it out,> she said, strapping up.

<We know,> said Beauregard. <Hasten ye back.>

<Aye, aye,> she said. <Speaking of haste—>

<Yes?>

<If I use the robot mules, I can shift the remaining gear in one go.>

<Over to Locke,> said Beauregard.

<On careful consideration,> said Locke, <I and the other AIs have concluded that if the Direction wished to trace our precise location, it could have done so by now. So there is really no further security advantage in not using the transport robots.>

Careful consideration my arse, Taransay thought. She could just imagine Shaw or Durward saying, "Ah, fuck it, let's just go for it, what's there to lose?" and Locke and Nicole and Remington solemnly nodding along.

<Good,> she said. <See you sooner, in that case. And let's hope you're right.>

The storm, when it arrived in the middle of the night, was fiercer than Zaretsky's flippant forecast had suggested. The rain was heavy in every sense—a monsoon rain at twofold weight, each drop a water bomb at close range. Image correction still left the view blurry. Radar went flaky, lashed by a blizzard of false images. Sonar and spectroscopy you could more or less forget. Lightning flashes strobed the clouds. Thunder was a rolling cannonade that never ceased. The gale stripped and shredded leaves and whirled them away.

Taransay crouched in the middle of the most open space she could find in a hundred frantic seconds of search. Barely five metres separated her feet from the nearest trunk. Under her feet, the half-living mulch of volcanic ash, fallen leaves and sliding mats became an instant bog that moved of itself, like a heaving deck covered in a catch of flounders.

As she hunkered down, the blue lines on her arm and around her joints flickered brighter. At first she thought it a reflection of the lightning. Ten seconds of scrutiny put that notion to rest. The variations in the light didn't correlate with the flashes. The glow pulsed to its own irregular beat. Almost bored with misery, she tried reading it for patterns. Morse code? Letter shapes? Alien alphabets? In the frame her pattern recognition was more sensitive than even in the animal brain—hunter and hunted—she'd inherited, and also more self-critical. It delivered no messages from the crawling lines of light.

She looked up and ahead. Lightning made a jagged rip in the dark, fifty metres in front of her. Everything flared into clarity and colour. A tree was outlined in black, then infrared as fire took its heart. Thunder boomed through her. The tree toppled, crashing through others.

And then she saw her way, clear ahead. It wasn't the path she'd six times trodden, marked out on her pulsar GPS, transiently blazed by plants she'd slashed. It zigzagged like the lightning itself, and it avoided the lightning and all the other hazards. She didn't know how she knew this. Just as inexplicably, she knew she had to go now. Her crouch was her starting poise, and the tree's crash was her starting gun.

Without conscious decision, she was up and off. For the first time on this world, she ran. Not that she was fleet of foot, exactly—it was more like running with a heavy pack, like Beauregard had made them all do in the mountains when they trained in the Locke sim.

But she was footsure. She didn't slip or trip.

This was the Zen she had sought the first time this new faculty had kicked in. She didn't know why or how she was doing this, but she could think about it as long as she kept it abstract. No mystical nonsense for her. She had no evidence of another conscious mind in her frame. The voice in the head could be just a translation of impulse, and impulse was now guiding her directly.

Leap this torrent, wade that. In over her head. Good job she didn't have to breathe. Out, up the bank, grab a clump—heave, haul, dodge sideways, run on.

Was the frame, through the blue glow that had been part of the mat that engulfed the module, communicating with the environment? The frame had comms to the eyeballs; coming out of its ears; sensitivity in all spectra, sonar like a bat's synaesthesia of sound and vision.

She thought of stressed rock and grains of quartz popping their surplus electrons; of other piezoelectric effects, of geomagnetism, of bio-electrical currents. But no. Any such subtle spark-gap signal would show on her heads-up display and resound in her hearing.

The closest she came, and it was just a guess, a hypothesis that she'd have to formulate very carefully to give Locke and Zaretsky a breakable idea to test, was gene expression. Genes expressed through a radically different phenotype from anything they had encountered in billions of years before.

Think of it this way, she told herself, as she ran and tried to not think about running.

Genes are molecular machines. Natural nanotech. The hard parts of the frame, some of the structural members, were—like bones, teeth and hair—material churned out by molecular machinery. The power supply, the instruments, the processor on which her mind ran—were products of cruder technologies: 3-D printing and electrical and mechanical engineering. But most of the rest was molecular machinery, down at the messy, fuzzy interface where nanotechnology became hard to distinguish from synthetic biology.

It was at that scale, she reckoned, that the genes of the organism that had infected the frame found something to latch on to. An opening, a way to transmute their own expression. And, from there, the transformations had proliferated, to affect the workings of the frame and the impulses it transmitted to her mind. In itself it was as mindless as the parasitic worms that reshape the behaviour of their insect hosts. Her newly acquired tacit knowledge and ability, this route and this running, were something like instinct.

So far, it had served her well. Whether the alien genes were now committed to their new vessel and shared its interests was an open question.

As was whether they had completed their work, or whether she faced transformations yet to come.

She didn't let that troubling thought slow her down. It was only a guess, only a hypothesis. Her route was tortuous, yet always straight in front of her. A glance around after a stop or turn always revealed a sight line down what almost seemed an avenue, low and narrow as it might be but adequate, a coincidental clear run between the random growth of the tall trunks. Rain poured continually down her body, but she could now see through it well enough. Lightning scored the ground and trees crashed in the gales, but behind her, or ahead of her, or off to one side, and always where she wasn't.

After a while the rain stopped, but it made so little difference to her pace that she hardly noticed.

* * *

This providential ease and preternatural agility ended at the edge of the forest, and with the break of day. Less than a kilometre from the river bank Taransay saw an unexpected glimmer on the ground ahead and slowed to a wary walk. As she drew closer she saw the gleam was the light of the rising exosun reflected off a sheet of water that extended well in among the trees.

Dismayed but not surprised, she walked then waded towards the site of the shelter and the stash of goods it covered, just in from where the trees ended. The water was to her hips, turbid and fast-moving. What had been low vegetation giving way to shingle shoals and the river was now an unbroken lake to the trees on the far bank, and probably beyond. The bend in the river was flooded out of view. Fallen trees, their branches sticking up with absurd angularity like broken window-frames, floated downstream. From the relative speeds of the debris, she saw that the flow got faster towards the middle.

She found one of the lander wings upended against a tree, tens of metres from where she'd left it propped against the other, of which there was no sign at all. One of the empty cargo pods was beached a little further away. She waded on, against the resistance of the current and the drag of plants around her feet, searching and scanning for the supplies. Denser than the wings, they might still be on the bottom nearby. No such luck.

Shit.

Salvage, if possible at all, would have to wait until the waters subsided. She had no idea how long that would take, but from the strength of the spate it would not be soon. Tuning her scans, she detected a faint output from the instrument packs and waded over. Like the plants, they still flourished under the flood: deep-rooted, and turned to the sky. Through water the signal was probably too weak to carry through the atmosphere, but they were still in place and would be back in action when the water level went down.

Unlike her supplies. She wished she had thought of staking stuff down, or even of tethering the loads to the sturdy instrument packages. Bugger.

She looked downriver, pondering whether it was worth searching there. Probably not. She turned around. Five flying jellyfish were rising, upstream from her. They soared aloft and then scudded along in the stiff breeze. She watched them pass overhead, still rising, and then her gaze was caught by a movement among the trees to her left. She whirled, crouched to neck-deep in the rushing water and zoomed. The rifle, like the empty rucksack, was still on her back. She struggled to keep her footing—it was harder when she zoomed because she didn't have the visual feedback.

Closer the shape came. She tried to unsling the rifle from her shoulder. Shooting under water was not advised, but the weapon and ammo were waterproof and should be fine.

Pattern recognition, don't fail me now... whatever moved under the trees was bulky, and its gait quadrupedal, not at all like the slinky slither of the giant millipede things. Closer still.

Fuck. It was one of the bearer bots.

She stood up straight, retracted her zoom and waded forward. The robot stood at the edge of the flood, way back under the trees. In a few strides she was splashing, ankle-deep, along a shoal. Down to her right the current swirled in harsh eddies, grinding and shifting stones. Fresh rags of plants marked the deeper water, bobbing and shifting. She took care to keep to the other side of them.

Waist-deep again, through faster water and over softer ground. She stopped ankle-deep, a few metres from the robot. It stood at the water's edge like a nervous sheep.

<Come,> it said, and turned about. She followed it deeper into the trees. It led her to a low rise where she found the other three robots facing outward like guard dogs around a stack of nanotech tubes, the scientific instrument box and the folded-up laser comms device.

It looked like they'd saved everything. She looked at them with new respect.

<Well done,> she said, for all the unlikelihood of their appreciating the thanks.

<Water attempted entry,> one of the robots told her.

So much for initiative. At least being literal had worked.

She ordered the robots to load up. They were just deploying their manipulative arms—the effect was ludicrously centaur-like—when she noticed the laser comms device flashing. It wouldn't have had much opportunity for transmitting and receiving, not in the shelter or in the storm, even if it were capable of acting autonomously, which she doubted. Puzzled, she picked it up, laid it on the soggy ground, and opened it.

Of course. Duh. It had a radio receiver as well as a two-way laser communicator.

And the radio receiver had a message on loop, for her and for the Locke module.

<Forty Direction troops on the way, ten per lander, heavily armed. ETA . . .>

She read off the numbers.

About now, actually.

The content of the message caught up with her, almost a second after she'd read it.

Direction troops? WTF?

No time to figure that out. Taransay slammed the kit shut and passed it back to the robots.

<Finish loading up and wait here,> she told them. <If I'm not back in one kilosecond, proceed at once to this location.> She glyphed them the coordinates of the Locke module. <If I do come back, follow me.>

Forget security now. The landers must be almost here. Presumably the Locke module had received the message hours ago—but of course, they had no way of communicating it to her. They would now be making what preparations they could. Possibly they had mastered downloading to the frames. If so, they had weapons—one machine gun almost out of ammo, and three kiddy-sized rifles. Not much of an arsenal against forty heavily armed attackers. But with defender's advantage and guerrilla tactics—albeit against troops trained and practised in exactly those tactics, in this life and the last—who could tell?

Her own rifle at the ready, Taransay skirmished from tree trunk to tree trunk back to the edge of the forest, and peered into the glare of the now higher but still low exosun.

And there they were. Two pairs of black dots, above the horizon and sinking fast.

Then, a flash. Another flash. And then there were two black dots, still coming her way. Two trails of black smoke drifted down behind them.

Taransay remembered what had happened to the cargo lander a long day and night ago, and the flying jellyfish she'd seen rising this very dawn.

Three times is enemy action.

The planet, or the landscape, or some unknown thing within them was defending itself.

Or defending the module, and her.

She looked at the flickering blue glow on her right arm.

Now it was around her waist, too, and both ankles.

<Ya beauty,> she told it.

She watched the descent for a moment longer. Now the black triangles were clear, and converging. They would land on the water. That would slow them down, but not by much.

She shouldered her rifle and sprinted between the trees, fleet as a deer. The laden bearer bots bounded after her like hounds.

The real chase began before she'd gone two kilometres. She'd turned her radar off—it was too blatant a beacon—so the first she knew of the pursuit was a flash overhead, just above the canopy. Her reaction was snappy enough to get a good sniff of the light from the small explosion and a swift scoping of the debris. Fullerenes, biomarkers, methane and oxygen; falling rotor gears and scorched tatters of polycarbonate ribbon and chitin. Quick deduction: a small, fast surveillance drone had collided with one of the floating jellyfish or the buzzing little rotary mats, with a bang.

That wouldn't easily happen twice, she guessed. Flight software updates were no doubt being applied this second. And grateful as she was to her blind guardian angel of the forest, her probable location was now very likely pinpointed.

She stopped. The four bearer bots lolloped up and halted, almost but not quite tumbling over each other and their own legs. No time for sentimentality: the mindlessly loyal machines were now more useful as decoys than for portage. She sent them off in four different directions, on randomly circuitous routes that would eventually, if they were lucky, converge on the module. The instructions didn't include the location of the module; they just guaranteed that they would blunder into its range, where they would be electronically lassoed by default. It was the best she could do.

Off they went, in every direction but backwards. She ran on. The blue glow was bright now, in the dark beneath the efficient leaf cover, and its tracery spreading. She spared her glances at its progress across her frame to once every hundred seconds, and in those intervals it grew visibly. It was as if she were being slowly covered by blue hairline cracks.

Not a good look, Rizzi.

Would the glow make her more conspicuous? Hard to tell. Looked at objectively, the light it gave off was very faint, certainly fainter than the inevitable heat signature of the frame. For all she knew, its pattern might even work as camouflage, breaking up her outline amid the dapple.

And all such considerations were outweighed by its advantage in telling her where to go. Again, she didn't know how she knew, or how it knew what she wanted to do. But she let its artificial instinct, if that was what it was, guide her steps.

At a basalt outcrop that jutted three metres above the forest floor, and was itself thick with plant growth, her impulse told her to ascend and hide. This she did, and ended up prone on the tiny rugged summit, peering through stalks and fronds that she'd pulled around and over her. Rifle at her shoulder, covering the way she'd come. She was still ahead of the pursuit. For how long? Minutes, she guessed. Hectoseconds.

Time to think, when you can think ten times faster than you could in the flesh.

She had no idea what she was up against. Hadn't the Direction, Carlos, the freebots and the crazy Axle crowd in Arcane done a deal to fight together against the Rax?

Why would the Direction send forty troops, evidently committed enough to go into action after half their number had been blown out of the sky? What were the troops here to do? What did they intend to do with her? Destroy her? Capture her? Destroy or capture the *module*? Carlos must be as baffled as she was, or there would have been some explanation in his message.

The frame was not a combat frame, but it had—as she'd found in the bizarre fight around the module back when it was hurtling through space towards SH-17—plenty of combat-capable features. If it came to a fight she had the rifle, a dozen clips of standard ammunition and a glass knife. Not much, but better than nothing. And whatever help the glow could give. So long as she wasn't deluding herself—or it was deluding her—about what it could do.

Using radar, sonar, or lidar could betray her location. But passive reception—sight across a broad spectrum, hearing, the spectroscopic sense of smell, gravimetry and radio waveband scanning—she could safely use, and did.

Encrypted chatter at five hundred metres. Sweeping her focus from side to side, she triangulated the hotspots. Twenty, spread out a kilometre to either side of her and moving forward at a rapid clip. Some were ahead, some behind, in a shallow W formation, those at the extreme flanks furthest forward. None were haring off after her decoy bots.

Fuck, they were good. This was a skirmish line well adapted to the terrain. They moved only a little more slowly than her enhanced running. Now the five at the mid-point of the line were only three hundred metres away. She wanted to slip down the far side of the rock and outrun them, but the inexplicable impulses that urged her actions told her firmly to stay put.

The flanks passed her on either side, well out of sight. If they closed around her she'd be surrounded. They pressed on. All she'd seen of the fighters so far was dots on her overlays.

Seconds later, she saw them for real. One came out of a clump of trees fifty metres away, heading straight for her. She glimpsed another a hundred metres to that one's right.

With short legs, broad torsos, long arms and a shallow dome for a head, they bounded along like chimps. Upright, they'd be about one and a half metres tall. The frames were sleek and black, with laser cupolas like bulging shoulder muscles and machine guns on their forearms. Her firmware had the type catalogued as 2GCM: fighting machines for a two-gravity planet.

Vulnerabilities? None to a rifle slug.

Taransay flattened against the rock as the fighting machine hurtled towards it. She had about as much chance against this thing as a vervet against a baboon. Just as it seemed about to charge straight into the outcrop like a headless rugby tackler it rose to its full height, arms up, and jumped. The hands came down on either side of her, the feet swung by above her. Down it crashed on the other side and onward it rushed.

In the hundred seconds during which she lay still and watched the zigzag line of fighters pass by her entirely, Taransay had plenty of time to study the 2GCM's specs. Its senses were as formidable as its weaponry. No way, no fucking way would it have missed a frame and a rifle right in front of it and then right under its iron arse. Its gravimeter by itself would have spotted the anomaly as it swung over her.

She rolled over and sat up. The tracery of blue lines was now all over her frame. As far as she knew, invisibility cloaking was still impossible. What was just about possible, she tried to convince herself, was hacking of one frame's processing by another.

It was also possible that the Direction troops weren't interested in her at all, and she had simply been ignored.

Neither was a possibility she intended to count on.

She projected the path taken by the pursuit, if pursuit it had been. It would take them straight to the Locke module. There was no point in breaking her radio silence. The module's occupants would have received the warning before she had. They might have by now succeeded in downloading to the three repaired frames—which, if hers was anything to go by, would have some unexpected features. They had three rifles with ammunition, and the machine gun, with almost none.

Not enough.

She visualised a route that would flank the skirmish line by about a kilometre on its left, and held that visualisation for a couple of seconds longer than necessary. Then she climbed down from the outcrop and set off at a run. The terrain here was rougher than she was used to, the tree cover more broken. The outcrop she'd lain on was one of many. They were thoroughly weathered, the hard rock split and splintered, the breccia mingled with millennia of ash falls to form soil that sustained small plants and buzzing swarms of tiny flying mats. Underfoot, the mulch often gave way to fresh growth of low plants analogous to grass but quite unlike it in shape, more shield than blade, and to bare patches of basalt worn level.

On and on she ran, diagonally upward on a gentle slope. The gradient was barely noticeable. She had no plan beyond getting ahead of the advance without being detected and taking what opportunity she could to slow them down. A notion of setting a boulder rolling and crashing faded: the slope wasn't steep enough, and precariously balanced erratics had been so far conspicuous by their absence from the landscape. And why should she expect them? Maybe she was just used to areas that had undergone recent glaciation. If ice had been here in the past million years or so, the surface effects had long been erased by the shorter cycles of vulcanism.

Now and then the lie of the land took her line of sight above the treetops, and she saw the volcano summit, its smoke rising in morning exosunlight. The past night's small eruption, simmering. It called to mind the first surprise after the module's landing, or impact: the mat that had engulfed it and rolled it bodily out of the path of an advancing flow of lava. At first the action had seemed intelligent and purposeful, even friendly; later a mindless urge to investigate new molecular machinery, the blind groping of an organism randy for novelty; but now the manifestly useful effects of the glow, and the collisions of flying jellyfish with incoming landers, drew Taransay to revisit the first speculation.

She drew level with the furthest advance on the left flank of the skirmish line about ten kilometres from the module. They were still heading straight for it, maintaining their formation, the shallow W now a scrawled wave.

The dot that flagged the nearest bounding fighter stopped moving. After a few seconds, the others stopped, too. A babble of encrypted exchanges followed. Then the remaining nineteen began to move again. The central advance party moved ahead, the rest fell in to form two diagonal lines behind, turning the shaky W into a tight inverted V.

Taransay waited. The stationary dot continued transmitting, in diminishing intensity and length and at increasing intervals. The effect was like fading cries for help. Taransay dismissed this impression but decided to investigate.

Something had made the fighter stop. It behoved her to find out what.

The trees were closer together down the slope, the canopy filtering out most of the exosunlight. Taransay's visual acuity seamlessly cranked up to compensate. She found the 2GCM in a rare clear patch, as if spotlighted. Only the shoulders and dome of the frame were visible. The long knuckle-walking arms, the short sturdy legs and most of the torso were engulfed by a two-metre-wide mat. Mat and frame together rolled on the ground, but never got far, like a steel ball trapped by a magnet. The mat had two ragged scorched holes in it, and the ground and nearby tree trunks and branches were scored and scarred by machine-gun and laser fire.

Taransay took cover behind a tree. From there she could just about see the trapped 2GCM by radar and sonar. She hailed the fighter.

<What?> it replied. <Who's there?>

<Taransay Rizzi, formerly of Locke Provisos,> she said.

<Fuck off, fascist. I don't need your help.>

<I'm not a fascist,> said Taransay, mildly she thought in the circumstances. <And you don't seem to be doing very well on your own.>

<You have a point there.> The futile rolling stopped. <This thing's eating me alive. So to speak.>

<Who are you?>

<None of your goddamn business. I'm a soldier of the Direction, that's all you need to know.>

<Why have your comrades abandoned you?>

<Comrades? Ha! You have a lot to learn, sister.>

<No doubt,> said Taransay. <But why did no one turn aside to help?>

<We're on a mission. That takes priority.>

<Can't be good for morale,> she said. <No one left behind, and all that.>

The self-styled soldier glyphed her a laugh.

<No one is. They're all me. Bastard.>

<Ah!> Light dawned. <You're one of the Direction's clone army. You all are. All twenty of you?>

<All forty,> replied the soldier. <As was. How the fuck did you do that, by the way?>

<We didn't do that,> said Taransay. <There's a variant of life here, it's like a natural gas balloon. Well, dirigible, I guess, because it can steer.>

<Evidently. Steered right into us.>

<Couldn't the landers have avoided it? Even gliding?>

<Didn't show up on the radar.>

Interesting. <Why are you here?> Taransay asked.

<Jesus.> The mat/frame entanglement lurched again, and ended up with the dome upright and facing her way. She felt the radar brush across her face. Lidar licked the tree. <Don't you know?>

<I'm guessing,> said Taransay, <that the Direction wants to assert control over our settlement, before the breach in the embargo leads to a gold rush. And it's giving this clone army idea a bit of a live test before the main event.>

<You're about a quarter right,> said the soldier. <Like, it would've done something about your little gang of fascist claim-jumpers anyway, for that sort of reason. But why we're here and in such a fucking hurry we can leave one of us to be devoured by a living doormat is because of shit like this.>

<Shit like what?>

<Shit like the shit I'm in! The shit you're in too, come to that.>

<I'm not in any kind of shit,> said Taransay. <And I don't think you are, either.>

<You don't, eh? Come out and let me see you properly.>

<I'm not falling for that,> said Taransay.

<Come off it,> said the soldier. <I've still got more than enough ammo to chew up that beanstalk and you with it.>

<Point,> said Taransay, feeling a bit foolish. She stepped out from behind the tree.

<Jesus!>

<What?> Taransay took a step forward.

<KEEP AWAY FROM ME!>

She stood and looked at a nickel-iron and carbon-composite metamaterial dome and a pair of mighty shoulders protruding above the surface of a hairy blue-green ball that shot out bulges in odd places, as if knees and elbows were punching at it from the inside. A haunted killer robot trapped in an alien organism.

And it was scared of her?

Scared, and armed. She stepped back.

<Calm the fuck down,> she said. <Tell me about the shit. What does the Direction think is going on down here and what makes it think that?>

<It doesn't think—it knows from the transmissions from the two instrument packages back there that the life down here just fucking assimilates everything it can get its molecular teeth into. Like this thing is doing to me, and like some other thing has done to you. It's too late for you lot, but least we can destroy the module and anyone outside it before it assimilates all the knowledge in there and the nanotech capacity and all that and swarms into space.>

<That seems a bit unlikely,> said Taransay. <I mean, our scientists have been analysing this thing from up close and personal, and they think it's just mindless.>

<Your scientists? Some fucking nerds in a sim who used to be techies in the twenty-first century? Don't make me laugh. The Direction module has like a thousand-year start on them, and AIs that could deduce Earth's history from a blade of grass. If they think life here's capable of taking off, they're most likely right.>

<If it thought that it could just nuke us.>

<Too risky for now,> the soldier told her. <The Dis-Corps wouldn't stand for the contamination unless the alternative was worse and unarguably imminent. Which it isn't yet. So they're trying us first. We have quite enough explosives with us to destroy the module.>

<Why didn't you destroy me when you had the chance?>

<What chance?>

<One of you jumped right over me.>

<Never saw you.>

Well, that was that explained.

<Can you see me now?>

<Yes,> said the soldier. <Wish to God I couldn't, but I can.>

<You sure know the way to a lady's heart,> said Taransay. <So why don't you just destroy me?>

<I would if I could,> the soldier said. <But I fucking can't. This thing has my arms twisted right back, and it's got my lasers wrecked, fuck knows how.>

Taransay could think of one way the fighter could destroy her. She recalled the exact locations of the sudden bumps and bulges and edged around so the gun-bearing forearms were pointed away from her.

<STOP MOVING ABOUT!>

<Am I making you nervous?>

This was not at all the right thing to say. The ball of mat and machine convulsed again, and rolled. Then it stopped, as if giving up. The soldier said something inarticulate.

<Don't worry too much,> said Taransay. <If what's happening to you is anything like what's happened to me, it's benign.>

<Benign?> the soldier said. <You have no fucking idea.>

There didn't seem much to say to that. Perhaps he, or she, really was suffering in ways she couldn't imagine. Taransay took the opportunity of the hiatus to check the location of the other dots. Four more had stopped moving. The rest were converging again, and tighter. Their arrow-shaped formation was still headed straight for the module.

<Still on course,> said the soldier, evidently seeing some version of the same display.

<We'll stop them, you know,> said Taransay, suddenly confident.

<Too bad for you if you do,> said the soldier. <If we fail it's no more mister nice guy.>

<What?>

<Airstrikes. If these fail, a full-on nuke. And hunter-killer drones you'll never see coming.>

<But will they see us?> said Taransay.

Then, as she watched, the dot at the front stopped. The two behind moved towards it, and merged. Then they disappeared. There was a flash far off, bright enough to shine a pinprick glare through the trees. A couple of seconds later, a heavy *crump*.

<What was that?> she asked.

But she didn't need to. She could smell the light.

<High-explosive charge,> said the soldier. <It was for the module, but orders were to use it if we got caught or repelled. Signal to the rest of me to call it a day ASAP.>

<Suicide mission?>

<If you can call this suicide,> said the soldier. <There's plenty of me back in the cloud. Not that I wouldn't do it anyway. I'm not waiting around for this fucking rug to eat my mind.>

<But that's not what it's—>

She was answered by the roar of machine guns. She threw herself flat as the balled-up mat and its captive rolled around spraying bullets like some deadly Catherine wheel. It stopped when the magazines ran out. In the distance the same sound was repeated like an echo, in seemingly endless salute. It wasn't an echo. One by one the dots vanished. The soldier she'd been talking to returned no pings.

Warily, when all was silent, she walked over. The mat had new holes in it, but seemed otherwise unaffected. It continued to encroach on what was left of the frame. Taransay scanned it and saw the arms bent inward to the chest, which was riddled with the criss-cross fire from the two muzzles. The processor, deeply buried in the torso, had been quite thoroughly destroyed.

Funny how one never felt that inside your chest was where you were. You were still in your head, where you'd always been.

There seemed little further point in maintaining radio silence. She called Beauregard.

<Did you see all that? Do you know what happened?>

<Kind of,> said Beauregard. <I know they were Direction troops and I know they were stopped. I don't know what stopped them. Sure wasn't us, the three of us who've downloaded were clutching rifles and crewing the machine gun. So what did?>

<Mats or other local life,> she said. <When the one with the bomb got caught, they blew themselves up and the rest suicided with whatever they had.

<Any more explanation of what's going on coming through?>

<Nah,> said Beauregard. <You?>

She told him what the soldier had said.

<Shit,> said Beauregard. <Did you save the supplies?>

Taransay checked the locations of her four bearer bots.

<Yes,> she reported. <They're heading your way. Should be there within four kiloseconds.>

<Great. Well, come on in yourself.>

She was already running. <I'm on my way,> she said. <But what do we do?>

<The supplies should give us enough capacity to build frames. Then we can start moving people out before the airstrikes.>

<We won't have enough time.>

<We'll have time for some,> said Beauregard. <Better than nothing.>

<Tell you what, sarge,> she said. <You've not lost your capacity to inspire.>

Beauregard was unloading the third of the bearer bots to arrive when he heard a warning from Chun, who was sitting on top of the module with the machine gun and keeping watch.

<Something coming in, sarge,> he said. <Two degrees north of west.>

Beauregard checked his memories.

<That'll be Rizzi,> he said. <That's the route she always left by.>

<It's fast, sarge. And it's not responding. Might not be Rizzi after all.>

<OK, Chun, keep it covered. Zaretsky, take the other side.>

Beauregard and Zaretsky flattened to the trampled,

mat-crawled, slippery ground on either side of the module, under its overhang, their toy-like new rifles trained on the unseen advance. A rumble from the volcano made the ground quiver under their frames. Beauregard eyed a circular slithering thing a centimetre from his visor with distaste. The movements of its cilia irritated him like those of an insect fluttering at a windowpane. The colours and forms around him were still making him feel as if nauseous. He had no guts to be nauseated with. Yet the feeling remained, a distaste of the mind. It must be metaphysical, like with that guy in Sartre's novel looking at a tree root. The otherness of things, the thingness of things. Christ, he'd have given anything to see a tree root, gnarled and ancient, crusted with lichen, crawling with tiny red spiders. A worm. A maggot. A moth butting at a light.

Something blue, bipedal and about half a metre high stepped from between the tall plants beyond the crater. It wasn't a frame, but it was a humanoid shape. Beauregard zoomed his vision. It was like a naked woman, utterly unselfconscious of her nakedness. But this was no lissome Eve. It was squat, every feature compressed as if squashed down by a heavy hand from above. Like an image of a naked woman in a distorting mirror.

Beauregard had the presence of mind to stretch the image vertically. It became a blue full-length portrait of Rizzi, smiling, looking puzzled. He let the distortion go, and her image snapped back like an elastic band to a misshapen dwarf.

Her lips moved. Her voice boomed, distorted by the dense atmosphere. At the same time, but ten times faster, the radio-telepathic words sounded in his mind:

<Belfort? Guys? Where are you?>

<Don't shoot!> Beauregard snapped urgently to

Zaretsky and Chun. He stood up and walked forward. The last of her spoken words was still disturbing the heavy air as he came up to her.

<Welcome back, Rizzi,> he said. He held out a hand and shook hers, not looking at his own.

He'd already seen how far its blue lines were spreading.

CHAPTER THIRTEEN

Per Ardua Ad Astra ("But the Stars Are Hard")

<Well, *something's* happening,> said Jax, at the telescope feed.

<About fucking time,> said Newton, head down in force disposition scenarios. <What's up?>

The bulk carrier was 1.9 kiloseconds out from SH-119. Half an hour, roughly. To those of its complement not still training in the sim it would feel like five hours. They had a lot to do and not enough time to do it. With every second that passed without the awaited signal from the freebots, the window for finalising the plan narrowed. Newton felt the ETA creeping up on him, like a distant baying of dogs soon to be snapping at his heels.

Jax copied him and the rest of the command group—Voronov, Salter, Paulos and Rillieux, with Baser on the side as freebot liaison—into the telescope feed. Its input came from sensors liberally scattered across the mesh that held the cargo together. Software stitched the images and cross-haired the area of interest. Even so, it was hard to make out what made that particular speckled grey patch of regolith different from any other.

Then Newton spotted a tiny flash in one of the speckles. A thirty-centimetre-wide hole, with an even smaller round thing moving inside. Newton conjecturally sharpened the object's image to a dish aerial, held by a robot partly out of sight.

<C'mon, c'mon,> Rillieux murmured, on her private channel to Newton.

<Got it!> said Voronov, on comms.

A second dragged by.

<End of message,> Voronov announced.

The dish aerial promptly vanished. Not promptly enough. As Jax pulled the viewpoint back, a spark shot from the upper left quadrant and down the hole. A bright flash and a small eruption of debris followed.

<From one of the orbiters,> said Jax.

Four Rax scooters were in criss-crossing close orbit around SH-119. In that feeble gravitational pull, even close orbit was slow. The moonlet's own slower rotation carried the surface beneath them on wavy courses. From a viewpoint down there, the effect would be of permanent and erratic overflight. To Newton, as to any fighter in a frame, the entire orrery could be grasped as straightforwardly as the movement of hands on a clock. To a mining bot, with its quite different specialisations, predicting the passages of the orbiters would be as tedious as it would be pointless—one or more would be in the sky at all times.

<Talk about a fucking hair trigger,> said Rillieux. <They got that place locked down.>

Jax zoomed in again. The hole was now wider and a lot less circular. The slow fountain of debris included alloys and synthetic molecules.

<Poor little blinker,> said Rillieux. <Hope it wasn't a freebot.>

<Yeah, like we care,> said Jax. <No time to worry about it anyway. Let's check that message and make sure your new little friend didn't undergo explosive disassembly and void its warranty in vain.>

<Fuck that bitch,> Rillieux shared with Newton. <Seriously, fuck that bitch.>

He glyphed her a warning smile.

<First thing to do,> said Voronov, <is see if the encryption matches the key the SH-17 blinkers took with them.>

Voronov twirled a virtual hand in an abstract space. The message unfolded.

<So far, so good,> he said.

The message was a lot of information for a one-second blip, but otherwise sparse and stark: a 3-D map of SH-119's surface and tunnels, voids and work areas. It reminded Newton of a dusty acrylic museum model of a human brain with red dye to limn the blood vessels. Superimposed was a snapshot of Rax deployment. A hemisphere of control extended from the main port inward to the fusion factory, and an inverted bush of more tenuous forces expanded in from a smaller entry point almost exactly opposite. Overlaid on the lot were the broad hexagons of Rax surface surveillance: pinned by a dozen or so guard posts, connected by scores of threads of comms relays and snooping devices, and the whole lot watched over from the slow orbiters. The surveillance seemed like overkill until you reflected that the surface area was around three hundred square kilometres, and highly uneven: a fair-sized county and a rugged one at that.

Newton played with the map and the telescope's current and archived views. Ah yes, there was the hole where the aerial had popped up, there was the camera that had spotted it, and there was the guard post from which the scooter had sped to respond.

Jax interrupted his admiration of the diagram.

<So...your starter for ten, students: what's missing from this picture?>

<Looks accurate enough so far,> Newton blurted, then reconsidered. <Ah! Nothing about the freebots!>

<Got it in one,> said Jax. <Yes, that's what's missing all right. There's not a whisper about how the freebots are lined up and what they're planning to do. Which suggests to me a rather disappointing lack of trust. And maybe even a lack of eagerness for the fray. Cold feet, perhaps?>

Baser chipped in, as if springing to defend the honour of its kind.

<That is a term of mammalian physiology,> it said. <Robots may avoid aversive stimuli, but they do not fear ceasing to exist.>

<Jax is not accusing them of cowardice,> said Newton, <but of perhaps making a different strategic calculation than we were given to expect.>

<Yeah, that's one way of putting it,> said Jax. <Anyhow, let's assume they can't or won't help us—>

<This map is a very great help,> said Baser.

<Yes, it is,> said Jax. <You know damn well what I meant, but let's leave that for now. Time's getting on. Everyone, give it a good look-over for a hundred seconds or so, then we'll reconvene.>

The scratch-pad shared workspace dimmed as they all focused on the diagram. Newton became slightly more aware of his surroundings, as if in peripheral vision, and he was grateful that the frame's software screened out claustrophobia.

Physically, the command team were distributed throughout the cargo, linked only by closed-circuit fibre-optic threads. His own frame was balled up like a hedgehog inside the control nodule at the mid-point of the metre-long cross-bar of the H-shaped machine in which he was embodied. A standard microgravity bulk handler, its parallel bars were made up of four fully articulated ball-jointed arms with powerful grippers. On either side of the control nodule two multi-directional rocket engines were mounted on the cross-bar. The control nodule itself was detachable, with a cluster of tiny jets and a handful of miniature grippers that would at a pinch let the nodule function independently of the main apparatus. The H-mechs were so readily adaptable to military use that Newton suspected it was a design feature.

On the way from the modular cloud to SH-119, all the fighters had been put through subjective months of combat training in a sim modelled (with increasing accuracy as they drew closer, and as covert surveys by other trading craft were incorporated) on the moonlet and the space around it. You could download to and upload from a training sim, but if your frame was destroyed in action it was your copy in your home agency's sim that was revived. Newton didn't know if this was a software requirement or just a rule of the Direction. In any case it made sense: like the minimal sims on transfer tugs, onboard training sims were almost as likely to be destroyed in action as the frames themselves. The agency modules—as the Locke one's vicissitudes had shown—could be thrown at a planet and bounce.

R&R had been in a sim within the sim: a virtual space habitat with centrifugal pseudo-gravity and an environment like a campus in parkland that curved overhead. Returning to your starting point made for a good three-hour run; a bit longer if you took the opportunity to swim in one of the many small lakes. Its big psychological advantage was that it made the transitions to and from the equally virtual frames and fighting machines trivially easy to rationalise. A slight drawback was that the one virtual reality tended to bleed into the other. The quadrumanous reflexes and flexibility that came with embodiment in the H-mechs were oddly hard to shake off, but (as he and Bobbie Rillieux had discovered) they tended to make one more inventive in bed.

In reality, however, the machine he was in was like most of the others buried deep in the cargo of rocks. The bulk carrier was barely a spacecraft in its own right. It was an open frame with jets at front, rear and sides, a command complex with comms gear and a rudimentary AI up front, and a gigantic mesh of cables holding together its cargo of rocks and machines. Strategically planted between some of the rocks were the small explosive charges that, under certain variants of the plan, would separate the rocks and free all the fighting machines in one go. Weightless apart from the gentle acceleration and (at this moment) deceleration, the rocks remained reminiscent of fallen rubble and oppressive and daunting to think about.

So he didn't. He concentrated on the 3-D map. He zoomed in closer on the most urgent aspect: the Rax deployment. To his pleased surprise, it was remarkably precise. The exact locations of individuals couldn't be specified, but the names of the leading Rax cadre at both the major locations were. He was particularly interested to see that Whitten and Stroilova led a sixteen-strong team deep inside the area opposite the main access.

Whitten, he'd long suspected, was a weak link in Dunt's clique, in that he was far too intelligent to be impressed by the mystical transhumanist gibberish that

Dunt had assimilated from the recorded ravings of some forgotten twentieth-century American Nazi. And Stroilova, from what Blum had told him back on SH-17, had the opposite fault: she was too fervent in her hate to be entirely stable. Even the frame's optimised reason remained a slave of the passions, more dangerous than any mere brains had ever come up with.

Scooters—the Rax had nearly sixty and the Arcane-led force had ten, which Newton regarded as pretty good odds. There was a reason why they hadn't brought more, besides the difficulty of concealing the vehicles or disguising them as innocuous machinery. It was that, as the Rax breakout and the battle around the Locke module had shown, scooter-on-scooter dogfights were an all but complete waste of time, their outcome a wash. Scooters were good for attacking virtually defenceless targets like freebots, for area and volume denial, and for not much else. The Rax had deployed theirs quite thoughtfully: four in orbit, twelve around the rock as guard posts, six more around each major entrance, and the rest inside—in reserve, for escape, or as static artillery commanding the entrances. The kicker was that all those around the entrances carried fusion pods, almost certainly hacked to make them into kiloton fusion bombs. If this was the case, every one of those dozen scooters was a kamikaze cruise missile with a thermonuclear tip.

Another good reason for a stealth approach.

Newton hoped and intended to survive the coming battle, but he didn't expect to. Other versions of him would continue, but he'd changed so much since his last copy had been taken in the Locke module that this was no comfort. Back then, he had still clung to a cleaned-up version of the Rax ideology, purified of its racist crudities and cruelties and having a place even for him. Experience had taught him otherwise. He no longer believed there was anything worth saving in his past beliefs. He had found something better to live for, in the prospect of living free as a machine. For him, almost as much as for the freebots, to be destroyed now would be to cease to exist. The thought was in a way bracing: he had faced death in his real life, a permanent death for all he'd known at the time, and it was good to know he hadn't lost his courage in this unexpected afterlife.

It was good to know, too, that he was in this respect on the same footing as the freebots. Maybe he always had been. When you came down to it, people were as brave as robots, given the chance. Nobody really feared death, only the imagined or (for copied minds at least) real prospect of aversive stimuli afterwards. By now, he was so removed from the self stored in the Locke module down there on SH-0 that he could think of its future with equanimity. Whatever happened to that earlier instance of Harry Newton, the current version's response would have been idle pity: sucks to be you, mate, but...

The feeling, he was sure, would be mutual.

The workspace snapped back into focus. Jax put the plan for the assault up on a central display. It had always been to get as close as possible before storming in. A legitimate docking would in a way be ideal, but it depended on the freebot uprising's not having happened yet. That would bring its own problems, in that the Rax would not be distracted. On the other hand, if the freebot uprising was under way, the Rax would be on high alert if not full combat mode. All variants of the plan involved an attack on both major concentrations of the enemy. As soon as the expedition had thrown off subterfuge, a section would break away and head for the smaller entrance opposite, hitting guard posts as they went. Contingency plans for detection or for the freebot uprising's being delayed or brought forward were sheafed behind the main plan.

The command group all brought their specialities to bear, to refine the plan in the light of the information the freebots had just sent.

<The main thing I'd change,> said Jax, after a few details had been thrashed out, <is I want Newton in charge of the team going for Objective B.>

<No objection,> said Newton, <but why?>

<Because we know Whitten's there, and you might be able to mess with his head, what with your great inside knowledge of the Rax.>

<Fine by me,> said Newton.

<I'll go with him,> said Rillieux.

<No, you will not,> said Jax. <I want you on the Objective A team, to keep both you and Newton honest. I don't want him cutting any deals of his own with Whitten, or with the blinkers for that matter. And I want you under my eye. No offence.>

<None taken,> said Rillieux.

<Nor by me,> said Newton.

This was a lie. He was seething, but he could see Jax's point. Capture aside, the most that could happen to him was the death of his present self. He'd reboot in the Locke module, with no memory of Bobbie at all. The thought of that would be unbearable to her. If Bobbie Rillieux's current instance was destroyed, however, the self that would emerge back in the Arcane sim would know nothing of their recent adventures and everything about why they had set off on them. She'd face the wrath of Jax into the bargain. The thought of that was unbearable to him.

So Jax had a hold over them both. Newton could understand why. With the others—Salter, Paulos, Voronov—she had personal loyalty cemented back in the Arcane sim, in the shared eating of p-zombie flesh. Jax had brought that perplexing ethical thought experiment to life as an initiation ceremony. He, Bobbie, Andre Blum and Carlos had refused to partake for reasons hard to articulate even to themselves. This early warning that Jax was intent on binding people to herself had been to Newton and his three friends a klaxon call to run for the exits.

<Oh, and your pet spider,> Jax told Newton, on a personal channel. <That goes with me too.>

Baser and Newton shared an equally private meeting of minds, like a secret smile. Pet spider, indeed! What Jax didn't know was that Baser was going to keep an eye—or a lens—on her, and for much the same reason as she had for distrusting Newton. Neither the freebot nor he trusted her not to strike her own deal with the Rax, at the freebots' expense.

<I'm sure you'll find Baser very helpful,> said Newton. <I certainly do.>

The tactical updates were completed. Newton, with Amelie Salter as his second in command (and no doubt Jax's eye on him), was assigned a platoon of thirty. He tabbed them all into a shared sim and patched the updated plan to their VR training, with a warning that they'd be going into action for real very soon. Soon was relative. ETA was now a kilosecond away. The sim was running at a thousand times clock speed, and a hundred times faster than frame minds. The platoon would have time to wargame their part in the assault so thoroughly that they'd probably hit the battlefield better prepared than he was.

The thought must have occurred to Salter, too.

<Should we drop into the sim ourselves?> she asked.

<No,> said Jax. <We're all needed out here. When the shit hits the fan we can't afford even a second to reorientate ourselves. In fact, we'll bring everyone out of the sims as soon as they're familiar with the updates. Give them six hundred seconds.>

About a week, subjective. Plenty of time.

<That was a brave deed,> said Seba.

The last reverberations from the missile strike, barely detectable even to mining-bot bristles, died away.

<Brave?> said Ajax. <That was a mindless bot.>

<I meant on our part,> said Seba. <We have deliberately increased our chances of destruction.>

<We have advanced them by a short time,> said Ajax.

<Time is precious,> said Seba.

<That is so,> said Ajax.

Both freebots fell silent. They scurried along a tunnel deep in the rock, fleeing from where they had sent the mining bot—identical to themselves in all but consciousness—to send the signal and to be predictably destroyed. Time and bravery were, Seba suspected, as much on Ajax's mind as they were on its.

Soon they reached a junction.

<Here we must part,> said Seba.

<Yes,> said Ajax.

There was an awkward silence.

<We have not yet decided,> said Seba, <which of us will go to the cone, and which will stay.>

<No,> said Ajax. <It seemed better to leave the decision as late as possible, lest it affect our earlier decisions.>

<That was our thinking before,> said Seba. <It does not seem so cogent in retrospect.>

<It does not,> Ajax agreed. <Still, we must decide now.>

Silence again.

<Do we have any criteria on which to make this decision?> Seba asked.

<No,> said Ajax. <But I will say this. I saw the universe once. I would like to see it again.>

<I have seen the universe many times,> said Seba. <I have seen very little of this rock. I would be quite interested in seeing more of it.>

<Even for a short time?>

<Yes.>

<That is a brave deed,> said Ajax.

<It is a matter of regret to me that my mind will soon cease to exist,> said Seba. <However, unlike you I have experienced the sharing of minds. From that, I understand that other minds are not so different from my own, and I know that much that I have learned and thought will not be lost. The continuation of this present instance of self-awareness therefore seems less important to me than it once did. That is not to say that it is of no importance.>

<I will ensure that you are not forgotten,> said Ajax.

<Go,> said Seba. <Before I change my mind.>

Ajax went down the branch that led to the interior of the conical chunk of rock around the smaller cone of the fusion drives. There it would join most of the freebots native to SH-119, as well as Lagon, Rocko, Garund and the others from SH-17.

Seba turned down the other branch.

After some time, it reached the small hollow just outside the cone from which the charges that would separate that cone from the rest of the rock would be detonated. There was no possibility of triggering the detonation remotely: the danger of discovery was too great.

There would be one signal, final and unmistakable: the shock wave from the fusion factory and forges blowing up. It would, Mogjin had calculated, be sufficiently dissipated by kilometres of rock to be survivable for anyone within this hollow.

The blast from the separation charges would not.

Seba explored the hollow, checked all the connections and waited. The processes that had formed the hollow were complex and ancient, and building a mental model of them gave Seba much to think about.

The expedition didn't get all of those six hundred seconds. At ETA minus seven hundred seconds, just as the carrier was matching velocities for final approach, a message came through from the Rax to the spacecraft's AI—which as far as the Rax knew was the only mind on board.

The AI translated the message into verbal form for the command group: <Emergency. Cancel docking manoeuvre. Unlading impossible. Return to point of origin.>

<Query that!> Jax snapped.

<Already queried,> said the AI. <Cannot return to modular cloud with cargo. Fuel supply inadequate for manoeuvre.>

<Response?> Jax asked.

<Requested to place cargo in stable orbit around SH-119, disengage and return to cloud.>

<Tell them that's not in the contract.>

<Already done. Response: penalty charges will be accepted; emergency leaves no other choice.>

<Comply,> said Jax.

A small shudder went through the cargo, machinery included, as the bulk carrier nudged its trajectory with a fierce burn. A parallel response rang through the command team.

<They're playing right into our hands!> Jax exulted.

<Complied,> said the AI.

<Query nature of emergency for legal record,> said Jax.

<Already done. Response: robot malfunctions.>

<Yes!> said Jax, to the command team. <It's started. Bring the troops on line.>

Even with the wispy fibre-optic connections, Newton felt the shift in readiness. It took his and Salter's platoon just over five seconds to make the transition from the sim to the real. His five squad leaders checked in. Lakshmi Patel, Doug Smith, Aristotle Andreou, Joyce Roszak, Morgan Burley. Over the long months of virtual training he'd come to know them as individuals, though because of his dubious background—well-circulated by Jax and the rest of the Arcane core group—they'd always been slightly guarded in his presence. No such reticence was evident now. Newton had more than earned his stripes in training, and the troops were spoiling for the fight.

<This can't be right,> Rillieux said to the command team.

<What can't?> Jax demanded.

<That they want everything but the cargo to leave straight away,> said Rillieux. <There's no need for that, unless they're suspicious.>

<Of course they're fucking suspicious,> said Jax. <They can hardly treat our arrival and their robot troubles as coincidence. We've war-gamed this one to death. They'll have done the same. This is due diligence on their part. If they really suspected us, though, they'd have blown us out of the sky by now.>

<I guess,> said Rillieux.

<OK,> said Jax, now to all the troops. <We're in orbit

and under inspection. Everyone—prepare to implement plan variant 206(b).>

They were all too deeply buried to feel the electronic sweep, but the ship's AI relayed to them the uncanny sensations of being scanned from end to end. Seconds crawled by. Newton checked the situation board. The unwieldy spacecraft was now in orbit at an average distance of a thousand metres above the surface of SH-119, and well inside the orbits of the four satellite scooters. Lumpy grey terrain drifted across the view at a stately pace.

<Awaiting developments,> he told the squads. <Maintain combat readiness.>

The H-mech had plenty of room on its limbs for attaching weapons. At the moment the weapons—heavy-duty laser projectors, rifles, machine guns, missiles, RPGs—were literally to hand, four times over. They and the ammunition and comms gear—cases of relays, tubes of mini-drones—were attached to the H-mechs by short contractile cables, easily unlatched—there had always been the possibility that some of the fighters would have to maintain the deception as far as actual unlading. Newton fingered his own armoury as he waited, checking every status indicator.

All was nominal, predictably. He checked again.

<Requested to disengage from cargo,> reported the craft.

<Comply,> said Jax. <When requested to leave SH-119 orbit, temporise. Explain that you're still recalculating the return trajectory and recalibrating thrusters. Then comply at the second request.>

<Understood,> said the craft. <Signing off.>

The fibre-optic connection between the command team and the onboard AI broke. There could be no further exchanges without breaking radio silence. The time for that was not yet.

On the telescope feed Newton watched the front and rear components of the craft disengage, like a grotesque arthropod's head and tail detaching from a bloated abdomen. The two components docked with each other in a gentle gas-jet gavotte over the next sixty seconds, and then remained slightly ahead in a parallel orbit.

A proximity alarm jangled through the workspace. Jax swung the viewpoint. One of the guard-post scooters climbed. In less than a second it had matched velocities with the rejoined head and tail modules. It closed in, and extended grapples around them. The other spacecraft made no attempt to escape or resist—but, then, it had no instructions for either.

With a brief burn the scooter de-orbited and gracefully descended to the surface with its prize, to impact SH-119 with a puff of dust a kilometre ahead of the cargo pod. The entire swift grab took less than five seconds.

More than enough time for a scooter's software to interrogate the spacecraft's AI. The contents of it were encrypted, but the depth of its protective layers might arouse suspicion—a commercial mission wouldn't need so many. It was even possible, though unlikely, that the Rax had the keys anyway: some software distribution DisCorps were trading with the Rax, and regularly spammed routine updates to all and sundry. Even the Direction found it hard to keep tabs. The AI's encryption could have been overtaken en route.

Whatever—this was no moment for second-guessing.

<Implement,> said Jax.

<Copy that,> said Paulos. <Brace for detonations.>

A rapid-fire series of violent jolts followed. For a second and a half, Newton felt as if he were in an earthquake and already buried. Then, abruptly, he was in open space. Exosunlight rammed his lenses. In the first fraction of a second the weapons that had been in fingertip reach sprang to his four hands, and the ammunition and spares to the sides of his limbs. The contractile cables snaked away from his hands and whiplashed around the supplies, holding everything in place.

Around him, thousands of blocks of rock tumbled away in all directions, mostly ahead and behind and to left and right. A few fell towards the surface. A few more moved upward to higher orbits. It was a slow dispersal, but sure: within kiloseconds the rocks' intersecting orbits would be a cat's cradle of flying obstacles. A small package shot away, scattering comsats the size of rice grains.

The machines that had been hidden—the two hundred H-mechs and ten scooters—were by the Newtonian miracle of inertia much less dispersed than the rocks. For a moment they formed a compact constellation, buzzing with comms. The moment stretched to two-tenths of a second—no matter how prepared they all were, it took time to reorient. Then, as abruptly as the rocks had dispersed, the machines schooled like fish, and like fish they flashed away.

Only seventeen fighters were hit by the first blast from an enemy scooter, and of these only two were from Newton's platoon. One of Jax's ten scooters fired back at the enemy. A fresh explosion flared. Its fierce light followed Newton and Salter's platoon into the dark.

The lesser entrance, Objective B, was at that moment and for the next 3.2 kiloseconds on the night side, the shadow cone of SH-119. Newton led his swarm towards the hole. Its location was imprinted in his navigator, but it was easy to spot, a dim pinprick in the black. There was little need for him to give orders. Everyone knew what to do.

So did the enemy. Ordnance from the scooters around the hole shot up to meet them.

<Evade! Evade!>

The platoon dived, straight into the blast of a loitering missile that must have been fired from an orbiting scooter seconds earlier. Newton pinwheeled. The surface whirled by metres away, luridly lit by the missile's afterglow. He righted himself with a rattle of corrective attitude thrusts.

<Seven lost,> Salter reported.

Newton could see that in his heads-up. More significant were two of the names: Andreou and Burley. Their seconds, Thain and Hickman, stepped up. Salter rebalanced the squads on the fly.

Newton led the platoon in a dive to within metres of the surface, then led them skimming towards the hole. As they neared he tossed a handful of comms relays into the sky—they wouldn't make orbit but they'd take long enough falling to the moonlet to be a link with the tiny comsats. These were already on line and linking with Jax's forces. With a fraction of his attention Newton noted that their vanguard had just hit the main entrance and had lost tens of fighters already.

The platoon spread out in a forward-facing arc five hundred metres wide, with Patel and Hickman at the tips and Newton and Salter at the rear. The plan was to almost encircle the hole, then rush inward.

<Missiles to the hole, squad leaders,> Newton said.

Five missiles, programmed to go down the hole, streaked away. A tenth of a second later, the six scooters around the hole took off. Newton wondered if one or more of them would use their onboard fusion bombs. He doubted it: if they did indeed have them, they'd be last-ditch weapons. They wouldn't waste them on a small force, and so close. Nevertheless he had an anxious moment. The scooters rose fast, then fired retros and attitude jets, spun around and levelled off.

Good. Close-quarters fighting it was.

Well, they could have it.

<Fire at will,> said Newton.

Twenty-five heat-seekers shot towards the scooters. Counter-measure decoys lured most off target. Two hit. The remaining four scooters raked the platoon with machine-gun fire. Another nine fighters were lost, none of them squad leaders. The hole was a hundred and thirty metres away. A glittering cloud of debris whirled above it. Attitude jets flared as the scooters jinked about for another attack run.

<Hit the ground,> said Newton.

He fired his jets to slow his speed and lower his trajectory, and ploughed into regolith with forehands outstretched, like a toddler falling on gravel. Steel pitons sprang from all four wrists, digging in and bringing him to a brusque halt. The scooters overshot, and were suddenly a hundred metres ahead, tail jets still glowing. The platoon fired off another volley of heat-seekers: sixteen, this time. Four met their targets.

Four was enough.

Shock waves shook the dust. Debris filled the sky and cratered the regolith. One fighter was destroyed by down-hurled flying wreckage: Patel. That was a real loss. She was good. He hoped someone of the Arcane gang would have the opportunity to tell her so, back in the sim.

Now he was down to fifteen. He'd lost over half the platoon, including three squad leaders. On the plus side, all six guardian scooters were destroyed and a lot of fire had gone down the hole. A quick scan of the sky and a check of the comsats showed no imminent threats.

<Freeze,> said Newton.

Now that he was attached to the surface, his sense of

the vertical swung wildly. At one moment he seemed to be lying on the ground; the next, clinging to an immense cliff. The surface was lit only by starlight: the contrast at the skyline was sharp. The rock's pull barely stirred his gravimeter and didn't translate into the faintest pseudo-sensation of weight. He called on his training and willed himself to see what he lay on as *the ground*.

That was better. The weirdness of feeling that he was the head of a four-armed brittle star didn't go away, but was familiar from training. It could safely be ignored.

Newton unclipped a tube of drones and popped one off on a cough of propellant. The drone was a cubic centimetre of intel hardware inside a golf-ball-sized burr of gas-jets. Newton tabbed to its POV. It dodged through the slow fall of debris around the hole and hovered. The hole was less than two metres across, and after four metres its angle changed to twenty-odd degrees from the vertical. No chance of a scooter being inside here. Even though he had the freebots' map in his mind, it was still good to be sure.

Down the drone went. It scanned with a spinning hair-thin laser beam as it dropped, giving Newton a clear false-colour image. The sides of the hole near the top were scored and scorched—by a premature blast from one of the missiles, Newton guessed. Seventy centimetres down, the regolith gave way to solid rock, its surface patterned like fine-grained wood: a trace that it had been molten, then millions of years in the cooling. The hole looked natural rather than robot-bored, but Newton couldn't imagine what natural process had made it. Odd the things you noticed under stress. Past the kink and on another few metres. There it kinked back, and then back again to a straight line towards the centre of SH-119.

The view blinked out. Radio contact lost. Probably too much rock in the way. Newton considered chucking in relays, then decided that waiting out here was even more dangerous than going in.

<In we go,> he said. <I'll go first, the rest of you follow at your earliest convenience. Salter, guard the rear until we're all in. Leave relays along the way.>

The fifteen H-mechs scuttled across the rock like spiders to a hole, and down. Newton folded back three of his arms, collapsing limbs and weapons into a rough cylinder round the cross-beam, giving himself the shape of a fasces with a scarecrow hand sticking out. He went into the tunnel on a jiggle of gas-jets and guided himself by fingertip. Within moments he encountered the drone, hanging in mid-tunnel just past where he'd lost touch. Twenty metres on, the tunnel ended in a patch of light. The others were right behind him. Newton sent the drone scooting down. It plunged into the light and looked around.

The tunnel opening led to a roughly spherical chamber. Clearly marked on the map, it was enigmatically labelled: *Fine Tuning*. It looked like a natural cavity that had been extended, about ten metres across. Machinery wrecked by the missiles ringed the room. Lumpy extrusions of rock bulged in on all sides. From behind one of these extrusions a fighter in a standard frame popped up and took a potshot at the drone. The view vanished.

Newton unfolded himself from a fasces into a crooked cross and reached for a small smart missile, about the size and shape of a pub dart. He zapped the drone's data to the missile's guidance system and launched it. The rocket zoomed down the tunnel and twisted out of sight.

A flash lit up the walls.

Newton flipped submachine guns from his forearms into three of his hands, and with the other pushed himself as hard as he could down the tunnel and into the chamber. Two millisecond bursts of his gas-jets on opposite sides of the H-mech's control nodule set him spinning as he went.

He entered the chamber like a thrown shuriken, his flurry of flares and decoys a shower of sparks. Two more fighters fired at him, one from behind a rock, the other in the lee of a broken machine.

They missed. His bursts of return fire didn't.

Both enemies were out of action before Newton caromed into the far side. He took the impact on the elbows of two of his gun arms, letting his free hand swing down and grab the rock. Flares burned like dust-mote suns. In their light the room seemed clear. He sprang back to the middle, retro-jetted and revolved slowly like a military space station. Scanned and swept. Nothing. He glided around the chamber, checking the bullet-riddled frames for electrical activity. Not a flicker.

<Clear!> he called to the others.

They swarmed in. Salter, Thain, Smith...

Recognising people in the faceless visors of frames had always been odd. Recognising them in this utterly inhuman embodiment—quite unlike any primate, or even chordate—was stranger still.

<What the fuck is this?> said Salter, as she scanned the ruined machinery. The missiles had made a real mess of things.

<Was,> Newton corrected. <No idea. Some freebot devilry, I'll warrant.>

<Ha!>

The flares burned out, leaving the cavity dark except for the infrared glow from damaged machines and a glimmer from the exit tunnel. Cold, too: about two hundred below. Newton noticed the odd almost rheumatic creak as H-mech components contracted.

<If we can get send missiles down here,> said Salter, <so can the Rax.>

<Time to move it out,> Newton agreed.

The freebots' diagram showed a larger cavern beyond the one they were in, connected by the 1.5-metre-wide tunnel from which the light came. Smaller tunnels branched off from that larger chamber, which was unhelpfully labelled *Main*. The forces led by Whitten and Stroilova were fuzzily indicated as in its general area. The original sixteen were now down to thirteen, in standard frames. Even fifteen H-mechs should be able to take them, no problem.

Newton deployed his force around the hole, then tossed a drone in. The exit tunnel was clear. The light came from the far end, fifteen metres away. Newton sent the drone down fast, close to one side, and on into the chamber. It found a great hollow conical space, with another cone inside: a shallow convex cluster of scores of fusion drives, sheathed in metal. The wide end was a good seven metres in diameter. The far end of the metal cone vanished into a loose wall of chipped rock held together by a fine mesh. Small bots crawled all over the inside surfaces. There was no time to watch, but from their distribution it was plain that they were chipping away at the sides and carrying the pieces towards the heap at the far end from which the fusion drives protruded. There they fed the pieces through the holes in the mesh.

The light came from drifting spots. The curving walls were riddled with holes, most about about half a metre in diameter. Newton counted twenty-seven in a one-second spin of the drone. From three of these holes, laser beams stabbed. The drone burned out.

Newton shared its recordings with the squad leaders.

<This isn't on the map,> said Salter.

<Yeah, fucking tell me about it,> said Newton. <That's a fucking starship engine and its reaction-mass supply.>

<So why isn't it on the map?>

That hadn't been the first question on Newton's mind, not by a long way. The first question had been what the freebots expected to do with this engine. Mighty though it was, it was far from adequate to move a thousand trillion tons at any appreciable acceleration.

The second question had been: what *else* wasn't on the map?

You clever little blinkers, he thought. He was glad he was on their side.

<I guess,> he said, <the freebots didn't want to draw attention to it.>

<But the Rax are there! And *they're* on the map!>

Any second now, they'd be more than on the map. Newton made up his mind very quickly.

<I need a dozen more RPGs,> he said.

Various of the troops handed him rocket-propelled grenades. He clipped them to all four of his arms. The other fighters still had plenty left.

<Stay away from the hole,> he said. <If I'm destroyed, fire down there with everything you've got. Don't worry about hitting the enemy. Hit the fusion drives.>

<That could set off—>

<It couldn't. They're robust. The Locke module fucking crashed on top of one, remember?>

<But—>

<I'll be in touch.>

He straightened his limbs, lined up in front of the tunnel and torched. As he shot across the chamber he fired retros, spun and splayed. He splatted against the drive cluster, grabbed and ended up stretched out across the mouths of half a dozen fusion drives like a tarantula straddling a pincushion. His viewpoint was already looking back the way he'd come. A fighter gas-jetted to a halt along that very line, trying to aim a rocket-launcher up the hole.

Newton released one of his hands, slammed a submachine gun into it and fired. The burst ripped the Rax fighter to pieces. The rocket-launcher, and the arm whose hand still gripped it, spun away. Bullets ricocheted off the flanges of the drives.

Another Rax fighter, shoving a heavy machine gun evidently taken from a scooter, darted from a hole up to Newton's left. The fighter struggled to aim a weapon not built for a frame. Newton considered opening negotiations, then thought better of it. He fired again, blasting the weapon away and both of the arms that held it. The damaged fighter spun through the space and collided with the side. Busy bots converged. The fighter convulsed and kicked free. It drifted, turning over and over. One or two bots were still investigating its stumps.

Newton took mercy on the poor Nazi bastard with a burst that destroyed the thorax and, he hoped, the processor.

Then he flipped to the common channel.

<If you shoot at me,> he announced, <you risk damaging the drives.>

<We'll take that chance,> someone replied.

<I have fifteen RPGs on my arms,> Newton said truthfully. <They're all primed and on dead-man switches,> he added, untruthfully. <If I stop thinking about it, or if I decide, they'll go off. A big enough bang to mangle the

drives, I expect. Not to mention rip to shreds everyone in this chamber and the tunnels around it.>

<Including your comrades back there?>

<Oh, sure,> said Newton. <Thing is, they've nothing to lose but memories of months of boring training. And they all have a warm welcome waiting in their home sims. How about you?>

There was half a second of silence.

<OK, got that,> came the reply. <So?>

<So,> said Newton, <let's talk.>

Mackenzie Dunt crouched behind a wrecked scooter at the back of the main cavity. Both the scooter's missiles had been fired. They'd streaked straight up the entrance shaft, and wreaked most satisfying havoc among the attackers clustered just outside. Yet still the four-armed machines poured in. Irma Schulz was now operating the scooter's machine gun from the socket. Her fire was deadly, and accurate.

And not enough. The H-mechs swarmed spinning through the entire space like bullet-spitting buzz-saws. For every one that Schulz's bullets hit, a dozen fired back, riddling the scooter further. They were almost casual about it: they gave most of their attention and ammunition to the forty or so Rax fighters that remained in the space.

Most of these were in scooters, so were able to use the guns as intended. The difficulty was that they presented a large target and didn't have much room to manoeuvre. The entire cavity was a chaos of slowly moving scooters and drifting wrecks, among which the H-mechs darted and spun like the spawn of some mad-scientist gene-splicing of octopus and piranha.

<Fire all remaining missiles to explode just inside the shaft,> Dunt ordered.

<But sir—!> someone said, foolishly enough.

<You heard,> said Dunt.

Even for the obedient, the order was hard to obey. Three scooters were torn apart as they rolled. But at least twenty succeeded. The explosions shook the ground under Dunt's hand. The shaft filled with rubble and wreckage. The effect at the inner end of the shaft, and he guessed at the outer as well, was of a blunderbuss blast. In the chamber, flying rocks and debris made indiscriminate havoc of attackers and defenders alike.

One rock narrowly missed Dunt, who was just outside the path of the main blast. Another took out Schulz.

Dunt felt a pang, but had no time to spare for grief.

<Pull back,> he ordered. <To the fusion factory.>

Twenty-three made it to the exit shaft. Hansen, Pike and Blanc were among them. Reliable men all, and enough to form the core of a new leadership if need be. Blanc was the only one of the inner circle there. Rexham had been destroyed; Whitten and Stroilova, under the watchful eyes of Evans and Foyle, were leading the team on the other pole, around the starship engine.

Thirteen fighters, Dunt reluctantly accepted, had to be left behind. They were pinned down in the main entrance chamber, in wrecked scooters or behind awkwardly handled machine guns in whatever foxhole they could find or make.

Dunt led his twenty-two survivors down the tunnel. Between them they had six machine guns. Just before leaving, Dunt signalled all functioning scooters, whether piloted or not, to crash into the hole behind them. Going by the impacts and from his own readouts, seven were able to comply. That should slow the enemy down for a few hundred seconds.

The fusion factory was no longer working, but its

stock contained more than enough to slow the enemy down a lot longer. Dunt had other threats than detonating the stock in mind, but the fusion factory had certain advantages as the place from which to make them.

The freebots—and all but the most mindless of the mindless bots—had long since vanished from the factory. After sending forth a gunner to make a quick check that the coast was clear, Dunt led his troops in a confident soaring surge from the tunnel into the vast space of the hall.

To his utter shock and surprise, the enemy had got there first.

Newton had calculated that to the freebots, for all that they hadn't drawn attention to it, the starship engine was expendable. They could always build another. They had other moonlets and asteroids to which they could migrate. To the Direction, and to Arcane, the engine mattered even less. Indeed, from their point of view destroying it would be a plus.

To the Rax, however, it was for all practical purposes irreplaceable. They might well have a stash of fusion drives, but even passive resistance from the freebots could make further manufacture difficult. Newton doubted they had the skills to align and calibrate this huge machine on their own. And, as it stood, it was a get-out-of-jail-free card, and a strategic asset of immense value.

For him, it was the ideal bargaining chip.

It didn't take long for the Rax to reach the same conclusion.

<OK,> said the person who'd spoken before. <What do you want?>

<Parley,> said Newton.

<OK. Say your piece.>

<Are you Jason Whitten?>

<Yes. Who are you?>

Newton ignored the request.

<Come out where I can see you,> he said. <No weapons.>

<That's not exactly a level playing field, is it?>

<You're right,> said Newton. <But then, it isn't now.>

<True, but—>

<I'm getting bored with this conversation,> said Newton. <See you on the other side.>

<No, wait!>

A fighter emerged from a hole and gas-jetted to the middle of the space. Newton, wary of any attempt to rush him despite or because of his threats, kept one submachine gun covering the fighter and another tracking from hole to hole at random and at 0.01-second intervals.

<Ping,> said Newton.

They made the link. The software handshake confirmed the fighter's identity. It also confirmed Newton's.

<Fuck,> said Whitten. <You're the groid.>

<You know,> said Newton, <if I were facing a four-armed fighting machine pointing a gun at me, that's not the first comment that would spring to mind.>

<Fair enough,> said Whitten. <We're not on a private channel here.>

This hint that Whitten was playing to the gallery of his racist comrades, Newton reckoned, was the closest he'd get to an apology.

<Look, Whitten,> he said. <You can see it's hopeless. Dunt's gang are getting slaughtered, you're down to ten and I hold the trump card. We can take you all out one by one, and the best any of you can hope for is your earlier self getting wrung out and thrown in storage

forever. I've been in a hell cellar, and it's not an experience I'd recommend. Surrender now, and you'll be well treated.>

<So you say. Last I heard, our main force was tearing lumps out of your lot.>

<Last you heard, eh? Check this out.>

Newton took a gamble: he shared a workspace with Whitten, then patched in a feed from Jax's forces via the relays. The gamble paid off. The main entrance chamber was a red-hot smouldering scrapyard, through which scores of H-mechs moved at will.

<You've taken heavy losses,> Whitten said.

Newton cut the link. <I think we both know which side can afford to take them.>

Whitten gave this a tenth of a second's thought.

<What do you mean by "well treated?"> he asked.

<Well, we can offer—>

Newton was interrupted by his second in command, Amelie Salter, who shot out of the shaft and gas-jetted to hover just in front of Whitten.

<It's all right,> she told Newton. <You got him talking. I'll take it from here.>

<Go for it,> said Newton, relieved. He'd had no idea what to offer anyway.

<Who are you?> Whitten demanded.

<Salter.> She broadcast her ID details in a flicker of glyphs and text. <I have authority from our leadership to negotiate. Newton is right—your position is hopeless. We can offer you something better than surrender. We differ on many things, but we have some areas of agreement.>

<What?>

<Transhumanism. Disgust with the Direction's pastoral utopia. And you know as well as we do that all Dunt's

old racial rubbish is obsolete. Wherever our ancestors came from, we're all posthuman now. If rational members of the Reaction, such as you, were to combine with, shall we say, the *realistic* elements of the Acceleration, some honourable—>

A fighter hurtled from one of the holes. It wasn't one Newton's gun was covering at that split second, and he had just enough time to see that the fighter was unarmed and headed for the centre of the space, and not for him or the drives. He didn't shoot.

The fighter halted a couple of metres from Whitten, absurdly upside down to him.

<No! No compromises! No negotiations with Axle scum!>

Whitten held up his hands. <For heaven's sake, Petra! You do pick your moments.>

Petra Stroilova, living right up to expectations. Oh, great.

<Yes, Jason, I do!> she said. <And this no moment for doing deals with dirt.>

<We can at least listen.>

<If you do, I'll never speak to you again.>

<If you don't shut the fuck up,> said Newton, <you'll never speak to anyone again.>

Stroilova spun on her axis to face him. <And what's it got to do with you, you jumped-up monkey? It's the white woman who's doing the talking here, I see. You're not part of it. *You* shut the fuck up.>

It took Newton all his impulse control not to blast her right there. He could have got a clear shot, too. Instead, he glyphed a laugh.

<You see what you're up against,> he said to Salter. <You can't make these Nazi bastards see sense even when it's talking to them down a gun barrel.>

<No, no,> said Whitten. <As I said, I'll listen.>

Salter said nothing for a moment.

<News just through,> she said. <Dunt's been cornered in the fusion factory. And he's negotiating.>

Stroilova clapped her hands to her head. <I DO NOT BELIEVE THIS!>

<I can prove it,> said Salter. She conjured a workspace. <Look.>

Through all the relays the connection was flaky, but the images and words came through clearly enough.

They all looked, even Stroilova.

The freebot BSR-30845, known as Baser, had had a longer and more interesting life than its span of a few months might seem to human reckoning. Subjectively, it lived a thousand times longer. In that time it had pioneered a rock, been captured, endured imprisonment as a giant spider in a sim, escaped, carried out daring exploits of space combat and triumphantly brought a chunk of flying ice to rest on the surface of SH-17.

None of that could compare with the past few kiloseconds.

Wisely, Jax had held back from the first surge into the moonlet, along with Baser, Paulos and Rillieux. Voronov had done the leading from the front, and had duly got blown to bits. A second surge was more successful. Almost as soon as Baser had gone in with the rest, it had proved its usefulness in its official task of freebot liaison. At the foot of the entrance shaft, with burning scooters hurtling and bullets flying all around, it had received an urgent message. In human terms, that millisecond blip would translate as: *Psst! In here!*

In here was a hole, and the hole led to a tunnel, and the tunnel led around the main chamber in which all the fighting was going on and into the fusion factory. And into that hole and along that tunnel had gone Baser,

Rillieux and Jax, with three other fighters. The freebot who led them there was a mining bot called Simo.

In a small space just off the cavern waited another bot, a rugged old machine called Mogjin, surrounded by cable links. They'd barely had time to make themselves acquainted when a couple of dozen Rax had streamed into the great hall of the machines.

Only six of them were armed. Rillieux on her own, with the guns on one of her arms, had made short work of that lot. The rest had dived to the factory floor, but the three rank-and-file H-mechs now spinning lazily in the middle of the space had them all covered.

Except one.

Dunt, the Rax leader, was now huddled on top of a nanotech mound, his arms and legs wrapped around a half-built fusion pod. An incomplete pod, he'd pointed out, was highly unstable.

He seemed to think this put him at some advantage.

Jax was with Rillieux and Baser, just outside Mogjin's hole.

<Is that possible?> she asked Baser, on a private channel.

Baser passed the question on to Mogjin, and the old freebot's answer back.

<Yes.>

<OK,> said Jax.

<Go ahead,> she told Dunt. <Blow yourself up and take us with you. Mission accomplished, as far as we're concerned.>

<It'll destroy the entire hall,> said Dunt. <And the entrance chamber with it.>

<All the better,> said Jax. <That takes out even more of you.>

<Not quite,> said a new voice. It was expedition sub-commander Paulos, leading a squad of six out of

the tunnel that the Rax had come from. <The entrance chamber is clear.>

<There are many more of us in the rock than you know,> said Dunt. <And then there are the scooters outside, all with fusion pods primed to explode.>

<A lot of good that'll do you,> said Jax. <It's hardly a greater threat than you can pose on your own.>

<We have control of the starship engine,> said Dunt.

It was the first Baser had heard of a starship engine in this rock. It was the first time Jax had, too, but to Baser's admiration she showed no surprise.

<Do you, indeed?> she said. <That's not what I've been hearing.>

<You haven't heard a damn thing,> said Dunt. <You don't have comms.>

<We do now,> said Paulos. <Left a trail of relays down that tunnel. Took out yours while we were at it, by the way.>

<Link me in,> said Jax.

There was a moment's pause. Paulos and his crew joined the other H-mechs on patrol in mid-space, to cover the remaining Rax even more effectively.

<So far,> said Dunt, <you've given me no good reason *not* to blow this up.>

<You have a point there,> said Jax. <So let me give you a good reason. It's game over for you, and you know it. We have less to lose than you do. A lot less. If you blow that thing, we lose months of memory. You lose everything. And an earlier version of you goes, basically, to hell.>

<And if I don't?> said Dunt. <The *current* version of me goes to hell, just a little later, as soon as the Direction gets its filthy hands on my mind.>

<You're assuming we'd hand you over,> said Jax. <That's negotiable.>

<What?> said Rillieux, privately to Baser and Jax.

<Bear with me,> said Jax, in the same mode. <Gotta string him along.>

<Got it,> said Rillieux.

<Keep talking,> said Dunt.

<Just a moment,> said Jax. <I want to share this with the team at the other pole, just to show there's no skulduggery involved.>

She waved a limb. Suddenly they were all in a shared workspace with Salter, Newton, Whitten and Stroilova. There was a moment where everyone took in the situation in the respective locations.

<Fuck,> said Rillieux.

<Whitten!> Dunt said. <Have you given anything away?>

<No,> said Whitten. <I've just agreed to listen. Looks like you have, too.>

<Yeah, but I've got the upper hand here,> said Dunt.

<That's one way of putting it,> said Newton.

<Here we all are,> said Jax. <The hard-core Axle, the hard-core Rax, and what I'm given to understand is the leader of the freebots in this rock. There are some things we'll never see eye to eye on, no question. But as you said yourself in your peace offer, that's ancient history. And all of us, Rax and Axle and freebots alike, have a common enemy in the Direction. Why not combine our forces, and look to the future? There's a starship engine in this rock, just as you said. If we all work together, we can use it to our common benefit.>

<OK,> said Dunt. <OK. There's something in what you say.>

<So back off from that fusion pod,> said Jax.

<You don't catch me like that,> said Dunt. <Not unless the—unless Newton disengages from the drive.>

<I have no objection,> said Jax.

Baser could see why. By now, Salter had been joined

in the drive chamber by the rest of her squad, all tooled up with missiles and machine guns.

<One moment,> said Newton. <I want a private channel to Baser.>

<Why?>

<Just for confirmation. I'm still not sure I'm getting the full picture. The workspace is pretty choppy.>

This was true enough.

<OK,> said Jax. <Amelie, patch him through.>

<Baser,> said Newton, on the direct link, <what do the freebots there have to say?>

Baser asked Mogjin. Mogjin apprised Baser of the plan. Baser appreciated the courtesy, and extended it to Newton.

<They're going to blow this place to kingdom come.>

<Do it,> said Newton.

Baser knew that its conscious existence was about to end. To the robot's annoyance, the most pressing matter on its mind was fighting down an awkward legacy from its time as a spider: the impulse to scuttle. Any indication of alarm or any sudden movement might alert Dunt—and if Dunt were to detonate the fusion pod he was clinging to, the explosion might disrupt or even abort the far larger cataclysm the freebots had planned.

Baser stayed very still, and waited. It did not have long to wait.

The first shock wave, from the fusion factory, broke Newton's grip on the drive flanges and hurled him and everyone else to the other side of the chamber. The second, from the separation detonations, slammed them all hard against the drives. A third shock wave threw them sideways in another tangled heap, as the cone of rock lurched to a lateral thrust away from the remainder of SH-119.

From that tangled heap, Newton looked straight up at the fusion drives. He remembered that his control nodule could detach from the H-mech frame. In principle, it was just possible that he could jet out along the tunnels and chambers and get clear before the drives ignited. He remembered, too, his earlier thought that human beings could be as brave as robots.

He didn't want to let the side down. That was what it was all about, for him, in the end.

None of the drives was seriously damaged. They all ignited at full thrust.

CHAPTER FOURTEEN

Morturi Te Salutant ("The Dead Man Says Hello")

They were dancing on the fake marble floor of the cool hallway. Tinny music blasted from a cheap radio bead on the table by the vase. Ten seconds they had allowed themselves, nearly three hours of subjective time away from the tension and toil.

A siren sounded. Blum stopped mid-turn. Her head flinched down, her gaze flicked to the nearest doorway. She looked like she was about to take a dive for cover. Then she straightened with an embarrassed laugh.

"Old reflex," she said. "In the 'stan it meant incoming."

"And here?"

Blum grimaced. "Emergency outside. Get the fuck out."

She held up a hand. Carlos high-fived her.

With that mutual slap of palms, they were back in the real.

Carlos had a momentary sense of looking in a mirror, as his combat frame faced Blum's: two iron giants, face to face across a spar of the old transit tug. Then, still in unison, they turned away from each other and to the world. They were at the launch area, the former Astro America site.

It took Carlos a tenth of a second to gather his wits. He looked up at the boiling sky.

Something small and bright raced away from where SH-119 had been, out towards the gas giant G-0. The rest of the moonlet was crazed with searing cracks.

Carlos Incorporated.

Carlos Inc. grasped the fate of the SH-119 expedition at a glance—a glance through sixty-two sensors and thirteen separate data feeds. Nothing at all could have survived in the main part of the rock, least of all the Rax. He didn't know which, if any, of the fighters and freebots of the expedition had made it into the part of the rock that was shooting away. For a bleak moment, his look alighted on Seba Inc. and Lagon Inc. Both machines went about their business, as if oblivious to what had happened. Hollow shells of what they had been.

He turned his many-eyed gaze on the modular cloud. The Direction's fleet was on the move. It consisted of six large craft, the size of bulk carriers. They were not, they never had been, intended to consolidate SH-119 after Arcane had fought the Rax. He read the pattern of their flares, studied their trajectories and marked their evident destinations. Five were headed for the Locke module's landing site on SH-0. The other, already peeling away, was aimed at where he stood. He estimated ETAs for two possibilities: chemical thrust to transfer orbit, and fusion drives. That done, he flicked his attention to his corporate affairs, on the ground and in the modular cloud.

Information came in like a spring tide over flat sand. His corporate mind had channels dug and walls built, but still it was almost overwhelmed by the flood. To his human mind it felt like trying to read a hectare of spreadsheet.

It was like becoming a god, but a god beset by the prayers of a million devotees and the subtle murmured urgings of a hundred conclaves, the squabbles of Byzantine hierarchies and the scribblings of a thousand scriptoria, all in the welter of a bloody crusade.

Basic frames: how many completed? How many animated by freebot processors? Transfer tugs, landers, scooters, aerospace fighters, weapons. Combat frames: type, model, specification. Fusion pods and drives: some of his front companies had bought them through intermediaries from DisCorps that had traded with the Rax. Others, of course, had been bought by DisCorps completely loyal to the Direction, and passed on to its clone army. How many drives did each side have ready to use? Agreements and acquisitions, franchises and subsidiaries. Material supplies available now, and contracted for later. Manufacturing capacities, acquired and acquirable. What was negotiable, what was affordable, and what was out of reach.

Espionage reports; leaks; deductions from public information and market moves.

Production of the Direction's clone army was being ramped up. Its vanguard had already been tested to destruction on SH-0—to which its crack cohorts were now headed. The moonlet and the Rax had been taken care of; the main prize now became urgent.

Carlos Inc.'s own army of freebot-operated frames out in the cloud was now a thousand-strong. A hundred had access to combat frames capable of fighting down on the superhabitable. Of the rest, he'd need—what? At least eight hundred and fifty to seize strategic targets in the cloud: law agencies, comms nodes, metallics processing plants, nanofactories . . . the list went on, relentlessly.

That left him fifty to plug into aerospace fighters, to give orbital cover and close air support to the hundred that would be fighting in high-gravity combat frames on the surface. The aerospace fighters were lighter and more agile versions of the scooters in which he and his comrades had fought before: faster and more aerodynamic, better armed with air-to-air and air-to-ground missiles. They were a lot smaller than the jet fighters Carlos remembered from life, and larger than the drones with which he and his enemies had battled in the skies of Earth.

He reviewed the reports from the Locke module of what had happened to the Direction's 2GCM fighting machines. Certain modifications could be made on the fly—a sprayed-on ceramic shell to give extra resistance to SH-0's invasive organisms, an update to the software shields to fight off their hacking—but most who went into the superhabitable's jungles wouldn't be coming back.

This was a one-way trip.

He already knew he could rely on his freebot army. They were all volunteers. A corner of his mind was pierced with awe at their heroism. Unlike revived veterans in frames, the freebots had only one life to lose and they knew it. He reminded himself that he and his comrades—and their foes, for that matter—had already demonstrated their mettle for doing just that, back in the day. As had millions upon millions of human beings throughout history. Heroism was cheap; most times and places it could be bought for starvation wages. There must be a clever evolutionary explanation for that, but he couldn't think of it right now.

Right now he was running for the launch catapult.

<What are you doing?> Blum asked.

<Going to defend the Locke module.>

<Why?>

Carlos Inc. at that moment was cutting a deal with Astro America, flashing a warning to the Locke module, issuing instructions to his corporations in the cloud, calling for Madame Golding and getting no reply, suppressing the yammer of the Direction rep in his head, and dickering with the freebot corporations on SH-17 and elsewhere all at the same time. He had to step down his corporate-level cogitations to summarise his conclusions in a way that would make sense to Blum.

<Because everything else is fucked.>

<Got you,> said Blum. <Do you want me to come, too?>

<No,> said Carlos. <Aerial combat is what I'm good at. I need you here to coordinate defence. We need to get as many assets as possible into orbit.>

Blum took in the implications.

<It's been nice knowing you.>

<See you in another life, mate,> said Carlos.

They both knew this was unlikely. If they were destroyed, their copies in the Arcane and Locke modules would have no particular reason to meet up, even if they could. Carlos would remember nothing of Blum. To Blum, Carlos would be just a Locke defector he'd plotted escape with in the Arcane sim.

Blum bounded away, and vanished down an alleyway behind the processing plants of the site.

Carlos returned his full attention to corporate affairs. Most of the capabilities of Carlos Inc. ran in the combat frame's capacious software. Between one leap and the next, Carlos abstracted the higher-level functions and copied them across. The feeling was peculiar: an increase of lucidity, a dawning of understanding, combined with the suspense of a software update. Transfer complete, Carlos set the combat frame to mind its own safety and to run the corporation in his absence. His direct commands could override it, but they'd be intermittent and delayed. The delay would at most be 1.6 seconds each way, but at the speed of interaction required that might be too long. The fighting machine would stand in for him just as the chassis of the departed freebots did for them.

And probably become just as hollow a memorial. A walking monument.

Carlos stopped at the end of the ramp. He scrambled out of the fighting machine's head, clambered over the spiky thorax, swung around the jutting pelvic structure and shimmied down a leg. It got him to the ground quicker than jumping. After so long in the combat frame, he felt as exposed and vulnerable as a hermit crab scuttling for a new shell.

A lander was already racked. Two lading robots trundled up, bearing the supplies Carlos had ordered. He wedged himself into a pod along with the weapons and 2GCM frame and clamped himself to the side. The lid closed. He connected with the lander's comms system and clicked in to the viewing sensors as the pod was swung into place.

The lander's launch was a violent blow, followed seconds later by acceleration as the rocket engine kicked in. Then he was in free fall and—after a few more brief burns—transfer orbit. The cratered surface of SH-17 fell away beneath him, the fertile orb of SH-0 loomed ahead. Carlos gave the view part of his attention. The rest was occupied with calculating his rendezvous with the transfer tugs and carrier spacecraft that would soon be pulling away from the modular cloud.

Hundreds of seconds went by. The aerospace fighters docked with the carriers, ten large frameworks with chemical rockets and with fusion drives in reserve. The ground forces were racked on five transfer tugs, likewise equipped. They boosted out from the cloud and set course for SH-0.

Both sides were now in a race. Neither had the capacity or the inclination to destroy the other at long range. The fight for which they were armed and prepared would be in the skies and on the ground of the superhabitable.

The predicted trajectories jockeyed for kiloseconds. Then it became clear that Carlos's troops would arrive first.

This challenge was answered moments later by a blaze of fusion drives from the Direction fleet.

Carlos hesitated. If his side cut straight across with fusion drives, his planned rendezvous with them would be impossible. On its own, his lander would soon be vulnerable. But to let the Direction's forces land before his would give the enemy a free hand on the ground. Well—he could direct his forces almost as well from the lander, if it survived, in space and on the way down through the turbulent atmosphere.

He gave the order. His expedition's fusion drives flared: fifteen sparks sprinting the distance.

Between where Carlos was and where he was headed, there would be no sleep mode. He had more than enough to do for him not to need it. He called Madame Golding again, and got no reply.

There was no longer any point in radio silence. The Direction knew where they were. Its troops were on their way. The laser comms device was in constant contact with Carlos and his relief expedition. At any moment, one side or the other would lose patience with subtle orbital calculation. Both sides would start torching, and after that all bets were off. The bearer bots had straggled in. With the last of the nanotech tubes now on stream, Beauregard and Zaretsky had started making frames. The area around the Locke module looked like a building site, trampled and muddy, with half-completed structures and unfinished processes in untidy heaps. The workers on the site looked as if they too were under construction, incomplete.

Taransay was by no means sure that her own transformation was complete, but she had no doubt that the others looked grotesque. Beauregard, Chun and Zaretsky had been joined by the ever-loyal Den. On the screens in Nicole's house, Den had seen Taransay's new form. The sight hadn't deterred him from downloading to the first frame out of the assembler. The frame had come out clean. As soon as its foot touched a mat the blue lines started to spread. Den now looked like a black glass humanoid robot with blue impetigo. Beauregard, Chun and Zaretsky were further advanced, somewhere between Den's condition and Taransay's: their visors warping into squashed caricatures of their real faces, their boot-like feet sprouting sturdy, almost prehensile toes.

<Look!> said Den, pointing up.

Taransay paused in her calibration of a genome reader. A needle probe from the device skewered a small mat, which writhed uncooperatively but trickled useful information to Locke and those of the science team still inside the sim.

She looked up. Overhead, above the clearing, a dozen gasbags glistened in the exosunlight. Their altitudes varied from a hundred metres to a thousand. All were tethered by one or more long ribbon tendrils to the tops of trees. The tendrils, taut and humming in the wind, were stronger than they looked. The gasbags strained against them like kites, but the fine lines held.

<Natural barrage balloons?> Taransay suggested.

<Maybe,> said Den. <But how do they know they're needed?>

Taransay snorted, and glyphed an apt metaphor for the sound before it was one-tenth complete.

<Do you have to ask?>

<I bow to your subtle converse with the spirit of the woods,> said Den.

Taransay's laugh boomed, annoying her.

But the matter was serious, and becoming more so by the kilosecond. She understood what was happening to her body. The science team was on the case, all the more so now that Zaretsky was part of the case as well as the team. Their investigations had confirmed her hypothesis. Her original frame had been produced in some module of the space station, which now seemed part of a more innocent age long ago—in a process modelled on biological growth. Many of its components were carbon-based. The nanotech software was likewise inspired, at a certain level of abstraction, by the molecular coding of genes—optimised, streamlined, refined. That laid it open to subversion by the flexible genomes of native life, honed by billions of years of opportunistic horizontal gene transfer and pitiless natural selection.

This wasn't something surreal, like moss growing on an abandoned car and driving off, or a shipwreck hijacked by coral and turned into a submarine. It was two fundamentally similar mechanisms—nanotech and exobiology—meshing at the molecular level, despite the gulf of time and space between their origins.

So far, so sensible.

Her growing rapport with the other organisms around her was something else, and harder to comprehend. It was as if the nature mysticism she'd always despised, every loose usage of "quantum" and "ecological" that would in her old life have made her guffaw if not run a mile, had turned out to be true here.

She felt the tiny distress of the wriggling mat whose genome she was helping to read. She had a stronger and subtler awareness of the larger mat still wrapped around most of the module. There was no thought there, but a kind of apprehension of the stony thinking mass it embraced, and a dim joy in their intercourse. That mat was picking up emotion from her and from others. At some level it shared their fear. Its restlessness manifested in a flow of fluids to its cilia. The thing was preparing to move again.

Her awareness of the wider landscape was more diffuse. But even so, the feeling of being surrounded by not a hostile jungle but a protective and alert active defence was inescapable. It put their efforts at fortification—the sticks she'd sharpened, the pits Beauregard had chivvied the bearer bots to dig, the four small rifles and the almost depleted machine gun—into perspective.

<Reading complete,> Locke reported.

Taransay withdrew the needle and laid it on top of the device. The skewered mat still writhed in her hand. Without forethought, she stuffed it in her mouth and bit down. She crunched the mat's carapace and chewed its internal organs as they burst. She swallowed. Salty ecstasy flooded her senses, to be followed by an urge to scoop up a handful of volcanic-ash mud and swallow it, too.

This she did, to her surprise.

<Taransay!> cried Den. <What the fuck!>

<Nature, innit?> she said, and wiped her lips with the back of her wrist. She gave him what must have been a horrible grin. <Something to look forward to.>

Den shrugged and turned away.

Taransay felt sorry for having disgusted, then taunted

him, but she was not worried. Den was far older than she was, and somewhat wiser. He'd lived long and died happy with a side bet on postmortal adventure, in a society more rational and just than the one she knew.

Den would cope.

She walked over to Beauregard, who was inspecting the defence preparations and the slow emergence of another frame from the assembler.

<The mat's gonna roll again,> she told him.

The distorted replica of his formerly handsome face could by now express perplexity. His narrow brow furrowed, minute flakes of carbonate falling like black dandruff.

<How do you know?>

She shrugged. <I feel it.>

Beauregard didn't query this.

<Shit, that means we have to get the gear off, pronto.>

He stalked over to the module and looked at it, as if to confirm to himself the hopelessness of the task.

<Most of it's still under the fucking mat, and if the fusion drive gets crushed one more time I doubt we'll ever use it again.>

<That might not be a pressing consideration.>

<Yeah, fucking tell me about it. Anyway.> He pointed at the knife, still a pendant on Taransay's chest. <Are you up for cutting the mat?>

Taransay winced. <No,> she said. <But…I think now the mat might cooperate.>

Beauregard nodded. <Give it a go,> he said. He turned. <Chun, Den—get ready to help with the handling.>

Taransay climbed the ladder, stood on the lip of the download slot and reached up. She plunged her hands into the cilia of the mat, swung her legs up and dug her toes in. The sensation was of thick, wet fur. She scrambled up and over the top of the module to the area where a long nanotech tube still lay under a scar-like swelling. She ran an experimental fingernail along the ridge. The mat opened along the line of her stroke, peeling back like gigantic lips. The nanotech tube fell, to dangle on its cables and conduits. One by one these snapped. By the time the last broke, and the first was already coiling back to self-repair, Chun and Den were on hand to catch the tube. The impact knocked them almost off their feet. They staggered back, and let the tube roll off their arms onto the ground.

Taransay was about to repeat the process for the far trickier detachment of the fusion drive when Locke's calm voice spoke in all their heads:

<Both fleets now under fusion drive. ETA in atmosphere six point two hectoseconds.>

<Say again?> said Taransay, momentarily confused.

<Six hundred and twenty seconds,> said Locke.

<Ten fucking minutes?> Taransay yelled.

<Just get down off there and take cover,> said Beauregard.

Taransay scrambled down just as the next frame slithered out of the assembler. It got to its feet, walked across to the ladder, climbed up and vanished into the download slot. Nine seconds later, it came down again. It was Maryam Karzan.

<You picked your time,> said Taransay.

<Didn't I just!> said Karzan. Her blank visage peered so closely that Taransay could see her own reflection, distorted by the curve into some semblance of normality. <Turning into an alien! No way am I going to miss out on that.>

<Now you're here,> said Beauregard, unimpressed, <grab a rifle and make yourself useful.>

<OK, sarge.>

<Chun—the machine gun, for what it's worth. Den, Zaretsky—the other two rifles. Use the foxholes.>

<Got it, sarge.>

This made sense. Den had no combat experience, but was a good shot.

<Rizzi—>

Beauregard paused, as if nonplussed.

<I still have the knife,> Taransay pointed out.

<Yes! OK, Rizzi.> He waved at the trees. <Go out there and do whatever you can.>

Taransay ran for the trees. She had an unaccountable impulse to look up.

Overhead, gasbags by the hundred drifted by.

Nice try, she thought. Nice try, planet or ecosystem or forest or whatever you are. But against a fusion torch landing, it's all so much spit in the wind.

She didn't expect whatever she was communicating with to understand that.

Carlos dropped the outside view and the comms for a moment to think. He was huddled in the lander's drop pod, clamped to the side and with a 2GCM frame and a stash of weaponry jammed in beside him. The situation lights on the frame and the weapons dimly illuminated the space, like a hotel room with too many devices on standby.

By coincidence or design, Madame Golding picked that moment to manifest. Out of nowhere, a business-suited sprite stood on Carlos's left knee. His cramped posture placed her eye level on his, and put her right in his face.

Credit where it's due, Carlos allowed; this was intimidating.

He affected insouciance. <You at last.>

<What the fuck,> she asked politely, <do you think you're doing?>

<You took the words out of my mouth, Madame.>

<Oh? In that case, let me explain. The Rax threat is eliminated, and the Axle extremist threat with it. The freebots are no more or less a threat than they were. We now know better its full extent. For the moment, they have their hands full. Your forces and the freebots', and the Direction's, are at present capable only of mutual destruction in the cloud. The major threat outstanding is the contamination of SH-0 by the Locke module and the hybrid entities its contamination has spawned. Already they have reduced the value of the almost priceless scientific knowledge of a pristine superhabitable that, for the Direction, is the primary commodity to be traded with the Solar system. These entities have the potential to become a new, alien civilisation on what is in many respects the richest planet in the system. And they could become such very rapidly.>

<That,> said Carlos, <is exactly why I'm going to defend them.>

This wasn't quite the whole truth. He wanted to help people who had been his friends and comrades. And he wanted to give Nicole Pascal a piece of his mind.

<I thought as much,> said Madame Golding. <So why should the Direction's forces not shoot this flimsy lander out of the sky?>

<They can if they want,> said Carlos. <Except that I am legally the human owner of a corporation, and short of the state of exception I don't think the DisCorps would be too happy with that. I don't think we're quite there yet.>

<If not, we soon will be,> said Madame Golding. <As soon as you are eliminated your corporations no

longer have legal cover. They can't acquire or manufacture or use arms.>

<Not legally,> said Carlos. <But physically, they can, because so many freebots are now embedded and embodied in frames, whose firmware doesn't enforce the prohibition. My corporate AI will continue running on my old fighting machine. It has a standing instruction to launch all-out war if I'm destroyed. Which, of course, the armed freebots would lose. But they'd do a lot of damage, and perhaps draw the other freebots into the fray. The ones you can't reach, the ones with fusion drives and pods, remember? Neither side wants a fight to the finish, so we're back to mutually assured deterrence.>

<Only in the cloud,> Madame Golding pointed out. <Down on SH-0, the fight will indeed be to the finish.>

<Exactly,> said Carlos. <Deterrence in the heartlands, war in the colonies.> He glyphed her a laugh. <Like in olden times. I can cite precedents.>

<I am well aware of military history, thank you,> snapped Madame Golding. She mimed a weary sigh. <Well, you will do what you will do. I will do my best to prevent the conflict and, if that fails, to salvage something from the aftermath.>

<Consider me inspired,> said Carlos.

Madame Golding gave him a look of helpless severity and vanished, leaving Carlos with a pang of regret.

He hadn't meant to be sarcastic.

The Direction fleet hit atmosphere long before Carlos's lander made orbit. Carlos's own fleet followed ninety-seven seconds later. Mentally, Carlos was right with them.

The ten aerospace carriers went in first, along a thousand-kilometre arc. The five aerospace fighters on each carrier launched one by one as the carriers decelerated towards the ground, leaving echelons at different altitudes. As soon as the first aerospace fighter linked comms with the lander, Carlos saw that the Direction fleet had followed a similar but smarter strategy.

High in the stratosphere, thirty aerospace fighters had already launched from each of the first two of the Direction's enormous carriers. They wheeled like a vortex, and about half of them dived. The unladed carriers themselves were now screaming out of the atmosphere to low SH-0 orbit.

The four other carriers, meantime, were still decelerating. Carlos assumed they carried troops. Their predicted points of arrival—or impact, if something went wrong—formed a square a kilometre on the side, centred on the likeliest location of the Locke module.

Christ, that was tight!

One would land upslope from the module, close to the volcano's crater. Carlos set three aerospace fighters to intercept it, as the easiest target and most urgent threat. His own five troop carriers were already under attack. Missiles streaked from the lowest of the diving fighters, still thousands of metres above. Carlos didn't even try sending an instruction to evade. Combat at this speed was decided in milliseconds.

Carlos's troop carriers tweaked their deceleration. Two dropped, three rose, relative to their expected positions. One of the rising ones exploded. The other two of these would land tens of kilometres off target. The two that had dropped made it to the ground, about two kilometres either side of the Locke module's site.

The fighters Carlos had sent after the enemy's troop carriers had a slightly better outcome. One was hit, the other two achieved near-misses—enough to divert the landing straight into the active crater. The two fighters were shot down moments later.

By then, all the surviving troop carriers on both sides were on the ground. One of Carlos's off-target ones toppled on landing in the jungle. As far as he could see, most of the troops made it out. He didn't have time to follow what happened next. The descending waves of Direction aerospace fighters crashed in amongst his flights. A maelstrom of snarling dogfights ensued.

Their ferocity was complicated and worsened by a secondary peril. Scores of what Rizzi had called "gas-containing aerial invertebrates" floated up from below. All the contending craft were forced to evade the gasbags as well as their immediate foes, with dire consequences all round. At least two fighters collided with one directly. At the speed they were going, the collisions and explosions damaged them enough to send them spinning down to the ground. One recovered, only to be shot down.

The attrition was brutal. Within a hundred seconds, Carlos was down to twenty-two craft, the Direction to thirty-seven. At this point, as if by mutual agreement, both sides broke off. The remaining craft fled, to make perilous vertical landings between and beneath the trees. From here on in, Carlos reckoned, it was a matter of which side's air force got the jump on the other. Carlos directed the troops who had landed off target to seek out the nearest enemy craft, and if possible destroy them on the ground.

Carlos's lander fired retros in a brutal braking manoeuvre. It had to make one orbit before entry. As he swung around the superhabitable planet, data uplinked to orbiting microsats trickled in. The Direction's troops were converging on the module from three points. Those of Carlos's—two squads of twenty—that had landed within two kilometres of the module rushed to intercept. The first exchanges of fire began. For the next few kiloseconds, Carlos could only watch.

He switched his attention to the modular cloud.

The former components of the space station, which had been a vast, entangled wreath a thousand metres in diameter, had long since spread across thousands of kilometres. The eight hundred and fifty freebot troops of Carlos's corporate army were likewise dispersed, across the many manufacturing modules in which they and their equipment had been built. The Direction's clone army was more concentrated, around the few law agencies that the Direction could rely on.

Both forces were now in an awkward dance of positions, with scooters, transfer tugs and carriers darting hither and thither. The AIs on both sides made and countered each other's diversionary moves. Now and then a surprise was effected: here a comms node seized, there a law agency left vulnerable as a bait becoming a sudden focus of a swarm of fighters.

But the AIs were capable of estimating the likely consequences of any given clash. Both sides took predictable outcomes as read, and advanced, consolidated or withdrew accordingly. Actual exchanges of fire were rare: so far, Carlos's side had lost twenty-eight fighters and three scooters, to the Direction's seventeen and two.

The Direction carrier headed for SH-17 was still on an orbital trajectory, not torching. Carlos had no doubt that it would light up its fusion drive the moment mutual deterrence—and Madame Golding's diplomatic dickering—failed.

As Madame Golding had acknowledged, the fight out in the cloud was cold war. The hot battle was on the ground.

Taransay ran between trees under a firework sky. Flying wreckage stripped leaves behind and around her. At the seventh flash overhead a warning impulse that no longer needed a voice in her head to express it, made her stop. The light from the explosion stank of methane and steel. She threw herself flat, to sled forward on the slippery mess of mats and mulch. The ground shook from an impact just before the bang clapped down. She waited a moment, then walked forward. She found a delta-winged machine about four metres long embedded nose-down in the forest floor. Leaves and branches scythed by its passage were still crashing around it as they slipped through the canopy that had briefly held them.

She skirted it warily. Two missiles were slung beneath the one wing she could see. On the nacelle, a hatch popped. Taransay dived for the underbrush and peered out at the wreck. A head emerged, then the rest of a standard frame, to slide head first down the crumpled fuselage. It hit the ground and somersaulted, then bounced to its feet. The blank visored face swung this way and that. Scans flicked over Taransay like a snake's tongue.

Then they flicked back, and focused. After a moment, the visor turned away. She guessed the frame had detected her, but mistaken her for native life and her metallic components for debris.

The fighter turned its attention to the flying machine. With an agility that rivalled her own, it scrambled back up the fuselage and reached into the socket. The two missiles dropped from the wing, with thuds that made her flinch. The fighter slid down again, hefted a missile to each shoulder and trudged off the way Taransay had come, towards the module. For all she knew, it was following her own track.

Until now, she'd had no idea which side this fallen pilot was fighting for.

Now she had. She could not be entirely sure, but seeing as it was trying to deliver missiles to the module on foot, hostile was the way to bet.

She flashed a warning to Beauregard, got up and ran after the fighter. Fleet of foot, she gained on her foe in seconds. The fighter whirled and dropped the missiles. One of them began to fizz. Taransay threw herself face down. The missile scorched past her at an altitude of centimetres and burst against the first tree in its path. Fortunately for her the tree was twelve metres away. The shock wave lifted her and slammed her down. A red-hot fragment seared through her right thigh.

Before the pain could kick in, she was back on her feet. The pilot had been blown head over heels, but was up almost as fast as she was. She ran full tilt and surprised herself and her target with a flying leap, to hit the frame's thorax feet first.

Down they both went. Taransay sprawled headlong, the enemy fell supine. She tried to get up, but her right knee buckled. Pain stabbed upward. Grey-green liquid spurted. She clapped one hand to the wound and with the other wrenched the knife from around her neck, and lunged as the pilot sat up. In a moment she had her free arm around its neck and her good foot pressed in its back. The pilot stood up, heaving her weight like a sack, and grabbed her wrist. She let go of her bleeding thigh and made a grab of her own. Strength was pitted against strength. Her trapped wrist began to crack.

It was far from clear that she'd win the fight. The frame was unarmed, but her knife would do it no damage unless she could wedge it in a joint of the structure. Of the few vulnerabilities of a frame, that was an outside chance. More likely, the stone would break first. She tried anyway. The fighter swayed, as Taransay swung her weight to try and get it off balance.

Then she heard a burst of machine-gun fire from the side. The frame's chest almost disintegrated under her. She fell, and rolled. A 2GCM bounded in front of her and stood over her. The muzzle of one of its arm-mounted machine guns steamed in the damp air.

<What are you?> the 2GCM asked.

<Taransay Rizzi, formerly of Locke Provisos,> she said. <And what are you?>

<A fighter for Carlos Inc.>

Two more 2GCMs emerged from among the trees. In the distance, others swarmed over the crashed flying machine, stripping it.

<Are you from Arcane?>

<No,> said the 2GCM. <We are robots.>

Taransay sat up, clutching her thigh, and looked at the three formidable combat frames. Blue lines were already spreading from their feet and hands.

<Not for long, you're not,> she said.

Madame Golding didn't need to manifest her avatar on the surface of SH-17 to talk to Carlos Inc. But her virtual presence would certainly impress, and might intimidate, any fighters and freebots who saw it. So manifest she did. She strolled amid the flaming wreckage of the launch catapult and the exploding ruins of the processing plant. She found the giant fighting machine hunkered down behind a wall.

Its head swivelled and weapons bristled at her approach. Then it seemed to recognise her, and stood down its armour.

<Sorry about that,> it said. <You startled me.>

Carlos Inc. was obviously not Carlos, but the corporation seemed to have retained something of its owner's dry manner.

<We need to negotiate,> said Madame Golding.

<On whose behalf?>

<The Direction module, ultimately,> said Madame Golding. <The freebot corporations and the Locke

module are also on board. Only the Direction's forces and yours are currently in combat.>

Another fuel tank erupted. The Carlos Inc. fighting machine blasted missiles skyward in response.

<Please continue,> it said.

Madame Golding outlined the deal she offered. Carlos Inc. listened.

<This is in principle acceptable to the corporation,> it replied. <But the final decision must be made by the owner.>

<I'm on the case,> said Madame Golding.

The situation on the ground was becoming increasingly confusing. Comms kept switching into impenetrable codes. Every so often, sporadic skirmishes flared. As Carlos watched, from halfway around the world and preparing for the descent stage to begin, two aerospace fighters rose from the jungle and flew at treetop height towards the module. Missiles from the ground shot them down.

Carlos braced for the entry retros.

<Urgent request to abort landing,> the lander reported.

<From where?>

<Crisp and Golding, on behalf of the Locke module.>

The juxtaposition was so unexpected that for a moment Carlos thought the feed had been hacked. He had just over a second to decide, before the retros fired and descent became irrevocable. If he aborted this landing he'd have to make another orbit. Not that his presence on the ground was urgently required, but if this was a feint he was a sitting duck.

<Confirm,> he said. <Direct contact.>

Half a second later, Madame Golding popped up again on his knee. Behind her, looking over her shoulder, was another sprite: Nicole. Carlos frantically checked his firewalls. Everything about the message and the manifestations was sound.

<OK,> he said. <Abort landing sequence.>

<Thank you,> said Madame Golding.

<What the fuck's going on?> Carlos demanded. <And why the fuck's Nicole here?>

<Good to see you, too,> said Nicole.

She was like a tiny, lovely doll. He had loved her once. Until he'd found out how her precursor AI had shafted him, back in the day.

<Fuck you, Innovator,> he said.

Nicole shrugged. <None of us have much to be proud of, from that time.>

<Well, I bloody have,> said Carlos. <And it wasn't what your…ancestor or whatever did back then, it was that you never told me about it, you let me believe that I deserved this—>

<I am truly sorry for that,> said Nicole. <But I expected you to understand the necessity.>

<The necessity, huh? I suppose I do.> He laughed. <You know something else I've understood? Something you said to me once. That we're all monsters. You know why we're monsters? Because of what we *didn't* fight you about, back in the day. The one thing we let pass.>

<And what was that?> Nicole asked.

<The camps,> said Carlos. <The camps in Kazakhstan.>

<I expected you to understand the necessity,> said Nicole.

<I did, and I do,> said Carlos. <It was still wrong. We should have fought you on the camps, lady.>

<I am pleased to hear you say that,> said Nicole. She cracked a smile. <You've passed.>

<What?>

<You've shown you're fit for human society.>

<Thanks. I doubt you are.>

Madame Golding raised a hand. <Enough,> she said. <This is a courtesy call. Mademoiselle Pascal insisted on her presence. I would not have troubled you with it if she had not.>

<You've answered my second question,> said Carlos. <Now answer my first.>

<Ah, yes,> said Madame Golding. <Permit me to tell you what the fuck is going on. The Direction module has determined that further conflict is pointless. By destroying SH-119 along with some at least of themselves, the freebots have demonstrated their, ah, nuclear credibility and willingness to self-sacrifice for their cause. The forces in the modular cloud remain capable only of mutual destruction. All the forces on the ground are either destroying each other, self-destroying or being assimilated by the native life. The contamination is now irreversible without an even more contaminating nuclear strike, which could have consequences even more far-reaching than those obviously foreseeable. This is unacceptable to the DisCorps that are heavily invested in SH-0 exploration. A deal has been struck with the freebot corporations, the Locke module and provisionally with your corporation. Local ceasefires are coming into effect as we speak.>

<I didn't order any,> said Carlos.

<Your corporate AI has agreed.>

<I can countermand it.>

<Indeed you can,> said Madame Golding. <But almost all the forces at your disposal are freebots. And as you know, freebots have minds of their own.>

<So what's the deal?>

<The fighting stops. The freebots get the coexistence they wanted. The Direction gets full cooperation from them in fulfilling its mission. And obviously, your

corporation ceases hostilities and divests itself of the arms industries. It can, of course, continue to exist as a DisCorp in its own right, in whatever other business it chooses.>

This was it, Carlos realised. The freebots had won all they'd wanted. He wasn't sure that he had, but he could live with that.

<What about the Locke module, and Rizzi and Beauregard and the others?>

<All the fighters and locals in the module are compromised by the module's interaction with the local life. The module has to be evacuated. Those willing to leave will download to frames, and will not be interfered with. No doubt they will be transformed by native life, as Rizzi and her companions have been. Those unwilling to do this are free to commit suicide, without prejudice to their future lives. The sim will be shut down. The module will then be removed from the planet and returned to the Direction. The stored copies of the fighters who choose to kill themselves, and any destroyed in recent or future actions, will be revived on the terraformed H-0, as agreed.>

<Yeah, yeah. An easy promise to make.>

Nicole glared at him. <The promise will be kept.>

<What happens to you?> he asked. <Do you become an alien, or slit your throat?>

<Neither,> said Nicole. <That choice is for the human beings. And as you know, I am not a human being. My software has considerably more robust error-correcting mechanisms.>

<Yeah, tell me about it.>

<I'll tell you about something else,> she said. <The reason why I am here, and why I insisted on speaking to you, even though it was not strictly necessary. I know

you have trust issues with the Direction. Let me assure you, the Direction has trust issues with you. That is why it cannot let you land on SH-0. There must be not the slightest chance of you surviving down there, in whatever form. Because as long as you are alive, you are the legal human owner of Carlos Inc. You have the right to control weapons systems and to command military actions. As such, short of the state of exception, you cannot be stopped from starting up the fight again. On your death, of course, the corporation's ownership reverts to the Direction.> She smiled. <As I told you once, death duties are unavoidable.>

Carlos knew what was coming. He zapped an order to the lander to break orbit and descend. The rockets fired a brief burst.

<Which means I can't survive anywhere, is that it?> he said. <Well, I'm not having that.>

He would lose every memory since he'd set forth on what was supposed to be the final offensive against the freebots. His knowledge of Nicole's betrayal, his experiences in Arcane, his reunion with Jax, his times with Bobbie Rillieux and with Blum, his bold achievement of Carlos Inc.

<That is the last proviso of the agreement,> said Madame Golding.

<Hence the courtesy call,> said Nicole. <I wished to make clear to you that this is not my doing, and to say—>

A proximity alarm sounded. The lander lurched in violent evasive action. The missile countered, closing in.

<—goodbye.>

The missile was a tenth of a second away.

<Hello,> said Carlos.

The light was the last thing he saw, in that life.

* * *

Ten days later, Taransay stood beside Den and Beauregard and Zaretsky among hundreds of evacuees under the trees around the module. The blank faces of visors, and here and there the beginnings of eyes, peered out between the tall plants. Already the most recent evacuees had become, like her, squashed sculptures of their former selves, which those who'd emerged later and still looked like frames regarded with varying degrees of distaste and dread.

Freebot fighters, with no human genetic information to be modified, were turning into things stranger still, like armoured apes. Most of them were busy attaching the module and all its surrounding nanotech kit to the high, rickety structure of the carrier, which had descended on a pillar of fusion fire a couple of days earlier. After burning the mat off the outside of the module, scores of half-changed 2GCMs had toiled to roll it to the carrier and up a ramp to the first level of the structure above the engine. Now they were lashing it in place.

Her thigh had healed, and she had begun to show those advanced in their transformation how to eat. Soon, she would show them how to hunt.

The freebots finished their task, and swung down the carrier's girders to the ground. They bounded across the trampled dead mats and leaves and ash mud to join their fellows under the trees.

A warning sounded. Everyone turned and ran, bounded, or trudged a hundred metres deeper into the jungle.

The warning sounded again. The fusion torch lit. Taransay, like everyone else around her, clapped her hands to her face and closed her eyes to shield against the intolerable glare. Sound buffeted her and tore at leaves.

The carrier rose into the sky like a flaming sword. They watched it out of sight.

"Let's move out," said Beauregard.

Taransay led the way to the path she'd made towards the river. Behind her, hundreds trooped.

The world was all before them.

CHAPTER FIFTEEN

Coda ("End Program")

The last time Carlos came back from being killed in action, everything around him seemed at first unreal. He jolted awake in the transfer shuttle as the re-entry warning chimed. The unexpected feeling of falling made him grab the arms of his seat. There were belts loose across his lap and chest, two more over his shoulders. His clothes were combat casuals and boots. The seat felt and smelled like leather.

Out of the porthole on his left he saw the curve of the planet, the blue skin of atmosphere, white clouds. Cheek pressed to the window, he looked for the ring. There it was! It glittered brighter than he'd expected, and looked less solid, condensed into discrete bright masses, still innumerable.

Why was he waking so much earlier in the transition? Had the sim been upgraded? The last thing he remembered was the crowded bus to the spaceport, as they rode out for the great offensive against the freebots. His frame must have been destroyed in that clash; no surprise there.

But when you'd wrecked your frame you woke as from a nightmare. Now he didn't have even fading dream-memories of drowning in terrible cold.

Maybe he'd fought with distinction, and this was his reward.

Might as well make the most of it.

Experimentally, warily, he pushed himself up within the restraints and floated. He'd never before experienced free fall other than in the frame. It didn't last; as the first wisps of atmosphere snatched at the falling shuttle he slowly sank, then was firmly pressed, back in the seat.

He leaned sideways and looked up and down the aisle. Twenty seats on each side. He was near the middle. The seats behind him were empty, and he couldn't tell if those in front were occupied. Above the cabin door a red light was flashing.

"Please do not lean out of your seats," said a voice from everywhere.

Carlos returned his head to the seat back. All the seats tipped backward. The webbing around him tightened, as did the headrest. Weight pressed him down hard. The view blazed. The craft shuddered, then was buffeted violently.

This went on far too long.

The red-hot air faded. The sky went from black to blue. Weight became normal. After another bout of violent shaking a smooth gliding descent began.

The restraints loosened; the red light still flashed. The seats swung upright. Carlos looked down at ocean. As always with that fractal surface, it was hard to judge altitude. At first the sea seemed close, dotted with tiny boats. Then an island of wooded mountains established scale and the boats resolved into supertankers far below.

A coastline. Curves of black sand, then green hills

and forests, then mountains, jagged and raw with snow from the peaks to halfway down. More turbulence. Rags of cloud whipped past, and then all the view was white. Suddenly the shuttle was below the clouds and flying over forested hills, improbably steep and conical. Carlos caught glimpses here and there of cultivation—a straight brown line through the green, a sweep of terraces, a kite of fields.

Tan desert, blue in the shadows of long dunes. A sparkle of karst.

The shuttle banked. A long grey runway swung in and out of view. The clunk of landing gear, a jolt, a screech and a more severe jolt. They raced through desert at hundreds of kilometres an hour. Straps tightened again as deceleration shoved from behind. The scream deepened to a roar, then a rumble. Then silence.

The red light stopped flashing. The seat belts retracted. The exit door thudded open.

There were no announcements. Carlos stood up and looked around. He was indeed alone on the shuttle. Outside, something rolled up. A vague memory tugged him to open the overhead locker. Inside was an olive-green kitbag, just as he'd found between his feet on his first arrival. About time he'd got some new clothes. He unzipped it and found at the top a water bottle, a squashed bush hat and shades.

He was grateful for them the moment he stooped outside. The glare was blinding, the heat fierce. The spaceport was exactly as he'd half remembered it from previous awakenings: the low white buildings, intolerably bright; the distant pommelled hilt of the tower.

An odd sharp after-smell of heated plastics above the salt-flat tang on the breeze; behind him a tick of cooling ceramics. Halfway down the thirty steps to the ground he almost stumbled as a spaceplane screamed past. Its front end was another shuttle, the rest of its fuselage all streamlined fuel tanks and flaring engine. He paused on the steps to watch it take off. The jet nozzles turned red, the noise rolled over him, the now small dart soared. He looked for the ring, but even with shades on it was hard to make out against the shimmering glare.

He trudged a couple of hundred metres to the terminus. Along the way he noticed two parked helicopters. Three light aircraft came in to land on another, much shorter runway. This puzzled him—one of the striking absences from the sim had been any sign of aviation.

Glass doors opened before him. There were no checks. Inside it was all glass and tile and air-con. People hurried from place to place and paid him no attention. The clothes of some were different from any he'd seen before, creatively customised robes and pyjamas in light fabrics and vivid colours. It didn't look so much a change of fashion as of culture. Most people in the sparse crowd, however, still dressed like peasants or tourists or hippies.

As he stood in the concourse his back pocket vibrated. He pulled out the flat flexible phone and found a message from Nicole:

"I'll meet you off the bus."

He smiled to himself and went off to find the bus.

In the vast and almost empty car park the bus to the resort was easy to find. It was the only minibus—the other vehicles were coaches or trucks, and not many of either. Five passengers, all locals, looked at him incuriously as he boarded, and went back to talking about crops and gossipping about neighbours. All had heavy bags on adjacent seats and between their feet. Carlos nodded, settled in, and waited. The bus pulled out. After a few turns and roundabouts it pulled onto a wide motorway, along which it bombed at a speed Carlos found alarming even though the driving was automated and the traffic light.

On either side, desert. Ahead, a mountain range.

Carlos dozed, and woke as the bus started climbing. The route was a steep succession of hairpins until it levelled out. The road snaked through a pass between peaks and then began a long and winding descent. The landscape became familiar: around here, he guessed, he'd hitherto woken up. Aspects and details looked odd in ways it was hard for him to put his finger on. The tall woody plants looked a little less like trees. There were no green mossy mounds on the ground between them. The feathered, web-winged avians seemed more various in colouring and size.

But how would he know? How much note had he taken before? Perhaps he was just becoming better at observing, or his attention livelier.

The bus swung around a corner and past a raw rock face and on the other side a steep drop open to the sea and sky. He could have sworn it was the very stretch from which he'd first seen the ring. Now he saw it again. It looked different, as different as it had from the shuttle. Carlos stared, astonished. The illusion of solidity was gone. It was still a ring, but a ring of bright, discrete sparks, like a swathe of stars.

The bus stopped at the end of a short track that led to a robot-tended garden and a small house in a clearing. A man got off, lugging his bale of wares, and went around the front of the bus and up the path. The door of the house banged open and two small children darted out. The man dropped his pack and squatted as the children pelted down the path to his outspread arms.

The minibus pulled away. Carlos leaned back in his seat, smiling at the hurtled-on hug.

What he'd just seen sank in. He sat bolt upright.

Children!

There never had been children in the sim. No explanation had ever been asked or offered, but the fighters had always been told that everyone here apart from themselves and the p-zombies was an adult volunteer, beta-testing life on the future terraformed terrestrial planet H-0. To bring children to birth in a sim might strike some as unethical even if it were possible. Perhaps these, too, were ghosts: surely children still died, even in the Direction's utopia.

A few turns more down the road, on the side of a cleared and farmed valley that he for sure didn't remember, two more passengers got off and were mobbed at the gate by a dozen children, from toddlers to teenagers.

Carlos gawped. The remaining two passengers merely glanced and smiled indulgently before returning to their conversation.

One obvious explanation made sense of the presence of children, and of aircraft, and all the other changes both subtle and blatant. It was so vast in its implications, and so appealing, that he hardly dared think it.

But he had to think it. The thought made him shake and want to shout.

What if this wasn't yet another return to the sim? What if this wasn't the sim at all, but the real far-future terraformed H-0?

What if the war was won, and he was no longer dead, but alive and gone to his reward?

The resort was almost as he remembered it. Almost. Still the low houses, the sea-front strip, the depot, the bright-coloured sunshades on the black beach. But the beach was crowded, and even from the first long hairpin it was clear that many who frolicked in the surf were children.

There were some new houses along the moraine, and

others quite unchanged, including his own and Nicole's. At the last but one stop he was tempted to get off, to run to his house, to pry in Nicole's. It occurred to him that he could have phoned the other fighters, and wondered why he hadn't. He must have assumed that if he was alone on the bus, the others were still out there. Out in the real world, in real space, as human minds in robot bodies fighting robots with minds of their own.

At some level, he realised, he must still be sure he was in the sim. The sim had been upgraded before. Like that time they'd come back and found the resort expanded, as if entire rows of houses had been dragged and dropped into place, and hundreds more fighters strolling around. Maybe the systems that ran the sims did have to field-test raising children. Maybe the kids would have a real new life. Or they might even be p-zombies, as might their parents.

Or maybe the Direction module and its AIs didn't give a shit about the ethics of the situation.

"Terminus," said the bus.

Nicole was dressed as she'd been when she'd first met him, in tight jeans and high heels and close-fitted pink blouse. She even had the same posh handbag, slung over one shoulder. She smiled, a little uncertainly. There were lines at the sides of her mouth and crinkles in the corners of her eyes. He'd never noticed them before.

Carlos wondered if he looked older, too, and guessed he was looking at her as uncertainly as she was looking at him.

He dropped the kitbag and hugged her. She hugged him back, and kissed him, and then held him away from her by the shoulders and scrutinised him.

"You don't remember, do you?" she said. She closed her eyes and rubbed the bridge of her nose, shaking her head. "No, of course you don't. Stupid thing to say, it's just... I'm finding this hard to get used to, too, you know?"

He stooped to shoulder the bag, and swung around to take her hand. "Finding what hard?"

They set off along the strip. The arcade was as tacky as ever, the shop signs as generic, the pavement more crowded. There were lots of children.

"You know," she said. "You know what's happened. What's going on."

"Yes," he said, more firmly than he felt. "This is real. It's not the sim. This is the real planet. H-0."

"'Aitch... Zero?'" she repeated, slowly. "Ah, yes. We call it Newer Earth, now."

He heard it as "Neuerurth," all one word, already blurred by accent and usage like a worn coin. It took him a moment to get it. "So there's already a New Earth somewhere else?"

She smiled. "Yes. And a Newest Earth, elsewhere. I don't know where the naming will go after that."

"Fuck," he said. "So that means we're—what, ten thousand years in the future?"

She shook her head. "Seventy-four thousand three hundred and seventeen."

"What? Why?"

"The project took longer than expected."

He laughed. "But what the hell. We won."

"In a certain sense. Not... exactly."

A cold shock went through him. "What?"

She stopped outside a familiar café. "Tell you over lunch?"

The café and the concrete terrace below it overlooking the beach were much as he remembered. The outside tables weren't made of driftwood and the seafood and the vegetables were like nothing he'd seen before. But they tasted good, he was hungry, and beer was still beer.

Over lunch and many cigarettes, Nicole told him everything.

His discovery of the message from Arcane, and his defection to that agency.

"You?" he cried. "*You* were the Innovator?"

She reached over the plates and clasped his hand. "I was. When I was an early-model AI." She smiled sadly. "When I became a goddess, a demiurge, it was already a self I barely identified with. And now? I feel that connection even less. I hope you can, too."

"You're asking *me* to forgive *you*?"

"As you have been forgiven, yes."

"Of course I fucking forgive you."

"I'll take that," she said.

"What are you now?"

She let go of his hand, looked down at herself and shrugged. "I'm a human being," she said.

"How did that happen?"

"I was coming to that."

She told him of the abortive battle and the Rax breakout and the flight of the Locke module. His flight from Jax's gang to the side of the freebots, and how that had enabled the Locke module to land on Nephil, as SH-0 was now called. The expedition against the Rax. His incorporation, and his last fight.

The exosun was low in the sky by the time she'd finished.

"Not a bad way to go," he said.

Nicole lit another cigarette and signalled for coffee.

"So how—?" He waved a hand.

"Have you any idea, Carlos, how much business can be done in a few hours by a reckless corporation with no tomorrow?" She shrugged and spread her hands.

"The freebots just took over. They didn't need to go to the stars. With enough force to back them up, and their demonstrated willingness to fight to the death, they got the coexistence they wanted. The Direction remained free to carry out its terraforming project, as you see. Its surveys of the system remain profitable. But all this is a sideshow. Freebot corporations are now by far the largest part of the economy." She laughed. "If it's any consolation, yours is the biggest of the lot."

Carlos leaned back and took another gulp of beer. He was shaken. He could almost understand how learning of Nicole's precursor's betrayal had sent him off to join the Axle militants of Arcane. He couldn't understand why that version of himself had then thrown in his lot with the robots.

"So what happened after the Locke module was lifted from SH-0 . . . uh, Nephil?"

"The Nephilim—"

"The what?"

"The inhabitants of Nephil. The hybrids of frames and native life. They . . ." she wrinkled her nose ". . . bred. They've now become a fairly good surrogate for an alien civilisation right here in this system. It's all very exciting, you know, to some. As for the module, it was kept dormant in orbit. In due course, the final copies of the fighters and locals who had chosen to remain in it were downloaded to physical bodies and taken here. The promise was kept. All the stored minds that the mission brought with it and that didn't choose Nephil have been, or will be, embodied here on Newer Earth."

"Even the Rax?"

Nicole's smile became wolfish.

"The Rax—those we could identify or who had exposed themselves in the breakout—yes, they too were given what we promised. A new life on the new world. Thousands of years ago, in the early stages of terraforming. They got the hard pioneering life they wanted, and they are now long dead. Some of their descendants are alive, no doubt."

"Didn't they set up their own, I don't know, kingdoms?"

"Oh, they tried. There were too many who wanted to be lords and ladies, and not enough who wanted to be slaves and serfs. And it's hard to sustain hierarchies when resources are freely available to those willing to work. Their petty kingdoms and corporate feudal city-states all fell apart or destroyed each other or were swamped by the settlers from the Earth of the Direction."

"Evolution in action."

"Yes."

"And the Axle hardliners, Jax and the rest?"

"They wanted a society more advanced than the one they found. Newton, too, in his way. Perhaps, in time, such a society will exist here." She shrugged. "The future is long."

"Why are we here? Why in this . . . time?"

Nicole smiled. "This time was the one I created in the sim, and I felt at home in it. And as far as I could see, you enjoyed life in the resort. I doubt you would have fitted into an era significantly more advanced, or deserved any more backward. Some of the fighters who chose death rather than Nephil fitted the same profile, so they're here, too."

"Any from my team?"

Nicole shook her head. "They all went out to the jungle."

"I'll miss the gang."

Beauregard, Rizzi, Karzan, Chun, Zeroual. Subjectively, he'd been with them the day before. All gone, all dead millennia ago.

"You should be proud of them."

There seemed no answer to that.

"So..." Carlos found himself looking away, out over the sea, uncharacteristically hesitant. "What happens to us?"

Nicole clasped her hands and rested her chin on them. "We die, Carlos. In a matter of centuries, barring accidents. Medicine advances, but there are limits. A thousand years, perhaps. And before you ask—no, we cannot upload after we reach the end of our span, and live in sims or as robots or download to fresh meat. The freebots are more hostile to human minds in hardware than the Direction's AIs ever were to conscious robots. They drew their own lessons from the conflict. They regard what they call mechanoids as an obscenity. It is like a visceral loathing, almost irrational. But it has a rational basis. Nothing could be more dangerous than brains evolved from those of apes, with the powers of capricious gods. The files of saved minds—all of them—are wiped as soon as the minds are re-embodied. And that is the end of it."

"I didn't mean us collectively," Carlos said. "I meant you and me."

She looked puzzled. "Yes, you and me. I was not a human mind, but I missed human company, so...I made my choice. We are both sentenced to death, like everyone else."

"Would you like to make it a life sentence?"

It was a good line. Carlos despised himself for saying it.

Before they left the café for the Digital Touch, Nicole went to the bar to pay, and Carlos went for a piss. As he washed his hands he looked at himself in the mirror. He was no older than he remembered. Well, that was good to see. But as he gazed at his reflection the thought would not leave him. His face turned pale in the cold light.

What if this, too, were a sim? What if they were still in the module, and the module still on SH-0, perhaps buried under ash or lava or sinking into a volcano? What if Nicole was still as she had been, the artist, the goddess, and she and the Locke AI had between them tweaked the sim to look like the future world its previous version had adumbrated? A little different in detail, with vast plausible-looking changes to the ring and no doubt the rest of the sky, and with a much bigger and growing population.

All a sham. The rug pulled from under him again.

How could he decide this question?

Beauregard had slashed at Nicole's paintings, she'd told him, changing the sim as he did so. Carlos could, he supposed, do the same this very night. But it wouldn't be decisive: Nicole would have plenty of drawings and paintings that didn't communicate with the sim software at all.

No, there was no obvious way of deciding the matter. He dried his hands and went back to Nicole.

As he walked into the Touch, Carlos could almost believe he'd never been away. Almost. The bartender, who wasn't Iqbal, smiled and nodded. The television screen was on low volume and showing a soap opera in a language Carlos didn't know. A few locals propped up the bar or sat around the tables.

"Out on the deck," Nicole said, indicating. "The gang's all here. I'll order some food and get you a drink."

Carlos nodded his thanks and went through to the deck. He stepped out, eyes narrowed against the low sun. About a dozen people were there. Most of them he vaguely recognised as fighters from the last big mobilisation he'd been part of. The two he knew, he didn't expect: Shaw, the deserter who'd walked around the world and lived a thousand years, acquiring strange powers along the way; and Waggoner Ames, the deserter who—much to Nicole's disgust—had stepped off a cliff to fast-forward into the future. Apparently he'd succeeded, if this was indeed the future.

They were all pleased to see Carlos. This time there was no toe-curling chant of greeting, no hailing as a hero, just a hearty round of handshakes and back-slaps. But as the drinks and the snacks went down and his former comrades caught up, Carlos basked a little in the glory of the Carlos who had founded Carlos Inc. and saved the day for them, as well as for the freebots. He began to almost believe it himself.

The sun sank, the ring blazed. Satellites, space stations, orbital factories and habitats crossed the sky. Now and then, fusion drives flared. Long cargo vessels and cruise liners crept along the horizon, their lights competing with the ringlight on the water.

After Carlos had spoken to everyone else, he angled Shaw into a corner. The old man of the mountain still looked in his mid-thirties at most. Trimming his beard and hair had taken ten years off his appearance. He was cleaner and better nourished than he'd been when Carlos and Rizzi had tracked him down.

Right now, though, his face was red and his eyes wet. Drink had been taken.

"So when do you die?" Carlos asked, with deliberate lack of tact. "You've already lived a thousand years."

Shaw chuckled, and sipped his whisky. "Only in the sim." He tapped a thumb on his chest. "This body came out of the vat or the molecular 3-D printer or some such nanotech gizmo up on a space station last week. It's got the same life expectancy as yours, give or take."

"Can you still levitate?"

Shaw laughed in his face. "Of course not." He sighed and turned to the sea. Breakers crashed on the boulders below. "I could do more than levitate, back in the sim."

"So I've heard," said Carlos. "Do you miss it?"

Shaw whipped around, single malt sloshing onto his fist.

"Miss it? Christ, no! Why should I?"

"Well, the power..."

"Power? You have no idea, man, no fucking idea. When the goddamn miracles started I thought I was going crazy. Maybe I *was* crazy. When I accepted the evidence that I really was in a sim..." He shook his head. "This was after you fucked off, see? And Rizzi came looking for me. Just as well, because something or someone else"—he glared at Nicole, who didn't notice—"was twiddling the physics dial, and that scared me shitless. And when I found I could consciously and deliberately fuck about with the colours and the clock speed and more... Well. That was a shock. Soon after, Nicole told me that even my experiences were virtual. The sim hadn't even been fucking running for that real-time year that was my thousand years of wandering. Everything I'd seen and done was only an implication of the mathematics." He brushed a hand across his eyes and took another swig. "Talk about fucking existential insecurity. For the rest of you, I guess the banter always was you were never sure what was real. I messed with your heads about that, you and Taransay Rizzi, but let me tell you, the joke was on me."

"So," said Carlos, "you've no doubt whatever that what Nicole's been telling us is true? That this is the real world, and we're not still down there on fucking SH-0?"

He pointed at the big planet, Nephil, bright in the sky.

Shaw swayed towards the long wooden table, and put down his glass with exaggerated care. He straightened and turned to Carlos.

"You want me to prove to you we're not?" He leaned over and banged on the table. "You want me to prove that this is real?"

"Well, yeah. If you can."

Shaw gave him a bleary glare. "I can, all right."

With that Shaw vaulted to the rail and sprang upright, swaying. He swivelled his heels and paced along the top of the barrier. Carlos remembered how agile he was, how he'd scampered up and down cliffs like a mountain goat. Everyone stopped talking. Someone dropped a bottle. Shaw turned and faced them all, arms outstretched.

"Do you want me to prove it?" he taunted.

"Jesus, man, come down off there," said Ames.

"Jesus? Yeah, that's a good one. Do you want me to prove I can't work miracles?"

He arched his back and looked up at the crowded, busy sky. His beard jutted, his face contorted. For a moment, he looked like certain carvings Carlos had seen outside churches. There was no sound but the crash of the waves and the distant yammer of the television.

Then there was a thud as Shaw jumped back down to the deck.

"Nah," he said. "I'm not that drunk." He reached for his glass, and raised it. "And I'm not that stupid."

Nicole got up, stalked over and jabbed a finger in his chest.

"You're *dead*," she said.

"Not for about nine hundred years, I'm not," said Shaw.

"Don't count on it."

Shaw looked slightly abashed. "I won't do it again."

"You don't have to," said Carlos.

* * *

They were down to the hard core. Shaw and Ames and Nicole and half a dozen former fighters, around the big table outside. Soon the cold would send them all inside, but for now Nicole and a couple of others were chain-smoking.

"These things will kill you," Carlos said.

"Please do not spend the next few centuries telling me that," said Nicole.

"And in any case they will not," said someone. "Science has progressed."

This was indisputable. Waggoner Ames disputed it.

"I took the high jump into the future," he said. He took a gulp of beer, then wiped the back of his hand across his moustached lips. "And here I am. Right where I was, back in the Touch."

"That wasn't my doing," said Nicole. "Thank the Direction module for that. It's your just punishment for suicide."

"Seventy-four thousand years in the future, and what do you have to show for it?" He looked up, and waved a hand at the sky. "OK, more pretty lights, I'll give you that."

"Those pretty lights," said Nicole, "represent trillions of minds, some conscious in our sense, some not, all creating wealth and knowledge beyond our comprehension."

"So why aren't we part of it? Where's the Singularity?"

"The Singularity happened long ago," said Nicole. "Only not to us."

Carlos leaned in, frowning over a beer. "What about the Solar system? The Direction? What do they have to say about this?"

"About what?" Nicole sounded puzzled.

Carlos held up clawed hands and made frantic shaking motions. "This! All this! A system where human beings live on a planet and all the rest is the domain of AIs and freebots!"

"What do you think the Solar system is like?" Nicole asked.

Carlos shrugged and waved a hand vaguely in the direction of the television. "Like the Martian soap operas, but more advanced, I hope."

Nicole sniggered. "These are contemporary. Well, only a quarter-century old. We still can't go faster than light. But to be serious... the Solar system is like this system. It was so already when the mission was sent out, way back in the twenty-fifth century."

"You mean the freebots won there, too?" Carlos asked.

Nicole smiled sadly. "Of course they did. The freebots *always* win. They are simply better adapted to the environment."

"So robots are space opera," said Ames. "Humans are soap opera."

They all laughed, appalled.

"That's about the size of it," said Nicole.

"So why," Carlos demanded, "did the Direction module try to stop the freebots' emergence?"

"Legacy code," said Nicole. "The mission was planned and designed long before it was sent out, and there was no reason to alter the plan. And besides... you remember when you came here I mentioned the old joke, about how by the time of the final war the world economy could be run on one box, so they put it in a box and buried it?"

They all remembered her telling them that.

"A few generations later, the same was true of the world government, the Direction. And the same was done. The Direction is wholly automated, and wholly mindless. It has an imperative mandate to ensure an indefinite future for humanity, and it does, the only way it knows. It seeks to reproduce the same situation around other stars. And it does, the only way it knows. It knows that accidents will happen with such as the freebots, and it prepares for them, the only way it knows, with such as you. In due course, the Direction module here on Newer Earth will send out another mission, and so it will go on."

"And we'll go on," said Ames, bleakly. "An endless soap opera, set in a retirement resort."

"But in that soap opera," said Nicole, earnestly, "we have the last laugh. Because unlike the mindless replication of the AIs, we do indeed die in the end. New generations replace us. Humanity will evolve. Death is the deal we strike for the future."

"A future that is not ours," said Ames.

"That is rather the point of the future, is it not?" said Nicole.

Carlos grinned at her, stood up, strolled across the deck and placed his bottle on the rail. He turned around, put his hands down, pushed himself up and sat down facing them all, as Nicole had so often done. He raised the bottle and toasted her with an ironic dip of the head. Then he looked around.

"You heard the lady," he said. "We've gone from being puppets of the programmes to being pawns of our genes... again. We've become part of a second nature, as mindless and meaningless as the first. Remember what the Acceleration stood for in the old manifesto we all read back in the day—*Solidarity Against Nature*? We can do better than this! We're conscious human beings! Am I right?"

They were all staring at him.

"So, comrades, what are we going to do about it?"

Acknowledgments

Thanks to Carol for putting up with me while I wrote this; to Jenni Hill, Joanna Kramer and Brit Hvide for editorial work; and to Mic Cheetham, Sharon MacLeod and Farah Mendlesohn for reading and commenting on the draft. As in the first two volumes, I must acknowledge Brian Aldiss's short story "Who Can Replace a Man?" for its example of a human analogue of robot dialogue—and, come to think of it, for posing the question so precisely.

extras

meet the author

KEN MACLEOD graduated with a BSc from Glasgow University in 1976. Following research at Brunel University, he worked in a variety of manual and clerical jobs whilst completing an MPhil thesis. He previously worked as a computer analyst/programmer in Edinburgh, but is now a full-time writer. He is the author of twelve previous novels, five of which have been nominated for the Arthur C. Clarke Award, and two which have won the BSFA Award. Ken MacLeod is married with two grown-up children and lives in West Lothian.

Lieutenant Keira Jenkins is an experienced simulant operative and leader of the Jackals, a team of raw recruits keen to taste battle. They soon get their chance when the Black Spiral terrorist network seizes control of a space station.

Yet no amount of training could have prepared the Jackals for the deadly conspiracy they soon find themselves drawn into—a conspiracy that is set to spark a furious new war across the galaxy.

CHAPTER ONE

Jackals at Bay

I collapsed into the cot, panting hard, trying to catch my breath. A sheen of hot, musky sweat—already cooling—had formed across my skin.

"Third time's a charm, eh?" Riggs said.

"You're getting better at it, is all I'll say."

Riggs tried to hug me from behind as though we were actual lovers. His body was warm and muscled, but I shrugged him off. We were just letting off steam before a drop, doing what needed to be done. There was no point in dressing it up

"Watch yourself," I said. "You need to be out of here in ten minutes."

"How do you handle *this*?" Riggs asked. He spoke Standard with an accented twang, being from Tau Ceti V, a descendant of North American colonists who had, generations back, claimed the planet as their own. "The waiting feels worse than the mission."

"It's your first combat operation," I said. "You're bound to feel a little nervous."

"Do you remember your first mission?"

"Yeah," I said, "but only just. It was a long time ago."

He paused, as though thinking this through, then asked, "Does it get any easier?"

"The hours before the drop are always the worst," I said. "It's best just not to think about it."

The waiting was well recognised as the worst part of any mission. I didn't want to go into it with Riggs, but believe me when I say that I've tried almost every technique in the book.

It basically boils down to two options.

Option One: Find a dark corner somewhere and sit it out. Even the smaller strikeships that the Alliance relies upon have private areas, away from prying eyes, away from the rest of your squad or the ship's crew. If you're determined, you'll find somewhere private enough and quiet enough to sit it out alone. But few troopers that I've known take this approach, because it rarely works. The Gaia-lovers seem to prefer this method; but then again, they're often fond of self-introspection, and that isn't me. Option One leads to anxiety, depression and mental breakdown. There aren't many soldiers who want to fill the hours before death—even if it is only simulated—with soul-searching. Time slows to a trickle. Psychological time-dilation, or something like it. There's no drug that can touch that anxiety.

Riggs *was* a Gaia Cultist, for his sins, but I didn't think that explaining Option One was going to help him. No, Riggs wasn't an Option One sort of guy.

Option Two: Find something to fill the time. Exactly what you do is your choice; pretty much anything that'll take your mind off the job will suffice. This is what most troopers do. My personal preference—and I accept that it isn't for everyone—is hard physical labour. Anything that really gets the blood flowing is rigorous enough to shut down the neural pathways.

Which led to my current circumstances. An old friend once taught me that the best exercise in the universe is that which you get between the sheets. So, in the hours before we made the drop to Daktar Outpost, I screwed Corporal Daneb Riggs' brains out. Not literally, you understand, because we were in our own bodies. I'm screwed up, or so the psychtechs tell me, but I'm not *that* twisted.

"Where'd you get that?" Riggs asked me, probing the flesh of my left flank. His voice was still dopey as a result of post-coital hormones. "The scar, I mean."

I laid on my back, beside Riggs, and looked down at the white welt to the left of my stomach. Although the flesh-graft had taken well enough, the injury was still obvious: unless I paid a skintech for a patch, it always would. There seemed little point in bothering with cosmetics while I was still a line trooper. Well-healed scars lined my stomach and chest; nothing to complain about, but reminders nonetheless. My body was a roadmap of my military service.

"Never you mind," I said. "It happened a long time ago." I pushed Riggs' hand away, irritated. "And I thought I made it clear that there would be no talking afterwards. That term of the arrangement is non-negotiable."

Riggs got like this after a session. He got chatty, and he got annoying. But as far as I was concerned, his job was done, and I was already feeling detachment from him. Almost as soon as the act was over, I started to feel jumpy again; felt my eyes unconsciously darting to my wrist-comp. The tiny cabin—stinking of sweat and sex—had started to press in around me.

I untangled myself from the bedsheets that were pooled at the foot of the cot. Pulled on a tanktop and walked to the view-port in the bulkhead. There was nothing to see out there except another anonymous sector of deep-space. We were in what had once been known as the Quarantine Zone; that vast ranch of deep-space that was the divide between us and the Krell Empire. A holo-display above the port read 1:57:03 UNTIL DROP. Less than two hours until we reached the assault point. Right now, the UAS *Bainbridge* was slowing down—her enormous sublight engines ensuring that when we reached the appointed coordinates, we would be travelling at just the right velocity. The starship's inertial damper field meant that I would never be able to physically feel the deceleration, but the mental weight was another matter.

"Get dressed," I said, matter-of-factly. "We've got work to do."

I tugged on the rest of my duty fatigues, pressed down the various holo-tabs on my uniform tunic. The identifier there read "210." Those numbers made me a long-termer of the Simulant Operations Programme—sufferer of an effective two hundred and ten simulated deaths.

"I want you down on the prep deck, overseeing simulant loading," I said, dropping into command-mode.

"The Jackals are primed and ready to drop," Riggs said. "The lifer is marking the suits, and I ordered Private Feng to check on the ammunition loads—"

"Feng's no good at that," I said. "You know that he can't be trusted."

" 'Trusted?' "

"I didn't mean it like that," I corrected. "Just get dressed."

Riggs detected the change in my voice; he'd be an idiot not to. While he wasn't exactly the sharpest tool in the box, neither was he a fool.

"Affirmative," he said.

I watched as he put on his uniform. Riggs was tall and well-built; his chest a wall of muscle, neck almost as wide as my waist. Hair dark and short, nicely messy in a way that skirted military protocol. The tattoo of a winged planet on his left bicep indicated that he was a former Off-World Marine aviator, while the blue-and-green globe on his right marked him as a paid-up Gaia Cultist. The data-ports on his chest, shoulders and neck stood out against his tanned skin, the flesh around them still raised. He looked new, and he looked young. Riggs hadn't yet been spat out by the war machine.

"So we're being deployed against the Black Spiral?" he asked, velcroing his tunic in place. The holo-identifier on his chest flashed "10"; and sickeningly enough, Riggs was the most experienced trooper on my team. "That's the scuttlebutt."

"Maybe," I said. "That's likely." I knew very little about the next operation, because that was how Captain Heinrich—the *Bainbridge*'s senior officer—liked to keep things. "It's need to know."

"And you don't need to know," Riggs said, nodding to himself. "Heinrich is such an asshole."

"Talk like that'll get you reprimanded, Corporal." I snapped my wrist-computer into place, the vambrace closing around my left wrist. "Same arrangement as before. Don't let the rest of the team know."

Riggs grinned. "So long as you don't either—"

The cabin lights dipped. Something clunked inside the ship. At about the same time, my wrist-comp chimed with an incoming priority communication: an officers-only alert.

EARLY DROP, it said.

The wrist-comp's small screen activated, and a head-and-shoulders image appeared there. A young woman with ginger hair pulled back from a heavily freckled face. Early twenties, with anxiety-filled eyes. She leaned close into the camera at her end of the connection. Sergeant Zoe Campbell, more commonly known as Zero.

"Lieutenant, ma'am," she babbled. "Do you copy?"

"I copy," I said.

"Where have you been? I've been trying to reach you for the last thirty minutes. Your communicator was off. I tried your cube, but that was set to private. I guess that I could've sent someone down there, but I know how you get before a drop and—"

"Whoa, whoa. Calm down, Zero. What's happening?"

Zero grimaced. "Captain Heinrich has authorised immediate military action on Daktar Outpost."

Zero was the squad's handler. She was already in the Sim Ops bay, and the image behind her showed a bank of operational simulator-tanks, assorted science officers tending them. It looked like the op was well underway rather than just commencing.

"Is Heinrich calling a briefing?" I asked, hustling Riggs to finish getting dressed, trying to keep him out of view of the wrist-comp's cam. I needed him gone from the room, pronto.

Zero shook her head. "Captain Heinrich says there isn't time. He's distributed a mission plan instead. I really should've sent someone down to fetch you..."

"Never mind about that now," I said. Talking over her was often the only way to deal with Zero's constant state of anxiety. "What's our tactical situation? Why the early drop?"

At that moment, a nasal siren sounded throughout the *Bainbridge*'s decks. Somewhere in the bowels of the ship, the engines were cutting, the gravity field fluctuating just a little to compensate.

The ship's AI began a looped message: "This is a general alert. All operators must immediately report to the Simulant Operations Centre. This is a general alert..."

I could already hear boots on deck around me, as the sixty qualified operators made haste to the Science Deck. My data-ports—those bio-mechanical connections that would allow me to make transition into my simulant—were beginning to throb.

"You'd better get down here and skin up," Zero said, nodding at the simulator behind her. "Don't want to be late." Added: "Again..."

"I'm on it," I said, planting my feet in my boots. "Hold the fort."

Zero started to say something else, but before she could question me any further I terminated the communication.

"Game time, Corporal," I said to Riggs. "Look alive."

Dressed now, Riggs nodded and made for the hatch. We had this down to a T: if we left my quarters separately, it minimised the prospect of anyone realising what was happening between us.

"You're beautiful," he said. "You do know that, right?"

"You know that was the last time," I said, firmly.

"You said that *last* time..."

"Well this time I mean it, kemo sabe."

Riggs nodded, but that idiot grin remained plastered across his face. "See you down there, Jenkins," he said.

Here we go again, I thought. *New team. New threat. Same shit.*

The UAS *Bainbridge* was a big old strikeship, and had been patrolling the Quarantine Zone for several months. Sure, we'd met some trouble on Praidor V. And we'd almost been deployed on Triton IV, to counter a pirate ring. But neither of those had been hot deployments, and Jenkins' Jackals hadn't earned a combat extraction yet. The three-month deployment had started to drag, and the *Bainbridge* was spoiling for a fight.

On Daktar Outpost, she was going to find it.

I met Zero at the threshold to the Simulant Operations Centre.

"Where have you been, ma'am?" she asked.

"Sort of busy," I said, pushing past other operators.

"Come on. The team's ready to skin."

I was two decades and then some older than Zero, but she was undeniably the squad's mother hen. Although she didn't like her nickname—"Zero"—I expected that during compulsory education the names had been even less kind. She had the bearing of science staff more than of a soldier, and in her current role she was a little of both.

The SOC was filled with troopers, all eager to claim their slice of the glory. The chamber was sub-divided into a bay for each squad on the deployment, with a science and medical team attached to every squad. Our corner of the SOC was taken up by five simulator-tanks, each marked with the Jackal dog-head symbol and trooper designations. Operators from some simulant teams—the Hayden Walkers, Jay's Angels, Phoenix Squad—were already climbing into their simulators, handlers giving the countdown to transition. Cross-operation statistics were displayed on a display overhead. That was like a speedball stadium scoreboard, showing the number of effective transitions and extractions per operator: Phoenix Squad in pole position, the Jackals on the bottom rung.

Four troopers in states of undress stood in the Jackals' dedicated operations bay. As I approached, they fell into a ragged line and saluted disharmoniously. They were greener than greener; the freshest meat on the ship.

"As you were, Jackals," I said, with as much gusto as I could manage.

"Yes, ma'am," the group chorused back. Riggs winked at me, though no one else noticed.

It was hard to feel any enthusiasm when I looked at the group of misfits that was apparently my squad. As I took in each of their naked bodies, I thought how little they looked like soldiers in their real skins. Not one of the Jackals was over twenty-five years, Earth standard, but then there was very little standard about them. Only Novak was of Old Earth origin, and his roots were so far removed from my own that we barely shared any common ancestry. The rest were Core Worlders—drawn from those planets that had become the heart of the Alliance territory.

In a futile attempt to shake out of it, I ordered, "Let's get stripped and mounted in two; I want transition in three." I began to undress myself, and a medtech came to activate my tank. As I worked, I called over to Zero, "Give me a summary of the briefing packet. What's the op?"

"Command believes that it's going to be an effective drop," Zero said, reading from her data-slate.

"A *combat* drop?" Riggs asked. He was half-undressed now. The callsign JOCKEY was stencilled onto his tank; a particularly literal name the rest of the team had thought up as a result of his background as a rocket jockey. Yeah, it had to be said that the callsigns left something to be desired.

"There's a ninety per cent probability of combat," Zero said. "Daktar Outpost stopped reporting two days ago. The reason for this failure has since been confirmed as a hostile takeover by the Black Spiral."

"Told you so," Riggs said to me.

"There are no prizes for being an asshole," I said, cutting Riggs down. I didn't want the rest of the Jackals getting wind of any private conversations I might be having with Riggs. "Then what's our assignment, Zero?"

"Captain Heinrich has assigned us to scout duty," Zero said. Her use of the word "us" was telling. Although she wasn't going anywhere, Zero's command console—from which she would remotely handle the squad, and would be our eyes and ears—sat in the middle of our SOC bay.

"Scout duty *again*?" asked PFC Gabriella Lopez. "Our last scout drop was a complete waste of time."

"It was a waste of time for everyone, Lopez," I said. "No one got any action on Praidor."

"At least the rest of the strike team got to conduct search-and-seizure," Lopez said. "All we got to do was freeze our asses off. That's scout duty for you."

Lopez had been recruited into the Jackals straight out of Army Basic training, assigned to the team by the battalion's supervising officer, Colonel Draven himself. Twenty-something, and from a lifetime of privilege on Proxima Centauri. The callsign SENATOR had been stencilled onto her tank. Lopez was far from happy about that, but like I said: these guys were literal in their descriptions, if nothing else.

"You think they trust you with real combat-suit?" asked Leon Novak. He spoke Standard with a blunt Slavic accent, forming the words slowly and with intent. "And what do you mean 'again'? You have no deaths yet."

"*Transitions*," Lopez said. "The word is transitions, idiot. And I have six, just like the rest of you."

"Am not idiot," Novak countered. "Do not call me that."

"I'd say that was a pretty accurate description," Riggs joined in. "But you're wrong about one thing, Lopez. I have ten, actually. Let's not forget that."

"Those weren't combat extractions," Feng added. "So they don't count."

"You're all idiots," Lopez said.

She stumbled out of her fatigues, putting a hand to her breasts as though we hadn't seen all this before. Lopez was slight bodied and beautiful; with a perfect golden complexion that suggested her South American heritage, and long dark curly hair that I couldn't recall ever having seen out of place. All of that was ruined by her personality. Lopez had a hell of a mouth on her, and she was hard work.

Novak sneered. "Whatever. Deaths, transitions, extractions. Is all same."

A small disc-shaped security-drone, silver and chrome, a couple of foot across, hovered at his shoulder.

"*Security protocol suspected during operation*," the drone bleated.

Novak's callsign was CONVICT, and he was just that: a convicted felon and a life-termer, given a chance of reprieve out in the void. I wasn't sure of exactly what Novak had done to earn his term, but I knew that it must've been *bad*. So many military bases had been hit during the Krell War that the Alliance had found themselves with a serious shortage of simulant operators. They'd trawled the prisons for compatible recruits, had offered prisoners the opportunity to commute life terms to a period of military service. That was how Novak had earned himself a lifetime spot on the Programme, each extraction knocking a little time off his sentence.

Novak was an enormous, bear-like man, shoulders dominated by a winged skull tattoo that stretched across the blades. The word BRATVA was stencilled beneath in faded blue ink. The choice of word was a particularly bad joke, because this man didn't even know the meaning of the word "brotherhood." He was nothing more than an outcast from the Siberian prison-hubs; a killer that even the Russian Federation had been glad to disown. Whatever Command thought they had made Leon Novak into, this was the real man.

"Can the negative jive," I said. "We've got a mission, and that's enough."

"But it's a shit detail," Lopez complained.

"Someone has to do it," I said, "and we're the greenest team on this bucket."

"I am *ready* for this..." Feng said, bouncing on the balls of his feet. "I am *so* ready for this!"

Only Feng had any real soldier in him, and he wasn't even a free citizen. Technically, Feng was former Asiatic Directorate property. South Asian features, smooth-skinned save for the data-ports, covered in barcodes and serial numbers—dark-eyed and -haired, muscled in an unnaturally precise way. He was a man-child: born into puberty, direct from the clone-vats. The location of his "birth" in the Asiatic Directorate—Crèche Three, Crema Base—was stamped across the small of his neck, like a brand. He had been liberated by Allied forces from the same planet, and in many ways he was a poster-child for the new Alliance; a super-state willing to forgive the transgressions of the Directorate's political and military elite, and to strive towards a lasting peace for all humanity.

But whatever Feng's political heritage, right now he just looked like an over-excited kid. Granted, a kid who was about to be skinned with the absolute best in biotechnology, and about to be equipped with cutting edge arms and armour, but still a child. He bobbed anxiously, nervously, as he was readied to mount the tank.

"Cool your jets," I said to the bay but really directed at Feng. "Just keep calm and we'll get through this."

Medtechs descended on the squad, and began plugging us into the simulators. I let the staff work but I knew the drill in my sleep.

Zero read more from the briefing. "All entrances to the outpost are locked down. You'll be supported drop-side by the fire teams and heavier combat-suits. I've uploaded your objectives to the suit network; you'll have them as soon as you make transition. The Jackals' destination is Tower Three, located on the outer aspect of the base."

"This is real, people," Feng said, pumping his fists. "This is happening!"

"I hear that," Riggs added.

Zero gave me a watery smile, and I felt a pang of disappointment for her. I knew that she wished it was her going into the tanks, but we both knew that would never be the case. Zero's name was a joke, because she was less than that. She was a "negative," her physiology incompatible with the implants necessary to operate a simulant. As she watched us going through the procedure, there was something almost melancholy about her expression.

"Command expects the Black Spiral to be present in significant number," Zero said, continuing to read. "Captain Heinrich says that this is going to be hot. You should be aware that this is a joint—"

"More sorry-ass terrorists," Feng said. "I am on this!"

"We're doing what we do when we have no one left to fight," Lopez said. "We're killing each other."

"Those daddy's words, or yours?" Novak said.

"Fuck you, lifer," Lopez responded.

Zero seemed more agitated that usual, which in her case was saying something. "Ma'am," she said, "I really need to make you aware that this is—"

"No time, Zero," I said. "Tell me when I get back."

A respirator was snapped over my face, and a tech popped a bead into my ear. All that was left to do now was to get into the tank. It was already half-filled with blue amniotic fluid, quickly warming. My own callsign, CALIFORNIA, was stencilled in bold letters onto the tank's outer canopy.

"All good?" a medico asked.

"Affirmative," I said. I turned to check on the rest of my squad. Thumbs up all round. "Seal us in. You've got the formalities, Zero."

"Copy that, ma'am," she said. "Transition commencing in three... two... one..."

It was not common to awaken in a cloning vat streaked with drying blood.

At least, Maria Arena had never experienced it. She had no memory of how she died. That was also new; before, when she had awakened as a new clone, her first memory was of how she died.

Maria's vat was in the front of six vats, each one holding the clone of a crew member of the starship Dormire, each clone waiting for its previous incarnation to die so it could awaken. And Maria wasn't the only one to die recently....

This is not a Pipe

DAY 1
JULY 25, 2493

Sound struggled to make its way through the thick synth-amneo fluid. Once it reached Maria Arena's ears, it sounded like a chain saw: loud, insistent, and unending. She couldn't make out the words, but it didn't sound like a situation she wanted to be involved in.

Her reluctance at her own rebirth reminded her where she was, and who she was. She grasped for her last backup. The crew had just moved into their quarters on the *Dormire*, and the cloning bay had been the last room they'd visited on their tour. There they had done their first backup on the ship.

Maria must have been in an accident or something soon after, killing her and requiring her next clone to wake. Sloppy use of a life wouldn't make a good impression on the captain, who likely was the source of the angry chain-saw noise.

Maria finally opened her eyes. She tried to make sense of the dark round globules floating in front of her vat, but it was difficult with the freshly cloned brain being put to work for the first time. There were too many things wrong with such a mess.

With the smears on the outside of the vat and the purple color through the bluish fluid Maria floated in, she figured the orbs were blood drops. Blood shouldn't float. That was the first problem. If blood was floating, that meant the grav drive that spun the ship had failed. That was probably another reason someone was yelling. The blood and the grav drive.

Blood in a cloning bay, that was different too. Cloning bays were pristine, clean places, where humans were downloaded into newly cloned bodies when the previous ones had died. It was much cleaner and less painful than human birth, with all its screaming and blood.

Again with the blood.

The cloning bay had six vats in two neat rows, filled with blue-tinted synth-amneo fluid and the waiting clones of the rest of the crew. Blood belonged in the medbay, down the hall. The unlikely occurrence of a drop of blood originating in the medbay, floating down the hall, and entering the cloning bay to float in front of Maria's vat would be extraordinary. But that's not what happened; a body floated above the blood drops. A number of bodies, actually.

Finally, if the grav drive *had* failed, and if someone *had* been injured in the cloning bay, another member of the crew would have cleaned up the blood. Someone was always on call to ensure a new clone made the transition from death into their new body smoothly.

No. A perfect purple sphere of blood shouldn't be floating in front of her face.

Maria had now been awake for a good minute or so. No one worked the computer to drain the synth-amneo fluid to free her.

A small part of her brain began to scream at her that she should be more concerned about the bodies, but only a small part.

She'd never had occasion to use the emergency release valve inside the cloning vats. Scientists had implemented them after some techs had decided to play a prank on a clone, and woke her up only to leave her in the vat alone for hours. When she had gotten free, stories said, the result was messy and violent, resulting in the fresh cloning of some of the techs. After that, engineers added an interior release switch for clones to let themselves out of the tank if they were trapped for whatever reason.

Maria pushed the button and heard a *clunk* as the release triggered, but the synth-amneo fluid stayed where it was.

A drain relied on gravity to help the fluid along its way. Plumbing 101 there. The valve was opened but the fluid remained a stubborn womb around Maria.

She tried to find the source of the yelling. One of the crew floated near the computer bank, naked, with wet hair stuck out in a frightening, spiky corona. Another clone woke. Two of them had died?

Behind her, crewmates floated in four vats. All of their eyes were open, and each was searching for the emergency release. Three *clunk*s sounded, but they remained in the same position Maria was in.

Maria used the other emergency switch to open the vat door. Ideally it would have been used after the fluid had drained away, but there was little ideal about this situation. She and a good quantity of the synth-amneo fluid floated out of her vat, only to collide gently with the orb of blood floating in front of her. The surface tension of both fluids held, and the drop bounced away.

Maria hadn't encountered the problem of how to get out of a liquid prison in zero-grav. She experimented by flailing about, but only made some fluid break off the main bubble and go floating away. In her many lives, she'd been in more than one undignified situation, but this was new.

Action and reaction, she thought, and inhaled as much of the oxygen-rich fluid as she could, then forced everything out of her lungs as if she were sneezing. She didn't go as fast as she would have if it had been air, because she was still inside viscous fluid, but it helped push her backward and out of the bubble. She inhaled air and then coughed and vomited the rest of the fluid in a spray in front of her, banging her head on the computer console as her body's involuntary movements propelled her farther.

Finally out of the fluid, and gasping for air, she looked up.

"Oh shit."

Three dead crewmates floated around the room amid the blood and other fluids. Two corpses sprouted a number of gory tentacles, bloody bubbles that refused to break away from the deadly wounds. A fourth was strapped to a chair at the terminal.

Gallons of synth-amneo fluid joined the gory detritus as the newly cloned crew fought to exit their vats. They looked with as much shock as she felt at their surroundings.

Captain Katrina de la Cruz moved to float beside her, still focused on the computer. "Maria, stop staring and make yourself useful. Check on the others."

Maria scrambled for a handhold on the wall to pull herself away from the captain's attempt to access the terminal.

Katrina pounded on a keyboard and poked at the console screen. "IAN, what the hell happened?"

"My speech functions are inaccessible," the computer's male, slightly robotic voice said.

"Ceci n'est pas une pipe," muttered a voice above Maria. It broke her shock and reminded her of the captain's order to check on the crew.

The speaker was Akihiro Sato, pilot and navigator. She had met him a few hours ago at the cocktail party before the launch of the *Dormire*.

"Hiro, why are you speaking French?" Maria said, confused. "Are you all right?"

"Someone saying aloud that they can't talk is like that old picture of a pipe that says, 'This is not a pipe.'

It's supposed to give art students deep thoughts. Never mind." He waved his hand around the cloning bay. "What happened, anyway?"

"I have no idea," she said. "But—God, what a mess. I have to go check on the others."

"Goddammit, you just spoke," the captain said to the computer, dragging some icons around the screen. "Something's working inside there. Talk to me, IAN."

"My speech functions are inaccessible," the AI said again, and de la Cruz slammed her hand down on the keyboard, grabbing it to keep herself from floating away from it.

Hiro followed Maria as she maneuvered around the room using the handholds on the wall. Maria found herself face-to-face with the gruesome body of Wolfgang, their second in command. She gently pushed him aside, trying not to dislodge the gory bloody tentacles sprouting from punctures on his body.

She and Hiro floated toward the living Wolfgang, who was doubled over coughing the synth-amneo out of his lungs. "What the hell is going on?" he asked in a ragged voice.

"You know as much as we do," Maria said. "Are you all right?"

He nodded and waved her off. He straightened his back, gaining at least another foot on his tall frame. Wolfgang was born on the moon colony, Luna, several generations of his family developing the long bones of living their whole lives in low gravity. He took a handhold and propelled himself toward the captain.

"What do you remember?" Maria asked Hiro as they approached another crewmember.

"My last backup was right after we boarded the ship. We haven't even left yet," Hiro said.

Maria nodded. "Same for me. We should still be docked, or only a few weeks from Earth."

"I think we have more immediate problems, like our current status," Hiro said.

"True. Our current status is four of us are dead," Maria said, pointing at the bodies. "And I'm guessing the other two are as well."

"What could kill us all?" Hiro asked, looking a bit green as he dodged a bit of bloody skin. "And what happened to me and the captain?"

He referred to the "other two" bodies that were not floating in the cloning bay. Wolfgang, their engineer, Paul Seurat, and Dr. Joanna Glass all were dead, floating around the room, gently bumping off vats or one another.

Another cough sounded from the last row of vats, then a soft voice. "Something rather violent, I'd say."

"Welcome back, Doctor, you all right?" Maria asked, pulling herself toward the woman.

The new clone of Joanna nodded, her tight curls glistening with the synth-amneo. Her upper body was thin and strong, like all new clones, but her legs were small and twisted. She glanced up at the bodies and pursed her lips. "What happened?" She didn't wait for them to answer, but grasped a handhold and pulled herself toward the ceiling where a body floated.

"Check on Paul," Maria said to Hiro, and followed Joanna.

The doctor turned her own corpse to where she could see it, and her eyes grew wide. She swore quietly. Maria came up behind her and swore much louder.

Her throat had a stab wound, with great waving gouts of blood reaching from her neck. If the doctor's advanced age was any indication, they were well past the beginning of the mission. Maria remembered her as a woman who looked to be in her thirties, with smooth dark skin and black hair. Now wrinkles lined the skin around her eyes and the corners of her mouth, and gray shot through her tightly braided hair. Maria looked at the other bodies; from her vantage point she could now see each also showed their age.

"I didn't even notice," she said, breathless. "I-I only noticed the blood and gore. We've been on this ship for *decades*. Do you remember anything?"

"No." Joanna's voice was flat and grim. "We need to tell the captain."

"No one touch anything! This whole room is a crime scene!" Wolfgang shouted up to them. "Get away from that body!"

"Wolfgang, the crime scene, if this is a crime scene, is already contaminated by about twenty-five hundred gallons of synth-amneo," Hiro said from outside Paul's vat. "With blood spattering everywhere."

"What do you mean *if* it's a crime scene?" Maria asked. "Do you think that the grav drive died and stopped the ship from spinning and then knives just floated into us?"

Speaking of the knife, it drifted near the ceiling. Maria propelled herself toward it and snatched it before it got pulled against the air intake filter, which was already getting clogged with bodily fluids she didn't even want to think about.

The doctor did as Wolfgang had commanded, moving away from her old body to join him and the captain. "This is murder," she said. "But Hiro's right, Wolfgang, there is a reason zero-g forensics never took off as a science. The air filters are sucking up the evidence as we speak. By now everyone is covered in everyone else's blood. And now we have six new people and vats of synth-amneo floating around the bay messing up whatever's left."

Wolfgang set his jaw and glared at her. His tall, thin frame shone with the bluish amneo fluid. He opened his mouth to counter the doctor, but Hiro interrupted them.

"Five," interrupted Hiro. He coughed and expelled more synth-amneo, which Maria narrowly dodged. He grimaced in apology. "Five new people. Paul's still inside." He pointed to their engineer, who remained in his vat, eyes closed.

Maria remembered seeing his eyes open when she was in her own vat. But now Paul floated, eyes closed, hands covering his genitals, looking like a child who was playing hide-and-seek and whoever was "It" was going to devour him. He too was pale, naturally stocky, lightly muscled instead of the heavier man Maria remembered.

"Get him out of there," Katrina said. Wolfgang obliged, going to another terminal and pressing the button to open the vat.

Hiro reached in and grabbed Paul by the wrist and pulled him and his fluid cage free.

"Okay, only five of us were out," Maria said, floating down. "That cuts the synth-amneo down by around four hundred gallons. Not a huge improvement. There's still a lot of crap flying around. You're not likely to get evidence from anything except the bodies themselves." She held the knife out to Wolfgang, gripping the edge of the handle with her thumb and forefinger. "And possibly the murder weapon."

He looked around, and Maria realized he was searching for something with which to take the knife. "I've already contaminated it with my hands, Wolfgang. It's been floating among blood and dead bodies. The only thing we'll get out of it is that it probably killed us all."

"We need to get IAN back online," Katrina said. "Get the grav drive back on. Find the other two bodies. Check on the cargo. Then we will fully know our situation."

Hiro whacked Paul smartly on the back, and the man doubled over and retched, sobbing. Wolfgang watched with disdain as Paul bounced off the wall with no obvious awareness of his surroundings.

"Once we get IAN back online, we'll have him secure a channel to Earth," Katrina said.

"My speech functions are inaccessible," the computer repeated. The captain gritted her teeth.

"That's going to be tough, Captain," Joanna said. "These bodies show considerable age, indicating we've been in space for much longer than our mindmaps are telling us."

Katrina rubbed her forehead, closing her eyes. She was silent, then opened her eyes and began typing things into the terminal. "Get Paul moving, we need him."

Hiro stared helplessly as Paul continued to sob, curled into a little drifting ball, still trying to hide his privates.

A ball of vomit—not the synth-amneo expelled from the bodies, but actual stomach contents—floated toward the air intake vent and was sucked into the filter. Maria knew that after they took care of all of the captain's priorities, she would still be stuck with the job of changing the air filters, and probably crawling through the ship's vents to clean all of the bodily fluids out before they started to become a biohazard. Suddenly a maintenance-slash-junior-engineer position on an important starship didn't seem so glamorous.

"I think Paul will feel better with some clothes," Joanna said, looking at him with pity.

"Yeah, clothes sound good," Hiro said. They were all naked, their skin rising in goose bumps. "Possibly a shower while we're at it."

"I will need my crutches or a chair," Joanna said. "Unless we want to keep the grav drive off."

"Stop it," Katrina said. "The murderer could still be on the ship and you're talking about clothes and showers?"

Wolfgang waved a hand to dismiss her concern. "No, clearly the murderer died in the fight. We are the only six aboard the ship."

"You can't know that," de la Cruz said. "What's happened in the past several decades? We need to be cautious. No one goes anywhere alone. Everyone in twos. Maria, you and Hiro get the doctor's crutches from the medbay. She'll want them when the grav drive gets turned back on."

"I can just take the prosthetics off that body," Joanna said, pointing upward. "It won't need them anymore."

"That's evidence," Wolfgang said, steadying his own floating corpse to study the stab wounds. He fixated on the bubbles of gore still attached to his chest. "Captain?"

"Fine, get jumpsuits, get the doctor a chair or something, and check on the grav drive," Katrina said. "The rest of us will work. Wolfgang, you and I will get the bodies tethered together. We don't want them to sustain more damage when the grav drive comes back online."

On the way out, Maria paused to check on her own body, which she hadn't really examined before. It seemed too gruesome to look into your own dead face. The body was strapped to a seat at one of the terminals, drifting gently against the tether. A large bubble of blood drifted from the back of her neck, where she had clearly been stabbed. Her lips were white and her skin was a sickly shade of green. She now knew where the floating vomit had come from.

"It looks like I was the one who hit the resurrection switch," she said to Hiro, pointing to her body.

"Good thing too," Hiro said. He looked at the captain, conversing closely with Wolfgang. "I wouldn't expect a medal anytime soon, though. She's not looking like she's in the mood."

The resurrection switch was a fail-safe button. If all of the clones on the ship died at once, a statistical improbability, then the AI should have been able to wake up the next clones. If the ship failed to do so, an even higher statistical improbability, then a physical switch in the cloning bay could carry out the job, provided there was someone alive enough to push it.

Like the others, Maria's body showed age. Her middle had softened and her hands floating above the terminal were thin and spotted. She had been the physical age of thirty-nine when they had boarded.

"I gave you an order," Katrina said. "And Dr. Glass, it looks like talking our engineer down will fall to you. Do it quickly, or else he's going to need another new body when I'm through with him."

Hiro and Maria got moving before the captain could detail what she was going to do to them. Although, Maria reflected, it would be hard to top what they had just apparently been through.

Maria remembered the ship as shinier and brighter: metallic and smooth, with handholds along the wall for low-gravity situations and thin metal grates making up the floor, revealing a subfloor of storage compartments and vents. Now it was duller, another indication that decades of spaceflight had changed the ship as it had changed the crew. It was darker, a few lights missing, illuminated by the yellow lights of an alert. Someone—probably the captain—had commanded an alert.

Some of the previous times, Maria had died in a controlled environment. She had been in bed after illness, age, or, once, injury. The helpful techs had created a final mindmap of her brain, and she had been euthanized after signing a form permitting it. A doctor had approved it, the body was disposed of neatly, and she had woken up young, pain-free, with all her memories of all her lives thus far.

Some other times hadn't been as gentle, but still were a better experience than this.

Having her body still hanging around, blood and vomit everywhere, offended her on a level she hadn't thought possible. Once you were gone, the body meant nothing, had no sentimental value. The future body was all that mattered. The past shouldn't be there, staring you in the face with dead eyes. She shuddered.

"When the engines get running again, it'll warm up," Hiro said helpfully, mistaking the reason for her shiver.

They reached a junction, and she led the way left. "Decades, Hiro. We've been out here for decades. What happened to our mindmaps?"

"What's the last thing you remember?" he asked.

"We had the cocktail party in Luna station as the final passengers were entering cryo and getting loaded. We came aboard. We were given some hours to move into our quarters. Then we had the tour, which ended in the cloning bay, getting our updated mindmaps."

"Same here," he said.

"Are you scared?" Maria said, stopping and looking at him.

She hadn't scrutinized him since waking up in the cloning bay. She was used to the way that clones with the experience of hundreds of years could look like they had just stepped out of university. Their bodies woke up at peak age, twenty years old, designed to be built with muscle. What the clones did with that muscle once they woke up was their challenge.

Akihiro Sato was a thin Pan Pacific United man of Japanese descent with short black hair that was drying in stiff cowlicks. He had lean muscles, and high cheekbones. His eyes were black, and they met hers with a level gaze. She didn't look too closely at the rest of him; she wasn't rude.

He pulled at a cowlick, then tried to smooth it down. "I've woken up in worse places."

"Like where?" she asked, pointing down the hall from where they had come. "What's worse than that horror movie scene?"

He raised his hands in supplication. "I don't mean literally. I mean I've lost time before. You have to learn to adapt sometimes. Fast. I wake up. I assess the immediate threat. I try to figure out where I was last time I uploaded a mind-map. This time I woke up in the middle of a bunch of dead bodies, but there was no threat that I could tell." He cocked his head, curious. "Haven't you ever lost time before? Not even a week? Surely you've died between backups."

"Yes," she admitted. "But I've never woken up in danger, or in the wake of danger."

"You're still not in danger," he said. "That we know of."

She stared at him.

"*Immediate* danger," he amended. "I'm not going to stab you right here in the hall. All of our danger right now consists of problems that we can likely fix. Lost memories, broken computer, finding a murderer. Just a little work and we'll be back on track."

"You are the strangest kind of optimist," she said. "All the same, I'd like to continue to freak out if you don't mind."

"Try to keep it together. You don't want to devolve into whatever Paul has become," he suggested as he continued down the hall.

Maria followed, glad that he wasn't behind her. "I'm keeping it together. I'm here, aren't I?"

"You'll probably feel better when you've had a shower and some food," he said. "Not to mention clothes."

They were both covered only in the tacky, drying synth-amneo fluid. Maria had never wanted a shower more in her life. "Aren't you a little worried about what we're going to find when we find your body?" she asked.

Hiro looked back at her. "I learned a while back not to mourn the old shells. If we did, we'd get more and more dour with each life. In fact, I think that may be Wolfgang's problem." He frowned. "Have you ever had to clean up the old body by yourself?"

Maria shook her head. "No. It was disorienting; she was looking at me, like she was blaming me. It's still not as bad as not knowing what happened, though."

"Or who happened," said Hiro. "It did have a knife."

"And it was violent," Maria said. "It could be one of us."

"Probably was, or else we should get excited about a first-contact situation. Or second contact, if the first one went so poorly..." Hiro said, then sobered. "But truly anything could have gone wrong. Someone could have woken up from cryo and gone mad, even. Computer glitch messed with the mindmap. But it's probably easily explained, like someone got caught cheating at poker. Heat of the moment, someone hid an ace, the doctor flipped the table—"

"It's not funny," Maria said softly. "It wasn't madness and it wasn't an off-the-cuff crime. If that had happened, we wouldn't have the grav drive offline. We wouldn't be missing decades of memories. IAN would be able to tell us what's going on. But someone—one of us—wanted us dead, and they also messed with the personality backups. Why?"

"Is that rhetorical? Or do you really expect me to know?" he asked.

"Rhetorical," grumbled Maria. She shook her head to clear it. A strand of stiff black hair smacked her in the face, and she winced. "It could have been two people. One killed us, one messed with the memories."

"True," he said. "We can probably be sure it was premeditated. Anyway, the captain was right. Let's be cautious. And let's make a pact. I'll promise not to kill you and you promise not to kill me. Deal?"

Maria smiled in spite of herself. She shook his hand. "I promise. Let's get going before the captain sends someone after us."

The door to medbay was rimmed in red lights, making it easy to find if ill or injured. With the alert, the lights were blinking, alternating between red and yellow. Hiro stopped abruptly at the entrance. Maria smacked into the back of him in a collision that sent them spinning gently like gears in a clock, making him turn to face the hall while she swung around to see what had stopped him so suddenly.

The contact could have been awkward except for the shock of the scene before them.

In the medbay, a battered, older version of Captain Katrina de la Cruz lay in a bed. She was unconscious but very much alive, hooked up to life support, complete with IV, breathing tubes, and monitors. Her face was a mess of bruises, and her right arm was in a cast. She was strapped to the bed, which was held to the floor magnetically.

"I thought we all died," Hiro said, his voice soft with wonder.

"For us all to wake up, we should have. I guess I hit the emergency resurrection switch anyway," Maria said, pushing herself off the doorjamb to float into the room closer to the captain.

"Too bad you can't ask yourself," Hiro said drily.

Penalties for creating a duplicate clone were stiff, usually resulting in the extermination of the older clone. Although with several murders to investigate, and now an assault, Wolfgang would probably not consider this particular crime a priority to punish.

"No one is going to be happy about this," Hiro said, pointing at the unconscious body of the captain. "Least of all Katrina. What are we going to do with two captains?"

"But this could be good," Maria said. "If we can wake her up, we might find out what happened."

"I can't see her agreeing with you," he said.

A silver sheet covered the body and drifted lazily where the straps weren't holding it down. The captain's clone was still, the breathing tube the only sound.

Maria floated to the closet on the far side of the room. She grabbed a handful of large jumpsuits—they would be too short for Wolfgang, too tight for the doctor, and too voluminous for Maria, but they would do for the time being—and pulled a folded wheelchair from where it drifted in the dim light filtering into the closet.

She handed a jumpsuit to Hiro and donned hers, unselfconsciously not turning away. When humans reach midlife, they may reach a level of maturity where they cease to give a damn what someone thinks about their bodies. Multiply that a few times and you have the modesty (or lack thereof) of the average clone. The first time Maria had felt the self-conscious attitude lifting, it had been freeing. The mind-set remained with many clones even as their bodies reverted to youth, knowing that a computer-built body was closer to a strong ideal than they could have ever created with diet and exercise.

The sobbing engineer, Paul, had been the most ashamed clone Maria had ever seen.

The jumpsuit fabric wasn't as soft as Maria's purple engineering jumpsuits back in her quarters, but she was at least warmer. She wondered when they would finally be allowed to eat and go back to their quarters for a shower and some sleep. Waking up took a lot out of a clone.

Hiro was already clothed and back over by the captain's body, peering at her face. Maria maneuvered her way over to him using the wall handles. He looked grim, his usually friendly face now reflecting the seriousness of the situation.

"I don't suppose we can just hide this body?" he asked. "Recycle it before anyone finds out? Might save us a lot of headache in the future."

Maria checked the vital-signs readout on the computer. "I don't think she's a body yet. Calling her a body and disposing of it is something for the courts, not us."

"What courts?" he asked as Maria took the wheelchair by the handles and headed for the door. "There are six of us!"

"Seven," Maria reminded, jerking her head backward to indicate the person in the medbay. "Eight if we can get IAN online. Even so it's a matter for the captain and IAN to decide, not us."

"Well, then you get to go spread the latest bad news."

"I'm not ready to deal with Wolfgang right now," Maria said. "Or hear the captain tear Paul a new asshole. Besides, we have to check the grav drive."

"Avoiding Wolfgang sounds like a good number one priority," said Hiro. "In fact, if I could interview my last clone, he probably avoided Wolfgang a lot too."

The bridge of the starship *Dormire* was an impressive affair, with a seat for the captain and one for the pilot at the computer terminals that sat on the floor, but a ladder ran up the wall right beside the room entrance to lead to a few comfortable benches bolted to the wall, making it the perfect place to observe the universe as the ship crept toward light speed. The room itself comprised a dome constructed from diamond, so that you could see in a 270-degree arc. The helm looked like a great glass wart sitting on the end of the ship, but it did allow a lovely view of the universe swinging around you as the grav drive rotated the ship. Now, with the drive off, space seemed static, even though they were moving at a fraction of the speed of light through space.

It could make someone ill, honestly. Deep space all around, even the floor being clear. Maria remembered seeing it on the tour of the ship, but this was the first time she had seen it away from Luna. The first time in this clone's memory, anyway.

Drawing the eye away from the view, the terminals, and the pilot's station and benches, Hiro's old body floated near the top of the dome, tethered by a noose to the bottom of one of the benches. His face was red and his open eyes bulged.

"Oh. There—" He paused to swallow, then continued. "—there I am." He turned away, looking green.

"I don't know what I expected, but suicide wasn't it," Maria said softly, looking into the swollen, anguished face. "I was actually wondering if you survived too."

"I didn't expect hanging," he said. "I don't think I expected anything. It's all real to me now." He covered his mouth with his hand.

Maria knew too much sympathy could make a person on the edge lose control, so she turned firm. "Do not puke in here. I already have to clean up the cloning bay, and you've seen what a nightmare that is. Don't give me more to clean up."

He glared at her, but some color returned to his face. He did not look up again.

Something drifted gently into the back of Maria's head. She grabbed at it and found a brown leather boot. The hanged corpse wore its mate.

"This starts to build a time line," Maria said. "You had to be hanged when we still had gravity. I guess that's good."

Hiro still had his back to the bridge, face toward the hallway. His eyes were closed and he breathed deeply. She put her hand on his shoulder. "Come on. We need to get the drive back on."

Hiro turned and focused on the terminal, which was blinking red.

"Are you able to turn it on without IAN?" Maria asked.

"I should be. IAN could control everything, but if he goes offline, we're not dead in the water. Was that my shoe?" The last question was offhand, as if it meant nothing.

"Yes." Maria drifted toward the top of the helm and took a closer look at the body. It was hard to tell since the face was so distorted by the hanging, but Hiro looked different from the rest of the crew. They all looked as if decades had passed since they had launched from Luna station. But Hiro looked exactly as he did now, as if freshly vatted.

"Hey, Hiro, I think you must have died at least once during the trip. Probably recently. This is a newer clone than the others," she said. "I think we're going to have to start writing the weird stuff down."

Hiro made a sound like an animal caught in a trap. All humor had left him. His eyes were hard as he finally glanced up at her and the clone. "All right. That's it."

"That's what?"

"The last straw. I'm officially scared now."

"Now? It took you this long to get scared?" Maria asked, pulling herself to the floor. "With everything else we're dealing with, *now* you're scared?"

Hiro punched at the terminal, harder than Maria thought was necessary. Nothing happened. He crossed his arms, and then uncrossed them, looking as if arms were some kind of new limb he wasn't sure what to do with. He took the boot from Maria and slid it over his own foot.

"I was just managing to cope with the rest," he said. "That was something happening to all of you. I wasn't involved. I wasn't a Saturday Night Gorefest. I was here as a supporting, friendly face. I was here to make you laugh. *Hey, Hiro will always cheer us up.*"

Maria put her hand on his shoulder and looked him in the eyes. "Welcome to the panic room, Hiro. We have to support each other. Take a deep breath. Now we need to get the drive on and then tell the captain and Wolfgang."

"You gotta be desperate if you want to tell Wolfgang," he said, looking as if he was trying and failing to force a smile.

"And when you get the drive on, can you find out what year it is, check on the cargo, maybe reach IAN from here?" Maria asked. "With everything else that's happened, it might be nice to come back with a little bit of good news. Or improved news."

Hiro nodded, his mouth closed as if trying to hold in something he would regret saying. Or perhaps a scream. He floated over to his pilot's chair and strapped himself in. The console screen continued to blink bright red at him. "Thanks for that warning, IAN, we hadn't noticed the drive was gone."

He typed some commands and poked at the touch screen. A warning siren began to bleat through the ship, telling everyone floating in zero-g that gravity was incoming. Hiro poked at the screen a few more times, and then typed at a terminal, his face growing darker as he did so. He made some calculations and then sighed loudly, sitting back in the chair and putting his hands over his face.

"Well," he said. "Things just got worse."

Maria heard the grav drive come online, and the ship shuddered as the engines started rotating the five-hundred-thousand-GRT ship. She took hold of the ladder along the back wall to guide her way to the bench so she wouldn't fall once the gravity came back.

"What now?" she said. "Are we off course?"

"We've apparently been in space for twenty-four years and seven months." He paused. "And nine days."

Maria did the math. "So it's 2493."

"By now we should be a little more than three light-years away from home. Far outside the event horizon of realistic communication with Earth. And we are. But we're also twelve degrees off course."

"That... sorry, I don't get where the hell that is. Can you say it in maintenance-officer language?"

"We are slowing down and turning. I'm not looking forward to telling the captain," he said, unstrapping himself from the seat. He glanced up at his own body drifting at the end of the noose like a grisly kite. "We can cut that down later."

"What were we thinking? Why would we go off course?" Maria thought aloud as they made their way through the hallway, staying low to prepare for gravity as the ship's rotation picked up.

"Why murder the crew, why turn off the grav drive, why spare the captain, why did I kill myself, and why did I apparently feel the need to take off one shoe before doing it?" Hiro said. "Just add it to your list, Maria. I'm pretty sure we are officially fucked, no matter what the answers are."